FOREVER

BY

LORI PRINCE PETERSON

LITTLE RED LEAF

For Mom

- Trevin and Teana

Little Red Leaf
Salt Lake City, Utah
First Edition: May 2016

All of the characters, organizations, and events portrayed in this novel are either products of the author's imagination or are used fictitiously.

ISBN-13: 978-0-9965206-5-2

ISBN-10: 0-9965206-5-1

Library of Congress Control Number:
Little Red Leaf, Salt Lake City, Utah

Printed in the United States of America

10 9 8 7 6 5 4 3 2

DEDICATION

Lori Prince Peterson's love for horses began at the tender age of five. That love took her to showing and 4H through her teen years, to racing horses with a young family, to finally passing that love of horses on to her children, especially her daughter Teana, as they pursued their own dreams.

Throughout the years, and the many different stories, there is one horse that will always stand apart from the rest for Lori. The one horse that strengthened a family, brought peace to her spirit, and taught people how to dream. That horse was Dash.

When she was bought as a yearling, the small filly didn't look to be anything special. But she was. She was special because she defied the odds, and she was special because of the impact that she was able to have on so many. Dash in many ways is a mirror image to Lori. Small in stature, many would not have assumed much of her. But Lori defied the odds; she was smart, working her way through nursing school to then having over 25 years as a successful nurse. She could haul hay better than any man; and without the whining that many would hear from one. She instilled hope, peace, and love in everyone that she came in contact with. She was the glue that held people together.

Inspired by the spirit of this horse, Lori set pen to paper and wrote. She wrote in the middle of a slow night shift at the hospital. She wrote after tucking her children into bed, she wrote this book for years, determined to share the unshakable bond between a horse and a girl.

In the fall of 2013, in the middle of an evening storm, the world was forever changed. Lori's horses had become loose in the midst of high winds and cracking thunder. Lori and her son, Trevin, struggled against the deafening winds to rescue the two horses. Scared and disoriented, the horses weaved dangerously back and forth on a busy, high speed, county road. Fearing for her horses, and the lives of those who would be injured in a collision with the 1200lb animals, she desperately tried to warn oncoming traffic. She was struck and killed by a vehicle that didn't see her in the dark and confusion amidst the chaos. None of her horses were injured, nor was her son or the driver of the vehicle.

The most important things in Lori's life were horses and people— her family. In honor of this brave and amazing woman, the woman who forever defied the odds stacked against her; her children are bringing her dreams to reality, by bringing her words, her story, to you…

FOREVER

CHAPTER 1

The sound of the auctioneer's voice rang melodiously throughout the room. The smells of clean sawdust and horses mixed gently with the light breeze floating through the doorway to the arena. A horse was entering the sale ring being led by a young stablehand. The colt's eyes widened as he looked anxiously toward the crowd.

Jace Brenton sat near the back of the room, his chair tipped back slightly from the table, his arms crossed in front of his chest. Horse sales were not new to Jace, he had been buying and training racehorses for the past ten years along with running the farm his father had left him. It was obvious, though, that his concentration was not completely on the sale. Quite often his eyes would glance toward the outer stalls, where rows and rows of horses were awaiting their turn in the ring. He caught a glimpse of the girl wandering from stall to stall. Quickly she would turn away only to again glance toward the man who watched her so intently.

Jenna had always loved horses as her mother had, but when her mother passed away, she had been sent to live with her Aunt Lorna.

Lorna dearly loved Jenna but felt that a stable was no place for a young girl. Instead Jenna learned to stitch, knit, sew and cook, none of which she cared for very much. But here she was, just where she had dreamed of being, back home with her father and in a barn full of horses.

Jenna wondered at herself and the mixed feelings she had concerning her father. She loved him, yet a part of her hated him. Or do *I?* She didn't understand why, if he loved her, he sent her away. He had given her numerous reasons, but still she didn't understand how he could hurt her that way. She remembered how she had changed the hurt to anger. It made it easier to deal with as she slowly convinced herself that she hated him.

Jace still watched her in glimpses. She had grown so much in the past two years that he felt he hardly knew her, but he remembered well the day he had sent her to live with her aunt.

She had just turned eleven the month before. Tears streaming down her face, she begged him to let her stay. He could still hear her words echoing in his mind and felt them tearing at his heart.

"I hate you!"

These were the last words he had heard from her until just yesterday. He was truly glad to have his daughter back home, but still he worried about a girl being raised only by her father. He had hoped to find someone to be a good mother to Jenna but had not been able to bring himself to even look at other women.

Jenna looked so much like her mother that his mind began to drift back, back to a time when she was being cradled in her mother's arms.

Jace was jarred back to reality by the slam of the gavel as the auctioneer closed another sale and announced a short break.

Heading toward the stalls, he could see Jenna stroking the nose of a bay filly. He enjoyed watching his daughter. The filly nuzzled Jenna gently, reaching through the rails, to gently brush her silken nose across Jenna's cheek.

"Did you get the two colts you wanted?" Jenna asked quietly as her father came to stand beside her.

The filly still reached toward Jenna as she turned to face her father. Her words seemed cold and Jace knew the only reason she had come to the sale with him was to see all the beautiful horses. After all this time, she still hated him, and he knew it.

"We got the brown gelding, but the sorrel won't go on the block until near the end of the sale."

Jace wondered if she even heard him as she had turned back to face the filly.

Jace let his eyes wander over the filly. *She is a fair size for a filly, but a bit thin,* he thought. *Besides, I prefer geldings. They are generally stronger, more muscular and aggressive. Fillies just can't run against geldings and win. Still, she is very straight in her legs with a nice slope on her shoulder.* The horse also had a slight scar on her left foreleg but it was hardly noticeable.

His eyes continued to inspect her, stopping at her hindquarters where the number "35" was painted on each hip. Slowly he walked back toward his table.

Tom sat at the table glancing through the sale book. Most people would think of Tom as just a farmhand. To Jace, he was his best, if not only, true friend. He had worked for Jace's father for many years, being more like the older brother he never had.

The sale was back in progress but moving quite slowly. One hundred horses were to be sold with short breaks after each set of twenty-five. Horse number 26 was just being led into the ring, a young bay filly by the name of Radiant Sunrise. She seemed nervous and danced uneasily around the ring. *Fillies are just too nervous and uptight,* Jace thought. He only bought mares for breeding.

"Jace? Did you hear what I said?" Tom asked, interrupting Jace's train of thought.

"No, I'm sorry, Tom. What was it you said?"

"Well, I was wondering about the filly in the ring. You are watching her so intently, I thought maybe you were thinking of buying her."

"No ... not her, but what do you think of this one?"

Jace's finger pointed to the page in the book where the number "35" was printed in the top left-hand corner.

Tom's eyes drifted over the filly's pedigree. She had good breeding, came from a good farm and was a spring baby born the first part of May.

"She looks real good," Tom replied, but Jace never bought fillies, so Tom turned his attention back to the ring as the next horse was brought in.

A sorrel horse colt walked calmly around the ring as the auctioneer coaxed for a higher price.

"So ... what do you think?" Jace questioned, still looking at the sale book.

"Well, you know, Jace, you usually don't look at fillies for running, but she's got real good breeding and, if she's anything like her name, maybe she'd be worth a look. "

Jace glanced at the name at the top of the page. "For Ever Dashin' " was printed in bold letters next to the number "35." It was a good name.

He glanced back over toward the outer stalls. Jenna no longer stood by the filly's stall; instead a couple of the hands from the owner's farm were brushing the horse off, preparing her for the ring.

Truly Rosy, an older sorrel mare, obviously heavy with foal, walked slowly into the ring as the auctioneer announced her history and breeding.

Jace could see one of the stable boys begin to lead the filly toward the ring. Turning, he glanced around the room, looking for Jenna, but could see no sign of her.

Another brood mare walked slowly into the ring, her bay coat shining. Her back sagged greatly from the weight of her belly.

Slowly the bidding came to a close and Jace could see the bay filly being led to the entrance of the ring— she stood tall and still. Her eyes glanced around the room with a steady calm, not at all like many of the other young horses.

The black mare was led out of the exit as the filly was led in. She walked calmly into the ring. The sun coming through the window highlighted her bay coat. The auctioneer called for a bid and slowly the price began to climb, then stopped. The auctioneer's voice continued to hum, calling for another bid.

"Well, Jace, are you going to get her or not?" Tom's voice broke Jace's trance.

He couldn't believe she was going for only six hundred dollars. *Paying seven hundred dollars would be a steal. The breed fee to her sire was double that.* Jace quickly nodded toward the auctioneer.

"Seven hundred, I have seven hundred, do I hear eight? Do I hear eight hundred?" The auctioneer's voice seemed to pound in Jace's heart.

He never bought fillies, but seven hundred dollars was too good a bargain to pass up.

"Seven hundred once, seven hundred twice. Sold to Jace Brenton for seven hundred dollars."

Jace felt someone standing beside him and turned to see Jenna.

Gently she put her hand on his shoulder. "Thanks, Dad. "

Jenna turned to leave but stopped as her father spoke quietly. "I still need the other colt, and I don't have enough help for three new horses. Do you think you can be responsible for her care and the cleaning of her stall?"

"Oh, yes! I'd love to."

It was more than Jenna could have ever hoped for or dreamed of.

Racing back toward the stall where the filly stood, Jenna exclaimed happily, "Oh, he bought you and you get to come home with us!"

The filly seemed to understand and gently nuzzled the girl standing before her.

Jace and Tom sat quietly at their table as the sale continued, waiting patiently for the young horse colt they also hoped to take home.

Jace glanced toward the filly's stall to find Jenna leaning contentedly against the rails, gently stroking the filly's nose.

A young colt was being led into the ring as Jace returned his attention to the sale. The colt walked straight and sure, gazing intently at the crowd. His muscles flexed rhythmically as he walked.

The auctioneer called for a bid, "One thousand, do I hear one thousand?"

The crowd waited quietly for the first bid. Jace nodded toward the auctioneer and the bidding began.

"I have one thousand, do I hear twelve hundred?"

A man near the front raised his hand.

"I have twelve hundred. Do I hear fourteen?" coaxed the auctioneer.

The room buzzed with voices as the auctioneer continued, pointing out the colt's fine pedigree, muscular development and flashy appearance.

He was quite striking. His sorrel coat glowed, the sunlight dancing with the movement of his muscles. His white stockinged legs carried him smoothly about the ring. His eyes glanced about the crowd, their darkness contrasting against the white blaze that ran to the end of his nose. His ears turned to listen to the auctioneer.

"Fourteen hundred, now sixteen hundred from the lady. Do I hear eighteen ... eighteen hundred?"

Jace turned toward the lady who was eyeing the colt. He hated to see such a fine animal go and again he nodded to the auctioneer.

"Eighteen hundred. I have eighteen. Now two ... two thousand ... do I hear twenty-two?"

Jace turned again to glance at the colt.

"I have twenty-two. Now twenty-four, twenty-four hundred, do I hear twenty-six? Twenty-six hundred, do I hear twenty-six?" the auctioneer asked looking directly at Jace.

"Yes, I have twenty-six!" the auctioneer's voice rang out as soon as Jace tipped his head. "Do I have twenty-eight?"

The auctioneer continued to coax as the room grew still, all eyes glancing between Jace and the lady who intently gazed at the colt.

"Twenty-six hundred once, twenty-six hundred twice ... sold to Jace Brenton for twenty-six hundred."

The colt was led from the ring, the white number seventy-five rippling with his muscles as he walked proudly through the doorway toward his stall.

The auctioneer announced a break, the crowd moving from the sale arena into the stall area and out into the cool breeze. The sun was beginning to dip into the mountains casting a golden glow across the land.

"Tom, if you'll get the trailer set up, I'll get the colts ready to load so we can head home. I'd like to get back before dark."

Tom nodded as he headed off toward the trailer. He felt good inside. The sale had gone well. They got the two colts and a nice young filly he felt might just surprise a lot of people, especially Jace.

Jenna was waiting at the stall when Jace came down the alley to get the filly.

"The colts are loaded so let's get her in the trailer and head for home."

Jenna nodded and opened the stall door so Jace could lead the filly out. His voice always seemed so angry when he talked to her and she wondered if, and why, he was mad at her. She hadn't asked him to buy the filly. She hadn't even said a word, but she was glad he had bought her.

Jenna loved the sound of the filly's hooves as she walked toward the trailer, her mind drifting with their echo. The filly walked quietly up the ramp, the sound of the trailer door shutting, breaking Jenna's aimless thoughts, was followed by her father's voice.

"Hop in, Jenna. We're ready to go."

In the truck, the silence seemed to close in upon them. Tom would come to the ranch tomorrow after he completed all the paperwork and got some supplies, leaving Jace and Jenna to themselves.

"Well, Jenna, she's yours to take care of if you want, but remember she's a racehorse not a pet. She needs regular meals, exercise, and specific training."

"Okay, I understand. I'll do my best. I want her to run like the wind, to fly like Pegasus."

Jace's mind began to drift as he drove for home, Jenna's words echoing in his head, *"... To run like the wind, to fly like Pegasus."*

Jenna's mom had said those same words about a dark bay gelding a long time ago. *Jenna is so much like her ...*

Suddenly he knew why he had bought the young filly. He had bought her for Jenna. He hadn't wanted to send her away. He had tried to explain to her that it was for her own good. It wasn't that he didn't love her; he didn't know how to raise a daughter. He was doing what he thought would be best for her and still she hated him ... or so he thought.

But now that she was here, he would do anything in his power to get her to stay, even if it meant buying a filly that Jenna liked. If she wouldn't stay because of him, maybe she would stay because of the filly.

His thoughts drifting, Jace knew in his heart why he had really sent Jenna away. She was so much like Shanna. He couldn't bear the pain, couldn't deal with the grief. It was easier to push it away, shut it out, and send her away.

Jace turned to glance at Jenna. She had listened to the mesmerizing sound of the tires rolling down the road, the breeze whistling through the window, until exhausted, she had drifted to sleep. Her head had tipped back to rest upon the seat, her long brown hair curling down her back stopping just short of her waist.

He turned his gaze back to the road as the sun slipped below the mountain ridge, leaving a glow of pink, orange and gold to blend with the evening sky.

The truck slowed, the brakes squeaking from the weight of the trailer, to turn down the gravel road leading to home. Large trees arched above the road, swaying slightly with the breeze. A couple of horses ran toward the truck, coming to a stop at the railed fence, before turning to follow the truck toward the barn.

Gradually the road came to a semi-circle where a giant oak stretched its large branches toward the sky with an old water well nestled beneath.

The well wasn't used anymore, but Jenna had always loved to make wishes, listening for the sound of the penny as it splashed into the cool water below.

Jace turned the truck toward the barn. It was not real fancy, but he was proud of the eight-stall horse barn with a run behind each stall, a large tack room, and one large foaling stall.

Jenna sat up slowly as the truck came to a complete stop. The horses shifting in the trailer caused the truck to rock awkwardly.

"Hop out and choose which stall you want for her and get it ready." Jace walked toward the back of the trailer, his voice trailing off as Jenna ran toward the barn.

She opened the large double doors and turned on the barn lights. A warm glow spread throughout and the smell of fresh sawdust and hay mingled with the breeze that flowed through the opened doors.

Walking toward the stalls, Jenna peered through the rear doors that led to the runs. She remembered that one stall had a large oak tree at the end of the run. Its branches spread almost protectively along the fence.

Gazing through the second stall on the right, Jenna glimpsed the tree through the darkness.

This is the one, Jenna thought as she quickly went to get the fork and ready the stall for the filly.

Jenna turned, her eyes searching out through the barn doors. Her father was unloading the three yearlings from the trailer, hooking them onto the walker.

She continued to watch as she got two buckets from the tack room and hooked them in the stall. She mixed up a special combination of oats and sweet feed with vitamins, filling the other bucket with fresh cool water. Jenna could hear her father in another stall and worked quickly to finish. Closing the rear door, she turned to evaluate her work.

Jace was coming down the alley toward Jenna carrying a large bale of hay. He stopped between the stalls to set it down, then cutting the twine, handed Jenna a portion for the filly.

Jenna loved the smell of the sweet hay and picked at a tiny purple blossom pressed gently in the leaves as she carried it to the filly's stall. Fluffing the hay, she let it fall gently in the corner of the stall, stopping to enjoy the sweet smell of clean sawdust, fresh hay and grain mingling with the cool night air.

"Well, Jenna, do you want to bring her in or should I?" Jace's voice broke through her daydream as she quickly rushed from the stall to get the filly.

Unhooking her from the walker, Jace handed the rope to Jenna. Standing back, he quietly watched as Jenna led her down the alley. The filly moved well and seemed to be at ease with the girl whose one hand gently stroked her neck, the other hand loosely holding the blue and white lead rope.

Coming to the open door, the filly stopped to look then followed Jenna cautiously into the stall. Flaring her nostrils, she sniffed toward the fresh hay and sweet grain. Patiently she waited as Jenna undid the buckle on the light blue halter, gently sliding it off her silken nose.

Turning toward the hay, the filly stopped to gently nuzzle Jenna. Blowing warm air from her nostrils onto Jenna's cheek, the filly carefully moved past her to enjoy the fresh hay and water. The trip had been long and the filly drank her fill of the cool water then continued to eat her hay.

Jenna gently patted her, then moved to close the stall door, leaving the filly to get used to her new home.

Jace was bringing one of the colts down the alley now and Jenna moved past to stand just outside the barn. Gazing up into the twinkling stars, she found the large bright star just above the old oak tree. Closing her eyes, she silently wished the wish she always made in her mind as the cool breeze brushed her face and danced lightly in her hair.

"Thanks for the help, Jenna. You did a good job." Her father's voice sounded gentle as she leaned quietly against him… if but for just a moment.

How I wish he would love me again or even like me enough to let me stay. But she was proud and thought; *I won't cry this time when he sends me back.*

Jace's hand gently caressed a curl in Jenna's hair before he stepped uneasily away.

"I'll unhook the trailer, Jenna. You better head in the house, it's getting cool out. I'll be in a minute."

Jenna rubbed her arms. She did have goose bumps, but she wasn't sure if it was from the cool night, the excitement of the day, or the gentle tone of her father's voice. Walking slowly toward the house, she paused at the porch to turn one more time and gaze toward the barn.

"Good night, sweetie," she whispered, thinking of the filly resting in her stall.

The large wooden door squeaked slightly as she entered the house, the light in the main room beckoned to her.

Jenna loved the old house her grandfather had built. The room was much as she remembered, the oak floors shining with the large soft rug in the center. The large rock fireplace framed on each side by oak shelves held all sorts of treasures. In the middle hung the picture she loved so much, her mother holding Jenna in her arms when she was a child.

Wiping a tear from her cheek, Jenna quietly walked toward the kitchen. Her stomach growled slightly. It had been a long day, and she knew her father would be hungry too. Quickly she made a couple of sandwiches from the roast that was in the fridge and poured two large glasses of milk.

The large wooden table looked just as she remembered except for the lack of flowers in the center. It felt good though to see the two places set across from each other, one for her and one for her father.

Jenna turned at the sound of the front door squeaking to see him standing in the doorway. He was quite nice looking. At six-feet three-inches in height, his slender yet muscular frame gave no hint of his thirty-seven years. His light brown hair was highlighted by the sun; a few stray gray hairs framing his tanned face. His blue eyes seemed tired as he gazed toward her.

Turning, Jace removed his boots to put them beside the door, a habit that Jenna's mom had encouraged to help keep the rugs clean and the oak floors shining. Hanging his Levi jacket on the brass coat rack, Jace moved through the family room toward the table in the dining room where Jenna sat quietly waiting.

Jace glanced around the room. The glow from the fireplace warmed the living room and spread toward the dining area. Pulling the chair out, he sat across from Jenna.

"Thanks, Jenna. It looks good, and the fire is nice."

Jenna turned to look toward the fire. She loved the way the flames reflected on the shining wood floor and gave a warm glow to the room.

"You're welcome," was all that Jenna could say and again an uneasy silence filled the room.

Finishing her sandwich, Jenna moved to the kitchen where she cleared her plate and finished the last of the dishes. Jace still sat at the table obviously deep in thought.

"Goodnight. Thanks again for buying the filly."

Jace stirred from his thoughts at the sound of his daughter's voice. It sounded soft, even loving.

"Jenna.... "

Jace stood and walked toward her. Leaning down, he gently placed a kiss upon her forehead.

"Goodnight, sweetie. I'll wake you in the morning for chores."

Ever so quickly, Jenna squeezed her father's hand, and then turned to dash up the stairs to her room. She didn't want her father to see the tears running down her cheeks. So often she had dreamed of her father kissing her goodnight just as he had before so long ago.

Jace stood somewhat confused as he watched Jenna run up the stairs, her brown curls flowing behind her.

Maybe I shouldn't have kissed her goodnight. He had wanted so to hold her in his arms. *If only she would forgive me.*

Turning, he strode, stocking footed, back to the living room. Sitting in the large rocker in front of the fire, he stretched his long legs out to rest them on the hearth and warm his feet.

The glow from the fire played lightly over the room, highlighting its contents as Jace gazed intently at the picture above the fireplace.

The glow from the fire enhanced the beautiful face that looked gently and lovingly at the child in her arms. *How I loved her and how I love Jenna.* Slowly Jace's head began to tip as his eyes closed and his mind slipped into an exhausted slumber.

CHAPTER 2

Jenna stirred slightly, noticing the light morning glow spreading throughout the room. Suddenly she thought of the filly. Jumping from the bed, she dressed and headed down the stairs.

"Jenna, come have some breakfast first, then we'll go do the chores."

Jenna turned back toward the kitchen. Her father, still in his clothes from the night before, stood in front of the stove scrambling some eggs. She could hear bacon sizzling as she walked toward the table, past the fireplace where a few embers still glowed from the night before.

The sun shone through the window, resting upon the table where her mother's beautiful white dishes sparkled, the light blue flowers decorating the edge. Jace smiled as he watched Jenna run her finger lightly over the flowers. He knew she had always loved the dishes, which was why he had unpacked them late the night before.

Breakfast over, the dishes done, Jenna and her father walked toward the barn. The sun, no longer resting on the edge of the mountains, now danced among a few fluffy clouds in an otherwise clear blue sky. Entering the barn, Jenna quickly ran toward the filly's stall.

"Well, Jenna, what are you going to call her? She needs to have a name and learn to respond to it. You can help me with the colt's names too if you would like. Even though they have their registered names it's good to have a simpler name, one that fits the horse."

Jace continued to walk past the filly's stall toward the colts, his voice echoing in the closed barn. "We need to open the doors to their runs so they can get out a little and let some fresh air in. You get the filly's, okay?"

"Okay," Jenna's voice drifted from the filly's stall where she was already opening the run door, the sun beaming in through the doorway. Gently the filly nudged at Jenna, pushing her toward the open doorway.

"Is it okay if I go out in the run with her?"

"Yeah, but remember she is a horse, and you need to watch her."

Jace could barely hear Jenna's reply as she was already outside in the run.

"Okay, Dad, I know."

Jenna climbed upon the fence rail to sit and watch the filly run and kick about. Stopping suddenly, the filly raised her head to sniff the morning air, and then turned to dash about the run some more. Jenna was so intent on watching her that she failed to notice her father come from the other run and stand beside her.

"Looks like she feels good. Why don't you just sit here and watch her? I'll get her hay and oats, then you can help me with the hose when I'm ready to water them all," Jace remarked as he turned to leave.

Jenna's smile was all the answer that Jace needed as he headed back into the barn, the sun's glow warming the back of his neck. In the barn, he turned once more to glance at Jenna and the filly, which nibbled gently at her shoes. He could hear Jenna's laughter mingling with the song of a bird perched in the oak tree, the leaves rustling in the light breeze. Smiling, he turned to continue his morning chores, enjoying the sweet sounds surrounding him.

Suddenly the filly stopped, turning her head toward her stall to listen. She could hear the sound of Jace pouring oats into her bucket. Moving quickly toward the open door, she turned to see if Jenna was coming, then moved to the corner where Jace had placed the fresh hay and oats. Eating hungrily, she forgot the girl who now stood watching from the doorway.

"Jenna, come run the hose for me," Jace's voice sounded somewhat angry, and she feared he was upset with her.

Quickly leaving the filly's stall, she moved to stand beside him. Grasping the end of the hose, Jace went from stall to stall while Jenna turned the water on and off. Spraying the alley lightly, Jace raked the dirt floor to leave the barn neat, clean, and smelling fresh.

Jenna had opened the extra stall windows, letting the sun and the light breeze flow throughout. Standing together at the barn doors, Jenna and her father took a moment to enjoy the stillness of the morning.

In the distance a trail of dust could be seen coming toward the farm along the gravel road.

"Dad, look! I think its Tom."

Jace turned to look out across the pasture toward the large three-quarter ton truck loaded down with bags of grain and other horse supplies as it slowly turned toward the farm.

Tom's tanned arm rested lazily out the window of the truck as he pulled up the drive toward the barn, whistling to a song on the radio. He gazed toward Jace and Jenna. They were his family, and it was so good to see them together again.

The morning sunlight danced through the leaves down onto the truck as it moved closer to where they stood. Bringing it to a stop, Tom climbed out of the truck, the wind blowing though his graying hair.

"You're up pretty early, Jenna."

"Yeah, Tom. Someone had to do your work," replied Jenna playfully running to hug him lovingly.

He was like a grandpa to her, and it felt good to be back at the farm with him and her father. Tom's arms held her gently as he spun her around, the breeze blowing back her hair that she had braided that morning.

Setting her back on the ground, he gently swatted her on the behind.

"Well, honey, I'm here now so you just head in the house and see what you can do in there, maybe you could add some female touches and remove some of the dust and clutter."

Jenna skipped toward the house giggling.

The gentle breeze blew through the open windows as Jenna spun happily about the room. The smell of flowers sweetened the air, their bright colors adding a lovely touch. The wood floor and shelves were polished and shimmering with bright highlights, the curtains parting with the touch of the afternoon air, allowing the sunlight to add a warm glow to the room.

Jenna had always hated to clean at her aunt's, but this was different. This felt good, and Jenna moved about the house planning little changes here and adding a fresh touch here and there.

Jace glanced toward the house as he and Tom headed for the barn. They had finished cutting the second crop of hay just in time to work with the yearlings. Tonight the yearlings would begin their training.

Jace liked to go slow with his horses so they could learn and feel comfortable with each new step in their training. Some horses learned faster and easier, and some needed a little more time, but patience was what Jace believed was important.

"Well, Jace, it smells like Jenna's been fixing something, " Tom commented as he sniffed the air and pointed toward the house.

Jace hadn't noticed the smell at first, but now he could almost see the fresh rolls and hot soup, their delicious aroma floating on the breeze.

"I'll say, it smells real good," Jace replied as he noticed Jenna standing by the barn waving to him and Tom.

"You know, Jace, she sure looks a lot like her mom," remarked Tom as he waved to the girl who smiled brightly at the two men as they came to stand beside her.

"Boy, do you two smell like you need a bath!" Jenna teased happily.

"Well, maybe I should just give you a big hug," Tom laughed as he moved toward Jenna.

Darting quickly she moved down the alley, glancing back to see Tom chasing after her. Giggling uncontrollably, Jenna stopped in front of the filly's stall.

"Okay, okay I give! You smell... well, okay."

Tom stopped just in front of Jenna to gently swat her on the hind end before moving on toward the tack room.

"Can I help with the filly, Dad?" Jenna's voice still had the hint of a giggle as she stroked the filly's velvety nose.

"Sure, Jenna, but remember to wait for me. I'm going to do the colts first, okay?" Jace replied.

His voice sounded tired yet gentle as he moved toward the colt. "Hello, boy. Oh, do you want some attention?"

The colt arched his neck as Jace scratched him vigorously before leading him from his stall down the alley to stand at the crossties. A rope from each side of the alley snapped to the side hook on the halter holding the horse in place. The colt stood waiting as Tom and Jace came toward him, Jace carrying a blue and white headstall in his hands.

Gently the two men moved to place the shiny bit in his mouth. It felt strange and he stepped back to get it out.

"Easy, boy, it won't hurt you." Jace's voice sounded so gentle that Jenna turned to watch the two men working with the colt.

Tom stroked the colt along his neck and around his head. Jace stood on the other side to gently place the bit again in his mouth.

"Easy, boy, easy. That's it," Jace's voice calmed the colt as his gentle hand held the bit in his mouth, the other hand slowly raised the headstall up and over his ears.

His nostrils flared slightly as he turned his ears toward Jace's voice.

"That's it, boy. It's not so bad now is it?" Jace praised the colt, which almost seemed pleased with himself as he arched his neck and stood proudly.

"That's good, Junior. Good boy." Tom also praised the colt as Jace began to lead him to the walker.

"Why did you call him 'Junior,' Tom?" Jenna asked as she walked toward the two men.

"Well, he looks just like his sire, only smaller, acts like him too. Real proud and sort of cocky, so he's a junior." Tom eyed the colt as he moved through the barn door.

"Sounds like a good name to me. What do you think, Jenna?" Jace questioned, his voice drifting back into the barn.

"I like it. What do you think, boy?" Jenna asked the colt as he pranced around the walker, slowing just a bit to glance at the girl who spoke to him.

"It looks like it's Junior." Jace turned to move toward the barn again where the brown colt stood, calmly waiting his turn. "Jenna, do you mind doing Junior's stall while we start the other colt? You just need to freshen the sawdust and get his feed."

Jenna headed back to the barn, skipping lightly. Junior watched her curiously as she disappeared through the barn doors.

"No, I don't mind," Jenna called back as she picked up the pitchfork, heading into Junior's stall.

Jace led the big brown colt out through the stall door. He moved cautiously as he eyed Tom moving toward him, carrying another blue and white headstall, the silver bit shining. The colt stopped at the crossties where Jace clipped the two ties to his halter.

Brushing the colt off, Jace spoke calmly to him. "You like to be brushed, huh? Does it feel good?"

The colt moved his hindquarters toward Jace as he ran the brush down over his rump. "So, you like your butt scratched, huh?"

The colt relaxed as Jace finished brushing, then moved to take the headstall from Tom.

Jace ran his hand gently down his soft nose, slowly bringing the bit toward his mouth. "Easy, boy, I won't hurt you," Jace coaxed as he eased the bit into his mouth.

The colt took the bit without a fuss and Jace proceeded to pull the headstall up and over his ears. Quickly the colt ducked back at the pressure on his ears. Patiently, Jace again brought the headstall up, gently scratching around his ears, to slowly pull the headstall up and over his ears. Again the young colt attempted to duck away.

"Easy, boy," Jace continued to reassure him as he gently prevented him from ducking out of the headstall and eased it into place. "That wasn't so bad now, was it?"

The colt's ears pricked toward Junior's stall where Jenna stood giggling quietly.

"What are you laughing about?" Jace asked slightly irritated.

"Well, the way he would duck and step back looked like he was dancing." Jenna had moved out from Junior's stall to stroke the brown nose of the colt. "You're just a little dancer aren't you, boy?"

The colt sniffed curiously at the girl talking so sweetly to him.

"Dancer, huh? Well, that sounds like a fitting name. What do you think, Tom?" Jace questioned as he led the colt to the walker.

Securing the clip, he stepped back to gaze at the colts as they pranced around the walker, the afternoon sun warming their sleek bodies. He didn't hear Tom's approval concerning their names because his attention was focused on the horses. They moved well, each seemingly content with the new bits held snugly in their mouths by the blue and white headstalls.

Most trainers used a specific color for their tack. Jace had used the blue and white colors ever since he and Shanna bought the two yearlings that changed his luck. Jace's thoughts drifted through a maze of memories. *A brown gelding and a pretty sorrel filly; which shined like a new penny in the sunlight. The blue and white tack Shanna gave me for Christmas that year. The sight of the brown gelding flying down the track to win by a length his first time out. The little sorrel filly finishing the day off with another win.*

Duckin' the Fog and Delightful Dot, they had been the start toward a dream. Shanna had loved the big brown gelding she called Duck and had worked him and Dot on the track. Jace remembered the tears in her eyes when he had sold the big gelding. He couldn't understand why she had cried so. He was just a horse. They needed to buy new yearlings, and she knew that Duck and Dot would have to be sold so they could start with some new stock.

After Shanna's death, Jace couldn't bring himself to sell the young mare. Dot was so much like his wife, small but strong and always willing to try anything, to do her best to please him. Sometimes when he watched the mare gallop in the pasture, he could almost see Shanna riding her, the breeze blowing through her golden hair.

"Are you coming, Dad?" Jenna's voice startled him. The vision in his mind changed from the sorrel filly to the colts moving around the walker. His thoughts back to the present, Jace headed toward the barn.

"Yeah, I'm ready, Jenna. You go get her and bring her to the crossties. I'll get a headstall for her."

Jace watched as Jenna raced down the alley to get the bay filly, poking playfully at Tom as she passed. Laughing, Tom turned to follow Jace.

"Well, Jace, what do you think about the filly?" Tom questioned as he held up a couple of bits.

One was just like the ones they had used on the colts; the other one had a thin rubber covering.

"She seems to have quite a sensitive mouth so I thought you might want to try this one," Tom suggested as he raised the black rubber bit.

Reaching for the bit, Jace began attaching it to another blue and white headstall.

"I haven't used this bit since Dot ran," Jace mumbled almost to himself as he headed toward Jenna and the filly, which stood patiently waiting at the crossties.

Jace handed the brush to Jenna, and then stepped back to lean against the stalls, enjoying the scene of his daughter brushing the bay filly. The sound of her sweet voice chatting lovingly to the filly teased at his heart.

"Well, Jenna, have you decided what you want to call her?" he questioned quietly, not wanting to break the peaceful spell that seemed to fill the barn.

"I want to call her 'Dash.' Partly from her name and partly because she likes to dash about in her run."

Jenna continued to brush her as she talked, walking up closer to her head. "What do you think, girl? Do you like the name Dash?"

The young filly turned her head to nuzzle Jenna affectionately.

"Dash is a good name, Jenna, I like it." Jace moved toward the filly, gently calling her by name, "Easy, Dash, that's a girl."

Slowly Jace placed the rubber bit in her mouth then pulled the headstall up and over her ears. She stood still not the least bit bothered by the new bit and headstall and seemed almost eager to move toward the walker as Jace unsnapped the crossties.

Once on the walker, she kept with the brisk pace, never falling behind, always consistent. Dash glanced toward Jenna each time she'd come around, but never slowed or broke her pace.

"She did good, Jenna, real good, " Jace spoke proudly of the filly as he admired her strength and poise. "Well, we better finish the stalls."

Jace patted Jenna lightly on the shoulder as he passed her and moved into the barn.

Jenna turned to look at Tom who was standing close by, a big smile on his face. "Have you ever seen a prettier horse, Tom? Isn't she beautiful?"

"Yes, Jenna, she sure is, and she did real good today." Tom turned and headed toward the barn. "Come on, Jenna, help me with the grain."

Turning, Jenna headed into the barn, stopping just inside the doors to glance back at the filly, then ran to get Dash's grain bucket from Tom.

The chores done, Jenna watched her father lead first Junior and then Dancer into their stalls. Waiting quietly, she moved to stand at the barn doors and watch Dash as she patiently walked around the walker waiting for her turn.

Unhooked, she calmly turned and walked toward the barn, Jace gently patting her on the neck. Stopping in front of Jenna, he handed the blue and white rope to her as she smiled from ear to ear. The two headed down the alley to leave Jace leaning against the barn doors.

"Well, Tom, let's get washed up and see what Jenna made for dinner. I'm sure it's better than either of us would fix ... you know what I mean?" Jace laughed lightly, then turned toward Jenna. "Do you need some help with her?"

"No, I'm corning. I'm just giving her a lovey good night." Jenna nuzzled the filly, closed her stall door, and then turned to rush past her father and Tom. "Give me a few minutes to set the table and maybe you could wash up a bit," she giggled happily.

"Do you think she meant something by that?" Tom laughed as he nudged Jace, both obviously aware of their physical appearances. "Tell Jenna I'll be there in about fifteen minutes or so, okay?"

Tom headed back toward the old bunkhouse that he and Jace had converted into an apartment for him. He loved it there. It wasn't real fancy, but he was with the only family he had ever known – the people he loved and was happy with.

Washing quickly, he put on a fresh shirt, brushed his graying hair and headed toward the house.

Jenna had set the table with three bowls of steaming soup, a plate of hot sweet rolls and a pitcher of ice-cold milk. She had put on a clean outfit, brushed her hair and sat quietly waiting for Tom and her father.

Jace moved down the stairs, thinking how long it had been since he and Tom had cleaned up much for dinner. Stopping a moment, he gazed at his daughter as the evening sun shone through the window, casting a golden glow about her.

"It sure smells good, Jenna. I hope Tom hurries."

With that, the back door opened and Tom stepped in the room. Jenna smiled, both men were clean, their hair combed, and clothes fresh.

"Well, Tom, it's about time! I'm starved and it's getting cold."

Jace moved to sit at the table next to Jenna as Tom sat next to Jace.

Hot steam drifted up from the soup, while the fresh butter melted slowly on the hot rolls.

"Oh, Jenna, this is the best I have tasted in a long time. Wouldn't you say so, Jace?" Tom continued eating not waiting for a reply as Jace relished the taste of Shanna's roll recipe. *It has been a long time.*

Dinner over and the dishes done, Jenna moved toward the stairs. Stopping at their base, she turned toward the two men sitting near the fireplace talking intently, not even aware of her presence.

"Good night, Tom. Good night, Dad," Jenna quietly spoke as she began to ascend the stairs.

The two men turned toward the soft voice to see Jenna moving sleepily up the stairs.

"Good night, Jenna," their voices rang out simultaneously.

Jenna stretched lazily in the soft covers turning in her bed to gaze out the window at the stars. The sounds of the night drifted in with the cool night breeze, lulling her into a peaceful sleep, mixed with dreams and memories.

CHAPTER 3

Jenna leaned lazily against the rail fence, gazing at the sorrel mare running casually about the pasture, seemingly for the pure joy of running. The sun gave her sorrel coat the shine of a new penny, highlighting her muscles as they rippled with her movement.

Slowly the mare came to stand in front of Jenna, her nostrils flaring slightly as she sniffed at the grain in the small hand.

"Hello, Dot. I'm glad you're back. Did they take good care of you? It sure looks like it."

Dot ate hungrily at the grain, Jenna's sweet voice reminding her of another sweet voice in her past. She nuzzled Jenna gently, searching for more grain, causing Jenna to giggle lightly.

"Do you want to ride her?" Jace's voice startled her and she turned quickly to see her father standing behind her.

His hair was slightly damp around his face and at the nape of his neck. He had taken off his shirt due to the extremely warm weather, revealing his brown muscular chest and shoulders. Jenna could remember how she had loved to place her ear against his chest listening to the steady beat of his heart. He would stroke her hair gently as he told her a bedtime story. It seemed like such a long, long time ago.

"Well, Jenna, do you want to go for a ride on Dot? I'll saddle her for you if you want." Jace's voice broke her trance and Jenna's eyes moved up to gaze into his.

"Oh, yes, if it's okay."

He nodded and Jenna ran toward the tack room.

"I'll get her and bring her into the barn, okay, Dad?" she replied happily.

Her voiced floated over her shoulder and back to Jace who had also turned toward the barn.

A smile played lightly on his face as he walked toward the barn. It made him feel good inside to see her happy again. The sparkle in her eyes he loved so much gave him hope that someday she would forgive him. The summer was quickly slipping by, increasing the confusion in his heart, wanting her to stay yet fearing the future.

She is so good with the yearlings, and Dash has especially become quite attached to her. He wondered what he or the filly would do if she decided to go back to Lorna and Wayne's at the end of the summer.

Dot saddled, Jace led her back to the pasture, Jenna skipping happily by his side. The grass in the pasture bent lazily in the breeze as Jace helped Jenna up into the saddle. The mare moved slowly away as Jenna urged her into a slow gallop along the railed fence.

Jace's eyes followed her hypnotically, the smooth movement of the mare and girl together as one, their hair flowing lightly in the breeze, the sun highlighting them in a golden hue. He felt a strange tightening sensation in his chest, his eyes having trouble focusing as he realized the emotions rising inside him. So many memories… so many dreams… so many feelings… so much confusion.

Uneasy, Jace turned and strode toward the barn, trying to shake the feelings inside.

Jenna continued to gallop around the pasture unaware that her father had left or why. *How I love to ride, to feel the wind in my hair, the sun on my face, the horse moving under me.* Her mother had often taken her for rides in the evenings as the sun began to dip into the mountains.

Tears came to her eyes as her heart ached for her mother and the memories they had shared. Bringing Dot to a stop, Jenna leaned against the mare's neck, her tears falling lightly into Dot's mane.

Leading Dot down the alley, Jenna's eyes searched the barn for her father.

"Dad, can you help me unsaddle Dot?" Jenna's voice drew Jace's attention away from Dancer who stood patiently at the crossties.

"Sure, Jenna, just hold her there a minute, okay?" Jace answered as he continued to work with the big brown colt.

Tom and Jace were easing the stock saddle off of Dancer. Soon the yearlings would be ready to be ridden. They had all progressed well with their training. Jace was especially pleased with Dash and Dancer.

"Tom, if you will put Dancer away for me, I'll help Jenna."

Tom brushed Dancer lightly and then led him inside his stall. Closing the stall door, Tom stopped to watch Jenna with her father. Jace was undoing the cinch on the saddle as Jenna stroked Dot's silky nose.

"Dad, what made Dot lose the baby?" Jenna's question startled him, and he paused from what he was doing.

"Um, Jace, I told Jenna about Dot losing the baby," Tom spoke as he began to walk toward them. "Jenna asked where Dot was, thinking maybe you had sold her, when she first came home. So I told her about the baby and that the vet was just watching her for a while to make sure she was okay. I hope you don't mind that I told her."

Tom stood uneasily, aware of the memories that would resurface.

"It's okay, Tom, really. Go ahead. We will come inside in a few minutes." Jace nodded at Tom, an uneasy smile on his face. "Really, Tom, it's okay."

Jace turned back toward Jenna as Tom left them to talk. "Jenna, sometimes mares lose their babies. We will try and breed her again next spring, okay?"

He stroked Dot's neck lightly as Jenna's eyes watched him intently.

"Is she going to get sick like Mom did?" Jenna asked, the question cutting deep into his heart.

He had expected the question to come up someday, but he still wasn't ready for it. Jenna stroked Dot's nose patiently waiting for her father to reply.

"Jenna, the doctors said that your mom was sick before she got pregnant. That's why she lost the baby, and then she just kept getting sicker. There are some sicknesses that doctors don't know how to cure. They tried, it wasn't their fault, and it wasn't the baby's fault. It's just something that happened," Jace's voice stayed calm, but his hand shook lightly in Dot's mane as he continued to stroke her neck.

Hesitantly, Jenna put her arms about her father, tears falling lightly on his chest. Slowly he brought his hand down to run his fingers through her hair. Holding back the tears, he felt a burning in his eyes. Dot nuzzled them gently sensing that something was wrong.

"Come on, Jenna, let's turn Dot out in the pasture." Jace moved uneasily away from her to untie the mare. He didn't want her to see the tears filling his eyes, the pain filling his heart. "Get her a scoop of oats and I'll meet you by the gate."

Moving toward the tack room, Jenna brushed the tears from her cheeks. Quickly she grabbed a scoop of grain and headed toward the pasture. The sun was dipping near the mountains, the evening breeze cooling the earth. Jace stood by the gate gently stroking Dot's head, resting against her, the evening sun silhouetting them with a golden outline.

Hearing Jenna's footsteps on the gravel road, he stepped back from the mare, forcing himself to push the memories back into the corners of his mind. "Jenna, pour the grain out here then turn her loose. You can ride her again tomorrow if you want, after we get done with the yearlings."

Jace's voice seemed cold and Jenna knew the great heartache her question had caused, but she needed to know, to understand.

Turning to walk toward the house, Jenna carefully slipped her hand into her father's. A warm glow filled her heart, easing her fears. Jace too felt a comfort from the gentle hand so small in his and squeezed her hand a little tighter, not wanting to ever let her go.

Entering the house, Jenna could see the flames dancing in the fireplace. The days were hot, but the evenings grew quite cool for August and the fire gave comforting warmth.

"Run upstairs and clean up, Jenna. I'll fix dinner tonight."

Jace gently swatted Jenna on her behind as she headed up the stairs. Turning, Jace moved through the living room toward the kitchen, stopping momentarily in front of the fireplace to gaze above at the picture of Shanna and Jenna. His heart ached longingly as he turned toward the kitchen.

Jenna woke with a start as the thunder shook the house with its powerful roar. The rain pounded on the window, the lightning illuminating her room momentarily, only to be followed again by another roar of thunder.

Jenna had always been afraid of the thunder and sat huddled in her bed watching the lightning dance across the midnight sky, the thunder rumbling loudly.

Suddenly the sky lit up illuminating her room so brightly she thought for sure it was just outside her window. Nervously, she waited in the silence for the thunder that would follow, but another sound could be heard echoing quietly just before the loud rumble shook the room.

Carefully as the rumbling subsided, Jenna moved toward the window where she slowly opened it so she could hear the quiet echoing better.

Suddenly Jenna's fear was pushed aside. It was Dash. She could hear her whinnying and kicking her stall in fear. Quickly Jenna grabbed a blanket and headed toward the barn. Stopping momentarily at the front door, she waited for a pause in the thunder, and then running barefooted, raced for the barn.

The wind was blowing so hard that Jenna could hardly get the barn door open, but once inside, she wiped the wet curls from her face and ran to Dash's stall.

The filly whinnied nervously as Jenna came to stand beside her, her side quivering, her neck lightly covered with sweat, her nostrils flaring with fear.

"Easy, sweetie. I'm here; it's okay now. I won't let the thunder get you," Jenna soothed the filly with the same words her mother had said to her so long ago.

Slowly Jenna opened the stall door, still talking to Dash. "It's okay. I'll stay with you."

Gently she stroked the filly's nose and slowly Dash began to relax, jumping only slightly when the next roar of thunder shook the barn. Junior and Dancer stood cautiously in their stalls, listening to the sweet voice echoing throughout the barn. They too had their fears eased and turned to lie down.

A half hour passed as Jenna sat sleepily in the corner of Dash's stall wrapped in her blanket, humming quietly to the filly. Dash, now relaxed, stood lazily above the small figure.

Slowly moving back a step or two, Dash very carefully so as not to step on the girl eased herself down next to Jenna to lie beside her.

Jace awoke to the knock on his bedroom door and a voice drawing him out of a deep sleep.

"Jace? Jace, get up. I want to show you something. Hurry." Tom's voice finally broke through his clouded dreams and Jace moved slowly from the soft covers.

"Come on in, Tom," Jace mumbled quietly, sounding somewhat annoyed at being disturbed so early as the sun was not even lighting the sky yet.

"What's wrong?" Jace questioned as Tom moved to stand by the man pulling on his pants and fumbling sleepily for his boots.

The sound of the rain still pattered lightly on the windows, the thunder and lightning long since ceased.

"Well, Jace, there's really nothing wrong, but there is something I thought you ought to see," Tom explained anxiously, knowing that Jace was irritated at being awakened so early.

The cool misty air greeted the two men as they opened the large wooden door moving across the yard toward the barn. Jace mumbled about the wet muddy weather.

"If there isn't anything wrong, then why couldn't this have waited a couple more hours?" Jace questioned Tom as he opened the barn door, causing a slight squeaking noise with its movement.

"And what in the hell are you doing up so early anyway?" Jace's voice sounded ornerier than he really was, and Tom paid no attention to the angry tone.

"Well, Jace, we were having a pretty bad storm whether you noticed or not." Tom jabbed Jace lightly in the ribs. "So I came down to the barn to check on the horses."

Tom stopped a few feet from Dash's stall.

"Well, Tom, what is it that you couldn't wait to show me?" Jace questioned standing impatiently in front of Dancer's stall who now stood at his door watching Jace intently.

"Okay, Jace, now be quiet so you don't disturb them." Tom moved quietly to open Dash's stall door as Jace's eyebrows raised wonderingly at Tom's request, not to disturb "them."

What does he mean by "them?" Stepping forward toward the open stall, Jace didn't quite know how to react to the sight before him. His first reaction was spoken lightly.

"What the hell is she doing in here?" Jace exclaimed as he moved forward into the stall, only to be stopped by Tom's dark, tanned hand placed gently but firmly on the younger man's chest.

"Jace, don't spoil the moment. Enjoy it." Tom's words stirred deep in Jace's heart, and he stepped back slightly to gaze within the stall.

Moving her head slightly, Dash acknowledged the presence of the two men.

"Easy, girl, don't move. It's okay." Jace's voice had lost its annoyance as he moved to crouch beside the filly.

Reaching slowly, he moved to lift the brown curl that lay against the filly's neck. Jenna's head rested on the filly's withers, her left arm reaching around the horse's girth. Jace stroked Dash's neck, gazing wonderingly at the sight before him.

Lifting her head, Dash turned to gently nuzzle the small hand resting across her chest. He was amazed at how gentle the filly was. She seemed very aware and concerned about the young girl deep in sleep and moved ever so carefully, so as not to disturb her.

"How long do you think they have been like this?" Jace questioned, turning to look at Tom who stood leaning against the stall door.

"I'm not sure but at least an hour or so," Tom answered quietly, not wanting to wake Jenna or disturb the filly. "I think Jenna must have heard the filly whinnying and came out to see what was wrong. I too had heard her whinnying and kicking and was about to go check her myself when she stopped. So I waited, listening and drifted back to sleep for about an hour. When I woke up, I noticed the storm had pretty well quit and, since I was unable to go back to sleep, I had decided to check on the horses. I looked in Dash's stall and there they were. They haven't moved since I found them."

Jace shook his head in amazement, wondering what kind of a horse, especially this young of a horse, would treat a child so gently.

"Well, Tom, we better move Jenna so Dash can get up."

Jace stood to move closer to Jenna, moving carefully around Dash as Tom too moved to kneel beside Dash's head.

"Easy, girl, hold still while Jace picks her up," Tom spoke gently to Dash, stroking her soft nose.

Jace had moved behind Jenna to slowly lift her in his arms. Turning subconsciously, Jenna wrapped her arms around her father's neck as he moved back around the filly. Dash lay quietly watching Jace as he moved toward the stall door.

Nickering softly she waited for Tom to step back, before she stood, moving to nuzzle Jenna lightly before Jace moved past the stall door, Tom closing it behind them.

Jace carried Jenna toward the house and marveled at how much she had grown. Her sweet face nuzzled into his chest as he mounted the stairs toward her room that faced out toward the barn. Gently he laid her on the soft bed where sleepily she rolled over into the warmth of the covers, drifting back into the comfort of her dreams.

Jenna woke slowly, the morning sun spreading its warmth throughout the room. Confused, she thought maybe she had had a strange yet wonderful dream. Sifting through her thoughts, Jenna realized it was almost 9:00 a.m. and quickly jumped from her bed to dress and head down the stairs.

No one had woken her and she had overslept by more than an hour. Quickly she looked about the kitchen, finding it empty except for a few breakfast dishes in the sink.

Stopping only for a glass of milk, Jenna then ran out the door toward the barn.

The air had a fresh clean scent as the sun gently dried the wet earth. Jenna stopped at the barn door to gaze up at the blue sky now clear except for a few small clouds.

Opening the door, she could see Tom and her father stacking the storage racks with bales of fresh hay. Tom glanced at her, and then moved toward the back of the barn to get a couple more bales off the truck parked at the back door.

Jace too was aware of Jenna's presence but continued working, intent on the many thoughts running through his head. Jenna had moved to stand at Dash's door, watching the filly run quickly about the run of her stall.

Slowly Jenna realized the presence of her father standing beside her and felt a strange tenseness begin to move inside her, filling her with a sense of dread.

Tom stood at the rear of the barn watching, hoping that for once Jace would not lose his temper— for once he would look at things from someone else's point of view and think about her feelings.

"So, Jenna, you decided to get up, huh?" Jace's voice had a nasty touch of anger.

Jenna was confused as to whether he was mad because she slept in or because she had been in the stall with Dash. She knew he had carried her to her room, she could still feel the warmth of his strong arms about her, hear the beating of his heart from her dreams as her head lay gently upon his chest.

"I'm sorry, no one woke me." Jenna's voice was quieter than usual, her mind spinning, wondering what her father would say.

"Well, Jenna, if you wouldn't have been out in the barn in the middle of the night, you probably would have woke up on time," replied Jace with a harsh tone.

Jenna's heart sank slowly as a lump rose into her throat.

"Dash was scared so I stayed for a little while so she wouldn't be frightened anymore," she spoke quietly, but the filly heard her sweet voice and headed into the stall toward Jenna.

"I didn't mean to fall asleep..." her voice trailed off.

"For hell's sake, Jenna, she's a horse not a scared little kitten. Besides you could have gotten hurt in there. How many times do I have to tell you that you can't trust horses? She could have stepped on you or kicked you!"

Jace's voice echoed loudly in the barn causing Dash to stop in her tracks.

Looking at the man and the girl, she tilted her head slightly in wonderment of the anger she could hear and feel.

"She wouldn't hurt me. She loves me," Jenna started to explain when Jace cut her short.

"Damn it, girl, she's a horse! She doesn't understand love. I don't know where you get some of your silly ideas." Jace's words cut deep into Jenna's heart. "And if you can't behave yourself and do as I tell you, I'll have to send you back to Lorna and Wayne's."

"I didn't hurt anything! I don't know why you are always so mad. You say Dash doesn't know anything about love, but she seems to know more than you do!"

Tears burning her eyes, Jenna turned to race out of the barn as they spilled down her cheeks. Running to the pasture, Jenna collapsed on the grass beside the rail fence. Sobbing uncontrollably, she felt a gentle nudge on the back of her head.

Dot had come to see why she was crying. Turning over, Jenna reached to stroke the soft nose of the mare.

"Why is he so mean, Dot? I didn't do anything wrong."

Jenna told Dot all the things in her heart that were troubling her, tears still streaming down her cheeks, the mare listening intently. "And he says horses are just dumb animals that don't understand, but you understand, don't you, Dot?"

Jenna stood to wrap her arms around the mare's neck as Dot nudged her gently, her tears beginning to subside.

"Well, Jace, if you are trying to push that girl away, you sure are doing a damn good job of it." Tom's voice startled Jace for he had forgotten the older man's presence behind him.

Turning to face him, Jace found the barn vacant as the back door to the barn closed with an echoing thud, leaving him to stand alone in the empty stillness.

The day seemed to drag on forever as the tension made working together uncomfortable. Jenna quickly did her evening chores, cleaning Dash's stall, changing her water and getting her fresh hay and grain. Quietly, she stayed back from her father, waiting for him to bring Dash in from the walker.

Once he had gone back outside, she ran to Dash's stall wrapping her arms around the filly who nudged her affectionately. Shutting the stall door, she raced from the barn toward the house not noticing Tom who had been watching her from Junior's stall.

Dancer came prancing down the alley with Jace at his side. Quietly, he spoke to the big gelding before turning him into his stall patting him lightly on the rump.

"You know, Jace, you treat those horses with more understanding than you do your own daughter." Tom's words cut the air like a knife, for Jace knew that Tom was right.

Turning, Jace continued his chores, a rush of mixed feelings and emotions swirling inside.

Finished, Jace noticed the sun was sinking low, the barn growing dim. Again he stood alone aware that Tom too had left.

Walking toward the house, he could see a warm glow coming from the window. He paused slowly turning the knob, the door squeaking slightly as he moved into the room. Glancing about, he noticed the fresh flowers in the center of the hearth just below Shanna's picture. He could almost hear her sweet voice. *"Jace, honey, you need to learn to relax, look past what you first see with your eyes and look further with your heart."*

Slowly Jace lowered himself into the large recliner in front of the hearth. Gazing up lovingly, he searched the depths of the blue eyes captured so well, their ever knowing light seeming to send out love and understanding.

"Oh, Shanna, I'm sorry. I try. It's just hard sometimes. I didn't mean to hurt her feelings. I'm just afraid she's going to get hurt, and she just doesn't seem to listen to me. It's only because I love her..." Jace's words trailed off not even realizing they were spoken out loud.

Soothing warmth spread through his heart reminding him of the comfort Shanna had always given him. Rising, Jace moved toward the kitchen, a slight rumble coming from his stomach, not noticing the girl who sat at the top of the stairs wiping a stray tear from her cheek before she tiptoed back to her room, her heart filled with confusion.

CHAPTER 4

Jenna stood by Dash's stall gazing out the rear window through her run. A cool breeze twirled the bright leaves as one fluttered lightly to the ground.

"Oh, Dash, I'll only be gone for a couple of days and then I'll be back 'til school starts." Jenna wrapped her arms around the filly's neck, tears falling lightly off her cheek to run down the filly's shoulder, falling into the fresh sawdust.

Jenna had cleaned her stall early since she wouldn't be there in the afternoon.

"You be a good girl, Dash, and I'll be back soon." Jenna turned at the sound of the car coming to a stop just outside the barn.

As Jenna moved through the barn doors, she could see her Aunt Lorna talking to her father. Hesitating momentarily, she moved toward them, first slowly, then quickly as she ran to wrap her arms around her aunt. It felt so good to have her aunt's arms wrapped around her, holding her close.

Jenna closed her eyes, a vision of her mother filling her mind momentarily until Lorna's voice broke the spell.

"Oh, Jenna, I have missed you so much."

Lorna stepped back to take a better look at the young girl before her. "I swear you look more like your mother every day, especially with your hair highlighted by the sun and your beautiful face all tanned."

Jenna smiled shyly. "I have missed you too."

And Jenna truly meant it. She missed the concern and affection her aunt expressed so freely and lovingly. On the other hand, she didn't miss the big city or the silly little rules Lorna had, such as always looking and acting like a lady, which meant dresses, not pants. It was hard to ride a horse in a dress.

Today though she stood quietly, her hair curled, a small ribbon holding the front curls back from her face matching the light blue dress.

"And, oh, don't you look beautiful," Lorna continued her appraisal of Jenna, and then realized Jace had begun to walk away. "Oh, Jace, I'll have her back Sunday after church!" Lorna yelled toward the man who was now almost inside the barn.

Turning in reply, Jace just nodded and waved, then turned again walking into the barn.

"Sometimes, Jenna dear, I don't think your father likes me much, but then your mother and I were always as different as night and day," Lorna spoke casually to Jenna not seeming the least bit affected by Jace's indifference toward them, but inside Jenna's heart was breaking.

He didn't even say goodbye. He just turned and walked away, she thought. Lorna could sense Jenna's hurt and quickly tried to soothe her feelings.

"Now, Jenna, don't mind him. Sometimes when men have a hard time facing something, they prefer to act like they don't care or like they didn't notice anything."

Lorna put her arm around Jenna as they walked toward the car. Once inside Jenna glanced back toward the barn to see Tom standing just outside the door. Seeing Jenna turn toward him, Tom raised his hand to wave and smile lovingly at her as they drove away.

Lorna's house was about three hours away, and slowly Jenna drifted into a restless sleep lulled by the hum of the engine. Memories and dreams drifted through her mind.

As they neared the last mile, Lorna noticed the restlessness of Jenna's sleep and patted the sleeping girl gently on the shoulder.

"Jenna, honey? Jenna, we're almost home." Lorna's soft voice soothed Jenna's mind and brought her gently from her restless sleep.

Moving to sit up, Jenna could see the house at the end of the street. The yard was neat and trim, the small freshly painted white fence surrounding the house. Uncle Wayne sat waiting on the porch, swinging slowly.

"Well, it's about time my girls got home. Come give me a hug, Jenna."

Wayne's voice had a gruff tone but the smile on his face and the twinkle in his eyes warmed Jenna's heart as she ran to hug him. He was so different from her father, shorter and somewhat heavyset, with dark hair and bright blue eyes. It felt good to be there, for Jenna truly loved Lorna and Wayne, but still her heart ached for her father.

Chores done, the sun resting on the mountains, Jace leaned against the rail fence talking to Dot.

"It's pretty quiet around here without Jenna, don't you think, girl?"

Dot raised her head at the sound of his voice, pausing from her dinner to gaze at the man curiously before she resumed eating the sweet grain.

Turning, he headed toward the house. He missed the warm glow that usually flowed from the windows, as Jenna would busy herself in the kitchen.

Reaching the door, he stepped inside, stopping momentarily to search the empty room. It seemed even emptier than he remembered it being in the past. Slowly he moved to the kitchen, noticing the flowers Jenna had placed in the center of the table before she left.

Leaning over the table, he pulled one of the fresh daisies from the vase. Smelling the sweet fragrance, he closed his eyes momentarily— sifting through the jumble of feelings within.

Jenna tossed in the bed unable to sleep; a mixture of thoughts and feelings busying her mind; making it impossible to find the peace of sleep.

She felt so torn inside. *How I have missed Aunt Lorna and Uncle Wayne!*

They had made her feel so comfortable and safe with none of the confusion and hurt feelings that she felt with her father. They had never been able to have children of their own; and Jenna knew she had filled an empty spot in their hearts.

But what about my father? Does he have a spot in his heart for me? Does he need or even want me in his life? And most of all, with all the confusion and hurt between us, why do I feel this overwhelming need to be with him, to reach out my heart to his? He seems to have shut his heart to everything around him; nothing seems to affect him anymore.

Slowly her mind began to drift sleepily from her father to the filly she loved so much.

Visions of Dash eased her heart, and she slipped into a deep peaceful slumber.

Jace moved slowly toward the barn, the sky receiving its first glow from the morning sun filtering dusty rays of light through the barn windows. Dancer paced impatiently and Junior anxiously pawed in his stall, waiting for their morning hay. Moving in a daze, he fed the two geldings, then moved toward Dash's stall.

She hardly paid attention to the man before her, but gazed past him down the alley searching for the sweet familiar face.

"Who are you looking for? Huh?"

Jace smiled as he stroked the filly's forehead turning to follow her gaze. "She's not here, Dash, but she'll be back tomorrow night. Now go eat your hay."

Gently Jace pushed the filly toward her hay only to have her move back, continuing to gaze searchingly throughout the barn.

"Well, suit yourself, but you might as well eat."

Turning, Jace moved out through the rear door, the sky now bright with the morning light, the earth responding to its sweet warmth. Soon the day would grow hot, the warm dry breeze mixing with the fresh cut hay as Jace and Tom cut the last twenty acres. This was the last crop of the season, for soon the touch of fall would fill the air.

Jace generally kept his second crop of hay, selling the first and third crops. This summer had been dry, and hay was in high demand. With Jace's wells and higher location, his crops had been better than he could have hoped. Already he had contracts for all the hay he could supply at top dollar.

Jace stopped momentarily to gaze about him. He felt good. His father would be pleased with his progress.

As his eyes surveyed the rolling acres, he found himself searching for Jenna. She often brought fresh lemonade to him and Tom. Today, he didn't notice his thirst, but instead the empty ache deep inside his heart.

Realizing the ache, Jace pushed it from his mind as he glanced toward Tom who watched him intently.

Uncomfortable with himself for letting his daughter cause such feelings within, he returned to the work at hand.

Jenna's mind reached through the sweet depths of sleep as she tried to orient herself to the bright room about her.

"Come on, Jenna, are you going to sleep all day?" Lorna's voice brought everything together in her mind as she realized where she was.

The room about her was just as she had left it not quite two months ago. Lorna opened the white curtains, embroidered throughout with little pink rose buds, allowing the room to flood with sunshine.

Dressing slowly, Jenna languished in the warmth and comfort surrounding her, but there was something missing. Carefully she picked up the porcelain, winged horse that sat on the dresser in front of the mirror. Gently she stroked the smooth white glossy finish as she glanced from it to the reflection of herself in the mirror.

She did look a lot like her mother, but in the reflection she could also see her father. Her heart began to ache inside, a lonely kind of ache as she gazed deep into the reflection of her eyes.

Aware of someone watching her, Jenna turned toward the door.

"I'm sorry, Jenna, I didn't mean to stare, I just wondered if something was wrong."

Uncle Wayne's voice was warm and gentle when he spoke to her, and Jenna couldn't help but smile as he moved from the doorway to stand beside her. Gently he put his arm around her shoulder, leaning to kiss her lightly on the top of her head.

"Everything will work out, Jenna, don't worry." Wayne gently took the horse from Jenna's hands, placing it carefully upon the dresser. "Come on, honey, breakfast is ready."

Then he turned and headed toward the door. Jenna took one last look at the image in the mirror, and then turned to follow.

Breakfast over, Jenna and Aunt Lorna headed into town. Lorna was always making or sewing something and, as usual, needed to buy some more material.

Jenna wandered throughout the store, somewhat bored with the whole thing, fingering materials as she waited. Noticing a bright blue fleece material, she moved closer to feel its softness.

"Lorna, could I buy a few things?" Jenna questioned quietly, somewhat unsure of herself, for even thinking of making something. It wouldn't be anything fancy or special, but she had an idea for a gift for her father.

"Why sure, Jenna, you know I have always tried to encourage you to make things." Lorna's voice had a hint of surprise in it as Jenna well knew it would.

Whenever Lorna had tried to involve Jenna or teach her some new homemaking skill, she had been less than interested and did only what she had to. But regardless of her disinterest, Jenna had learned quickly and done quite well at cross-stitching and sewing.

"What are you going to make?" Lorna questioned.

"Well, it's kind of hard to explain, " Jenna answered, not really wanting to tell her, afraid she would not be very interested, since it was something for the horses.

"But, Jenna, it would be very helpful in deciding how much material you need if you would tell me what it is you want to make."

Lorna noticed the shy hesitation in the young girl, who stood nervously before her, gazing at the bright blue material, fingering it lightly.

"Jenna honey, it's okay. You can tell me. I promise I won't make fun of it. All I want to do is help you make what you want and have it look the best, okay?" Lorna's soothing voice and reassuring words comforted Jenna as did the gentle squeeze Lorna gave her shoulder.

"I guess you're right, since I'm not really sure how to make it. I just know what I want to make," Jenna quietly spoke as she turned to gaze up at Lorna.

"It's okay, Jenna, I'll help you. Now tell me what it is you want to make."

Aunt Lorna's voice was always so sweet and understanding. Jenna so dearly loved her.

"I want to make a set of shadow rolls, two sets of leg wraps and a matching saddle pad for the horses." Excitement began to rise in Jenna's voice as Lorna smiled lovingly at her.

"Okay, Jenna, we can do that. But I'm not sure what shadow rolls are. I know what the wraps and the saddle pad are so you need to tell me what the shadow rolls are and we will figure out what we need. Okay?" Lorna's voice became a bit excited too with the thought of Jenna wanting to make something, anything.

Lorna had seen a definite talent in the young girl and was pleased at the thought of Jenna doing something, even if it was for the horses.

"The shadow rolls are what go over the horse's nose covering the noseband of the bridle," Jenna began to explain to Lorna, envisioning in her mind what they would look like when they were finished.

Lorna listened intently as Jenna described in detail what she wanted them to look like, how big they should be, and how she wanted the leg wraps and the saddle pad to match.

Writing some figures on a piece of paper and making the final choice on the materials and threads with Jenna, Lorna handed the material to the clerk along with the measurements. Glancing at Jenna, who stood anxiously watching the clerk cut the beautiful white and blue materials, Lorna was pleased to see the bright twinkle lighting Jenna's beautiful eyes.

"I bet they will look just beautiful, Jenna."

Lorna turned to hand Jenna the package full of material, which she hugged lovingly to her chest.

Jace and Tom finished the last load of hay then headed from the hay barn toward the horse barn. They had both been unusually quiet, neither man knowing quite what to say to the other.

Tom gazed toward Jace, wondering what the younger man was thinking, if he too missed Jenna. Tom felt he knew Jace quite well, but since Jenna had come for the summer, Jace had seemed to even shut him out. Unsure of his place to question him, Tom had suffered in silence most of the day. He had waited for Jace to say something, anything about Jenna, but now something would have to be said if not by Jace then by himself.

Heading down the alley of the barn, Jace moved to get Dancer from his stall as Tom moved to get Junior from his. Then both men led the colts out to the walker into the evening sun.

"Well, Jace, I guess I have an extra stall to do tonight since Jenna's gone," Tom joked lightly, hoping to ease some response from Jace.

But instead Jace's voice was quite somber, his reply not at all what Tom expected. Standing by Junior's stall Tom wondered at the younger man's mood.

"Uh, Tom, listen, I'll do the filly. You look like you have had quite a day, and I don't mind." Jace headed toward the filly's stall seeming lost in thought as he gently reached to place the halter on Dash who gazed down the alley.

Jace glanced about her stall as he stroked her forehead.

"Come on, Dash, you've hardly eaten any of your food. What am I going to do with you?"

He continued to stroke the filly's head, content to stand close to her as she gently nuzzled him before she turned again to gaze down the alley toward the door.

"She can't always be here to feed you and if you don't eat, she'll think I didn't take good care of you."

Jace turned to lead Dash from her stall as Tom quickly turned back to his work, not wanting to make the younger man uncomfortable at being watched.

Almost through with the chores, Tom and Jace leaned against the barn watching the yearlings circle on the walker. Dash continued to look toward the house with each turn but kept her stride even and strong.

"She sure is looking for Jenna, wouldn't you say, Jace?" Tom's question broke the silence, speaking the same thoughts Jace was having.

"Yeah, I guess so. It does kind of look like the filly's gotten a bit attached to her."

Jace continued to watch Dash, thinking how much he too had become attached to her in such a short time.

"Well, we just might have to keep Jenna here I think. I know I like having her around," Tom gently coaxed Jace, but the younger man just gazed at the filly, watching her rippling muscles shimmer in the evening sun.

Tom, feeling uncomfortable with the silence, moved to get Junior off the walker. Jace continued to gaze entranced by the actions of the filly, her steady gaze intent on searching for the one thing that he too longed for.

Jace, aware of Tom's uneasiness, tried to ease his concerns though he was unwilling to admit his feelings about Jenna.

"I'm sorry, Tom, I guess I'm kind of tired today. Let's put her away, and I'll fix us some dinner."

Jace moved to lead Dash from the walker back to her stall. Once inside, she again turned to gaze about the barn before she took a small bite of the fresh hay.

"That's a good girl. Eat your hay and she'll be back tomorrow evening." Jace stroked her neck then turned to follow Tom toward the house.

Stopping momentarily, he glanced back at the filly who stood gazing toward him not the least interested in her hay or grain. Shaking his head to himself, Jace turned again toward the house, wishing Jenna was there so the filly would feel at ease.

Stepping up onto the porch, Jace opened the front door letting Tom go through first, almost dreading the emptiness within.

Jenna sat swinging in the porch swing, her eyes closed, listening to the sounds of the night. They were so different here in the city, even though it wasn't a very big city. Busy cars driving past were about the only thing she could hear. She missed the sounds of the crickets singing in the evening, the echo of the owls' hooting drifting through the night air, and longed to hear the horses nickering to one another as the cows' mooing drifted from across the field in a soothing lullaby. The night breeze caressed her face as her mind drifted through the sounds she longed to hear.

Uncle Wayne stood in the doorway watching Jenna, sensing her loneliness. He understood the sad look he could see on her face. Even though she loved it here with him and Lorna, her heart belonged somewhere else. Jenna had such a passion in her heart for horses, perhaps a special gift from God, and horses loved and responded to her as well. But then Wayne too had become very attached to her.

It would be hard, but he knew Jenna should be with her father. They needed each other whether they knew it or not. Suddenly Wayne noticed a single tear drifting down his rugged cheek and turned toward the kitchen where Lorna stood at the sink doing the dishes.

Stopping behind her, Wayne gently wrapped his arms around her holding her back to his chest.

"We need to let her go, Lorna. She belongs with her father, they need each other."

Wayne's voice echoed in her mind, coming to rest deep in her heart. She had been feeling the same way but had tried to ignore the feeling, hoping she was wrong. Turning to face Wayne, she buried her head in his arms as the tears trickled down her gentle face.

"I know, Wayne, but what if Jace doesn't want her to stay? What if...?"

Wayne's gentle fingers on her lips hushed Lorna's words lovingly. "He wants her, honey, he wants her so bad it scares him. He is afraid of being hurt, afraid of caring. But he needs her as much as she needs him. We just need to help each of them to see it. Give things time, and they'll work out."

Wayne always had a way of making things look better, and Lorna squeezed him gently as he wiped the last few tears from her cheek.

"With a little help, things will work out for the best." With that Wayne headed back to the front door, walking slowly out onto the porch.

The sound of the door stirred Jenna from her thoughts, and she turned to see Uncle Wayne coming to sit beside her in the swing. Gently Wayne pulled her to lean against him, his strong arm holding her gently.

"Aren't the stars pretty, Jenna?" Wayne asked as he tipped his head back and gazed at the twinkling lights in the night sky.

Leaning back against his arm, Jenna followed his gaze into the night's endless stars.

"They look the same, even though everything else is different." Jenna's voice, low and soft, spoke the words she was thinking, not realizing they had escaped her troubled heart.

"That's kind of the way life is, Jenna." Wayne stroked her hair lightly. "Wherever you go there are some things that always stay the same. Just like while you've been with your dad, you were somewhere different. But we love and think about you all the time and that is something that will always stay the same."

Jenna gazed at Wayne then back at the stars, trying to understand what he was saying.

"What do you mean?" Jenna asked, not sure if she should.

"Jenna, honey, I know you like it here, and I know you like it with your dad and the filly Lorna was telling me about. Sometimes it's hard to know what you should do. Now I don't want you to think we don't want you here because we do, but we know you miss being home with your dad, and that's okay, Jenna. A daughter should be with her father."

Wayne waited patiently for some sort of reply from Jenna, the night breeze swaying them gently as Jenna brushed a tear from her cheek.

"But, he doesn't want me. Remember? He sent me away," slowly Jenna's words faded, her shoulders trembling uncontrollably with the tears that ran freely down her cheeks.

"Oh, Jenna, don't cry." Wayne held her close as he gently wiped the tears from her face. "Your dad does want you, maybe he just doesn't think you want to be with him. Give things time, honey, they'll work out."

Slowly Jenna's tears subsided, her head resting gently on his shoulder.

"It's getting pretty late, Jenna. Come on and I'll tuck you in."

Wayne helped Jenna to her feet still holding her close to his side as they headed into the house, the swing swaying empty in the cool night breeze.

Not really feeling any energy within, Jace stretched slowly as he gazed toward the barn. The morning sky had a beautiful golden hue as the sun moved from behind the large mountains to announce the beginning of a new day. Stepping from the porch, he mentally scolded himself for being so lazy, not that he was really being lazy; he just didn't feel like doing anything.

Grasping the handle, Jace pulled open the alleyway doors to allow the sunlight to spread within. Immediately Junior and Dancer whinnied at the man who moved toward them, watching him intently. Dash too glanced at him momentarily, and then gazed past him, searching again for Jenna.

"For hell's sake, Dash! I take it I'm not good enough, huh?" Jace reached through to stoke her gently on the nose. "Well, it's a good thing she's coming home today because I can see you haven't eaten much again. What am I going to do with you?"

Dash turned her attention back to the man standing before her. He was leaning against the stall, a lost and lonely look upon his face. He also missed her, she sensed it and nuzzled his arm gently, and understanding better than he, the common bond they shared.

Tom paused quietly at the barn door enjoying the scene of the man and the horse before him. *They share a special bond between them,* he thought. *They both love Jenna awful bad. Only difference is Dash openly shows her feelings where Jace tries so desperately to hide them.* Tom shook his head thinking to himself, *If only Jace could open himself up to his daughter the way he's able to with the horses.*

Slowly Tom began to walk toward the horses drawing Dash's attention away from Jace.

"Good morning, Tom." Jace turned from the filly to face the older man who now stood beside him.

"She still hasn't eaten much has she?" Tom questioned as he gazed into the corner of the stall, still half full with hay.

"No, not much."

Jace moved toward Dancer's stall not really wanting to go any further with the conversation. They both knew why the filly wasn't eating, and Jace was afraid Tom would be able to tell just how much they both missed her if anything more was said. But Tom wasn't blind, no words needed to express what he already knew.

Jace led Dancer down the alley to the walker, while Tom slid the blue halter over Junior's nose, before leading him to join Dancer on the walker. Dash impatiently paced her stall. She hated being the last horse out and kicked the panel of her stall with her powerful hind legs.

"What's the matter? Didn't I take you out first?" Jace teased as he slid the halter snugly on her head.

She waited patiently for him to step from in front of the doorway then moved quickly down the alley, Jace walking close by her side. Dash loved the mornings and moved quickly about the walker kicking out her hind legs enjoying the cool morning air.

Jace and Tom quietly went about their chores. Done, they went to lean lazily against the barn to watch the yearlings.

"Aren't they beautiful, Tom?" Jace questioned, his gaze lingering appreciatively over each of the horses. He loved to watch them move, their muscles flex as the sun danced over their sleek coats, enhancing their strength and beauty.

CHAPTER 5

Jenna dressed slowly, a bit unsure of herself. She felt more comfortable in pants and hesitated as she slowly finished tying the bow on her dress.

"Are you ready, Jenna?"

Aunt Lorna's voice drew Jenna's attention from the mirror and her own reflection to the doorway where Lorna stood. Lorna always looked so nice, just as she did this morning.

"You look very pretty, Jenna."

Lorna stepped forward to run her hand lightly over Jenna's hair, its soft curls falling down her back. Gazing into the mirror she pulled Jenna to her, smiling at their reflection. *How I love her,* Lorna thought. She had always wanted a daughter and she gently pulled her yet a bit closer, knowing that today they would take her back to her father.

"Well, don't you two look pretty."? Wayne's voice drew their attention from their reflection to the man who stood beside them.

"Aren't you coming to church with us?" Jenna questioned Uncle Wayne as she wrapped her arms lovingly around him.

"Now, Jenna, you know if I walked into a church, the whole building would cave in," Wayne teased as he tickled her lightly along her side.

Giggling softly, Jenna turned to gaze at Lorna who stood smiling at them, shaking her head slightly.

"Oh, Lorna, honey, don't shake your head at me like that. You know it's true. It's been so long since I have been in a church..." Wayne's voice trailed off not knowing what else to say.

He had his reasons, and she knew that.

Lorna stepped close to Wayne, gently kissing him on the cheek.

"Maybe another time," she always said, maybe another time, but she would never force the issue, only hope in her heart that someday he might go. She knew he was a good and loving man, and God would know that whether he went to church or not.

"Come on, Jenna, or we'll be late." Lorna squeezed his hand lovingly as she turned to leave.

Smiling at the love and understanding they so obviously shared, Jenna moved to lightly place a kiss upon his cheek, then turned to quickly run down the stairs to catch Lorna's hand lovingly before they stepped from the front porch into the warm sunlight together.

Jace sat at the kitchen table surrounded by a jumble of papers, each filled with numerous figures.

"Well, Jace, I just thought I would check and see if you wanted to go to church with me?" Tom asked even though he already knew the answer.

Jace smiled and turned from the pile of papers before him.

"You know, Tom, I'm almost tempted today, just to get away from all this paperwork, but I think I'll pass anyway. "

"So how do the accounts look?" Tom asked pointing to the papers before him on the table.

"Things look real good this year. We came out better than I could have hoped, what with the price of hay up and the supply down." Jace thumbed through the livestock reports as he continued, "And the cattle sales were pretty good. I hope that bull can produce more calves next year."

"This was his first real season, Jace, I'm sure his production rate will increase next spring," Tom replied as he headed toward the door. "Well, I better go, or I'll be late."

Jace nodded and turned his attention back to the papers before him, his mind wandering. Tom had always gone to church. For Tom, it brought a great sense of comfort and peace within his heart. But for Jace, the peace and comfort wasn't there. Since Shanna's death, Jace had not set foot back into the beautiful oak chapel, his heart haunted by the tormenting memories. *The pain and loss of Shanna are so overwhelming that my heart seems lost, never to be at peace again. She was my comfort, my peace, and God has taken her from me. Why?* Jace shook his head, bringing his attention back to the many papers.

Tom had looked back momentarily, seeing Jace's head bent low to the table, resting heavily in his tanned and callused hands. *How I wish I could comfort Jace, to put his heart at peace.* But he knew it was only Jace himself who could open his heart and let the peace come in. Tom stepped quietly from the house, gazing wistfully up into the clear blue sky and past into the heavens.

Jenna packed her clothes carefully into the leather suitcase running her fingers lightly over the soft blue material before gently closing the lid. She had it all planned out, how to make the shadow rolls and wraps. They wouldn't take long and she could use her mother's sewing machine while Jace and Tom were in the fields. In her mind, she envisioned how beautiful they would look on the horses, especially Dash.

Her heart ached with a longing to please her father. *What if he doesn't like them?* Tears burned her eyes as she stared off into space, her mind wandering.

She didn't understand her own feelings sometimes. *Why do I love my father so much and feel such a need to be with him? He sent me way, and now I am so torn inside. I missed Aunt Lorna and Uncle Wayne when I was gone, and now I miss the ranch, Tom, my father, and most of all, the filly. Dash seems to understand me and comforts me, as words never could.*

Reaching to wipe a stray tear from her cheek, she remembered Uncle Wayne's words as they echoed in her mind.

"Give things time, Jenna, they'll work out."

Turning once more to gaze about the room, Jenna grasped the suitcase and headed down the stairs. Uncle Wayne stood at the bottom waiting patiently for her. He sensed her troubles and took the suitcase in one hand while he gently wrapped his other arm around her small shoulders.

Jenna gazed up into his loving eyes. No words needed to be spoken. She sensed his love and knew as he did, that given time, things would work out.

Moving together they stepped from the porch beside the car. Lorna sat patiently in the driver's seat because Wayne didn't care to drive. Jenna slid in next to her, making room for Uncle Wayne to then sit beside her. She felt so safe, sitting there between them, their presence such a comfort. Soon all her concerns seemed to fade away as she gazed at the passing world through the windows.

Jace moved about the barn with no real purpose to his actions, for the chores were all ready done. Junior and Dancer were eating contentedly. Dash had even eaten a little, but now stood watching the man pacing about, wondering at his mood.

She sensed something and now paced about her stall anxiously, gazing out through the barn door.

"I'm sure they are just running late, Jace. You know how Lorna always runs late." Tom's voice startled Jace, as he was unaware of the other man's presence.

"Oh, I know, I'm not worried. I just thought they would be here by now." Jace turned and walked toward Tom who now stood leaning against the barn gazing at the beautiful sunset.

Tom knew better. He knew Jace was worried and that was okay. He too was a bit worried and searched the gravel road for any signs of the car.

Dot stopped grazing. Raising her head from the grass, her eyes searched intently and a loud whinny filled the air's stillness. Jace turned to see the mare running toward a small trail of dust slowly moving toward them. Her tail held high, the beautiful mare floated along the rail fence coming to meet the car now moving down the lane.

"Well, I'll be damned! That girl's even got Dot under her spell. Did you see her take off when she saw the car?" Jace laughed, a big smile forming on his tanned face.

"It's probably because of that extra grain Jenna sneaks out to Dot every evening. But isn't that a pretty sight?" Tom pointed toward the mare running abreast of the car alongside the rail.

Dot's mane and tail were flowing behind her, her gaze locked on Jenna, who had moved to lean out the car, the sound of her voice dancing melodiously through the breeze.

Jace's gaze followed the mare's flight, coming to rest on Jenna; his heart pounded so hard he thought it would burst. The sight of her brought his emotions to the surface as he desperately struggled for control. *Oh, how I have missed her.* Shaking his head slightly, trying to clear his mind, Jace moved toward the approaching car.

Tom smiled to himself. Jace had maintained his composure, but not before Tom had glimpsed his heart melting, if only for a moment.

Jenna glanced past Dot to find her father and Tom moving from the barn door toward them as the car slowed to a stop, the dust floating in the air.

Jumping lightly from the car, Jenna ran to the rail where Dot stood anxiously waiting, her nostrils flaring slightly with each breath as her eyes shone brightly with anticipation. Jenna reached into her pocket pulling out two small cubes of sugar. Dot's gaze followed Jenna's hand as it moved toward her until she could devour the sweet treat while Jenna lovingly scratched her head.

"So that's what you've been giving her," Tom laughed as he moved to stand next to Jenna. "You've got yourself a sweet tooth, huh, Dot?"

The mare's eyes searched Jenna for any sign of a second helping, waiting patiently as Tom too stroked her lightly on her neck.

"Well, Jenna, it's good to have you back."

Jace moved to lightly put his arm around her shoulder just long enough for a little squeeze.

"I know someone else who will be glad you are back. I don't know what you've done to that filly, but she doesn't think Tom and I are good enough," Jace teased lightly as he moved toward the barn, the sound of Dash's hind foot connecting loudly with the panel of her stall. "Hell, girl, you better go see her before she puts a hole through that panel."

Jace smiled at Jenna as he motioned her toward the barn.

Jenna glanced about at Lorna and Wayne, who stood smiling at her before she dashed toward the barn door, her sweet voice calling to the young filly, "I'm home, Dash! I'm home."

Jenna's words warmed not only Dash's heart but her father's as well—the words echoing in his mind. *She had said, "I'm home." Does she really mean it? Does she feel this is home?*

Jace moved toward the barn, the others following close behind.

"You know, Jenna, she sure missed you. We could hardly get her to eat. Could we, Tom?" Jace gestured toward Tom, his mind racing.

I can get her to stay. I'm sure of it. She called this home, and if she knows how much the filly has missed her, and if I word it right, I'm sure I can get her to stay.

"Yeah, Jenna, it's true. She was always looking for you."

Tom glanced at Jace, knowing what the younger man was thinking. "I think maybe you better stay here and not go back to school in the city. That filly can't stand to have you away."

Wayne could see the look in Jace's eyes, even if he didn't realize it was there. He wanted her home just like Wayne had thought. He just didn't know how to get her to stay. Wayne smiled lovingly at Lorna, squeezing her hand lightly as they stood together, watching Jenna, who now stood with her arms wrapped tightly around the filly's neck.

Dash lovingly nuzzled her, nickering softly.

"You know, Jenna, I think Tom's got a point there. I think you are needed here a lot more than you realize."

Jenna turned to gaze at Uncle Wayne, his words stirring deep within her. *Is what he said true? Do they really need me, want me?* Jenna glanced shyly at her father, wishing he would tell her he needed her, if not for himself, for Dash.

Jace smiled at the two older men. *How can I ever thank them? They both set it up so perfect for me. Why is it so hard?* His mind clouded with thoughts, he hardly realized he was speaking until he heard the sound of his own voice.

"Well, Jenna, you know you are always welcome to stay. I have to admit you're a much better cook than either Tom or I and the school's not too far. I'm sure we could get you in for this year. Besides, I don't know if that filly will eat if you're not here."

Jenna paused, unsure of his words. They sounded cool, distant. Nervously she searched the faces before her, wondering if they too noticed. *Or am I being silly? What does it matter? He is saying I can stay. That is what I wanted.*

Sensing Jenna's confusion, Dash nudged her gently, reminding the girl of her presence, almost encouraging her.

"You know, Jenna, it would be nice to have you here," Tom spoke encouraging her, sensing Jenna's thoughts. "We would both really like you to stay. Wouldn't we, Jace?"

Tom knew in his heart what Jenna wanted to hear, but he knew too, how hard it was for Jace, at least for now to admit how much he needed her.

"Yeah, Tom," was all that Jace could say.

His heart was pounding. *What is wrong with me? This is what I wanted. Why am I now panicking inside, fear building within?*

"You know, Jace…" Wayne's voice broke his trance as he came to put his arm around the younger man, "that girl of yours kind of grows on you."

Wayne leaned close whispering, "Just give things time. "

Then he quickly stepped away letting the words sink slowly to the depths of Jace's heart.

"What do you think, Jenna? Would you like to stay?" Wayne questioned, glancing lovingly at Lorna who stood quietly watching, understanding well what he was trying to do.

She knew he was right. This was where Jenna belonged. They needed her here and even if Jace couldn't say it himself, he wanted her here. Lorna could see it in his eyes.

"Well, Jenna, dear, what do you think?"

Lorna moved to gently stroke her hair, knowing Jenna's need to know from her that it would be okay. "That filly does look quite attached to you."

Jenna turned from Dash to gaze lovingly up into Lorna's eyes. "Well, I would like to stay, if that's okay with everyone."

The smile on Lorna's face warmed Jenna's heart. Lorna knew how Jenna felt; she could see it in her eyes.

"Well, that sounds good to me," Tom spoke lightly wanting to ease the mood. "Jace and I put a little something together for dinner, and I'm sure you are probably all hungry. Jenna, tell that filly you are going to stay so she will eat something and then we can get something to eat. I'm starved."

Wayne smiled at Tom, the two older men pleased with themselves and each other. In just that simple gaze, they both knew that, given time, things would work out.

Jenna kissed Dash gently on the nose, and then latching the stall door, turned to follow the others who were heading toward the house, their idle chatter floating through the air.

Stopping at the well, Jenna reached into her pocket to pull out a handful of coins. Closing her eyes wistfully, Jenna tossed them lightly into the well, wishing her wish, and then waiting for the sound of their bright musical tone as they came to rest in the cool waters below.

"Are you coming, Jenna?" The sound of his voice so close almost made her heart skip a beat as she turned to gaze into the eyes of her father.

How I have missed him, how I want to wrap my arms around him, to feel his arms around me.

"Is something wrong, Jenna?" Jace was confused by her silence. *She looks so sad. Has she changed her mind?*

"No, I was just thinking." Jenna tried to sound casual, not wanting to give away her feelings.

"Well, let's go eat then, okay?" Jace gently put his arm around her shoulder drawing her toward the house.

The simple touch ran through him coming to rest in his heart. *How I have missed her; and now she is going to stay. Maybe Wayne is right; given time, maybe she will forgive me.*

Jenna walked slowly beside him, content with the feel of his arm about her.

Approaching the porch, Jace moved to open the door, not wanting to let go of her, he reluctantly let his hand slide down her shoulder lightly, touching her silky hair as she moved past him into the house.

Dinner through, Jenna ran quickly up the stairs to the guestroom. Opening the door, she could see the evening rays of sunlight floating in through the open window, the breeze gently blowing the soft peach curtains.

The room was freshly cleaned, a vase full of fresh flowers sitting on the dresser before her. Seeing the room all ready, Jenna turned, skipping down the hall, to meet Wayne, who was bringing up a small suitcase in one hand and Jenna's in the other.

Happily she took her suitcase, continuing down the hall to her room. Stopping momentarily, Jenna slowly opened the door, the sunlight spreading from the window to fall before her feet, dancing along the soft wood grain on the polished floor. Glancing up, she gazed about the room, her eyes greeted by the fresh bright flowers centered before the dresser mirror, their reflection mingling with hers as she gazed lovingly about the room.

Slowly Jenna reached to pull a single flower from the vase, enjoying the sweet aroma before she carefully threaded it through her hair. Gazing at her appearance in the mirror, Jenna saw something reflected behind her.

Turning, she caught a glimpse of her father as he quickly stepped from the doorway so not to be seen. Smiling to herself, she felt a warm glow spread through her. She knew who had fixed the rooms. *He does care!* The rooms were filled with warmth and love. *Maybe my father really does care!*

Jace stacked the wood carefully in the fireplace, his mind wandering with so many thoughts. Striking the match, he gazed at the flames as they spread across the wood, dancing, pulling his mind deeper into the mixture of feelings within him.

Why are some things so hard for me? Why can't I say the things I feel? How he had tried as he cleaned and readied the rooms, thinking of Jenna the whole time. The flowers and their aroma filled his senses reminding him of her, their bright color filling his thoughts, slowly changing to the bright flames still dancing before him.

"Well, Jace, everything looks really nice and it feels so good to be here." Lorna gently ran her fingers through his hair at the base of his neck as he slowly rose to stand beside her, feeling a bit uncomfortable by her touch.

But Lorna was always one to hug and touch. It was her way of expressing love and caring. It was nice to know she cared, but he glanced away uncomfortably to gaze at the flames as they spread over the wood, sending their warmth throughout the room.

"Thanks, Lorna, but Jenna did most of the house before she left."

Jace gazed down at the small woman beside him, her eyes gazing up at him. She always made him feel uneasy for he sensed she could almost see inside him, could read his thoughts.

Lorna knelt down, reaching her hand toward the dancing flames before her. "The fire sure is nice."

"Thanks. I thought Jenna might like it." Jace moved to sit in the recliner, stretching his stocking-covered feet toward the warmth.

The sound of Jenna's voice floated down the stairs as she and Wayne descended into the room. The fire's glow spread across her features, causing Jace to gaze admiringly.

She really looks pretty, he thought, her sweet gentle warmth mingling with that of the fire. Wayne moved to stand next to Lorna, bringing his arm lovingly around her shoulders drawing her close.

"Thanks for inviting us to stay, Jace. This is really nice."

Wayne moved to the couch drawing Lorna down beside him. "The farm looks really good. Can I ask how you have come out this year?" Wayne questioned, honestly interested.

"We did really good this summer, actually better than I could have hoped."

Jace watched Jenna as she curled up in the soft chair, noticing how tired she looked, then turned back to answer the questions Wayne asked concerning this and that. Jenna listened to the hum of their voices as she slowly drifted into an exhausted slumber.

A cool breeze drifted in as Tom closed the door, moving to stand by the fire, enjoying its warmth.

"Well, I just wanted to say goodnight. I really enjoyed visiting with you." Moving toward Wayne, he extended his hand as Wayne rose from the couch to accept it warmly.

"Goodnight, Tom," were all the words that Wayne spoke, but the strength of his grasp and the light in his eyes said so much more, and Tom knew this, understanding the deep bond of friendship they had.

They both loved Jace and Jenna and wanted the best for them. Turning quietly, Tom stooped carefully over Jenna to place a light kiss upon her forehead.

"Well, Jace, she sure looks peaceful, doesn't she?" Tom whispered as he moved to the door.

"Goodnight, everyone." Tom's words left the room in silence after the door closed with a dull thud.

The cool air dancing lightly across Jenna's bare arms caused her to cuddle up tighter for warmth.

"Well, I think I better carry Jenna up to bed."

Jace moved to place his arms gently under her, lifting her carefully from the soft chair. Instinctively, she wrapped her arms about his neck, nuzzling into the warmth of his chest, her mind in a deep and peaceful slumber.

Carefully, he carried her up the stairs to her room, enjoying her arms about his neck, for they seemed to ease all the aches from within him with their very touch.

Placing her gently on the bed he slowly ran his fingers over her silky hair, watching her for a moment before he tucked the covers close about her, then turned to leave the room.

Wayne and Lorna had both seen how gentle and loving Jace had been with Jenna as he carried her up the stairs. Smiling at each other, they moved toward the stairs.

Lorna yawned deeply. "Wayne honey, why don't you stay a bit longer? Maybe Jace will come back down."

Wayne knew what she was thinking. *Men sometimes need to talk to men without women about.* Smiling, he stooped to kiss her sweetly on the cheek. *How I love her. She always seems to sense the thing to do,* and Wayne trusted her senses. *I'll relax by the fire for a while; maybe Jace would like some company for a bit.*

Stepping back from the stairs, he watched Lorna move to the top and then around the corner out of sight before he moved to sink down into the softness of the couch by the warmth of the fire.

Jace glanced about the room as he slowly descended the stairs noticing Wayne reading by the fire.

"I thought you had gone to bed, Wayne. I hope I'm not interrupting you." Jace's voice drew Wayne's attention from the book as he moved to sink slowly into the comfort of the recliner, enjoying the warmth of the fire.

Its yellow glow danced across his tired face.

"No, Jace, actually I was hoping you would come back downstairs," Wayne spoke quietly, but his words drew Jace's attention away from the fire to the man beside him.

"Oh?" was all that Jace could manage to say, his thoughts racing, wondering what Wayne was thinking.

He had known Wayne for about sixteen years now. They had met when he had married Shanna. Wayne and Lorna had been married for a couple of years, living just a few blocks from the home where Lorna and Shanna had grown up.

The only two children, they had been so different, Lorna always so proper and loving the city life and Shanna so impulsive and wild, loving the country, animals, and wide-open spaces. But in spite of their differences, they had been very close, both beautiful in their own way.

The past years raced through Jace's memory as he realized he really didn't know Wayne that well. Wayne had always been so quiet, and they really hadn't had much interaction, but Jace felt a kindness and understanding as he turned to gaze questioningly at the man beside him.

"You know, Jace, I'm really not one to step in or say much, but I want you to know I feel you are a good man. Sometimes I think you are too hard on yourself. You worry too much about your feelings showing," Wayne paused momentarily as he noticed Jace's discomfort with the conversation, his gaze moving from Wayne back to the fire.

"But, Jace, having feelings doesn't make you less of a man, you are more, and sometimes feelings hurt, but if you shut them out, you will lose a part of the man within you. Jenna loves you, Jace, let her love you."

Wayne rose to stand beside Jace whose gaze was fixed on the flames before him. "I hope I haven't said anything wrong, Jace. I know things are hard sometimes. But give things time ... they'll work out. "

The room became quiet except for the sound of Wayne's footsteps moving toward the stairs. Stopping momentarily, Wayne gazed back at the man deep in thought.

Jace's eyes were burning from the warmth of the fire before him, *or is it tears trying to break free from their long held bounds?*

Finally Jace turned to gaze about the room, finding himself alone. He felt more alone than he had in a long time, *or am I just feeling what has been there for so very long?* Slowly he gazed up at Shanna's smiling face, not realizing the stray tear that escaped to roll slowly down his tanned face.

Jenna leaned against the rail fence still waving to the car that was turning from the lane onto the main road. She could barely see Uncle Wayne's arm waving out the window as he and Lorna headed for home. Dot had come to stand next to her, hoping for a sweet treat, drawing the young girl's attention away from the road as the car turned the corner, moving out of sight.

"Hello, Dot." Jenna smiled as she reached to scratch the mare lovingly on the forehead. "Sorry, girl, I don't have a treat right now, but I'll bring you one later."

Dot seemed to understand and returned her attention to the sweet grass, staying close enough for Jenna to pet and scratch her, for she enjoyed the attention.

Running her hands through Dot's mane, Jenna gazed off into the distance. The morning had gone by so fast. Lorna had fixed a big breakfast, and Wayne had even come out to help with the chores in the barn. Her father had seemed so quiet, and Jenna caught him gazing intently at her only to quickly turn away. She was confused by the quietness that surrounded her, almost like everyone knew a secret but her, each afraid to say anything. So the morning passed with idle chitchat till Wayne reminded Lorna they needed to get back.

How I wish they could stay, Jenna thought and hung on tightly to Uncle Wayne as he hugged her goodbye. Sensing her fears, he had whispered softly in her ear, and Jenna could still hear his voice, "Give things time, Jenna, they'll work out. I know they will."

Jace stood by the barn door as he watched Jenna, wondering what she was thinking. He had seen the tears in her eyes as Lorna and Wayne drove away. *Has she changed her mind? Maybe she doesn't want to stay after all.*

Jace cursed himself silently. *What the hell's the matter with me? Why can't I say what I feel inside? Why can't I tell her how much she means to me?*

Sensing his gaze, Jenna turned to see her father watching her, an intent look upon his face.

Slowly he began to walk toward her, causing Jenna's heart to pound in her chest as he drew closer. He always seemed so ornery, but now his expression confused her, for a soft smile replaced the usual hard expression.

Stopping before her, Jace moved alongside her, drawing her toward Dot, who stood watching them both intently. Slowly Jace reached to scratch Dot on her neck as the mare gently nuzzled the young girl beside him.

Jenna held her breath waiting quietly for her father to say something, anything, afraid, yet comforted by his presence. Slowly Jenna felt her father's arm wrap around her shoulder, pulling her closer to his side as he gently kissed her on the top of her head. Holding her close, his mind tried to say the right words, but they just wouldn't come. Squeezing her gently, he turned and headed toward the barn, disappointed with himself.

Jenna turned to watch her father as he slowly walked toward the barn. He confused her.

She didn't understand why he had held her close, then turned to leave, never saying a word.

CHAPTER 6

Jenna gazed intently at the night's stars dancing in the early morning sky as the sun slowly rose from behind the distant mountains to dispel the darkness of the night, the stars fading with the light. She had awakened early, unable to sleep, her mind filled with thoughts and worries.

The weeks had flown by, seeming but a blur, and now school was starting. Today would be the first day. Her heart pounded and her stomach seemed to rise up to sit in her throat. *What if the kids don't like me? Maybe they won't like the way I look or dress.* Slowly she turned from the window to gaze into her closet.

Jace and Tom had taken her into town to buy school supplies and some new clothes. Now here she stood fingering through the many hangers, trying hard to decide. Slowly she pulled a blue and white sweater from its place among the others. Lightly she fingered its softness, the blue almost matched the blue cloth she had bought and tucked carefully under her bed.

Jenna held the sweater to her chest squeezing it slightly. She would wear this one. Its hue warmed her heart, it was her favorite color, and her father had picked it out. Pulling on a pair of Levi's from the lower dresser drawer, she dressed and began fixing her hair as the sun's morning rays filtered through the window to brighten the room about her.

Quietly, she gazed at her reflection in the mirror as she brushed her hair, pulling it back a bit from her face to be held by a blue ribbon trimmed with lace.

"Are you ready to go?" Jace's voice startled her as she quickly turned to find him leaning against the door, a slight smile upon his face.

But Jenna had a hard time smiling, for again the feeling of butterflies filled her stomach.

"I guess," Jenna's voice quivered a bit, betraying her nervousness.

"It'll be okay, Jenna." Jace moved to stand beside her, and brush a stray curl from her face. "You look very pretty, so don't worry. Now come on or you'll be late."

Squeezing her lightly, he turned to leave the room.

"I'll start breakfast," his voice faded down the hall as Jenna glanced about the room, grabbed her jacket, then follow her father down the stairs.

Picking lightly at the biscuit and eggs, Jenna watched her father across the table. He ate quietly, not seeming to remember her presence, but glanced through the paper. Jenna took a few more bites, and then moved to leave the table.

"Jenna, is that all you're going to eat?" Jace questioned, still gazing intently at the paper before him.

"I'm not very hungry," Jenna answered quietly as she carefully moved toward the kitchen.

"Well then, head out to the truck, I'll be there in a minute."

His voice seemed a bit gruff, and Jenna quickly headed out to the barn, wanting to see Dash before leaving.

Jenna opened the front door. Scattered rays of sunlight fell about her feet as she stepped into the cool morning air. The leaves on the trees were turning bright colors of orange, red and yellow. Many had already been shed, now resting on the cool earth.

Pulling her jacket tight about her, she quickly ran toward the barn. The sound of rustling leaves announced her approach to the filly within. Dash raised her head from her morning hay to nicker softly as Jenna moved down the alley.

"Good morning, Dash. I see Tom fed you." She stroked Dash gently on the neck as the filly listened intently to her soft voice.

"I have to go to school today, but I'll be back soon..." Jenna stopped at the sound of her father's voice echoing in the morning's stillness.

"Jenna, come on. It's time to go."

Jace smiled as he stood by the truck, knowing well Jenna was just inside the barn wrapping her arms about the filly one more time before she left.

"Bye, Dash."

Jenna lightly blew into Dash's nostrils as the filly blew back a sort of goodbye kiss, before Jenna turned and raced toward the truck where her father stood waiting.

The sound of voices drifted from the large brick building as Jenna paused at the *door,* her heart pounding. She turned one more time to wave to her father as he pulled away. Slowly opening the *door,* her eyes scanned the halls as she moved forward, her stomach slowly rising to sit in her throat.

The voices hushed as eyes turned to watch the new girl before them, only to be interrupted by the sound of the bell ringing, its tone echoing loudly in the halls. Suddenly she was alone; the halls now empty as everyone had moved into their classrooms.

"You must be Jenna."

The sweet voice broke Jenna's trance as she turned to face the woman beside her. She smiled warmly at Jenna, her blue eyes twinkling as she moved to gently place her arm about her.

"I'm Mrs. Stewart, and I'll be your teacher this year. I spoke with your father the other day, and I'm so pleased you will be in my class…" her voice hummed in Jenna's ears as she walked down the hall beside her, the gentle tone of her voice soothing Jenna's fears.

Opening the door, Jenna hesitated, but Mrs. Stewart gently squeezed her hand as the hum of voices within drew quiet, and all eyes turned to gaze upon her.

"Good morning, class. This is Jenna Brenton."

Mrs. Stewart led Jenna down the aisle as she continued to tell the class about Jenna, their eyes all following them to the empty desk near the back of the classroom.

"Here, Jenna, you may use this desk. Now, class, please turn your math books to today's lesson."

Mrs. Stewart handed Jenna a math book, then moved to the front of the class as Jenna nervously slid into the seat, then cautiously gazed about her. Many of the other students still gazed at her. Jenna smiled a shy smile. There were so many smiling faces about her that she wondered why she had been so nervous.

Mrs. Stewart's voice hummed soothingly and the lesson drew the class' attention from her. Soon she too was moved into the flow of the class activities, and the time passed quickly.

Suddenly the bell rang, and Jenna glanced at the clock. She was surprised at how fast the day had gone. Turning, she found herself surrounded by smiling faces and laughing voices.

"Now, kids, don't miss your busses."

Mrs. Stewart's voice barely broke through the hum, but slowly everyone moved toward the door, gently carrying Jenna with them.

The days passed quickly as the fall nights began to leave a subtle frost upon the fallen leaves. Jenna watched the morning frost warmed by the sun as it slowly turned into dewy puddles that ran down the windowpane as she glanced toward the barn.

She loved Saturdays and had been looking forward to today. Over the past few weeks, Tom and her father had broke the yearlings to ride and were now breaking them to the chariot.

Using Dot as a teacher, they would hitch one of the yearlings beside her, a large leather collar about their necks, the leather harness snug about their bodies to hold them close to one another. The iron tongue of the chariot became a part of the team, tethered closely between them.

Jace and Tom would stand in the chariot behind the horses, guiding them firmly with the reins. Dot would respond quickly while the yearling, learning from her, would respond somewhat slowly and awkwardly, not sure of himself or what he was supposed to do.

Jenna glimpsed a movement in the field, turning her gaze to watch Tom and her father riding in the chariot. Dot and Dancer worked together, their warm breath dancing mistily about their noses in the cool morning air.

Dot moved strongly with a steady pace as Dancer fought uneasily with the leather lines, uncomfortable with their restraint.

"Easy, Dancer, work with her." Jace's voice drew Dancer's attention as his ears turned to listen searching their meaning, listening and responding.

"Dot!" Jace's tone scolded the young mare, as she pulled hard on the reins, wanting to run with the young colt.

"Not now, Dot, he's not ready yet." Jace's gentle touch on the reins mixed with his voice brought the mare back to a slow and steady pace as they headed toward the barn, the wheels of the chariot breaking through the frosted earth.

Jenna enjoyed watching her father work with the horses. She could almost hear his words as they moved toward the barn.

Quickly she grabbed her jacket and gloves and headed for the barn, just as Jace and Tom brought the chariot to a stop in front of the hitching post.

"You are just in time, Jenna. Go get Dash, and we'll hook her up next."

Jace moved to unhitch Dancer as Jenna ran down through the alley to Dash's stall, almost missing his last words.

"Do you want to come with me in the chariot?"

His words drifted down the alley stopping Jenna in her tracks as her heart jumped into her throat.

"Oh! Can I?" Jenna turned to see her father coming toward her.

He had hooked Dancer on the walker and now walked toward her carrying Dash's blue and white headstall. His stride was a bit rough, the ache in his knees reflecting in his walk. A hint of a smile played upon his face, his heart warmed at the shine in her eyes and the smile on her face as she opened the door to Dash's stall.

Reaching to slide the light blue halter over Dash's head, Jenna anxiously anticipated what lay ahead.

Grasping the halter, Jenna led the filly from her stall to stand before her father. He gently placed the rubber bit into Dash's mouth, pulling the headstall snugly over her head into place.

"Go fix her stall and feed her. Tom and I will get her hooked up," Jace's voice seemed a bit gruff, but Jenna's excitement over-rode his gruffness as she hurried about her chores.

Once done, Jenna waited patiently for Tom and her father to finish hitching up the filly who stood anxiously, impatient to be out in the field. Dash enjoyed pulling the chariot and stepped back slowly with Dot, turning the chariot to pull alongside Jenna who stood waiting by the barn door.

"Well, hop in," Jace coaxed, reaching his hand out, helping her into the chariot to stand behind him.

Grasping the reins with both hands, he moved Dot and Dash into a smooth gallop, the cool air blowing through their manes and tails as they moved across the frosted earth.

Jenna loved the rolling of the chariot, the sound of the horses, and the feel of the cool breeze blowing her hair behind her, and the closeness of her father as they moved about the field.

"Jenna, come stand in front, and you can help me drive them. "

Jace raised his arm to enable her to move in front, having her place her hands in front of his. Holding the reins firmly in her hands, Jenna felt the strength of the beautiful animals before her. They worked together as a team, their heads tucked, necks arched, muscles flexed and rippling smoothly with each movement.

Jenna leaned back, her arms stretched holding firmly on the reins, her back resting against her father's chest. The caress of the morning sun warmed her face as she closed her eyes, feeling the splendor of the moment.

Jace brought Dot and Dash around through the gate to the hitching post. Jumping lightly to the ground, Jenna ran to gently stroke Dash's nose while Tom and her father unhooked the harnesses. The horses' sides heaved slightly, their hair damp with perspiration.

"Well, they looked real good, Jace. This filly sure seems to be catching on quick, " Tom commented casually while he lifted the leather harness from her back leaving her free to shake, the steam rising from her, to disappear into the cool air.

"Yeah, Tom, she's doing real well," Jace replied as he turned from Dot to set her harness aside.

"Jenna, put Dash on the walker when I put Dot on."

Jace turned to lead the mare to the walker as Jenna quickly untied the filly who danced about anxiously.

Turning to lead Dash toward the walker, Jenna felt a bit nervous as Dash pranced about, still pumped with adrenaline from the morning workout.

"Easy, Dash," Jenna coaxed as the filly pulled on the lead rope.

Jace turned impatiently to see what was keeping them. Suddenly a dark shadow filled his face as he strode toward them, reaching to take the rope from Jenna, abruptly turning with Dash to move quickly to the walker.

Jenna turned slowly to brush the tear from her cheek, her eyes burning, her heart sinking. She didn't understand her father's actions. *What did I do wrong? I'm doing the best I can. Just because I'm not always fast enough or strong enough or whatever it is he wants, doesn't he realize I'm trying?*

Slowly Jenna moved toward the barn glancing back at the man who walked toward her. He seemed so angry and she quickly moved into Dash's stall to finish her morning chores.

The stall clean, the water changed, Jenna moved to get Dash her hay just as her father led the filly down the alley. Dash glanced at Jenna as they passed, but her father acted like he hadn't even noticed her. Turning Dash into her stall and closing the door, Jace moved down the alley past Jenna as she struggled with the twine on the bale of hay.

How I wish he would help me! The twine cut into her hands, bringing tears to her eyes as she pulled it off the end, allowing the bale to open. Grasping an armful of hay, she headed toward Dash's stall. The filly seemed to sense Jenna's feelings, nudging her gently before turning her attention to the fresh hay Jenna fluffed in the corner.

Jenna stroked her neck lovingly before she moved to leave the stall, but Dash sidestepped over a bit blocking the door with her hindquarters.

"Now, Dash, move your butt so I can get out," Jenna scolded as she slapped her lightly on her rump, causing the filly to lift her head from the hay, an almost mischievous look within her eyes.

Jenna pushed again on Dash's hindquarters, coaxing her to move, but Dash ignored the gentle push continuing to eat her hay, still watching Jenna out of the corner of her eye.

"All right, Dash, you win. I'll scratch you some more, but then you move so I can finish my chores."

Jenna began to scratch the filly's neck, running her fingernails firmly against the soft hair. Dash stopped chewing, slowly arching her neck to lean in toward the girl, a low moan of pleasure rising deep from within her throat.

"Okay, girl, now I have to go, so let me out," Jenna scolded lovingly as she stopped scratching the filly.

Slowly Dash moved away from the stall door, returning to the sweet hay before her.

"You sure are spoiled, Dash!" Jenna teased as she slapped the filly on the rump and darted past, noticing the hind leg that Dash kicked out toward her in a playful manner.

Jenna laughed as she closed the stall door, and then turned to see her father and Tom finishing the last of the chores.

Tom smiled lovingly, acknowledging her as she moved toward them. Jace noticed her, but moved to leave the barn, embarrassed by his gruffness with her, and a bit unsure himself concerning his mood. Tom gently squeezed her about the shoulders, not knowing what to say, but sensing her troubles, before he too turned to leave the barn. Jenna gazed about the barn feeling very lonely and confused.

Jace sat quietly on the bed cradling his head in his hands, running his fingers firmly through his hair. He felt so confused inside, troubled, yet almost angry with himself. *Why is it Jenna can touch my heart and make me melt inside, yet make me so angry with her? It isn't that she does anything wrong. It's more me, or something deep within me.*

"Oh God, what is wrong with me?"

Jace raised his gaze from the soft carpet toward the ceiling mumbling the closest thing to a prayer he could, before he rose and moved toward the bedroom door.

Moving down the hall, he paused at the closed door beside him. Raising his hand to knock, he stopped at the sound that drifted through the door to tear at his heart.

Jenna tried not to cry, but she was so confused and hurt. *Yes, hurt.* Her father's actions hurt her, and she didn't understand why he treated her the way he did. *He is never really mean to me; he just isn't very nice sometimes. One minute he makes me feel needed or even wanted, the next I feel that I am just in the way, not doing things right or good enough. I am trying hard to do things right and I am going to try even harder to make him happy, to please him in some way.*

Feeling useless, Jenna slowly buried her head in the soft pillows on her bed muffling her sobs.

Jace clenched his fist, his jaw going tense as he turned away from the closed door to stride down the hall. The echo of his steps was followed by the loud thud of the front door as he brushed past Tom, who stepped aside, wondering at the foul mood of the younger man.

Jace quickly climbed into the truck, spraying gravel from the tires as he drove down the lane. He wasn't sure where he was going, but he needed some space, some time to think. He didn't know how to handle Jenna's tears.

Even with Shanna, he had had a hard time knowing what to say. Slowly his mind drifted through a fog of memories as he drove down the road. The cool breeze blew lightly on his face, clearing a memory, the events becoming fresh in his mind.

Shanna's face— her tears, his anger, not at her, but at himself. She had come to him and still he tried to move away, uneasy with her emotions, compounding her tears with anger.

"Jace, don't you walk away from me! You wonder why I think you don't care how I feel? Well, if you cared how I felt, you never show it. You never ask what's wrong, you never try to comfort me; you just turn and walk away. How do you think that makes me feel?"

Shanna's words pounded in his head as he continued down the road more aware of his memories than where he was going.

"Shanna, I know what's wrong. I sold Duck. But you know why."

His voice had been hard and angry— angry with her for being able to express her feelings, for being able to let others see how she felt. He couldn't. He had been raised differently, and he honestly didn't know how.

His memory fogged, but he remembered trying to explain, trying to say the right thing, trying to justify what he had done that had hurt her so much. He remembered how she had moved to gently place her finger on his lips, hushing his words, her touch tearing at his heart.

"Jace, I'm not asking for an explanation or a justification, I just want you to acknowledge my feelings. Show some caring. Sometimes all I need is a hug, and it wouldn't hurt you to say you're sorry, at least sorry that what you did hurt me so."

He could remember how he had moved to gently wrap his arms about her trembling body, the touch of her reaching deep inside him.

As he drover he could almost feel her arms about him, feel the warmth within his heart. Slowing the truck, Jace gazed about; amazed at the distance he had traveled.

Bringing the truck to a stop along the side of the road, he looked off into the distant mountains. He needed to be more patient and understanding. He needed to remember to try and see things from Jenna's point of view.

Turning the truck, Jace headed for home. By the time he would get there, it would be time for dinner, and he slowly increased his speed.

Hearing the sound of the truck leaving, Jenna moved to the window to search the gravel road. Wiping the tears from her cheeks, she followed the truck, blurred by the tears still filling her eyes, until it moved from view.

She felt so lonely. She wanted so much for her father to just hold her, to feel loved and protected, safe in his arms.

Slowly she moved to kneel beside the bed, pulling the small box from beneath. Opening the lid, she gently lifted the soft blue material to hold it close, caressing its softness, her thoughts drifting with a mix of memories and dreams.

She remembered when her mother had given her father the blue and white headstalls and blinkers. He had smiled sweetly as he wrapped his arms about Shanna holding her close, obviously very pleased with the gift.

Slowly the memory turned to a dream as she envisioned a Christmas yet to come, of her and her father, as he would open the gift from her. The blue and white shadow rolls, leg wraps and blanket tucked carefully in the box, their rich color and fine stitches bringing a smile to his face as he removed the lid from the box. His arms would wrap about her holding her close to his chest. The gentle strength of his touch, spreading through her like a warm fire, the sound of his heart beating, telling her the things she longed to hear but were too hard for him to say.

Blinking back a tear, Jenna picked up the box and headed to the spare bedroom where her mother's sewing machine sat empty in the corner of the room. The blue thread was still threaded through the machine, waiting for her return.

The sound of the sewing machine hummed softly throughout the house as the clock ticked gently in rhythm.

Lifting her eyes to gaze out the window, Jenna was surprised by the amount of time she had spent, for the sun was gently resting on the mountain ridge, a golden hue spreading across the late afternoon sky. Quickly she finished the last shadow roll. Pleased with the results, she quickly replaced the material, and shadow rolls with the leg wraps and blanket.

Placing the lid gently over the treasures, she cleaned the cabinet, and removed the blue thread from the sewing machine. Moving to the door, she turned gazing about, a feeling of pride and accomplishment filling her. Replacing the box beneath her bed, Jenna rushed down the stairs to start dinner.

She had already planned and prepared most of the meal, all she had to do was turn the roast in the oven and put the potatoes and carrots on the stove. Satisfied with her work, Jenna quickly donned her jacket and headed to the barn, stopping momentarily to search the road for any sign of her father's truck.

"Jenna, honey, don't worry about your dad. We can do the chores without him." Tom's voice drew her attention away from the empty road as she turned to see Tom leading Dancer from the barn to the walker.

"Can you bring Dash out?" Tom questioned as Jenna headed into the barn, a smile spreading across her sweet face.

Tom watched her skip happily down the alley enjoying the freshness that Jenna brought with her. She loved the horses, they loved her, and the interaction between them was truly magical. Leaning against the side of the barn, Tom waited for Jenna and Dash to come down the alley, the two walking side by side into the golden hue of the early evening sun. The combination of the two was beautiful. The filly towered over Jenna, prancing excitedly, neck arched, muscles flexed as her bright eyes watched the girl beside her, frail in appearance yet strong in heart. Love and gentleness, not strength, controlled Dash as they moved to the walker beside Tom.

"You sure have a special touch, Jenna." Tom squeezed her gently as the walker began to turn leading the two young horses around the circle. Dash continued to watch Jenna as she and Tom turned toward the barn.

Jenna's heart was soaring inside. She had done real well with Dash, and Tom hadn't even had to help her. Since Dash had begun her training, the extra grain and exercise had made her friskier and harder to handle. Jenna kind of missed the way Dash had been before, but enjoyed watching the excitement and enjoyment the filly showed with the training.

Horses that loved and enjoyed the work did better on the track, and Dash truly loved to work and run.

"Do you want to lead Junior out too?" Tom's voice startled Jenna from her thoughts, making her heart skip a bit with the thought.

Junior isn't quite as gentle as Dash. What if I can't handle him?

"No thanks, Tom. I better not." Jenna's voice sounded somewhat sad. "He might get away from me, and I wouldn't want him to get hurt."

"Oh, Jenna, I'll help you. We'll just take it slow. I'm sure you will do just fine." Tom sounded so sure and eager that Jenna reluctantly agreed.

"First give him a handful of oats and just pet him for a minute," Tom coaxed Jenna as she moved to stand beside the gelding.

Petting him gently, she spoke softly, her voice teasing lightly at his ears as they turned to hear the words being spoken to him.

"Now, Jenna, he doesn't get as anxious about getting out of his stall as Dash does, but he does get a bit excited once he sees the others, but I'll be right beside you, okay?"

Tom stepped aside as he handed the lead rope to Jenna who smiled nervously as he opened the stall door, looking at Junior. Jenna continued to talk softly, drawing his attention to her as they moved from the stall.

Her heart pounding, she glanced out of the corner of her eye, assuring herself of Tom's presence as they moved down the alley.

"Easy, Junior," Jenna coaxed as they neared the barn door, her sweet voice competing with the sound of the other horses on the walker for Junior's attention.

"Be good for me, okay, boy?" Jenna continued to coax as he sidestepped and began to prance excitedly, causing Jenna to quickly look for Tom.

"It's okay, Jenna, you're doing fine," Tom reassured as he moved a bit closer to Jenna. "Give him a little more rope so he won't accidentally step on you. Just keep talking to him, he's listening."

Tom slid the lead rope gently in Jenna's hands, allowing a bit more slack, continuing to coax and reassure her as they moved through the barn doors to the walker.

Bringing Junior to a stop, Jenna waited nervously as Tom stepped away, moving toward the walker. Talking softly, she stroked the white softness of Junior's nose, distracting him slightly with her gentle touch and sweet voice.

"Okay, Jenna, hook him on." Tom's voice broke the trance as Junior stepped quickly toward his spot on the walker, Jenna by his side.

Her hand shaking slightly, Jenna struggled with the snap, trying to hurry, knowing Junior felt he had been good long enough. Slowly, Tom's tanned hands reached on top of hers, steadying their trembling as they fastened the snap. Squeezing her hand gently, they moved to turn the walker on, allowing the horses to move about.

They shared their excitement with each other as they spun, kicked, and ran about, confined only by the lead rope pulling gently from the walker.

Stepping back, Jenna breathed a sigh of relief as Tom wrapped his arm about her small shoulder.

"See, I told you; you could do it," Tom smiled lovingly as he and Jenna paused to watch the beautiful horses before them.

Jace stepped back from the corner of the barn to lean momentarily against the cold rough wood. He had driven in to find Dash and Dancer on the walker. Walking toward the barn doors, he stopped at the sound of the voices from within. Not wanting to interrupt, he stood quietly listening and watching, being careful not to draw any attention to himself.

The jealous feeling that filled him as he watched how gentle and patient Tom was with Jenna surprised him. *What is wrong with me? Why can't I be more like Tom?*

Moving carefully, Jace headed toward the back of the house as Jenna and Tom came through the barn doors with Junior. Slipping through the back door, he stopped momentarily before the fireplace, a mixture of feelings spinning within him as he glanced at Shanna's picture.

Turning slowly, Jace moved through the front door, letting it shut with a loud thud.

"Well, there you are."

Jace's voice drew Tom and Jenna's attention away from the horses to face the man walking toward them. Jenna was pleased to see her father yet somewhat nervous, considering his distant mood and impatience towards her.

Shyly she stepped back a bit as Tom replied, "When did you get here? We didn't hear the truck pull in. Did we, Jenna?"

Tom rambled on unsure of Jace's mood since earlier in the day, but truly hoping it had improved.

"You got here just in time to do the stalls with us," Tom chuckled as he slapped Jace lightly on the back.

"You mean you don't have the stalls done yet? I guess maybe I should have taken longer," Jace returned jokingly as he and Tom moved into the barn, leaving Jenna behind them.

She wasn't sure what to do and stood nervously alone.

"Well, Jenna, just because I'm back doesn't mean you're through," Jace teased, turning back to wrap a gentle arm about her shoulder, pulling her into the barn, a confused look upon her face.

CHAPTER 7

The days passed quickly, and soon the first signs of winter touched the farm, blanketing everything with its white splendor. Jenna gazed out the window, letting her mind drift with the snowflakes that floated gently to rest upon the windowsill.

She loved the snow, for with it would come Christmas. Kneeling beside the bed, she pulled the box from beneath, wanting to glimpse the gifts within. She couldn't wait for Christmas so she could give them to her father.

Replacing the box, she moved to quickly grab her coat, heading down the stairs and out onto the porch. Tilting her head back, Jenna closed her eyes letting the snow fall gently on her face, enjoying the touch of the cool morning air. The snow sparkled in the sunlight filtering through the few clouds that remained still sending forth a few fresh snowflakes.

Moving toward the barn, Jenna noticed Tom leading Dot from the pasture, her warm breath blowing out about her face, her eyes blinking with the touch of the snow falling upon her eyelashes.

"What's the matter, Dot? Don't you like the snow?" Jenna teased as Tom and Dot came up beside her.

"Oh, Jenna, you know Dot doesn't like to get wet," Tom reminded. "Besides, you know your dad doesn't like his horses left out in a storm when there is room in the barn."

"Do you have a stall ready for her?" Jenna questioned as they entered the barn, drawing the attention of the other horses that whinnied and nickered, welcoming Dot.

"No, but if you'll dry her off a bit, I'll get it ready for her."

Tom hooked Dot to the crossties, and then headed toward the empty stall on the other side of Dash, leaving Jenna with the mare who nuzzled her pocket gently smelling the sweet sugar within.

"Be careful, Dot, you'll get me in trouble," Jenna whispered as she held the sugar cubes out for the mare to nibble eagerly.

"All right, you two, who do you think you're fooling? Both Tom and I know about the sugar cubes."

Jace's voice startled Jenna almost making her drop the sugar cube still in her hand.

"It's okay, Jenna. Just don't give her too much and none to the yearlings, all right?" Jace's voice seemed gentle with a touch of humor.

"Okay," Jenna answered quietly her heart still pounding as she noticed Tom step from within the stall to smile and wink at her, knowing well her answer.

Jenna continued as Tom watched on, "Dash and Junior don't really like the sugar. Dancer does, but I won't give it to him anymore."

Quickly Jenna stepped around to the other side of Dot, continuing to brush her, hoping to escape any wrath that might come from her father.

"Jenna, what am I going to do with you?" Jace's voice was strangely gentle with a hint of laughter, causing Jenna to glance toward him over Dot's back.

There seemed to be a new light in his eyes that touched her heart. Jenna smiled as he unhooked Dot, leading her to the fresh stall where Tom had finished putting her hay in the corner.

Jenna moved to stand beside Dash's stall stroking her gently on her silky nose.

"She sure is looking good, Jenna. Don't you think?" Jace commented as he too moved to stroke the filly who turned to nuzzle him.

Looking from Dash to Jenna, Jace slowly wrapped his arm gently about her holding her close for a brief moment, before he turned and left the barn, remembering Shanna's words.

"You don't always need to say something, sometimes a hug can say so much more. " His heart felt strangely warm and content as he stepped from the barn into the cool air, the snow still falling gently about him.

Jenna leaned against Dash burying her head into her silken mane. *Is it too good to hope for? Does my father really care about me? Maybe even love me?* Jenna felt warm inside yet unsure as a strong hand reached to rub her gently on the back. Knowing Tom's touch, Jenna turned to accept the gentle hug. He sensed her uncertainty as he tilted her head back to gaze into her eyes.

"Remember, Jenna, just like Wayne said. Give things time, they'll work out." His gentle voice eased her fears as they too moved toward the house where they could see a faint trail of smoke rising from the chimney.

Jace relaxed by the fire, the glow warming him as he stood by the window, gazing out at the bright stars dancing in the velvety blackness of the night. Jenna had long since gone to bed, leaving him alone with his thoughts. *I am glad she is here with me; sometimes I don't realize just how glad I truly am.*

Gazing at the stars, he could envision her image, her sweet smile, and the twinkle in her eyes, as she would caress the filly gently on the nose. *She has a special touch with the horses; it's almost magical.* He loved to watch her with them.

Slowly another image filled his mind as he realized even more how much like Shanna she truly was. Sometimes it was almost scary how much of Shanna he saw in her. The image changed slowly to show another sweet face, stroking yet another horse, only bigger and darker with a snip of white upon the tip of his nose. *Shanna and Duck shared the same kind of magical bond between them that I can now see between Jenna and Dash, something truly special that is hard to explain ... perhaps a bond of the heart.*

Slowly he felt his chest tighten as the images touched deep into his soul. *Maybe that is why I keep my distance from Jenna. I don't like the pain brought forth by the memories. I loved Shanna so much, but never truly realized how much until it was too late. How it tore the pain, the hurt, the sorrow, and me apart.*

His eyes began to cloud and again he fought the emotions building inside, turning them into something he could deal with, anger -- anger at God for taking her away, anger at the doctors for not saving her, and yes, at Shanna for leaving him. *How could she leave me? Especially with a young daughter to care for?*

His eyes began to clear as he mentally used his anger to deal with the pain inside, his adrenaline rising, his muscles tightening as his fist clenched. Raising his gaze into the heavens a hoarse rasping sound escaped as the pain rose from deep inside, trying to break free, the anger ever forcing the pain deeper into his heart.

"Damn it, God! Why?"

His fist came down hard on the windowsill, causing a numbing sensation to spread through his hand, a small twinge of pain bringing him slowly back to reality. Sensing something, Jace turned to find the room empty, not noticing the small shadow that crossed the top of the stairs, creeping slowly down the hall where Jenna slipped quietly into the comfort of her covers, confused by what she had seen.

Jenna turned restlessly in her bed, pulling the covers back to cool herself, feeling unusually warm. Her head ached as she slipped back into an erratic slumber filled with strange dreams, darkness and confusion.

She could hear a voice drifting in and out of her dreams, yet preferred to slip back to the depths of slumber, turned and burrowed deeper into the softness of her bed.

"Jenna? Jenna, honey… "

Jace's voice drifted through the darkness, echoing softly as a strong hand shook her gently.

"Jenna!"

Jace shook her harder, trying to rouse her from her troubled sleep. He had heard her mumbling as he passed her room, her sweet voice slurred and rambling, a mixture of memories and feelings slipping forth from her fevered mind.

Jace's heart began to pound as he gently stroked her forehead, surprised by the intense heat that radiated forth. Gently he lifted her from her bed, moving to place her carefully in the center of his bed. She was so hot.

His mind spun, wondering what to do. *I'm not good with people when they get sick. I know what to do for horses, but what should I do for Jenna?*

Quickly he went to the bathroom, returning with a cool cloth, gently placing it on her forehead.

Stirring lightly, Jenna reached for the man beside her. She was so tired, yet felt a comfort from his presence next to her as he whispered softly in her ear.

"Jenna? Come on honey, wake up," Jace coaxed gently trying to rouse her.

Slowly the heavy lids of Jenna's eyes strained to open, seeing her father, if but for a moment, before their heaviness became too much and again the darkness closed in.

Adjusting the cool cloth upon her forehead, Jace turned to pick up the phone. Dr. Glenn lived about a mile down the road and Jace hoped he wouldn't mind the early morning call.

The voice on the other end of the line sounded a bit groggy, but understanding, and to Jace's relief, he was willing to stop by on his way into town.

After phoning Tom, Jace watched through the window for the older man as he hurried for the house. Moving into the room, Tom reached to caress Jenna's forehead.

Jace paced about the room as the sun began to lighten the night sky, the stars fading from sight. It seemed to take forever, but finally Jace heard the sound of a car and moved down the stairs to greet Dr. Glenn and lead him up the stairs to Jenna.

Waiting impatiently, Jace paced about the room some more while Dr. Glenn checked her. He said she showed early signs of pneumonia and would need lots of rest.

She flinched at the pain that broke through her fogged sleep as he gave her a shot. Turning toward Jace, Dr. Glenn handed him a list of things to do and some medicine. His voice buzzed in Jace's ears as concern filled his heart.

"Jace, she will be fine." Dr. Glenn patted him gently on the shoulder as he turned to follow Tom from the room, leaving Jace to hover lovingly over Jenna, who moved restlessly in the large bed.

Jenna stirred slowly, her body stiff and aching. She was confused by the appearance of the room about her and searched her memory trying to orient herself to her surroundings.

Sitting up slowly against the soft pillows, she reveled in the glow from the fire spreading lightly about the room intermixing with the morning sunlight that peeked through the curtains.

Her father lay sleeping uncomfortably in the recliner not far from the large bed where she lay wrapped in the soft covers. A hoarse cough racked her small body, causing her to shake with its intensity, the sound rousing Jace from his sleep as he quickly moved to sit beside her.

"How are you feeling, honey?" His voice was gentle, and Jenna melted toward him, desiring the comfort he offered as he tenderly wrapped his arms about her.

"I have been so worried about you. Don't scare me like this, okay?" Jace teased, relieved by the smile upon her face.

Gently he stroked her forehead, his heart truly elated by the sweet warmth that radiated forth instead of the previous intense heat.

"I'm sorry, Dad, I didn't mean to get sick." Jenna's voice was low and quiet, tearing a bit at his heart as he remembered Shanna's words so long ago.

"It's okay, honey. Now you rest, and I'll get you some soup. "

Jace moved slowly toward the bedroom door, glancing back to see her eyes flutter closed as she drifted back into an exhausted slumber.

Jace moved down the alley, enjoying the cool fresh air, the smell of the hay, and the horses about him. The day had passed slowly as he watched lovingly over Jenna. She seemed to be feeling better, but still slept deep within her troubled thoughts, tossing and turning in the soft covers.

Tom had come into see Jenna early that morning finding Jace beside her.

"Why don't you get out for a bit? I'll watch her, besides it looks like you need a break," Tom whispered quietly not wanting to disturb her.

Gently he brushed a loose curl from the side of her face, causing her to stir briefly as Jace moved slowly away from the bed.

"Are you sure you don't mind?" Jace stretched a bit, his body stiff from sitting so long.

"Well, actually, Jace, I saved Dash for you," Tom's voice lightened with a hint of humor. "You see, she seems to be a bit upset about Jenna not coming to the barn, almost like she senses something is wrong. Every time I go into her stall, she kicks out her hind leg at me. I don't think she wants to kick me, if she meant to, she would. I think she just wanted me to know she was upset."

Smiling back at Tom, Jace could almost see the filly raising her hind leg to kick out at the older man.

Jace opened Dash's stall door allowing her to extend her head through the doorway to gaze down the alley, searching for Jenna.

"Sorry, Dash, Jenna's not here. She's sick, but she'll be better soon." Jace spoke gently to the filly as he led her down the alley through the barn door.

Stopping, Dash turned looking toward the house as Jace watched her intent gaze and tense manner.

"Dash, come on. She'll be okay. Maybe she can come out for a while tomorrow. Now come on."

Glancing once more at the house, Dash turned and moved toward the walker, seeming to forget the girl as she moved briskly about, enjoying herself.

Jace leaned back against the barn relaxing in the quietness. His thoughts drifted aimlessly, the late afternoon sun warming his tanned face. Watching Dash, he wondered at her manner. She seemed to sense things and understand so much.

How much does she really understand? Why does there seem to be such a strange— yet magical— bond between her and Jenna?

As if sensing his thoughts, Dash paused, holding the walker still for a moment, the gears straining against her strength.

"Dash, get going!" Jace yelled, causing her to start walking again, though she continued to gaze back at him.

His thoughts disrupted, Jace headed into the barn to do the chores, noticing the amount of time that had passed. He hadn't realized it had gotten so late and quickly moved about the barn, his thoughts and concerns returning to Jenna.

A warm glow flickered about the room and down the hall as Jace moved toward his room. He could see Tom placing another log upon the fire as he moved to sit carefully beside his daughter.

Gently he placed his hand on her forehead, carefully brushing back her brown curls.

Jenna stirred, her mind fogged as she struggled to respond to the gentle touch.

"Easy, sweetie. Just lie still," Jace coaxed as Jenna strained to sit up. Slowly she leaned back against the strong arms that gently lowered her back into the softness of the bed, her head spinning.

"Do you want some soup, Jenna?" Tom asked as he moved to stand next to Jace, his heart comforted by the sweet but tired smile upon her face.

Nodding, Jenna tried to speak, only to hear a strange croak and notice the dry burning ache that radiated down her throat.

Jace reached for the small glass on the bedside table, gently encouraging her to sip slowly of the cool juice. The burning eased and Jenna realized she truly was hungry and ate slowly of the warm soup, until exhausted; she lay back upon the soft pillows.

"You rest, Jenna, we'll be right here."

Jace brushed a loose curl back from her tired face as she again drifted back to sleep.

"Well, Jace, I guess I'll head home. Call me if you need me."

Tom moved to kiss Jenna gently on the forehead, his voice drawing Jace's attention away from Jenna for a moment.

"Thanks, Tom, I appreciate the help," Jace spoke quietly not wanting to disturb Jenna as she burrowed deeper into the covers, comforted by their softness.

Tom quietly left the room, concern still filling his heart, yet with a sense of joy as he watched Jace lovingly care for his daughter.

Jenna awoke slowly, the morning sun falling lightly upon her face, drawing her from a peaceful slumber. The room was empty around her as she gazed about, comforted by the warmth the room held.

"Oh, you're awake."

Jace moved through the doorway pleased to see the sparkle back in her eyes as she stretched slowly in the large bed.

"How are you feeling?" he questioned lovingly, still concerned as he reached to gently place his hand upon her forehead.

"I feel much better." Jenna's voice was quiet, yet sounded more like the Jenna he loved so much as a sweet smile spread across her face.

"Eat some breakfast and then we'll get you cleaned up a bit, okay?"

Jace moved toward the bathroom, his voice fading slowly as the sound of running water filled the room.

"A good hot bath will feel good and then maybe I'll sneak you out to the barn before that filly goes nuts."

Jenna turned toward her father at the mention of the filly.

"Is she acting up?" Jenna questioned softly, a smile spreading across her face at the thought of Dash missing her.

"Well, Jenna, the first couple of days she wasn't too bad but I think she's a bit annoyed with me." Jace's voice was light with humor as he remembered Dash's actions that morning as she looked from him to the house and back to him as if to question him concerning Jenna's whereabouts.

"Days?" Jenna questioned as she searched her memories, *or were they dreams? How long have I lain in this large bed?* Her head pounded as she tried to remember.

"Two days, Jenna." His tone was soft as he remembered the past couple of days.

He had hardly left her side and had even called Lorna to ask her advice. Two days that seemed more like a week.

"Hurry and finish your breakfast before your bath gets cold. When your hair is dry, I'll take you out to the barn to see Dash, but only for a moment.

Jenna's head spun as she tried to comprehend what her father had said. *How sick have I been? All I can remember are strange dreams, soft voices, and feeling so very tired.*

Quickly she finished the last of her breakfast, her heart soaring with the thought of the filly as she moved to stand, suddenly aware of how weak and tired she really felt.

Jenna's heart warmed with her father's tenderness as she leaned contentedly against his chest, listening to the steady beat of his heart while he carried her down the stairs. Placing her carefully in the large chair before the fire, he wrapped her in a large quilt. Kissing her softly on the forehead, he turned to answer the phone as its ring broke the silence.

Jenna gazed sleepily at the fire, enjoying its warmth as she listened to the hum of her father's voice, not really hearing his words.

"Jenna?"

Jace's voice brought her attention away from the fire to see him standing beside her, extending the receiver toward her. "Jenna, it's Lorna."

Jenna's heart soared. *How I long to see Lorna. I have truly missed her.*

"Hello." Jenna's voice was soft and weak as she waited to hear Lorna's voice.

"Oh, honey, I'm so glad you are feeling better. We have been so worried about you. When your father called, I offered to come, but he wanted to take care of you, and it looks like he has done a wonderful job... "

Lorna's voice hummed on as Jenna concentrated on what she had said, *"He wanted to take care of you." Instead of sending me away or wanting someone else to care for me, he had wanted to!*

Lorna's voice continued to hum lovingly in her ear. "Your father has invited us for Christmas dinner. Isn't that wonderful? I can't wait to see you, but that will be a couple of weeks away."

Excitement filled her at the thought of seeing Lorna and Wayne.

"I miss you, and I can't wait to see you. Give Uncle Wayne a hug for me, okay?"

Exhaustion showed in Jenna's voice as she tried to cover a yawn, not wanting Lorna to know how tired she truly was.

"Well, honey, I'm glad you're feeling better. Now get some rest and we'll see you soon." Lorna finished the call sensing Jenna's fatigue, though Jenna reluctantly handed the receiver to her father.

Jace smiled at his daughter as she snuggled deep into the quilt before the fire. Exhausted, she quickly slipped into a peaceful slumber.

Jenna stirred slowly in the chair, stretching as she sat up to gaze about. The fire flickered, casting warm highlights about the room. Jace was moving down the stairs, his fleece jacket on, his arms carrying her coat, gloves and scarf.

"I was just coming to wake you."

He smiled lovingly at her, relieved to see the smile upon her face, the color in her cheeks.

"Now you can't be out there very long, but the fresh air might be good for you."

Kneeling beside the chair, he gently slipped her coat about her, wrapping the scarf snugly about her neck as she pulled the gloves on her shaking hands. Wrapping the rest of her in the large quilt, he gently lifted her into his arms, carrying her toward the door.

"Thanks, Dad," Jenna whispered softly in his ear, her head resting upon his shoulder as they moved toward the barn.

Tom turned to see what the fuss was as Dash quickly spun about her stall, kicking the side panel. Then suddenly she stopped, gazing toward the open barn door. Following her gaze, Tom could see Jace carrying Jenna toward them.

"Well, I'll be damned, Dash. You knew they were coming long before they even got near the barn. Is that what you were fussing about?"

Dash turned her head toward Tom acknowledging the words spoken to her. Impatiently she moved to bump the stall door with her strong chest, trying to coax Tom into letting her out so she could get to Jenna.

"Easy, Dash, she's coming. You'll just have to wait a minute," Tom soothed the filly, stroking her affectionately on the forehead.

Patiently Dash gazed down the alley to watch the man carrying the young girl she loved so much.

"Hell, Jace, she heard you coming long before you even got close to the barn," Tom laughed amused, yet touched with the filly's deep concern.

"Well, Dash, I told you I would bring her out as soon as I could. Here she is."

Jace moved close to the stall, enabling Dash to nuzzle Jenna in a motherly fashion, like a mare would her foal.

Opening the stall door, Tom stepped aside, allowing Jace to move into the stall, Jenna cradled gently in his arms.

"Easy, Dash," Jace gently coaxed as he moved along her side.

Jenna's heart swelled as her father gently placed her on Dash's back. *How I love to ride this filly, to even just sit on her, to feel her warmth and strength beneath me.* Leaning slowly, Jenna brought her head to rest on Dash's neck as the filly turned her head back to tug playfully with the corner of the quilt. Jace stayed close, but smiled, shaking his head slightly.

It is amazing the tenderness between these two. Love and affection, a simple and natural thing, yet it is something so hard for me. Why? He wondered, searching within himself if but for a moment.

Dash seemed to sense Jace's uneasiness and turned to nudge him gently. She felt the goodness and love in his heart and in her own way tried to show him it was there.

Petting her gently, Jace reached to lift Jenna off the filly's back.

"Come on, Jenna."

Dash turned her head to carefully hold the sleeve of Jace's coat in her teeth, trying to keep him by her side.

"Now, Dash, let go. I'll bring her out again tomorrow. "

Jenna wrapped her arms about her father's neck.

"Come on, Dash, let go," Jenna coaxed, stroking the filly on her nose as Dash reluctantly let go of Jace's sleeve, content with the attention and seeming to understand.

As Jace carried Jenna from the barn, the filly's gaze followed until they disappeared from view.

Jenna lay on the couch gazing at the glow of the fire as it intermixed with the light of the TV, the low hum of the show being the only sound in the room, except for an occasional crack or pop from the fire.

A light knock on the door followed by the low creak drew her attention toward Tom as he stepped into the room.

Removing his jacket and boots, he moved to kneel beside her.

"You know, Jenna, it sure is funny the way that filly worries about you. For the past few days she's been real uptight and now she's all stretched out dozing in her stall."

Tom enjoyed the smile that spread across her face as he gently ruffled the front of her hair, then moved toward the kitchen, the sounds of pans and dishes echoing out into the dining room.

"Would you like some help?" Tom questioned drawing Jace's attention toward him. "I could set the table if you'd like. "

"Well, I thought we would just eat out by the fire so Jenna won't have to get up and we could all just watch TV together for a while," Jace replied, as he glanced toward his daughter, noticing her soft laugh rising above the hum of the TV.

"It sounds like there's maybe even something good on for a change," Tom smiled at the idea.

He never watched TV much and savored the thought of lounging by the fire watching some TV with the people he loved.

The evening passed pleasantly, the glow of the fire, the hum of the TV, and the warmth of love filling the room. Jenna dozed sleepily, her father's watchful eye constantly glancing over in response to any movement or cough as his thoughts drifted with memories of the past few days. His heart felt full and warm, and he had a smile upon his face as he noticed Tom watching him.

"Well, Jace, I think I'll head to bed. I really enjoyed the evening. Thanks for inviting me to stay."

Tom moved toward the door, donning his jacket and boots, and then turning in response to Jace's reply.

"Tom, you know you are always welcome here at any time. You're family." Jace's words seemed to float across the room, their warmth reaching deep into Tom's heart as he quickly turned to leave, tears filling his eyes.

How much I love them both. Taking a deep breath, Tom moved slowly down the steps, gazing back at the warm glow radiating from the windows.

CHAPTER 8

Jenna busied herself about the house. She had begun to feel more like herself, but Jace kept her home from school and only allowed her to visit Dash for a short time each day, explaining she was still sick. Wiping the moisture from the bedroom window, Jenna gazed toward the barn, watching the horses move about the walker.

Opening the window a crack, she whistled, the sound breaking the silence of the evening. Dash turned, pricking her ears to follow the sound, her eyes searching the house.

"What's the matter, Dash? Did you hear Jenna?"

Dash turned spinning about on the walker, first searching the house, then turning in response to Jace's voice, his words teasing, "Well, where is she?"

The filly again turned to gaze at the house, her eyes focusing on the image in the window. Reluctantly, Dash turned away as the walker gently pulled her around its circle, only to again gaze intently at the window.

"Oh, you see her, do you? Do you want me to get her?"

Jace was amazed at the response of the young filly, she seemed to understand what he was saying as she began nickering softly.

Shaking his head, Jace moved toward the house as Dash became more and more excited. Opening the door, he called for Jenna as he moved to the base of the stairs.

"Jenna? Jenna, you can come out for a little while if you want," his voice echoed up the stairs to greet Jenna as she raced from her room.

She had seen him heading toward the house and had anxiously grabbed her jacket, hoping he was coming to get her. Running down the stairs, Jenna came to a halt beside him. He stood straight and somber, his expression blank, making it hard for Jenna to judge his mood.

Jace instructed her to bundle up and put on her boots. His voice sounded kind of gruff or maybe she just perceived it that way. Not wanting to anger him, Jenna quickly turned to put on her boots and wrap her scarf snugly about her neck. He stood calmly at her side, waiting to walk back to the barn with her.

Opening the door, they moved onto the porch, the cool air lightly touching her cheeks. She enjoyed being outside and quickly skipped toward the walker where Dash and the others moved quickly about, each turning their heads to gaze at her as she stood beside the barn.

Dash slowed, holding the walker still as she neared Jenna, who smiled lovingly at her.

"Dash!" Jace yelled, scolding the filly with just the tone of his voice, causing her to quickly move forward.

Moving into the barn, Jace passed Jenna without saying a word. She watched him pass, then turned to follow, but paused in the doorway, unsure if she should help or stay out of the way. He seemed to be kind of ornery and Jenna had learned to be careful not to anger him.

So, unsure, she slowly moved to Dash's stall, finishing the last bit of the chores.

"Jenna!" Tom's voice broke the silence, causing her to turn around to see his smiling face as he leaned against the stall door.

"Hurry and finish up. We thought we would go out and cut a Christmas tree. Does that sound okay?"

Jenna's heart soared with the thought, and she smiled happily as her father moved to stand beside them, the filly at his side waiting to move into the fresh stall.

Jenna stepped aside as Jace released Dash, sending her into the stall with a swat on her rump. The filly moved quickly to the sweet grain waiting in her bucket. Moving along the filly's side, Jenna stroked her silken nose as she leaned to kiss her quickly, aware of her father and Tom waiting at the door.

"Come on, Jenna, let's go if you want to get a tree," Jace growled slightly as he turned away from the stall.

He liked horses and enjoyed them, but felt it was a bit silly for Jenna to insist on kissing the filly goodnight all the time.

Sensing his disapproval, Jenna reached to quickly unbuckle the light blue halter, letting it slide off the filly's nose. Looking about, Jenna quickly kissed the filly one last time before she moved to the stall door where Tom stood waiting, his smile warming her heart.

"Well, honey, it sure is good to have you back out in the barn, but we better hurry so you don't get chilled again. "

Tom drew the young girl close, his arm about her small shoulders as they moved toward the barn doors. Jace had moved the truck, the engine running, to wait impatiently.

Hopping into the truck, Jenna realized she was indeed cold as she hovered close to the warm air blowing from the vents. Her father seemed angry as the truck moved down the lane toward the back fields where the road ran along the foothills, the trees framing the farm with a mix of pines, oaks and maples.

Tom too sensed Jace's mood and spoke lightly, hoping to ease the tension that seemed to fill the truck cab.

"It sure is a pretty evening, don't you think, Jenna?"

Jenna gazed about to notice the sun's glow as it spread across the field, casting a golden hue upon the fresh snow. It truly was a beautiful evening and she smiled as they neared the edge of the field, a row of pine trees rising next to the rail fence, reaching to meet the evening sun.

Jace too looked at the trees before him, his mind drifting with memories of past Christmas trees, of sunsets turning the snow to shimmering gold. Fighting the memories, Jace tried not to think of Shanna, her excitement and happiness concerning Christmas -- without her it just wasn't the same.

Slowing the truck, he pulled along a nice six-foot pine, pointing out its nice size and shape, his voice sounding empty.

But Jenna was too excited to notice as she jumped from the truck. The tree was perfect, just the right size, full and green. Tom walked around the tree, Jenna following by his side.

"What do you think, Jenna?" Tom turned to face her, noticing the sparkle in her eyes.

Gazing at the tree, she envisioned in her mind how it would look in the corner of the living room, the decorations adding to its beauty.

"So, Jenna, is that the tree you want?" Jace moved to stand beside the two of them, a large chainsaw in his hands.

Jenna nodded smiling as her father moved closer to the tree, pulling the cord to start the saw. Quickly she stepped back to watch as Jace began to cut, the saw buzzing as small chips flew from the trunk. The tree fell into the soft blanket of snow as Jace and Tom moved to carry it to the truck, sliding it into the back.

"Hurry and get in the truck, Jenna, so you don't get too cold."

Jace slammed the tailgate shut, then moved to climb back into the cab where Jenna and Tom now waited. Starting the engine, the truck moved down the back lane past the field and exercise track to pull up in front of the house.

Jenna ran excitedly to open the front door, allowing her father to carry the tree in, setting it in the stand that waited in the corner.

The smell of dinner mingled with the fresh pine that filled the air. The fire crackled, its flames casting a warm glow about the room. Jenna waited excitedly as her father moved down the stairs, a large box cradled in his arms. Tom followed closely behind, his arms also filled with a large box.

Setting the box on the couch beside Jenna, Jace quietly moved toward the kitchen.

"Aren't you going to help, Dad?" Jenna questioned, her excitement filling the air as she began removing the shimmering decorations from their boxes.

"No, Jenna, you go ahead. I'll finish dinner."

Turning away from the living room, Jace busied himself in the kitchen, reminding himself how he really didn't care for Christmas. Memories of Shanna with Jenna as a small child decorating a similar tree haunted him as he glanced toward his daughter as she and Tom began streaming the lights about the tree.

Jenna finished the dishes, content with the evening. She was feeling much better even though she seemed to be overly tired all the time. Moving into the living room, she climbed into the large recliner, pulling the quilt up above her shoulders.

She enjoyed watching Tom and her father as they played a game of chess. She knew how to play chess, but had no real interest in playing. She was content to lie in the chair, watching the twinkling lights as her mind wandered with hopes and dreams.

Lorna and Wayne would be arriving in two days, staying overnight for Christmas day then going back home the following morning. It would be a short visit but Jenna's heart was filled with excitement. She had gotten Wayne a new belt and made a cross-stitched plaque for Lorna, something she was sure would please and surprise her.

Glancing at the tree, she gazed at the three packages beneath. She had wrapped hers earlier that day, choosing special paper with matching ribbon. Her eyes drifted from the largest present to her father as she wondered what his reaction to the gifts would be. She hoped he would like them, but worried, always unsure of her father.

Yawning sleepily, she moved quietly toward the stairs, her mind fogged and sleepy.

"Jenna, don't I get a kiss goodnight?" Tom's voice brought her back from the foot of the stairs to stand sleepily beside him.

Leaning close, she lightly kissed him on the cheek, then paused beside her father, unsure whether to kiss him or not. His gaze was fixed on the chess set before him, seemingly unaware of her presence beside him. Shyly Jenna bent and kissed him lightly on the cheek before turning quickly toward the stairs.

"Goodnight, Jenna. I'll wake you in the morning." Jace's voice seemed warm and Jenna turned to see him smiling, a loving gaze shadowed by his tired eyes.

Morning came and the day passed quickly. Jenna busied herself cleaning the house, making the finishing touches. Lorna and Wayne would be here tomorrow afternoon.

Jace had been gone most of the day, returning late in the evening in a somewhat foul mood, confusing Jenna and making her worry. Not wanting to irritate him, she had slipped up the stairs unnoticed.

Snuggling deep within the covers, her mind drifted into a peaceful slumber as she dreamed of things to come.

Jace fumbled with the wrapping paper, feeling very clumsy as he tried to wrap the box before him. He had never been good at Christmas shopping, and always waited till the last moment. In fact he had almost forgotten. For the past few years, Christmas celebration had all but disappeared, but Jenna had brought the magic back with her presence.

Jace paused to gaze about the room. The fire's glow added a warm touch to the decorations surrounding him. The tree now stood in the corner of the room, the lights twinkling, the decorations reflecting the magic about them.

He had enjoyed watching Jenna decorate the tree, even though he resisted her pleas to help. Shanna had always had to drag him to the tree refusing to let him miss the moment.

His mind drifted back to past Christmases, even to his childhood. He didn't know why but he never really cared for Christmas. He didn't seem to remember it being a happy time, but more of a sad time.

Finishing the present, Jace placed it carefully beneath the tree. Jenna loved sweaters and Jace had known the minute he had seen the white sweater with the light blue flowers that Jenna would love it. Still he had felt a strong desire to give her something truly special and searched through the many stores, not sure what he was really looking for, only to run out of time, returning home with only the sweater for Jenna and a shirt for Tom.

Leaning against the fireplace, Jace gazed lovingly at Shanna's picture, his fingers caressing the frame as he searched the image. The love between mother and child was captured by the magic of an artist's hand. Slowly his fingers moved upon the canvas lightly caressing the child, and then moving to Shanna's cheek and neck coming to rest upon the golden necklace.

His heart paused as his thoughts spun. *I gave Shanna that necklace for Christmas when she was pregnant with Jenna and she had worn it always.* His fingers ran back and forth across it, remembering Shanna's surprise as she had opened the small box, never expecting to see the golden horse she had admired so many times in the jeweler's window.

He had pretended not to notice her interest and had even smiled secretly when she had noticed it gone from the window, never suspecting Jace to be the buyer.

His heart pounding, Jace moved toward the stairs. His hand shook slightly as he opened his bedroom door. The room was dark except for the moon's glow that spread throughout, casting a silvery light.

The dresser was neat and clean as Jace reached for the wooden box in the center. Holding the box, he slowly moved to the window, his gaze searching through the window into the stars and beyond.

It had been so many years ago that he had placed the golden contents onto the velvet lining of the cedar box. Many times he had held the box, his emotions tearing at his heart, wanting so to gaze upon it. Yet fearing the pain of the memories it held, his strength would fail, and he would return the box to the center of the dresser.

Holding the box close, his soul searched farther past the stars, his heart swelling within his chest.

"Oh, Shanna!" the strangled cry broke free as a single tear rolled down his face.

His arms shaking from the strain, he slowly lifted the small lid on the box, stopping, as his throat seemed to close. His heart pounded loudly, the sound echoing in his ears as he took a deep breath and removed the lid to reveal the golden horse.

Holding his breath, Jace waited for the pain, waited for the sorrow. Instead, a strange warmth spread through his heart as the pounding slowed, his soul soared with comfort. Holding the small charm in his hand, the golden chain swung slowly.

It was nothing fancy, but it was Shanna, simple yet beautiful. Holding it close to his heart, he felt only comfort and peace, not pain. In fact the pain he had thought was there, was gone. Slowly he eased himself into the chair, emotionally drained, wondering why he hadn't opened the box sooner.

Enjoying the comfort and warmth throughout his soul, he closed his eyes, the small charm enveloped in his large hand. Shanna's image filled his mind, easing his troubled thoughts as he drifted into an exhausted peaceful slumber.

Jenna ran from the barn, her heart filling with joy at the sight of Uncle Wayne and Aunt Lorna. She was so excited. Wrapping her arms about them, she reveled in their love. *How I have missed their hugs!*

Her mind drifted with thoughts of her father. She honestly felt he loved her, but sometimes wondered if he was unhappy with her. He confused her with his moods and distance. *How I long to understand him, to share a closeness, a bond of the heart.*

Closing her eyes, she pictured his arms about her, holding her, making her feel safe and loved. She was reluctant to let Wayne's arms release her, but slowly stepped back, her happiness reflecting in her eyes.

"You look so pretty, Jenna," Lorna inspected her lovingly, noting her still pale complexion and slightly hollow cheeks. "I'm so glad you're feeling better."

Wrapping her arms about Jenna's shoulder, they moved toward the house. Wayne followed close behind, a large travel case in one hand and a bundle of presents in the other.

Jace stood by the barn door watching his daughter. He knew how much she cared for Lorna and Wayne, yet felt a twinge of jealousy at the ease with which they expressed their love. So often he longed to hold her close. He fought with his past, remembering the distance his father insisted was proper, yet wondered why.

Feeling it senseless to torment his mind and heart, Jace pushed his thoughts aside, preferring to finish the last of the chores.

Entering the house, Jace could hear the buzz of voices coming from the kitchen. Wayne placed the presents beneath the tree, and then turned at the sound of the door closing.

"Jace, thanks so much for inviting us. It's really nice to be together as a family."

Wayne moved to give the younger man a strong hug, continuing to talk, his voice humming in Jace's ears.

Wayne's hug felt good, expressing sincere warmth and friendship in a simple physical action. Why didn't my father ever hug me?

Jace's mind searched for explanations to his inner turmoil, unaware of his own words as he moved toward the stairs, his voice sounding strange to his ears.

"It's really nice to have you and Lorna here. I'm going to shower and I'll be right down."

Moving up the stairs, his mind continued to swirl with discontented thoughts. *Maybe it seems silly, but I have this strong desire to change. I have always been cool and distant, not that that is terribly wrong, but I have a strong desire for something more.*

The shower warmed him as he closed his eyes, the water beating gently upon his skin. Fear began to rise within his soul. *Closeness often leads to pain. After losing Shanna, I swore I would never go through that again, it just hurt too much. Yet my heart feels so empty and alone.*

Slowly the water became cool, bringing him from his distant thoughts. Finishing quickly, he was surprised how long his thoughts had wandered. Dressing, he pushed his thoughts aside.

Lorna gazed at the man moving down the stairs. She had a love for him that he would never understand, and so she kept it to herself. It was not the kind of love between a man and a woman, but a lover deep and intertwined. He had a part of Shanna deep within his heart. Though Shanna was goner her love was something that would last forever.

Jenna too had a part of Shanna within her. Just being with them warmed Lorna's heart, for they were all of Shanna that she had left.

Lorna and Shanna had always been very close. They had known each other's feelings and thoughts, their hopes and dreams. Glimpsing the sadness in Jace's eyes, Lorna's heart ached to comfort him, like she had comforted Shanna so many years ago. But things were different, for Jace had to come to terms with himself, then the pain would leave, allowing the love to heal his troubled heart.

They all shared a special bond— a bond of love for Shanna and each other, yet even stronger was the love from Shanna— a part of her to live forever in their hearts, binding them together deep within their souls.

Sensing Wayne beside her, Lorna turned to squeeze him gently. Smiling, she dismissed her thoughts as everyone moved to sit around the table. Enjoying the meal, they talked late into the night, the Christmas lights twinkling brightly.

The sun rose to a clear blue sky, radiating its warmth upon the earth. Jenna scrambled from her bed, dressing quickly in her excitement. She couldn't wait for everyone to open presents.

Running down the stairs, she could smell breakfast cooking and hear the sound of Lorna's sweet voice humming softly.

"Good morning, Jenna," Lorna greeted without turning from her cooking.

She had heard the light footsteps sneaking up behind her before Jenna's arms wrapped about her from behind.

"Isn't it a beautiful day?" Jenna questioned.

Turning about the room, she danced amongst the rays of sunlight flowing though the window, her voice chatting lightly with her excitement.

"Jenna, honey," Lorna interrupted, "your father said to tell you to come help with the chores. Then we'll have breakfast and open presents after. I'll start the turkey and we'll have a big supper around two o'clock. Does that sound okay?"

Jenna nodded smiling at Lorna as she continued, "Well, then hurry out to the barn and help your dad."

Running from the house; Jenna's excitement radiated in her eyes.

Dash turned at the sound of Jenna's voice calling her name, "Dash!" Stopping in front of the stall door, Jenna wrapped her arms about the filly's neck. "Merry Christmas, sweetie."

Kissing the filly lightly on the nose, Jenna continued talking to her as she filled the water bucket, and then tossed a portion of fresh hay into the corner.

Jace watched from the back door of the barn. He enjoyed watching Jenna and the filly, even if their actions seemed a bit silly, the love they shared was special. Love, simple without restrictions or expectations.

Smiling at the constant chatter, he shook his head. *Who's to say they can't understand each other?* He thought to himself as he walked toward the pair.

"Are you ready for breakfast?" His voice was soft and quiet as it touched her ears.

"Yeah," she replied, smiling happily at her father.

Turning toward the house, she slipped her small hand in his.

"Is Tom coming?" she asked, glancing about for the older man.

"He just went to change first, then he'll come up to the house."

Jace too gazed about searching for Tom as he answered her question. Moving through the front door, he was surprised to see Tom already waiting with Lorna and Wayne at the table.

"Boy, you were pretty quick," Jace commented, smiling at Tom as he stood up from the table, his arms opening toward Jenna.

Her hand slipping from Jace's, she ran to Tom hugging him tightly.

"Well, let's eat so we can open the presents," Tom's voice showed his enthusiasm as he motioned Jenna to her chair.

Jenna's excitement mounted as everyone gathered in the living room. A small fire flickered, mingling with the glow from the Christmas lights. Glancing out the window, she could see small snowflakes floating gently to the ground. *This is a perfect Christmas,* she thought and couldn't have been happier.

Kneeling beside the tree, Jenna picked up the presents for Lorna and Wayne. Handing the presents excitedly to each of them, Jenna waited impatiently as other presents were passed to everyone, excitement and pleasure showing upon their faces.

Jace carefully gave his present to Jenna, his heart pounding nervously. Pulling the paper back, Jenna gently lifted the lid, revealing the beautiful sweater within.

Holding it up, she hugged it snugly to her chest. The gifts were all so wonderful— the porcelain horse from Lorna and Wayne and the light blue earrings from Tom.

Nervously Jenna placed the large box in her father's arms, noticing Lorna's knowing smile.

All eyes focused on Jace, causing him to pause nervously as he slowly peeled the paper back. Opening the lid he hesitated at the sight of the rich blue and white material. His heart swelled as he reached to touch the softness of the shadow rolls.

Lifting the gifts from the box, memories flooded back of another Christmas. *A large box filled with a set of blue and white headstalls and blinkers, Shanna's eyes gazing at me lovingly as I drew her close.* Blinking his eyes, Jace fought to control the emotion building inside as he struggled for the words.

"Thanks, Jenna. They're... really... nice." His voice sounded cool, the words strange. *That isn't what I wanted to say, what I feel inside.*

Disappointment showed in Jenna's eyes as she searched her fathers' face. She wasn't sure if he liked the gifts or not. Blinking back a tear, she tried not to over-react. He had said they were nice. Her mind wandered as the hum of voices echoed in her mind.

She was happy though. It was a wonderful Christmas and she was with the people she loved.

The day passed quickly, and Jenna fought back the tears as Lorna and Wayne packed to leave. Holding the plaque lovingly, Lorna kissed Jenna lightly on the forehead. Thanking her for the new belt, Wayne moved to hug her tightly.

Jenna watched the car until it disappeared from view. *How can I be so happy, yet so sad at the same time?*

Jenna walked quietly into the barn, her thoughts drifting aimlessly with the evening breeze. She was a bit confused with herself and the mixture of emotions tugging her heart.

Smiling at Dash, she wrapped her arms about the filly's neck. Dash seemed to sense Jenna's melancholy, nuzzling her gently. Resting her head in Jenna's arms, Dash enjoyed the attention, seeming to be a bit melancholy herself.

Raising her head from Jenna's arms, Dash searched the alley for Jace. She knew he was near, she could sense his presence.

Turning to follow the filly's gaze, Jenna found the barn empty.

"What's the matter, girl?" Jenna asked as she stroked her silky mane, content to feel Dash's warmth and softness.

Jenna felt comforted by the filly, her troubled thoughts drifting slowly away.

Dash stood still not wanting to disturb Jenna as Jace quietly moved down the alley. He had been outside the barn for quite some time, trying to organize his thoughts.

Holding the wooden box, he had gazed at the golden horse. The delicate details, the mane and tail flowing, the nostrils flaring slightly, the wings adding magic to its beauty. Shanna had always liked Pegasus.

Stroking the wings gently, he remembered Shanna saying Pegasus was an angel from the gods, sent as a horse to watch over Perseus. Gazing at the golden angel, he turned his attention to his daughter and the young filly.

Their interaction touched his heart, their gentleness, their love and understanding. Bowing his head slightly, he spoke softly, his words for no one near, but for one far away.

"Who's to know, Shanna? I'm sure God sends angels in all forms."

Closing the box gently, he moved into the barn still unsure of what he would say to Jenna.

He now stood close behind her, the box held tightly in his strong hands.

"Jenna?"

His voice shook a bit with emotion, and he struggled to cover his nervousness. "I wanted to tell you thank you for the gifts. They are very special and I like them a lot."

Jenna turned to gaze into her father's eyes, only slightly startled by his quiet approach. She had noticed Dash's interest toward the barn doors, sensing herself a presence beyond.

"I'm really glad you like them. I wanted something really special for you." Her voice was soft with a hint of reservation.

Her eyes shone bright, a smile spreading across her sweet face. *He really did like the gifts.* Joy filled her heart as she longed to wrap her arms about him, but she held back. She was never sure of his mood, or how he would react.

Pausing she glimpsed the wooden box, still held tightly in his hands.

Jace fumbled for the words he felt in his heart as he gazed about the barn. The moon's glow was beginning to spread its silver light throughout, moving magically with the yellow glow from the barn lights.

Stepping closer to Jenna, his voice mingled lightly with the soft breeze gently touching her ears. "They mean more to me than you will ever know…" leaning yet closer he kissed her tenderly on the forehead as he slid the wooden box into her small hands. "And so do you!"

Turning quickly, he left Jenna holding the small box as tears filled her eyes. She could almost feel her heart swelling up into her throat as she lifted the lid to gaze upon the golden horse she remembered so well.

Jace took a deep breath of the cool air, his head spinning, and his heart pounding. *Why had it seemed so hard?* Emotions turned within tearing at his soul as he gazed into the stars.

Was it really that hard? No, not really, he thought to himself. *What had been hard was holding back the feelings inside, letting my feelings out had been easy, had even felt good.* Breathing deeply, he enjoyed the feeling as it warmed him throughout.

CHAPTER 9

Slowing Dot to a stop, Jenna jumped lightly to the ground. The sun warmed her face as she climbed to sit along the rail, scratching the mare's forehead.

The days had flown by as the snow melted, the earth warming to a new spring. Plucking at the branch above her head, she fingered the new leaves, noticing a small-white blossom.

Reminiscing, Jenna remembered how Dot had often waited by the rail, as she would pluck a sweet apple from the branches above.

Looking back toward the exercise track, she could see her father exercising Dancer on the track. She was really amazed at how fast the past three months had gone. The yearlings were already working well in the exercise saddle preparing for the races in May.

Soon Don, a young man a few years older than she, would be corning to gallop the yearlings. He had galloped horses for Jace for the past couple of years. Don was just the right weight and had a good gentle hand.

Looking wistfully at Dot, Jenna longed to gallop around the track on Dash, feel her speed and strength beneath her.

Slipping the bridle from Dot's head, Jenna headed toward the barn. She was a good rider, had ridden since she could barely walk. *I know I can handle*

Dash. Sighing to herself, she moved quietly up behind her father, who now stood unsaddling Dancer.

"Hi, Dad," she almost whispered as she slid her arms lightly about him, squeezing him quickly before she turned to skip down the alley.

Dash watched Jenna, and nickered softly, then gazed past her toward Jace. Moving to the stall door, Dash pushed impatiently against it.

"What's the matter girl? Are you jealous?" Jenna teased, knowing well the filly was.

Dash wanted to go out on the track and felt it was her turn. Becoming more impatient, she reared up to gaze over the top of the stall walls.

"What's the matter, Dash? Can't you wait?" Jace asked noticing the filly's impatience. "Well, just a minute."

Turning toward Jenna, he smiled as he moved down the alley, his voice drifting back to question her as he led Dancer to the walker. "Jenna, do you want to get Dash out and hook her at the crossties?"

He enjoyed Jenna's presence even though he sometimes felt unsure or confused by her actions. *Just like the small squeeze she just gave me. It had felt good, but still I'm not sure how to react, or what to say.*

Moving back toward the crossties, he could see Jenna brushing the filly who stood eagerly waiting. Saddling Dash, Jace felt a bit uncomfortable.

He had snapped at Jenna the day before while saddling Junior. It wasn't really her fault, but when Junior stepped forward onto his foot, he had turned to Jenna cussing loudly.

Tears had filled her eyes as she struggled to control the excited yearling. Gazing at her now, her eyes had a hint of sadness, yet a slight smile played lightly upon the corners of her mouth.

She loved to help her father and longed to please him, yet felt saddened when she failed. But she did the best she could do and had begun to realize it wasn't really her he was yelling at. She was just the one that happened to be there. Stroking the filly gently she glanced toward her father.

"Dad, can I ride her?" she asked longingly as he turned to gaze into her eyes, knowing now why the smile had played upon her lips.

"Okay, Jenna, I'll let you ride her out of the barn," Jace replied, charmed by her smile, feeling a bit of guilt from the day before influencing his decision.

Disappointed, yet pleased, Jenna knew better than to complain. A ride down the barn alley was better than no ride at all.

Raising her left leg back, Jenna waited as her father lifted her up onto the filly's back, his hand gentle about her small leg. *Oh, it felt good.* Leaning forward, Jenna grasped the reins in her hands as her father led Dash from the barn.

It felt so good, the filly moving beneath her in a strong and steady stride. Dash turned her head to gaze back at Jenna sitting ever so lightly upon her back. Prancing lightly, she enjoyed the feel of Jenna upon her back; the thought of moving around the track excited her even more.

"Easy, Dash," Jace spoke firmly to the filly, noticing her excitement. "Maybe you better get off now, Jenna."

He turned to ease Jenna gently from Dash's back as he continued to hold her still beside him.

"Do you want to walk back to the track with US?" Jace questioned Jenna as he eased himself into the saddle, Dash sidestepping slightly at the weight of the man upon her back.

Smiling up at her dad, Jenna reached to pat Dash lightly on the shoulder. The sound of the birds chirping mingled with the musical echo of Dash's hooves upon the gravel road as they moved toward the track.

Jenna rushed down the alley, the early morning breeze kissing at her cheeks. She had overslept, enjoying the comfort of her soft covers to find her father and Tom gone.

A note on the table read briefly:

"Jenna, having trouble with a cow calving. Please feed the horses before you leave for school, Dad."

The horses whinnied as Jenna entered the barn, each moving toward the front of his stall to watch Jenna as she scooped up the buckets of grain.

Moving closer to Dash's stall, Jenna noticed the filly wasn't watching from her door. In fact, Jenna couldn't see her at all. Dumping Junior and Dancer's grain into their buckets, Jenna moved to Dash's stall.

A strange feeling crept slowly through her body, coming to rest uneasily in her heart. Glancing through the upper rails Jenna could see Dash standing in the corner of her stall.

Her head hung low, facing toward the back wall of the stall, seeming not to even notice Jenna's presence.

"Dash, what's the matter, girl?" Jenna questioned as she tried to coax the filly toward her. "Come on, girl, don't you want your grain?"

Jenna shook the bucket rapidly as she moved to open the stall door.

Slowly Dash raised her head, a far and distant look deep within her eyes. She acknowledged Jenna but remained still, her head lowering again as she continued to gaze at Jenna.

Moving closer, Jenna ran her hand down Dash's neck, her voice soothing her as she continued to question and coax the filly. "Come on, sweetie. What's wrong?"

Tugging gently on her mane, Jenna tried to pull her toward the center of the stall. Hesitating, Dash stepped cautiously only to stop, nuzzling her head into Jenna's side.

Confused Jenna gazed about the stall. The sawdust was piled high here and dug down low there. The grain bucket lay empty on the ground, the hook broken.

Hurrying from the stall, Jenna ran to grab the halter hanging in the tack room. Rushing back to the filly, she slid the halter on, her hands shaking.

"Come on, girl, please."

Jenna tugged firmly, causing Dash to stiffly turn her body toward her. Jenna's heart sank as she gazed upon the filly's right front leg. No longer shadowed, Jenna could see the open flesh oozing, the hair matted with dried blood. The knee was twice its normal size.

Tears burned her eyes, the vision of Dash's knee blurring as her mind spun, horrible thoughts consuming her. *What if the knee is torn apart? Would they have to put her to sleep? Could she ever run if she got better?*

Blinking back the tears she gazed about her. *What should I do now? Why isn't my father here when I need him?*

Panic taking hold, Jenna bolted for the house, leaving the stall door open. Dash watched as she disappeared from sight.

Tears cascaded down Jenna's pale face, her heart pounding as she burst through the front door.

Fingers shaking, Jenna dialed the number listed on the board for Dr. Daines. He had been the vet her father used for as long as Jenna could remember. He had even taken care of Dot just before Jenna arrived last summer.

"Dr. Daines, this is Jenna Brenton. Our filly tore her knee open and Dad's not here. Can you come over please? I don't know what to do!" Her voice cracked as she fought back the sobs rising in her throat.

"Jenna, it's okay. I can be there in about twenty minutes. Just keep her still, okay?" His voice was kind and comforted Jenna as she replied, a sob the only sound able to escape her strangled throat.

"Now, Jenna, where is your dad?" Dr. Daines questioned his voice reaching through her muffled sobs.

"He's out in the back field with Tom. There's a cow having trouble calving," she answered quietly, as anger began to build within.

She was mad, mad at her father for being out with a dumb cow. *I need him here. Dash needs him.*

"Could you get out to him? Jenna? " His voice broke through her thoughts as she slowly realized what he had said.

Struggling to control her emotions she replied, her voice still quivering, "I could ride Dot out to him."

"Okay, Jenna, that would be good. Now listen, can she put her weight on her leg?" he questioned his voice gentle yet firm.

"Yes, but it hurts her real bad. I had to pull her around so I could see what was wrong," she answered quietly trying to maintain control.

Dash needs me. I need to be tough, to do what needs to be done. "What can I do for her?"

"Just put her food and water where she can reach it. That way she won't have to move. Then ride out to your dad and I should be there by the time you get back. She'll be okay, Jenna, I promise."

He wasn't really sure why he had said that, and hesitated as he replaced the receiver. Saying a silent prayer, he hoped he hadn't promised Jenna something he shouldn't have.

Stumbling on the steps, Jenna struggled to gain her balance, still unnerved by everything. Running to Dash, she quickly placed the hay and water close to the filly.

"I'll be right back, sweetie." Hugging Dash she ran to grab Dot's bridle, turning once more toward the filly. "Just stand still."

Racing from the barn Jenna's words echoed back to Dash, who nickered softly as the young girl raced toward Dot. "I'll hurry!"

Jenna's heart pounded as she struggled with Dot's bridle, the mare standing patiently, sensing Jenna's distress.

"Come on, Dot."

Jenna led Dot from the pasture to stand along the fence. Climbing quickly, she leapt from the fence to land gently on the mare's back. Kicking

Dot's sides, she urged her into a gallop as they passed the barn to head down the gravel lane.

The cool breeze cleared her head as Dot increased her speed. Taking a deep breath Jenna pulled the reins tighter, her heart pounding faster in rhythm with Dot's stride. She was surprised at the speed the mare had, Dot's muscles working smoothly against her tight legs.

Nearing the back field, Jenna pulled firmly on the reins, but Dot continued at her steady speed. Jenna's heart raced as she struggled to slow Dot, the wind teasing the tears from her eyes. Gasping for air, she searched the field for signs of her father and Tom as she continued to pull back on the reins.

"Easy, Dot. Come on, girl, slow down so I can catch my breath."

Her words teased lightly at Dot's ears as the mare pricked them back listening to Jenna's sweet voice.

"Easy, girl, that's a good girl," Jenna praised Dot as the mare slowed her gallop, allowing Jenna to relax, her gaze searching the field.

Jace glimpsed the figure moving down the lane. Searching the image, he froze in disbelief. The young mare was into an open run, a small figure bent low along her bare back.

For hell's sake, what is Jenna doing?

"Tom! Something's wrong!"

Pointing to the figure moving toward them, Jace turned away from the cow and her calf now standing beside him.

Tom followed quickly behind Jace as they broke into a run, both fearing Jenna's ability to stop the mare who showed no sign of easing her pace.

Fear tore at his heart, his lungs beginning to burn as he neared the fence. Dot was nearing them, Jenna beginning to pull her up, slowing her into a smooth gallop.

Reaching out Jace grabbed the reins as Jenna pulled the mare to a stop beside him.

"What the hell are you doing? You know you shouldn't ride Dot without a saddle, especially at a dead run down the lane."

His voice began to soften as he reached to stroke the tear-stained face of his daughter who sat, shaking, astride the mare before him.

"Honey… I'm sorry; it's okay. Just tell me what's wrong."

Struggling to control her sobs, Jenna became aware of how much she was trembling, her voice shaking with each word.

"Oh, Dad… it's Dash! She tore her knee open. Please hurry, Dr. Daines is coming… "

Pulling on the reins, Jenna turned Dot, wanting to hurry back to Dash, her words trailing off.

"No, Jenna, leave Dot with Tom. We'll go in the truck. We can get there faster."

Jace helped Jenna to the ground as Tom moved to take the reins, Dot dancing impatiently.

Wrapping her arms tightly about the mare's neck, Jenna thanked her, then moved quickly toward the truck.

Her heart pounded as she explained to her father what was wrong, her voice sounding strange and distant. Jace listened as the truck sped toward the barn. His expression seemed calm and unconcerned, yet deep inside, his heart sank as fear filled his soul.

What can I do? What will this do to Jenna? His mind thought the worst, his heart aching.

Searching the distance, Jace could see Dr. Daines' blue and white truck turning from the main road as he stopped the truck by the barn door.

Dash stood exactly where Jenna had left her, moving only her head to search for the familiar figure now running toward her.

"I'm back, Dash, and Dad's here, too. Soon Dr. Daines will be here," her voice soothed Dash as she gazed lovingly at the filly.

Stroking Dash's nose, Jenna wiped a tear from the filly's eyes, noticing the pain and sadness deep within.

Jace moved to kneel beside Dash, gently examining the swollen knee. Flinching slightly, Dash stood fairly still, allowing him to check her leg; the pain filled her mind, yet she knew he was there to help.

"Easy, girl," Jace spoke softly, his heart sinking.

The knee looked awful. It was so swollen he could hardly tell what she had done.

"Jace?" Dr. Daines' voice echoed down the alley drawing his attention away from the filly.

Moving down the alley, Jace helped Dr. Daines with his equipment. *Now the work will begin, and no matter what it takes, we will do it, we have to… for Jenna.*

Jenna could hear the hum of their voices as they moved closer. Straining to hear what they were saying, she listened carefully, catching only a word here or there.

"It's okay, Dash, they'll make you better," Jenna cooed softly as she cradled the filly's head in her arms.

"Dad, can he give her something for the pain?" Jenna questioned her father as he and Dr. Daines moved into the stall beside her. "It hurts her real bad."

"Jenna, I'm sure he can give her something for the pain," Jace answered calmly as he turned to Dr. Daines, who nodded as he began to draw up a syringe.

"This will make her feel better, Jenna," Dr. Daines spoke gently as he moved to search the filly's neck for her vein. "Hold her still for me, okay?"

Holding her gently but firmly, Jenna stroked her nose, her voice humming in the filly's ears as the vet injected the medicine. Slowly, Dash began to relax as it flowed through her veins, easing the pain.

"Dad, look!"

Jenna reached to pull her father toward her, pointing to the teary stream trickling from the filly's eyes.

Jace wiped the moisture from one of Dash's eyes, noticing the painful sadness reflected in its warm depth.

Shaking his head slightly, he wondered at the sight before him.

"I think if she could, Jenna, she'd crawl in your arms, but she seems content for you to cradle her head."

Dash jerked slightly, the pain breaking through the comforting fog as Dr. Daines probed gently at the swollen tissue.

"Hold her still, Jenna." His voice was firm but calm as he worked on the swollen knee.

Carefully, he eased the torn flesh to rinse the wound. Working quickly, a smile began to spread across his face.

"She'll be okay, Jace. There's no internal damage. She's torn the outer flesh and has a lot of swelling, but the joint isn't injured. I'll give her a couple of shots, and then you'll need to give her one a day for a week. We'll wrap the knee lightly and you'll need to clean it and rewrap it twice a day. Once it scabs over you can leave the wrap off and just put the medicine on… "

His voice trailed off in Jenna's mind as tears of joy spilled lightly down her cheeks, her arms squeezing the filly's head closer into her chest, relief spreading through her.

"Jenna?" Jace repeated her name, drawing her from her distant thoughts. "Can you hand walk her each day? We need to keep her moving, but not too fast. Dr. Daines will give us some medicine to put in her grain to calm her down for awhile, and if anyone can get Dash to behave, it's you."

Jace smiled at Jenna as tears trickled down her face. Reaching to draw her close, he cradled her head lovingly in his arms.

"It's okay, honey. She's going to be fine."

"But will she be able to run?" Jenna questioned softly, dreading the answer.

"Well, Jenna, I don't see why not. Like I said, the joint is not injured. She tore the flesh, but not very deep. If you take good care of her and work her back slow, I don't see any reason why she can't run," Dr. Daines answered, feeling good about the filly as he finished wrapping her knee.

"When is her first race?" he questioned looking toward Jace.

"Well, she needs a couple of schooling races before we can run on a recognized track. I have her entered in a futurity the middle of May."

Jace mentally figured the time and the work that would need to be done. He truly doubted that she would be able to run in Mayas he stared at the swollen knee. He had paid four hundred dollars to put her in the race, but if she wasn't sound, he wouldn't risk running her.

"Let's see how she does in the next few days. That will give us about two months and she just might be ready, especially with all the TLC I'm sure Jenna will give her."

Dr. Daines winked at her as he handed Jace the medicine and other supplies explaining how they should be used.

"I'll stop by on the way home tomorrow and check on her. If you have any questions, just give me a call."

CHAPTER 10

The days turned into weeks as Jace and Jenna worked with Dash. Twice a day they soaked her leg in ice water to reduce the swelling, and then cleaned, medicated and rewrapped the knee. Jace was amazed at the results as the swelling reduced rapidly. Dr. Daines had stopped by a few times and was also quite impressed.

Jenna continued to hand walk her, adding a small amount of distance each day.

Dash was walking quite smoothly now, the swelling all but gone, the open wound now closed with a fair sized scab. They had begun walking her on the walker by herself, allowing her to stretch and kick a bit. But Jace always stayed close by to be sure she didn't get carried away.

Soon they would begin leading her around the track with Buck. Jace had had Buck for years. Jenna could remember riding on him with her dad when she was quite young. The big gelding was an awesome sight, seventeen hands high, strong but gentle, and one of the prettiest buckskins she had ever seen. But Buck was Jace's horse and no one rode him but Jace.

Buck had been mistreated before Jace bought him at a sale. With time and proper handling, the gelding grew to trust him, and only him.

Jace headed down the lane on Buck; Dash walking by his side. Running to the rail fence, Jenna watched as they moved onto the soft track. The young filly kept pace with the large gelding as they moved into a slow gallop.

Jace would only work her one lap, real easy, moving up slowly during the week. If she did well, he would put Don back on for works, but for now he would keep any weight off her back.

Jenna smiled as she watched Dash float alongside of Buck. Dash moved smoothly, seeming to glide across the track, her hooves barely touching the soft earth beneath her.

"She's doing real good, don't you think?" Jenna questioned as she moved to take Dash from him.

Dismounting from the large gelding, Jace quickly checked Dash's leg for any heat or swelling.

"She looks real good, Jenna, but we don't want to push her. If we take things slow, we just might get her ready in time for that futurity. Now, Jenna, I know how much you want her to run, but if she's not ready, we won't run her, okay?" Jace explained to Jenna sensing full well her anticipation and excitement.

How I long to watch Dash run, Jenna thought, for she had all the confidence in the world where Dash was concerned, feeling sure the filly could outrun anything.

"Jenna, could you finish with her while I work Dancer and Junior? Just walk her a minute, put the medicine on her knee, then put her in her stall. I think Tom has everything else done."

Jace led Dancer from his stall, handing the rope to Tom, who now stood waiting by Buck. Mounting the big gelding, Jace turned to glance at Jenna and the filly moving slowly into the barn, before he turned to take the rope from Tom.

"Thanks," Jace smiled as he moved toward the track, the young gelding beside him, pulling on the lead rope.

Jenna led Dash to her stall speaking softly. Dash had worked real well on the track, but had seemed to be lacking some of her usual enthusiasm.

"What's the matter, girl?" Jenna questioned as she turned her loose inside the stall.

Dash turned to nuzzle Jenna, her head low enough to be cradled in the crook of Jenna's arm. Stroking her gently, Jenna cooed in her ear whispering sweetly, the filly obviously enjoying the attention.

Tom came to stand by the stall enjoying the sight of Jenna and the filly together.

"She sure is looking good, Jenna, don't you think?" Tom questioned drawing Jenna's attention away from Dash.

"Oh, Tom, she looks wonderful!" Jenna smiled as he moved to stand beside her in the stall. "See how good her knee is healing, there's hardly even a scab left."

Jenna gently stroked her knee as Tom knelt down beside her for a closer look.

"It's healed up real good. Better than I ever hoped it would," Tom commented as he squeezed Jenna about her shoulders. "You've done a real good job." He smiled as he left the stall. "Keep up the good work."

Smiling back at Tom, Jenna watched him walk down the alley before turning her attention back to Dash.

Nuzzling her gently, Jenna stayed, cooing softly in her ear, "What's the matter, girl? Huh?"

Dash seemed somewhat sad, a distant look reflected deep within her eyes. Sliding down against the stall wall, Jenna sat in the softness of the fresh stall.

"Come on, girl," Jenna patted the sawdust beside her, encouraging her to lie beside her.

Dash sniffed the sawdust, turning about the stall to position herself. To Jenna's surprise, she watched the filly carefully maneuver herself to lie beside her. Leaning back, Dash brought her head to rest gently in Jenna's lap.

"Oh, you silly girl," Jenna teased as she stroked her neck. "Just crawl on my lap why don't you?" Jenna giggled softly, enjoying herself as she cradled Dash's head gently in her arms.

Jace glanced about the barn searching for Jenna as he turned Dancer into his stall. Seeing no sign of her, he headed for Dash's stall where, just as he suspected, he found her with the filly.

"What are you doing?" he questioned as he gazed at his daughter sitting in the stall, the filly still lying beside her.

"She seems kind of sad. When she worked today she just didn't seem to have her heart in it."

Jenna glanced up, her eyes meeting his as she struggled for the words. She didn't want him to laugh at her, so she spoke slowly choosing her words carefully as she gazed back at Dash.

"Well, I think maybe something else is hurting her. We have been treating her knee, but maybe her heart needs some healing too."

Pausing Jenna gazed up into her father's eyes, not sure of his thoughts as his expression seemed not to have changed.

"Whenever someone is physically hurt I think their heart hurts too. For Dash to be her best her heart needs to be as sound as her leg."

Jace smiled at Jenna, a bit amused, yet touched by what she said. It wasn't really something he would have thought of, but some of what she said made sense.

"So, Jenna, what do you do to heal a hurting heart?" he questioned curious about her treatment.

"Some extra love and tenderness. If you fill her heart with love, then she has something to give out… "

Jenna's words trailed off feeling uneasy as her father moved into the stall to kneel beside her.

"Well, Jenna, don't be too long, and please remember to be careful, she is a horse."

He patted her lightly on the shoulder then turned to gently stroke the filly's nose before leaving the stall, the sound of his steps echoing in the stillness.

His thoughts wandered as he moved toward the house. Some of the things she said made sense, even tugged a bit at his heart. Pausing he gazed back toward the barn, the image of Jenna with the filly still clear in his mind.

CHAPTER 11

Jenna's heart pounded as she gripped the rail in front of her. Her eyes were fixed on the starting gates in the distance, as the last horse was loaded. Holding her breath, she waited for what seemed like an eternity for the gates to open releasing the powerful horses within.

The first glimpse of Dash's head, rising from behind the opened gates, brought joy and fear to Jenna's heart. She could hear her voice screaming; feel her eyes brimming with tears as Dash flew down the track. With each powerful stride, Jenna watched her front leg, afraid the knee might blow, but exhilarated by Dash's strength and beauty as she crossed the finish line.

Relief and joy filled Jenna's heart as Dash rounded the corner coming back to accept the applause from the crowd. Running down the grandstand, Jenna raced toward her father who stood waiting on the track for the filly slowly loping toward him.

Jenna's enthusiasm broke free as she threw her arms about her father's neck.

"Oh, Dad, she did it! She won!" Jenna's voice burst with excitement as she too turned to wait for Dash.

Jace pulled away from Jenna, uncomfortable with her show of excitement, moving toward Dash, who now stood before him. Her sides heaved slightly with each breath, a light sweat covering her silken body, her eyes shining bright with excitement as she posed for the win picture.

Turning to lead Dash from the track, Jace left Jenna standing alone as the other horses and trainers weaved around her. Feeling awkward, she too headed toward the barns her excitement dampened by emptiness as Jace continued on, leaving her far behind.

Dancer would be next to run with a couple of races in between his and Dash's. Jenna hoped he would do as well as Dash, but honestly felt he just couldn't compare with her.

Arriving at the barns, she could see Dash moving briskly about the walker, obviously not too worn out from her race. The filly watched intently as Jenna moved closer, nickering softly as she slowed her stride, trying to pause the walker.

"Dash! Get up!" Jace's voice rang loudly through the air, causing the filly to again move quickly around the walker.

Dash's eyes still followed Jenna as she moved toward her father anticipating his next words, directed somewhat angrily at her.

"Jenna, come help with Dancer. You've got him so spoiled he won't hold still without you baby-sitting him."

His words stung, but she tried not to let it bother her. She knew he was nervous and a bit stressed and reminded herself of the influencing factors that surrounded him.

Dancer was hard to get prepped for a race. He did as his name implied, dancing and moving about, making it quite hard to wrap his front legs.

"Jenna, come hold him still!" Jace yelled again, not realizing she was already standing at Dancer's head trying to convince the eager gelding to be still.

"Easy, Dancer, be a good boy," Jenna whispered softly, stroking his nose as she gazed into his nervous eyes.

He wasn't trying to be difficult, he was just nervous, the new surroundings and strange noises scaring him. She continued to whisper softly, drawing his attention to focus upon her. His eyes relaxed, his breathing eased as he listened, the softness of her voice, if not the words, easing his fears.

Jace stood up from beside Dancer's front legs, the wraps snugly in place. His tension seemed to radiate from him as he stepped outside the stall leaving Jenna a bit uneasy as she continued to sooth the young gelding.

Soon they would be taking Dancer to the paddock to saddle him for his race. She would just stay by him, and keep herself out of her father's way. She could hear Jace and Tom talking outside the stall, their voices drifting to her.

"Dash did real good, Jace. Do you plan on running her in the futurity?" Tom asked.

"I think so, but until I see how her leg is tomorrow I won't make a definite decision." His voice seemed distant as Jenna strained to hear what else he was saying.

Moving to the stall door, she peered out to see her father leading Dash from the walker to her stall. "That futurity is about two weeks away, and even though she won this, we have to remember this was just a schooling race. The other horses in this futurity have had a lot more races and Dash hasn't had half as much experience."

Pausing to scratch the filly's neck, he turned his comment toward the filly, "Well, Dash, it all depends on you. "

Tom smiled as he began walking toward Jenna, causing her to move back to Dancer's head. She didn't want them to know she had been listening and began whispering again to Dancer, who had begun to fidget again.

As Tom neared, she could again hear his voice and her father's as they discussed Dancer and Junior. Junior had run earlier in the day, finishing fourth in his race. Jace was truly disappointed in the flashy gelding, but had high hopes for Dancer.

"Well, it looks like it's time to go. Jenna, bring Dancer out." His voice still seemed gruff, but she reminded herself he was probably just nervous.

She also got nervous, with each race her stomach would move to sit in her throat. Just her father's words and the tone of his voice started her stomach to flutter and rise. Unhooking the lead rope, Jenna began to lead Dancer from the stall as Tom opened the stall door.

Leaning close to Dancer's head, Jenna whispered quietly, "Go get 'em, boy!"

Kissing him lightly on his cheek, she handed the rope to Tom who led him toward the paddock, Jace following alongside on Buck. Jenna watched them move away feeling somewhat hurt. They seemed to completely forget her, not even looking back to see if she followed.

Quietly she headed for the grandstand, going around the paddock where she stopped to watch the horses being saddled.

Dancer caught a glimpse of Jenna by the rail as they saddled him for the race. He longed to get closer, to hear her soft voice, and lunged toward her. Jace held him tight as his saddling was completed.

"Easy, Dancer. Easy, boy," Jenna's words floated from the crowd to Dancer's ears.

Slowly he calmed, his eyes searching for the source. Jace too heard her voice and turned to find Jenna standing along the rail. He marveled at the effect she had on Dancer, who now walked calmly beside him.

Turning to lift the jockey onto Dancer's back, Jace heard the sound of the bugler, calling the horses onto the track. Dancer moved closer to Jenna, following in order the other horses as they moved onto the track.

"You can do it, Dancer!" Jenna coaxed as he passed by, his eyes fixed upon her, until he had to turn as the jockey urged him gently away.

Running to stand at the finish line, Jenna waited just as she had with Dash's race. All the nervous feelings were the same, and again it seemed like forever before the gates opened.

Dancer broke straight, the horse next to him bumping him off balance. Continuing to move forward, he seemed more determined to push past the horse beside him. The two of them were out in front; the others close by their sides.

Jenna could hear herself screaming, her excitement rising as the two young horses fought for the lead, looking to be but a blur as they crossed the finish line together.

The announcer's voice hushed the crowd as everyone waited to find out the winner, the race too close to call. They would have to wait for the photo to declare the winner.

"The photo results show the number four-horse— Ramblin' Storm the winner," the announcer's voice brought cheers of joy and sighs of disappointment from the crowd.

Jenna paused a moment, the gelding's real name sounding strange. They never called him anything but Dancer; it seemed to fit better than Ramblin' Storm.

Quickly she rushed to the track to meet her father and Tom who now stood with Dancer at their side.

Moving close to Dancer's head, Jenna praised him enthusiastically, "Good boy, Dancer. You did real good!"

Turning toward Tom, Jenna wrapped her arms about him wanting to share her happiness with someone. Sadly she glanced toward her father, she loved him dearly but he seemed cold and distant, uneasy with her hugs and affection.

The win picture taken, Jace turned toward the barn, leading Dancer away.

"As soon as Dancer's cooled off, we need to head home, so get things ready." His voice sounded harsh as he continued walking toward the barn.

Glancing up at Tom, Jenna knew her father was talking to her, even though he didn't say her name. Jace wouldn't talk to Tom like that. Tears stung her eyes as she rushed away from Tom, not wanting him to see her cry.

I don't understand why my father has been so ornery lately. Is it the pressure of the races? Is it something I did or didn't do? All I ever try to do is help, to do what he wants.

Gathering up the tack, Jenna noticed a few men stopping to talk with her father about the races. His voice seemed quite pleasant. He even laughed and smiled as they talked about the horses. *How I wish he would laugh and smile at me.*

He had his moments though. She remembered that evening in the barn, his gentle touch and soft words. Reaching to caress the golden horse about her neck, she smiled to herself. *He does love me;* she felt it deep inside her heart.

It was hard though, for she didn't understand his moods, but maybe he didn't understand them either.

Stopping in front of Dash's stall, she smiled lovingly as Dash reached her head out through the opened upper door to gently nuzzle her.

"You did real good, sweetie. I knew you could."

Jenna's words were cut short as Jace questioned her, "Have you got everything loaded?"

"I've got all the bridles, the two tack containers and the carrier," Jenna answered proudly, pleased with the fact that everything was neatly loaded in the trailer.

"Well, Tom, if you'll get Junior, I'll get Dancer. We'll load them first, then Dash," Jace hollered toward Tom as he unhooked Dancer from the walker.

Jenna stood quietly watching her father from Dash's stall. He seemed tired and somewhat unhappy. She was confused.

The horses had done quite well, and even if they were just schooling races, you would think he would be pleased.

"Jenna, bring Dash and let's get her loaded so we can head home," Jace yelled as he stood waiting by the trailer.

Quickly she hooked the lead rope to Dash's halter, opened the stall door, and headed toward the trailer. Dash moved briskly beside her, anxious to load in the trailer and head for home. Jenna handed the rope to her father as the filly stepped up into the trailer. Stepping back, she watched her father as he tied the lead rope through the side ring, and then gently patted Dash on the neck, before moving to shut the rear door.

Sliding into the truck, Jenna sat between her father and Tom. Her excitement only slightly dampened by her father's mood, she began chatting lightly about the races. Not talking specifically to either Tom or her father, she began summarizing the day, her excitement and happiness showing in her voice.

"Oh, they all did so good today! Even Junior did good; at least he tried. His legs are just kind of short and he has to run two strides for each one of the other horses. But, oh, didn't Dash look beautiful? I knew she could run. She seemed to just float down the track, her hooves barely touching the surface. And Dancer sure showed that other horse a little bump wasn't going to bother him," Jenna's voice continued, becoming but a hum in Jace's mind.

He felt good about the day, yet kind of empty. *How I long to feel as Jenna does. She seems to see so much more than just a race, like she can tell how the horses really feel. Who knows, maybe she really can? She seems to have a bond with each of them, an understanding and caring, that they too share with her. Maybe she just opens herself up to them.*

His mind drifted as he remembered little things about the horses. At the time he hadn't paid close attention to them, hadn't opened himself up. Visions filled his thoughts mixing with the road before him.

The scene of Dancer anxiously moving about while he had tried to wrap his legs drifted through his thoughts. *Dancer wasn't trying to be obnoxious; he was just nervous, maybe a bit scared. Yelling at Jenna hadn't helped either, but her gentle touch and soft words had.*

His mind projected the image of Dash leaving the starting gates as he stood behind her. *I noticed her strength, but failed to see the beauty as she truly flew down the track, her hooves barely skimming the soft surface.*

The brightness in her eyes flashed through his thoughts. *She had loved it… the race, the crowd, all of it ... it had showed in her eyes.*

Jenna glanced at her father. He hadn't heard her question. He hadn't even seemed to notice anything she had said.

Tom gently squeezed her arm drawing her attention from him. He smiled softly, understanding her thoughts.

"He's just got a lot on his mind. I'm sure, if she's not sore tomorrow, he'll run Dash in that futurity. She did real good today. Too bad Dancer's not paid into it instead of Junior. I really don't think Junior's going to be able to run with the other horses."

Jenna was comforted by Tom's words. It was nice to have someone interested in what she thought.

"Well, Junior didn't seem to grow as much as Dash and Dancer. He tries real hard though."

Tom smiled at Jenna, a vision of Junior running down the track in his thoughts.

"You know you're probably right, Jenna. As a yearling he had been a good size and Dash was kind of small. Now that they are all two-year-olds, he still looks about the same, but Dash and Dancer are quite a bit bigger."

Smiling, Jenna leaned her head lazily against his shoulder. "You know, Tom, it's hard to believe they are already two, that I have been here almost a year."

Squeezing her gently, Tom smiled lovingly at the girl beside him. Glancing at Jace he could see a smile playing quietly upon his face. He had paid attention, Jenna's words bringing the smile to his tired face.

The sound of the truck turning onto the gravel road stirred Jenna from her thoughts. As she had leaned against Tom's shoulder, the excitement of the day caught up with her. She enjoyed listening to the songs on the radio, the memories of the day's races playing over and over in her mind.

Searching the dusky pasture for the sorrel mare, Jenna slowly remembered Dot wasn't there. Her father had taken Dot back to the stud farm to be bred. She was excited about a new baby for the next year, but worried about possible problems.

Looking away from the pasture, she turned toward her father.

"Dad, when will Dot get to come back?"

She hoped soon for she missed the mare. Dash was her favorite, but she loved all the horses.

"Probably two more weeks. Actually I thought we would pick her up when we go to the track for the futurity. It's just along the way, about a mile from the track," Jace answered as the truck slowly stopped in front of the barn.

CHAPTER 12

The weeks passed and before she knew it they were back at the track. Dash and Junior stood quietly in their stalls. They had hauled them to the track the day before the races so the horses could rest overnight. Dancer had fussed and whinnied loudly as Dash and Junior were loaded into the trailer.

Gazing out the motel window Jenna said a little prayer in her heart. She always asked God to watch over the horses.

She never dared pray for them to win, even though she hoped with all her heart they would. Instead she prayed for God to keep them safe. That was truly the most important thing— that they did the best they could and not get hurt.

A vision passed through her mind. She had seen a horse go down at one of the schooling races. Just thinking about it made her heart pound faster, her stomach knotting. She could still see the sorrel filly coming down the track.

They were done running for the day, but Jenna had wanted to watch a couple more-races before they headed home. She had stood by the rail, halfway between the starting gates and the finish line.

The filly came out strong-and fast. She wasn't very tall but she was quite muscular, a real nice looking filly. She had seemed to shy at the crowd as she twitched her ears, her eyes widening.

With the next powerful stride, the filly fell forward, her silken nose slamming into the dirt. The jockey flew through the air as the other horses passed by.

Jenna had frozen, her heart seeming to stop, the scene before her tearing at her as the filly staggered to stand. Men were rushing toward her, seeming to be in slow motion.

Jenna was sickened by the sight, but couldn't take her eyes off the filly. With that last powerful stride, she had completely separated both front knees, the lower portion of her legs hung loosely, attached only by the flesh.

Tears stung Jenna's eyes, the filly seeming to blur before her. Still standing on the stumps that had been her knees, the filly tried to get away from the pain, away from the men.

The pain of the needle wasn't even noticed as she struggled in agony, the men gently trying to get her to lie down.

The filly's body was slanted at an awkward angle her front end being almost half the height of her hindquarters. Slowly she had gone down, the pain easing from her, her breathing slowing as her soul left the broken body.

Looking at the lifeless filly, Jenna realized she had fallen to her knees, her body trembling as the tears flowed freely. She hadn't known the filly, but she could still feel a sharp pain deep in her heart, an empty sadness within.

The strong arms of her father coaxed her to her feet, leading her back to the trailer. He squeezed her gently not sure what to say. He really didn't know her thoughts or feelings, but he knew her tender heart.

Kissing her on the forehead he had whispered softly, "I'm sorry, Jenna, you shouldn't have seen that, but, honey, it does happen."

"Oh God, please don't let Dash or Junior get hurt. Don't let Dash blow her knee," quietly she prayed as she gazed out into the heavens, the stars blurred by the tears filling her eyes.

She felt strange inside, a mixture of feelings tearing at her heart. She loved the races, but always right before each of their races, her heart would pound with fear and anticipation.

Her father had assured her of the unlikelihood of something like that happening again. The filly must have been sore or hurt before. He would never run a horse that wasn't sound and fit. He had tried to explain the risks of racing and help her realize accidents do happen. You can only do your best to keep your horse safe and sound.

The morning passed quickly and again she found herself waiting in the grandstands. Her father went down to the gates explaining to her that if he "tailed" the horses it usually helped them to get out quicker.

In quarter horse races, the race could be won or lost at the gates. The average race for two-year-old quarter horses was generally a sprint of 350 yards, leaving no room to make up for a slow start.

Jace had explained to her that, by holding the tail and pulling it just right, it would cue the horse to stand up on all fours, and center itself just right in the gate. That way, the horse would be ready to spring when the gates opened.

Tom too had gone down to the gates, leaving Jenna to stand alone. She gazed about at the people around her, as the horses were slowly loaded into the starting gates. Again her heart began to pound furiously with both fear and excitement.

Finally the last horse was loaded, and the starter waited patiently for the horses to all be ready, wanting to give an equal chance for each horse. He pushed the button, the bell ringing loudly as the horses lunged forward. But the gates had remained closed as the headers in the gates struggled to control the confused horses.

It was the headers' job to center the horses' heads forward in the gates, letting them go as the gates opened, the jockeys driving them to the finish line.

Settling the horses, the headers turned to each other, to the trainers behind the gates, and to the starter. All seemed confused.

The hum of voices in the crowd buzzed loudly in Jenna's ears as the announcer's voice broke through, announcing a malfunction in the gates. Someone would have to climb up into the top section of the gates to reset the line. The crowd waited anxiously, all eyes on the young man climbing carefully above the nervous horses.

Jockeys waited, their positions relaxed upon the horses shifting their bodies anxiously.

Suddenly the gates opened, not all together or quick, but slow and erratic. The jockeys, not being ready, scrambled to control their horses as they tore down the track. Jenna's heart sank as Dash ran down the track coming across the finish line— fourth.

The starter stared in amazement at the empty gates. He hadn't pushed the button; the bell hadn't rung. The jockeys had been told to relax until the gates were reset, then they could retake their starting position.

No one had been ready. Most of the jockeys fumbled for their reins, struggling to keep their seats on the fast-moving animals beneath them.

The announcer's voice again broke through the confused hum rising from the grandstand, "Due to mechanical failures the clock did not start when the gates opened. The start was uneven and therefore unable to be hand timed. The race will be void. All horses in the gate will be refunded their entrance fee."

In large futurities, the horses were divided into equal gates, each timed. When all the races were completed, the horses with the ten fastest times would run again in two weeks for the total purse.

Jenna's heart sank; she knew Dash could have run fast enough to be in the top ten. She just knew she could have. But at least they would get the $450.00 entrance fee back. Disappointed, Jenna walked quietly back to the barn alongside Dash and her father.

"You know, I have the worst luck at this track. I don't know why I even run here," Jace bitched loudly, extremely displeased with the events of the day so far. "I don't know why it couldn't have happened when Junior was in the gates instead. He doesn't really stand a chance, but Dash did."

Jace turned his attention toward Tom, who had joined them as they moved closer to the barn.

"You know, the jockey said he couldn't believe her power, said he thought for sure they could have won. He thought they would have if she hadn't left the gates so fast; damn near left him behind. He had to pull himself up off her butt by the reins to get in the saddle, by then he couldn't catch the others, but she was moving up on them. Damn! Of all the luck."

Junior's race went uneventfully, the sorrel colt finishing second to last. Jace was quiet as he led the young horse back to the barns. Jenna too remained silent, sensing her father's foul mood. She couldn't blame him though, for she too felt as though a black cloud was hanging over them.

The ride home seemed to last forever, silence filling the cab of the truck. Stopping to pick up Dot at the stud farm had been the best part of the day. The mare looked wonderful as she anxiously walked toward the trailer, seeming to know she was headed home.

Off and on Jenna would gaze wonderingly at her father. His thoughts seemed to be far and distant as his eyes searched the road before him.

She wanted so to ask him what his plans for Dash would be. *When will we run her again?* She knew Dash could do well, but since she wasn't entered in any other futurities, they would just have to enter her in open races.

Tom seemed to sense and share Jenna's thoughts and questions, he himself wondering the same things.

"So, Jace, what are your plans for the filly? I think she's got some real possibilities."

Jace glanced away from the road just long enough to look at Tom and Jenna, who both stared at him waiting anxiously for his reply.

"They have got some good open races next week at Greenland Downs, and since it's a pari-mutuel track, we won't have to pay entrance fees. I thought we could enter both Dash and Dancer."

Jenna smiled as her father returned his attention back to the road. Tom's voice hummed quietly in her ears as he agreed with Jace decision.

Visions of Dash racing down the track filled her thoughts as the truck left the highway to travel the last twenty miles to home.

Dot moved smoothly along the pasture rail, the young girl moving as one upon her silken back. Jace had reassured Jenna it wouldn't hurt Dot to be ridden; in fact the exercise would be good for her.

Jenna had gone without the saddle though, wanting to feel the powerful beauty of the horse beneath her as they moved smoothly about the pasture.

The large trees filtered the morning sun, which broke through to dance upon horse and rider. Jace stood alongside the rail, quietly watching, his figure obscured by the tree beside him.

Jenna rode real well. No one had really taught her, she just seemed to have that natural ability. Smiling to himself, he remembered a few times Jenna had gotten dumped off when she was younger. Even if she had gotten hurt a bit, she would still get right back on.

She seemed to learn from the horses, taught herself with experience. Smiling to himself he watched as Jenna brought her legs up into the jockey position, the strength of her legs holding her up for just a minute before she would slip back down upon Dot's back.

"If you want, Jenna, you can put the exercise saddle on Dot and practice. I'm sure it would be a lot easier with the stirrups." His voice broke through the stillness, startling Jenna as she moved closer.

Pulling Dot up from the slow gallop, she slowed her to a stop.

Stepping up to the rail, Jace leaned close to the mare, now standing before him.

"You ride her real well," Jace commented, smiling slightly.

"Thanks," was all that Jenna could say as she watched her father cautiously.

She wasn't sure what he was thinking, not daring to hope he would teach her how to ride like a jockey. She was even a bit embarrassed that he had seen her trying, especially without a saddle.

"Well, should we put the exercise saddle on her?" he asked again. "I guess it wouldn't hurt to teach you how to ride jockey style. I might even put you on the others sometime if you do good enough."

Jenna smiled happily her mind envisioning exercising Dash on the track.

"Oh, can I, Dad? That would be great!"

Turning, Jace headed toward the barn. "Well, bring Dot in the barn and we'll saddle her up."

Hurrying, Jenna jumped lightly to the ground, leading Dot toward the barn.

Tom turned toward the two of them as they moved inside. Smiling to himself, he anticipated what Jace would say. He had been watching them for a few minutes while he did some things in the barn. He too had seen Jenna try to ride in the jockey position without a saddle.

Shaking his head to himself, he smiled as Jace motioned toward him.

"Tom, will you get the exercise saddle for me? We're going to saddle up Dot and teach Jenna how to exercise racehorses. Maybe we'll even put her to work if she's good enough," Jace smiled teasingly at Tom then added as an afterthought. "And get the helmet too!"

Jenna glanced at her father. She hated the jockey helmet. It was too big, so to keep it on, she had to keep the chin strap real tight, and it made her head sweat.

"I don't need the helmet, Dad, really I don't," Jenna coaxed.

"If you want to ride on the track, you will wear the helmet! Do you understand?" Jace's voice was harsh and firm as he turned to gaze at his daughter.

She is just like her mom. Shanna had hated the helmet too. No matter how much I tried, I could never get Shanna to wear it. But Jenna is my daughter; she doesn't have a choice.

Tom handed the helmet to Jenna, winking at her lovingly, a sympathetic smile upon his lips.

"Jenna, he just doesn't want you to get hurt in case you fall off. Besides Don always wears his, doesn't he?"

Jenna nodded slowly, knowing Tom was right, as she tightened the chinstrap.

"Well, let's go," Jace hollered back over his shoulder as he led Dot out of the barn. "Tom, leg Jenna up here and we'll walk her out to the track."

Tom eased Jenna up into the saddle, and then squeezed her leg gently. He didn't need to say anything; she knew what he was thinking.

Jace's voice brought Jenna from her thoughts. The words seemed cold and a bit harsh. But she realized he didn't really mean them to be that way, it was just his way of making sure she paid attention to what he was saying.

Listening, she wished he could speak a bit kinder; she would listen and take him seriously. But she knew he just wanted to make sure.

His words seemed to thunder in her ears as she began to get nervous. Dot had spied the track and began to prance excitedly.

"Now, Jenna, remember what I told you. She remembers the track and she can run, so keep her under control. It's a lot different on the track than in the pasture. Some horses act like a totally different horse when they move onto a track. Now, if you do get into trouble, just keep your feet solid in the stirrups and lean back like you do when you water ski.

"Now, there is no way you can pull her up with your arms, you're just not strong enough. If you'll talk to her though, she'll listen and you can talk her down."

His voice became a buzz in Jenna's mind. *Do I really want to do this?*

She remembered the day she had ridden out to the back field to find her dad when Dash had gotten hurt. She had felt Dot's power, her speed. She remembered how wonderful it had felt, the power beneath her, the wind as it blew across her face.

Suddenly she realized her father and Tom had stopped walking beside her. Dot was already moving into a smooth trot waiting for her cue to move into a gallop.

"Remember, Jenna, just a nice gallop. Hold her at a good speed and you'll do just fine," his voice calmed her nervousness.

His words weren't cold and harsh but warm and encouraging.

Urging Dot into a gallop, Jenna raised herself off the mare's back. Her legs flexed, her knees in place alongside Dot's withers.

Her father's voice echoed in her mind, reminding her not to sit back down upon her back while she was in a gallop. That was a cue to increase her speed, to run.

If her legs got tired she was supposed to stand straight up and lean back holding the reins firm. Otherwise she had to keep her hands along Dot's neck, the reins crossed over, held firm but not too tight.

Jenna had watched Don lots of times, thinking how easy it looked. She was surprised how much work it took to stay in the squat position, leaning forward above Dot's neck. She could feel the strain in her legs as Dot moved down the backstretch of the track.

Dot increased her speed, wanting to run and causing Jenna's heart to pound faster.

Quietly, Jenna began to talk to her.

"Easy, girl, take it easy. Just a nice slow gallop, okay?" Jenna coaxed, her voice causing Dot to turn her ears and listen intently.

Slowing her pace, Dot moved into the corner not far from where Tom and Jace stood watching. Jenna continued to talk to Dot, probably more for her own sake than Dot's. It eased her nervousness and seemed to relax Dot as she eased into a smooth gallop; the reins firm but looser.

Jenna relaxed her grip as she began to feel the rhythm. Closing her eyes for just a moment, she felt just like she was flying.

Passing Tom and her father, Jenna glanced toward them. They leaned casually against the rail each smiling to the other as she passed by.

"Pull her up, then turn her around and trot her back," Jace yelled, his voice mixing with Jenna's as Dot too listened.

Seeming to understand what he had said, Dot eased her stride, slowing herself into a smooth trot.

Jenna praised the mare as she pulled her up even more, slowing her to a stop. Sitting down upon Dot's back, she could feel a warm burning deep in her thighs, her arms aching. She hadn't realized how much work it was to exercise the racehorses.

Turning Dot back toward her father, Jenna moved her into a smooth trot, again raising her seat off the mare's back. The burning in her legs eased as she relaxed with the smooth movement beneath her. Smiling proudly, she stopped Dot in front of Tom and her father.

"Well, how did I do?" Jenna questioned as she searched their eyes.

"You did pretty good, and you will do even better next time. You just need to relax a bit. It will make it easier and it won't wear you out so much," Jace spoke quietly as he began to lead Dot from the track, Jenna still sitting upon her back. "You just need to move with the rhythm of the horse. Yet always be ready, always be in control."

Jenna gazed from her dad to Tom who also walked beside her and Dot.

"You did real good!" Tom mouthed quietly not wanting Jace to hear.

"Can I take this helmet off now?" Jenna questioned as she began undoing the chinstrap.

Gazing back, Jace chuckled to himself, "Yeah, Jenna, you can take it off now."

CHAPTER 13

The days passed quickly, blending into weeks, a mixture of working, training, racing and farming.

Jenna sat along the rail fence watching Dash. Jace had turned her out in the small pasture letting her run about, enjoying the open space. She loved to watch her run, moving at her pleasure, no restrictions, and no controls.

Turning she noticed her father had come to stand beside her.

"What are you doing?" Jace questioned quietly, his voice sounding tired and distant.

Turning her gaze back toward the filly, Jenna hesitated. She had so many thoughts, so many feelings about things. Her father and she had been getting along quite well lately. She had learned to watch his moods and understand them.

Gazing up into his eyes, he seemed to be in a good mood. Focusing her eyes back on Dash, Jenna let her thoughts spill forth.

"I was just watching Dash and thinking how amazing horses really are. How strong and beautiful, yet how delicate they can be." A vision of the fallen sorrel filly came to mind. "And I just thought what a miracle they truly are. "

Jace turned his attention toward Dash. He really hadn't thought about it that way, at least not for a long time.

"You know, Dad, if you look around you, you can see a miracle in just about everything -- the sky, the clouds, the mountains, the trees, everything around us."

Jenna spun slowly around as she gazed about her.

Watching his daughter, Jace felt a little tug at his heart. *There really are so many miracles, and maybe, just maybe, I have forgotten most of them. Jenna herself is a miracle.* A vision of her as a small infant held awkwardly in his arms blurred with the image of his young daughter still smiling before him, her voice continuing to hum in his ears.

"Like when Dash hurt her knee, maybe it was a miracle that it wasn't worse. When the gates malfunctioned, a miracle that none of the horses or riders were hurt. Sometimes what seems bad, may really be a miracle…" Jenna's voice trailed off embarrassed by the way she had rambled on, feeling a bit silly.

Jace stood quietly beside her, his thoughts reflecting Jenna's words as he sifted through them. *She is right, quite wise for one so young, she will only be fourteen in a couple of weeks.* Drawing her to him, his arms held her close as he thought of what a true miracle she really was.

She can touch my heart with a look or a smile. She knows so much more than she probably realizes and reminds me of how much I have forgotten.

Kissing her upon the forehead, he whispered softly, then turned and headed back to the barn, leaving Jenna alone.

His words seemed so soft, so gentle, yet they burned deep within her heart.

"You are my miracle, Jenna."

His words echoed over and over in her mind as tears filled her eyes.

Watching her father disappear into the barn, Jenna turned her attention back to the filly who had come to stand beside her.

Dash nudged her gently. She had sensed Jenna's tears and had come to comfort the girl. Nickering softly, she brushed Jenna's cheek gently with her silky nose.

"Oh, Dash, you sweetheart. What would I do without you?" Jenna sighed as she wiped the tears from her cheeks. "You mother me like a mare would her foal."

Wrapping her arms gently about Dash's neck, her father's words still echoed softly in her mind. *"You are my miracle."*

"Oh, Dash, I think you are our miracle, mine and Dad's."

Visions of the past few weeks replayed in her mind. Dash had way surpassed their wildest expectations. In the past three races, she had won two and ran second in the other. In spite of being bumped by horses or other negative influences, she rallied through, pushing harder and faster. She seemed to run with her heart, giving her all.

Looking deep into her big brown eyes, Jenna sensed a warmth and comfort. Dash's eyes seemed so intense as though she could see into Jenna's soul, understanding everything about her. It was a strange feeling, yet comforting.

"Jenna?" Jace voice echoed loudly, drawing her attention back from the depths of Dash's eyes.

Dash too raised her head, looking to the man walking toward them.

"Jenna, her stall is ready so let's put her away for the night."

His words were kind, in spite of the fact that she had not come and helped. He had watched her from the barn as she had caressed the filly, the tenderness touching him. He had his days; and on another, it might have made him angry, but today he preferred to watch, enjoying the moment.

"Oh, Dad, I'm sorry I didn't mean to be out here so long. I just lost track of the time.... "

Her words were hushed as her father drew nearer.

"Jenna, it's okay, really it is."

He smiled tenderly as he slipped the halter in place, leading Dash toward the gate.

"Jenna, get the gate, then you can put her away." Jace handed the lead rope to Jenna, and then turned toward the house. "Hurry in, there's something I want to talk to you about."

Jenna wondered what he wanted, worrying somewhat as she led Dash into the barn.

Tom stood by Dancer's stall stroking the gelding on the forehead.

"You know, Jenna, that filly is different, kind of special. I think she would do anything for you," Tom commented as he moved to open Dash's stall door for her.

"What do you mean?" Jenna questioned, curious about his meaning.

"Well, there seems to be more to that filly than meets the eye. She is so gentle and careful, yet strong and aggressive in a race. She seems to understand so much and be so comfortable with herself. She never seems to be unsure, just confident..." his words trailed off. "Oh, Jenna, I don't know how to explain it. She's just different, special, all heart."

Jenna smiled as she leaned against Tom, her head resting upon his chest, her arms holding him close.

"She is special, isn't she, Tom? Almost like a miracle."

Squeezing her back, Tom agreed as they turned to leave the filly, who now stood contentedly eating her grain.

"Tom?" Jenna questioned, "Do you know what my dad wants to talk to me about?"

Her voice seemed nervous as Tom turned to look into her worried eyes.

"It's okay, Jenna, really it is. He just wants to talk to you about a futurity he's thinking of putting Dash in," Tom answered trying to reassure her.

Stopping in front of Dancer's stall, Jenna thought about what Tom had said as she scratched the young gelding firmly on the neck.

"But, Tom, I thought all the futurities were closed. Doesn't it cost almost double to pay in late?"

"Well, one of them is still open and the other one he would have to pay the late fee, but Dash has got a real good chance," Tom tried to answer her questions, but not say more than he knew for sure. "Your dad can answer you better. We talked about it, but he really hasn't decided yet. He wants to see what you think."

Jenna smiled, the idea of her father caring what she thought, pleasing her greatly.

"Well, Dancer, I guess I'll go see what Dad wants." Patting him firmly, Jenna headed toward the house.

Listening quietly Jenna tried to absorb everything her father was telling her.

"You see, Jenna, it will cost one thousand dollars to put Dash in late. There are only twenty-five horses entered, though, so she would have a real good chance of getting into the final gate of ten horses. The purse for the final gate is ten thousand dollars and the winner would take about six thousand of that home," Jace continued as he watched a smile spread across her face.

"If she makes it into the final gate, it would run the same weekend as your birthday. I wanted to make sure you wouldn't mind spending your fourteenth birthday at the races."

"Oh, Dad, are you kidding? That would be the best birthday ever. Can Lorna and Wayne come too?" Jenna exclaimed excitedly as she wrapped her arms about him.

Jace smiled, gazing across the room at Shanna's picture as he held Jenna firmly, his strong grip lifting her off the floor.

"Yes, Jenna, that would be real nice if Lorna and Wayne could come."

"So when are the trials for the futurity?" Jenna questioned, her excitement showing by the way she wiggled, finding it hard to stand still.

"They are July twenty-seventh and the final gate would run on August third, the day before your birthday."

Jace spoke quietly enjoying Jenna's excitement as he continued; "I also plan to put her in a futurity scheduled to run September fourteenth. Payments are just starting so there wouldn't be any late fee on that one. I think I'll enter Dancer for that one too."

"It sounds great, but what about Junior?" Jenna questioned remembering the sorrel gelding.

"He just isn't doing that well, Jenna. We'll run him in some open races that I don't have to pay entrance fees on and just see how he does." After answering Jenna, he moved toward the stairs. "Well, sweetie, I'll call and get her entered tomorrow but I'm heading to bed. Don't stay up too late, okay?"

Blowing Jenna a kiss, he disappeared up the stairs the soft whisper of a yawn drifting down to Jenna causing her to also yawn sleepily.

Jace leaned against the old well slowly dropping pebbles, listening to the distant splash that would intermix with the soft music of crickets humming in the late night breeze.

He had not been able to sleep, and after what had seemed like hours, had slipped on his pants to get a breath of fresh air.

The night air was a bit cool, but he enjoyed the feel of it blowing gently across his bare chest. Tilting his head back, he breathed deeply of the fresh air as he gazed into the starry sky.

He was a bit confused with himself lately, not understanding his moods. It wasn't a bad mood; it was just different. He seemed to always be thinking, and about things he hadn't thought of for a long time.

Like tonight, that was why he couldn't sleep. He was thinking about little things. The little things that maybe he had forgotten to notice; like the sound of pebbles splashing in the water, the sound of the crickets, or the feel of a cool breeze upon his face and chest.

Shaking his head, he moved toward the pasture just listening and looking, enjoying the peaceful night. Stopping at the rail he whistled for Dot, who raised her head, searching for the source of the sound.

Jace whistled again, the moonlight brightening the night as a small cloud passed by, revealing the man and the young mare only a dozen yards apart.

Dot trotted smoothly toward him. She knew him well, for often in the past he had come to stand beside the rail.

Moving to climb the fence, Jace stubbed his toe. He had not even realized he was still barefooted and cursed himself quietly for not wearing his boots.

Dot nudged him gently as he stroked her on the neck. He enjoyed the feel of her, the softness of her hair, the strength of her muscles beneath his hand. Clasping her mane, Jace swung himself easily up upon her back.

He had no bridle, no rope or halter, he didn't want one, didn't need one. Urging Dot forward, they moved into a gallop, both free, as they floated along the rail. Closing his eyes, Jace let himself feel— feel the breeze, the movement of the horse beneath him, her warmth and strength. Let himself hear, really hear the sounds around him— the crickets, the cows distant mooing, the sound of Dot's breath, and her hooves as they moved through the grass.

"Whoa, Dot," Jace breathed deeply as she slowed to a stop.

How good that had felt. Petting her lightly, he again breathed deeply. "Oh, Dot, I guess I'd almost forgotten how good some things feel, really feel. Thanks, girl."

The morning dew still lingered slightly, the sun sparkling in the moisture as it began to warm the earth.

Jenna watched Don eagerly as he worked Dancer on the track. It seemed to take no effort from Don at all as he and Dancer galloped past. They each seemed to be at ease, enjoying themselves completely.

Jenna turned at the sound of footsteps to see her father and Tom.

"There you are. I should have known you'd be out here," Jace teased lightly as he stopped beside her.

"Are you learning anything from watching?" he questioned.

"Yeah, I think a little," Jenna, answered as she turned and pointed toward Don. "He just makes it look so easy."

"Well, he will be the first to tell you it isn't," Tom, commented his eyes focusing on the young man as he turned Dancer to come back.

"That's true, Jenna, in fact I was talking to Don and he said he would be happy to teach you. So we thought it would be good to have you gallop Dot while he gallops Dash. That way they can work together and Don can see how you are doing; maybe give you some tips. What do you think? Want to give it a try?" Jace asked watching her expression.

Turning toward her father, Jenna couldn't believe what he was saying.

"You mean I can go out with Don when he works Dash? Really?"

Jace smiled as he winked at Tom. "Yeah, Jenna. Dot and Dash are already saddled and waiting in the barn."

"So, is she coming out with me?" Don questioned as he rode up on Dancer.

The young horse's nostrils flared as he danced impatiently at the rail.

Smiling nervously Jenna turned from Don back to Tom and her father.

"You mean you guys had this all planned?" Glancing again at their faces, Jenna smiled happily.

"Well, come on, Jenna, they're waiting." Jace turned toward the barn. "How did Dancer work, Don? He looked real good. "

"He worked like a dream, almost as good as Dash, but not as strong, " Don answered as he and Jace moved toward the barn.

"Come on, Jenna, let's get your helmet while Don and your dad get Dancer on the walker, then your dad and I will walk you and Don back out to the track, " Tom said.

Jenna loved working on the track with Don. He honestly seemed pleased to have her alongside him, even gaining respect for her desire. He had always felt no one could love horses the way he did. But Jenna did, he could see it in her eyes, and hear it in her voice. She seemed to feel the same things he did as they moved around the track, yet Jenna would freely express her joy and feelings, where he had only thought them to himself.

"Oh, Don, don't you just love the feel of the sun upon your skin, the breeze across your face and most of all the glorious feeling of a living, breathing animal moving beneath you? It almost makes you feel a million miles away from the rest of the world!" Jenna exclaimed as the horses moved side by side down the track, the sound of their powerful hooves breaking rhythmically through the peaceful morning.

Don smiled to himself as he glanced at the girl next to him.

"It is a wonderful feeling, isn't it? You know, Jenna, as well as you are doing, maybe your dad would let you breeze Dot down the backside of the track with Dash."

"Breeze her down the backside?" Jenna questioned unsure of Don's meaning.

"Well, Jenna, most of the time the horses are worked at a good gallop. When you breeze a horse down the backside, you are putting them into a brisk run down the straightaway, then you slow them down at the corner, to a strong gallop for the rest of the work. It helps build up their wind and increase their speed for a race," Don explained.

"But what if Dot won't slow down? What if she wants to keep running?" Jenna asked; a bit worried at the thought.

"She will stop. She knows the track and the routine. If you stay calm, she feels secure and comfortable, but if you become panicky or frightened, Dot will sense that and become uneasy herself. Besides I'll be right beside you. I'll talk to your dad about it. He had planned on having me blow Dash tomorrow anyway and I think it would be good to work Dash against Dot. He said we would give Dash a day off after the blow, then a light work the day before you leave for the races on Friday," Don finished talking as he moved Dash to a stop, pausing to pat the filly affectionately on the neck.

Jace had liked the idea of breezing Dash with Dot. It would be good to let Dash really stretch out and work alongside another horse. Doing it now would be just right for the race trials, and Dot wasn't far enough along that it would be a problem for her. *Besides,* he thought, *mares run in their pastures all the time.*

Jenna struggled with the helmet as it slipped slightly on her head. It just didn't fit and even tightening the chinstrap didn't help much.

"Dad, do I really have to wear this helmet? It doesn't fit very well."

"Jenna, you know very well you have to wear it, especially breezing those two down the backside, " Jace answered firmly as he turned to leg her up onto Dot's back.

"Dot may not have breezed for a long time, but you better hold on tight because she can move! Remember that day running her out to the back pasture? Well, she's on the track now and that will make a difference, so keep your seat flat on her back and lean in along her neck. Keep her going straight, right alongside of Dash. Dot may start out faster, but Dash will catch her.

"Try to keep them paced together. When you move into the corner, rise up off her back and pull firmly back on the reins, keep them snug but allow her to slow her pace gradually. Just follow Don and you'll do great."

Jace released Dot sending her in the direction of the track alongside of Dash and Don.

"Warm them up, keeping their gallop slow. When you come out of the corner, come out straight side by side, adjust your reins, then drop your seat down onto her back. Believe me, Jenna, she'll know what you want."

Jace smiled as he caught a glimpse of the nervousness Jenna tried so hard to hide.

Moving alongside of Don, Jenna's nervousness was eased somewhat by his compassionate smile.

"You'll do great, Jenna, and believe me you're going to love it! "

Before Jenna realized it, they had moved into the corner of the track, the two horses moving smoothly beside each other.

"Adjust your reins, Jenna, and lean in just a bit," Don instructed.

Tightening her reins slightly, Jenna was surprised by the change in Dot. It was like she knew what was about to happen. Suddenly she seemed to pump herself up, every muscle becoming taut and ready.

"Are you ready?" Don's voice broke through her thoughts as she realized they were almost into the straightaway.

The two horses moved alongside each other, no longer relaxed but ready to explode, just waiting for the cue.

Nodding at Don, Jenna dropped her seat onto Dot's back.

"Dash, get!"

The sound of Don's voice broke the invisible gate that held the two horses at bay as they exploded down the track.

Jenna gasped for breath as Dot flew down the track, the wind bringing tears to her eyes. She knew Dash was alongside as the two horses literally tore down the track, dirt flying from their hooves.

Suddenly they were into the corner as Jenna realized she had been holding her breath. Breathing deeply, she relaxed her stance, rising up off of Dot's back as she pulled back on the reins.

Don was right alongside, a big smile spreading over his face.

"So what did you think, Jenna?"

"Wow, it was awesome! The power and the speed were more than I had ever imagined. I swear I can still hear my heart pounding, even though I know they can go even faster. The sound of the two of them side by side, stride for stride, breathe for breathe.... "

Jenna smiled at Don as the two horses continue to slow their stride. "I loved it, Don. Thanks."

Don smiled back at Jenna as the two turned, heading back toward Jace and Tom, who stood waiting at the rail.

"Not bad, Jenna, not bad at all," Jace praised, and then turned his attention to Don. "Dash looked real good, Don. We'll give her a day off, then a light work before we head for Greenland Downs.

"She looks ready, don't you think?" Jace questioned.

"She sure worked good and strong. Having Dot next to her seemed to give her that extra drive to stay ahead. Boy, that Dot sure can move for an old mare, and Jenna did a real good job. I hope she doesn't get too good, I would hate to lose my job."

Don smiled back at Jenna making sure she had heard him and could see the pleased look upon his face.

CHAPTER 14

Jenna waited anxiously in the grandstands as the trumpet announced the horses moving onto the track. The musical sound echoed; sending goose bumps to rise then run clear down to her toes.

The horses moved excitedly, their necks arched, bodies pumped, eyes shining as they gazed about them. The announcer's voice broke through the hum of voices to announce each horse.

Jenna loved to hear the sound of Dash's name, her eyes fixed on the filly as she moved gracefully before the grandstands.

"The number two-horse is For Ever Dashin', owned and trained by Jace Brenton, ridden by Tomme Day," the announcer finished with Dash then went on to announce the other eight horses in the gate.

Smiling, Jenna was pleased to see Tomme ridding Dash. As one of the leading jockeys at the track, it would possibly give them a bit of an edge in the race.

Don too had come to watch the race. He seldom rode in the races, preferring to mostly exercise the horses. He had a special fondness for Dash though and just couldn't miss being there for this race.

Waiting, Jenna watched as the horses moved away in a smooth gallop to warm up on the backside of the track. People rushed past, heading toward the betting windows.

Jenna had coaxed Tom into placing a small bet for her since she wasn't old enough. It wasn't so much that she wanted to bet, but to show her faith in the filly.

Holding the ticket tightly in one hand, Jenna reached to caress the golden horse hanging loosely about her neck with her other hand.

Rising from behind the open gates, Dash sprung to the lead, the number one-horse close by her side. She dug deep and strong, with each stride widening the distance between her and the other horse. The one-horse struggled to catch her as the jockey tapped him firm with his whip.

Leaning in, Tomme flagged his whip along Dash's side never touching her silken hair, only the sound of the whip whistling at her side and Tomme's strong arms pushing against her neck, driving her on.

Dash and the one-horse had a good length and a half over the rest of the field as they neared the finish line. Tapping Dash once on the shoulder with the whip, Tomme coaxed her for a bit more. The one-horse fought to stay with her as she slowly drew away leaving him a length behind and the other horses two or more lengths in the distance.

Rising up off Dash's back, Tomme raised his arm in victory as they passed the finish line. The cheer of the crowd almost drowned out the announcer's call, proclaiming For Ever Dashin' the winner by an impressive lead over the rest of the field; the one-horse, Bofus, running second and Katy Kirk finishing third.

Jenna ran to the finish line as tears filled her eyes. Her heart pounded as she waited impatiently in the winner's circle for Dash to return, being led by her father. Tom stood beside her squeezing her tightly as friends moved into the circle, waiting for Jace to bring Dash into position to take the win picture.

Jace patted the filly on the neck as Tomme exclaimed what an awesome ride it had been. Jace was listening as he led Dash to the winner's circle. Suddenly his heart seemed to rise into his throat, the cheers of the crowd seeming to fade as he paused, his gaze fixed on the figure in the distance.

Dash nudged him gently on the shoulder, confused. *Why has he stopped?* She seemed to know the routine and was eager to move into the circle. Taking a deep breath, Jace shook his head, clearing the image from his mind. Bringing Dash into position, Jace turned to face the cameraman.

Jenna moved to wrap her arms about Dash as Tomme jumped lightly to the ground to remove the saddle.

Again a loud cheer rose up from the crowd as Dash's win time lit up the tote board. She had the fastest time so far with only one more trial race to go. The time of 17:93 was her fastest race yet and pretty well guaranteed her a position in the final gate.

Jace turned to lead Dash toward the test barn.

"Jenna, stay and get the time on the next race, then come to the test barn and help me with Dash."

Jenna smiled, knowing well the routine. Each winning horse had to go to the test barn for a blood and urine test before they could be released from the track. These tests helped keep racing safe for horses, riders, and owners, making sure no illegal medications were given to the horses.

Jace moved Dash into the test barn area where she was given a drink of water before they drew the tube of blood from her vein. Hooking her on the walker, Jace moved to sit upon the bench off to the side. Dash would be cooled down on the walker then moved into the barn to get a urine sample. All he could do was wait.

Suddenly it was there again; the image, the woman. Jace's heart felt near to exploding, his breath caught in his chest.

The young woman leaned over the rail at the saddling paddock to watch the horses being saddled for the next race. He could almost hear her laughter as she smiled at the man beside her. Jace couldn't believe the resemblance as he felt a strange emptiness within.

The woman looked to be taller than Shanna, but her face, the color of her hair, the look in her eyes, even her smile seemed to reach deep into his mind drawing Shanna's memory to blend and mix with the woman in the distance.

The trumpeter announced the next race as the horses moved out onto the track. Turning, the woman moved toward the grandstands, her image floating away in a wave of people.

"Jace, will you bring your horse into the barn?"

The vet's voice drew his attention from the blurring vision of people as the woman disappeared from view.

Nodding, Jace moved to lead Dash into the barn. Waiting patiently he could hear the hum of the crowd as the announcer's voice caused a nervous twinge to run through him. The woman forgotten, he listened intently for the call of the race.

The sound of the bell rang clear as the horses broke from behind the opening gates. It was hard to hear inside the barn, but he caught the general results of the race as the announcer's voice rose above the crowd.

"The winner looks to be MaKayhan by a head. Please hold all tickets till the race is official."

Taking a deep breath, Jace hoped for a fairly slow time. He had seen races in the past where the last trial race had been run so fast it had bumped winning horses out of the final gate.

"She's all done, Jace. You can take her back to the others barns now."

Dr. Summers smiled at Jace. He had been the track vet there for the past two years and knew Jace quite well.

"Good luck, Jace. I hope to see you back here in two weeks."

"Thanks, Doc. We'll see you later."

After thanking Dr. Summers, Jace led Dash from the test barn. He too hoped to be back in the test barn in two weeks.

Looking up, he could see Jenna running toward him.

"Dad, she's in! She's the third fastest qualifier. That last race had more of a tail wind, so they ran a bit faster. MaKayhan won it in 17:85 and Noble

Dash ran 17:90, so Dash is third with 17:93. Oh, she did wonderful didn't she?"

Reaching into her pocket, Jenna pulled a small bundle of bills, waving them excitedly toward him.

"Tom bought me a two dollar win, place, and show ticket. It paid a total of $62.50. Not bad, huh?"

Turning toward Dash, Jenna patted her lightly on the neck. "Oh, sweetie, you did wonderful!"

"She sure did, Jenna, she sure did!" Jace answered as his thoughts of the race drifted, mixing with the image of the woman once again.

CHAPTER 15

The breeze blew across his face as Jace closed his eyes, the movement of the horse beneath him rocking him slightly with its powerful stride. A sweet voice floated through the air as a young woman moved alongside, drawing his attention toward her.

Her long blonde hair flew luxuriously behind her as the wind played with her curls, the rock of the horse bouncing her gently. Her eyes shone brightly as he gazed toward her.

Moving toward the stream, they left the horses to graze beneath a large oak tree. The long grass swayed in the breeze, the sound of the stream singing musically.

Reaching to touch a blonde curl, he drew her close, the smell of her perfume tantalizing him. She spoke softly, her words caressing his mind as he reached to touch her soft lips, silencing her as he leaned to kiss her tenderly.

Her closeness made his head spin— the sweetness of her lips, the softness of her skin. Moving his hand slowly, he caressed her neck, his lips following to gently kiss the soft hollow of her throat.

Her fingers ran gently through his hair, causing a chill to run through him.

His hands seemed to burn, his heart pounding as he slid her blouse from her shoulders. His lips hungered for her flesh as he savored its softness, lingering along the edge of her breast.

Gently she pulled him with her to the shelter of some small trees, the softness of the grass welcoming them.

His hands continued to glide tenderly across her flesh, enticing him further as they traveled to her small waist, her lean stomach and slender hips. Her fragile beauty entranced him, the feel of her lean muscles beneath his hands arousing him even more.

Her hands had moved to caress his back, their touch sending warm shivers throughout. Her lips now caressed his neck, his chest, and their warmth reaching deep into his heart.

Burying his head in the crook of her neck, he closed his eyes, the silkiness of her hair, its freshness, teasing at his senses. Moving gently upon her, his heart pounded yet louder, his head spinning as the warmth of their flesh blended as one.

Breathing deeply of the fresh air, Jace opened his eyes, the darkness about him confusing him as his mind struggled. His body tingled, his heart pounded as he breathed slowly, trying to regain his senses, to understand.

The room about him was dark and empty, the only movement that of the curtains blowing lightly in the breeze. The scent of her perfume seemed to linger about the room.

Moving to the window, he searched the heavens. The dream had seemed so real. He could almost feel her presence, not beside him but deep within his heart, filling his soul.

How I miss her, long for her! Yet stronger than the ache within his loins was the ache within his heart.

Leaning on the rail, Jace savored the cool night air, trying to clear his head. Haunted by the dream, he had left the house trying to sort through his feelings.

Dot had come to stand at the rail. Sensing Jace's mood, she nudged him gently.

"So, Dot, what do you want, huh?" Jace spoke softly as he stroked her on the forehead.

Her closeness comforted him, as he stood surrounded by the peacefulness of the night.

"Do you miss her too?" Jace questioned as he gazed into the depths of her eyes.

She couldn't speak, yet she could say so much with the warmth and caring in her gaze.

Time seemed to stand still as his mind drifted, filling with memories far and distant. Suddenly a loud thud echoed, breaking through to the present.

Dot raised her head, looking toward the barn, her ears pricked forward listening as again another thud echoed in the silence.

Turning to follow her gaze, Jace heard still yet another loud thud echo from deep within the barn.

"Well, Dot, who do you think is making all that noise, huh?" Jace asked, a smile upon his face. Patting her on the neck, he turned toward the barn. "I guess I better go see what the problem is."

Dot watched Jace as he disappeared into the barn. A warm glow from the lights drifted out the door as they illuminated the barn within.

Dash stood near her stall door as she watched the man moving toward her and her back hoof hit the panel yet one more time, the thud echoing within the barn.

"Hey, Dash, what's the problem?" Jace questioned as he reached out to stroke her silken nose.

A low nicker vibrated deep within her throat as her eyes gazed into his. Her warm breath caressed his neck as she snuggled her nose in along his shoulder, gently nuzzling him.

"You are a strange horse, Dash. Did you just want some company?" Jace teased as he continued to stroke her neck, enjoying her attention.

Stepping inside the stall, he leaned against the panel to slide down to sit in the fresh sawdust, suddenly realizing how tired he was.

"Now don't step on me," Jace warned as Dash circled the stall, positioning herself to slowly lower herself down next to him.

A contented moan escaped her from deep within as she laid back, her head resting near his leg.

She gazed back at him as his words touched her ears, his voice quiet and gentle.

"So, Dash, what was all that ruckus about, huh?" Jace asked as he stroked her silky neck.

It was nice in the barn, the warm glow of the lights mixing with the night, the smell of fresh sawdust and sweet hay mixing with the cool breeze drifting through the open barn windows.

He felt at peace sitting there as the filly's nose nudged his leg gently.

His thoughts drifted with the dream, of Shanna, of the many things that troubled him.

"It seemed so real, Dash. I could have sworn it was real, and the past had been the dream."

Dash lifted her head to gaze at the man. Her eyes touched his with their mysterious aura as he continued to talk.

"You know, Dash, Shanna would have really liked you. She was so good with horses. It's funny, I think back now and there are so many things that are so clear, like it was only yesterday. She could look at me with her beautiful eyes, and I swear, she could read my mind, see right into my heart. She knew the things I couldn't or wouldn't say."

Gazing up at the rafters in the barn, Jace's throat grew tight as his eyes burned with held tears.

"I only hope she knew how much I truly loved her, for I know I didn't say it near enough."

Dash stretched slightly, moving her head to where it now rested in his lap. She enjoyed the man and sensed his troubles. She nickered softly trying to comfort him in the only way she knew how.

"It's funny, girl, I don't think I've really talked much about it to anyone, and now here I am talking to a horse."

He watched her quietly for a moment as the words searched slowly for a way out. "It's always been too hard to talk about ... that last day. For so long I had kept telling her to hang on, to fight harder. Then that day, she had looked at me, those eyes tearing at my heart. 'I'm so tired, Jace. I'm just so tired of it all.' I knew what she meant and God knows how it tore me apart.

"I sat by her for what seemed to be hours instead of just a couple of minutes and somewhere in that period of time God gave me the strength to let her go, to tell her it was okay. The words seemed to come from somewhere else as I told her it was okay.

"Go to sleep. I'll stay with you." As her eyes drifted shut, I sensed an emptiness I'd never felt before. Leaning over I kissed her gently on the forehead, telling her how much I really loved her. I was never sure if she heard me."

Dash nudged his hand gently the way a mare would comfort her foal, her low nicker caressing his heart. Jace fought back the tears as he leaned to rest his head along her side. He could feel the beat of his heart pounding in his chest, the sound of hers pounding in his ears.

Closing his eyes, he was comforted by the sound, the closeness, the warmth, the strength and gentleness of the horse beside him.

Raising his head, Jace again gazed into the rafters now highlighted by the sun's morning rays. He felt a warm comfort and sense of peace he hadn't felt for a long, long time.

Jenna woke to find the house empty. Rushing out to the barn, she found the horses already on the walker, her father and Tom sitting on a couple of bales of hay, just watching the horses. She hadn't slept in. In fact she was up early, so she was somewhat confused to see Tom and her father just sitting in the early morning sun.

"Do you want me to get the hay?" Jenna questioned as she came to stand in front of them.

"No, that's okay, Jenna, they're all done," Jace answered looking up at his daughter.

"I couldn't sleep, so I came out early. Come sit down." Jace patted the bale of hay next to him.

Sitting by her father, she enjoyed the warmth of the morning sun on her face. She loved to watch the horses as Dash, Dancer and Junior moved briskly about the walker.

Occasionally one of them would kick and spin about, wanting to go faster than the speed of the walker would allow.

A loud, deep whinny broke through the stillness of the morning, drawing everyone's attention toward the front pasture. Buck stood near the rail watching the younger horses, Dot just a few feet to his side.

"What's the matter, Buck? Hasn't Jenna brought your treat to you?" Jace asked teasingly as he glanced at Jenna.

He knew she would always bring Dot some grain and Buck some apples. It was kind of funny that Dot just would not eat the apples; she preferred a small handful of grain. Jace had often watched Jenna from a distance as she would sneak out of the house with a couple of apples, stop at the barn for some grain, then head to the pasture where Buck and Dot would be waiting.

"Well, Jenna, you better run get him a couple of apples," Jace commented as again Buck's deep whinny rang through the air, this time followed by Dot's.

Tom laughed lightheartedly as he and Jace watched Jenna run to the house.

"She sure has a way with horses. I didn't think Buck would ever like anyone but you, Jace," Tom commented as he watched the gelding's gaze follow Jenna till she disappeared into the house.

Smiling to himself Jace agreed, nodding slightly. *I understand just how the big gelding feels, for Jenna has a way of sneaking into your heart before you know it. Shanna had been that way too. She had stolen my heart before I knew what was happening. She could brighten my day with just a smile. Oh, how I miss her smile!*

Jace's thoughts had drifted and suddenly he realized Jenna was already back at the pasture rail feeding Buck and Dot.

Turning to glance at her father, Jenna smiled happily as Buck nudged her gently coaxing her for the other apple he knew she held hidden behind her back.

She has the same smile, the same glint of warmth and love in her eyes. She is the one part of Shanna I have left, so much a part of her that I can't imagine her not being here, not being with me. He even wondered how he ever could have sent her away.

Tom quietly watched Jace. The younger man had changed lately. He seemed to be living, feeling, caring, and yes, loving. He could see the love in Jace's eyes as he watched Jenna.

Smiling to himself, Tom thanked God for bringing them back together. Yet he could still see the caution the two of them seemed to feel. Often he would see one of them look at the other when they weren't looking. For some reason people seem to feel the need to hide their feelings, but Tom could see it in their eyes. Maybe, in time, that too would change.

Dash nickered softly as Jenna came toward the walker, wondering if Jenna had a treat for her. She never seemed to whinny, just nicker in a deep warm tone.

"Someone's a little jealous, Jenna," Jace commented as he watched the filly, her deep nicker coaxing.

Glancing first at Jenna, Dash then looked toward Jace throwing her head slightly as she passed by.

"I'll shut the walker off and you can take her in." Jace's words were well understood by Dash, who turned impatiently as the walker came to a stop.

Nickering still softly, she waited as Jenna reached to unhook the snap.

Leading her into the barn, Jenna smiled warmly to Tom and her father as she passed. "Do you think she can win the race, Dad? "

Jace moved to follow Jenna and Dash into the barn, patting the filly lightly on the rump. "Well, Jenna, I guess we will find out in two weeks."

His words sounded warm and confident as he moved closer to Dash's head. Stroking her nose gently, their eyes met with an understanding warmth.

Jace whispered in the filly's ear as they stood waiting in the stall at Greenland Downs, "Well, are you ready, girl? I've done my part, now it's up to you."

Dash nudged him eagerly, pushing him toward the stall door.

"Not yet, girl. Now hold still while I check your leg wraps. "

Jace knelt down to carefully squeeze her front legs, making sure the wraps were snug but not too tight. He had wrapped a light cotton padding covered with a snug vet wrap to protect and strengthen her front legs.

"Jenna, do you have her blinkers and girth cover?" Jace questioned, his voice traveling through the stall door toward Jenna who stood nervously waiting with Tom.

"I've got them," Tom answered smiling at Jenna.

"Well, Jace, it's about time to head to the paddock. Are you ready to bring her out?"

Jace opened the stall door leading Dash out; her ears pricked forward, her eyes alert and searching.

"Horsemen, bring your horses to the paddock for race number four, " the announcer's voice carried from the grandstands to the barns along the speaker system as horses began to move toward the paddock.

Jace and Dash carne into the saddling paddock; followed by MaKayhan and a couple of other horses. The ten saddling paddocks were full with young horses that danced eagerly about, anxious to be on the track.

Jenna stood nervously with Lorna and Wayne as Jace and Tom got Dash saddled. She glanced from Dash to each of the other nine horses. They were all real nice horses, each with strong potential. They had to have to have made it to the final gate.

She knew Dash could win it though, she just knew it, but as each horse moved onto the track Jenna felt her heart rise into her throat. MaKayhan was favored as the fastest qualifier, and he looked real good. Dash would be coming out of the five hole with the big sorrel gelding right beside her in the four hole.

Jace smiled to Jenna as he hopped into the truck to go to the gates. Dash moved easily down the backstretch to warm up, Tomme upon her back in the black racing silks. The pony-rider kept Dash's lead tight; holding her alongside the pony-horse as they neared the gates.

Nervously Jenna watched from the grandstands with Tom, Lorna, and Wayne at her side. She hated this part— the wait as the horses circled momentarily behind the gates before being loaded one at a time.

Jenna could see the horses loading, first the one, then the two, and so on down to Dash. It seemed to take forever for the last horse to load. Holding her breath, Jenna waited for the gates to open.

Suddenly she saw the six-horse rear up in the gate, crash against the sides, thrashing frantically about before falling to the ground, his powerful body trapped by the metal frame of the gates. He struggled fiercely on his side trying to get up. His strong legs kicked and thrashed erratically.

Quickly the gate workers rushed toward the fallen horse as Dash's header tried to calm her, for she had begun to dance about nervously in her gate.

Jenna's heart sank, as tears burned her eyes, her voice frantic, "No Please, God, no! Get him off of her, please, get him away from her!"

She could see the gelding's powerful hooves striking Dash's legs as the filly tried desperately to move.

"Oh, Tom, they've got to get her out! He's kicking her legs."

Tom could only wrap his arm about her shoulders as he too stood desperately watching the scene before him. Lorna had turned to grip Wayne's arm as she searched his eyes wonderingly; unsure of what was happening.

Jace yelled frantically at Dash's header and the race steward beside him.

"To hell with him, get her out before he hurts her! Those other guys can take care of him."

Throwing the latch to the back gate, Jace swung the door open as the header guided Dash back, Tomme trying to calm her.

Dash moved quickly backward, the pain of his hooves catching her one more time as she turned to bolt away.

"Easy, girl, easy."

Jace quickly grabbed Dash's reins as Tomme worked gently to control her. "That's a girl. Whoa. Let me check your legs," Jace coaxed as he stooped to run his hands down each leg, slowly, gently.

"Is she okay, Jace?" Dr. Summers, the track vet, asked as he stood beside the filly, stroking her on the nose.

"I think so. She has a couple of scratches on her right hind leg, but they aren't bleeding much. The right front leg looks like it got hit, but the wrap protected her. It is torn a little bit but most of it is in place," Jace answered as he continued to check Dash over.

Dr. Summers knelt to check Dash's legs as Jace turned his attention to those around him.

The six-horse was out of the gate and being led away from the track, while the other eight horses circled anxiously, confused at being unloaded from the gates.

"Well, Jace, the starter scratched the six-horse. If you don't want to run your filly, I'll give you a vet scratch for her, but she looks okay to me."

Dr. Summers patted Dash gently on the neck as she moved anxiously toward the gates, her pain forgotten.

Looking deep into Dash's eyes, Jace felt a warm glow of excitement and desire radiating forth.

"Okay, let's load her back up," Jace spoke to her header and Tomme, who both smiled confidently.

"Oh, Lorna, they're loading her back in. She must be okay. "

Tears still moistened Jenna's cheeks as she squeezed Lorna's hand, waiting nervously. Reaching subconsciously, Jenna wrapped her fingers tightly about the golden horse.

The gates flew open, the ring of the bell breaking through the air to mingle with the announcer's voice as he called the race. Jace had held his breath as he watched Dash crouch back, and then explode forward, dirt flying from her hooves as she tore down the track.

Jenna screamed, cheering loudly as Dash broke from the gates. MaKayhan had beaten her out, but she moved strongly along his side. Tomme tapped her encouragingly on her right hip and shoulder. It was a tight race as Dash and MaKayhan battled each other for the lead. Noble Dash moved on strong on the inside of the track from the two hole as Kizzy Pic led the outside from the eight hole.

"Come on, Dash, you can do it!" Jenna screamed as she continued to hold the golden horse tightly in her small hand.

"Come on, come on, girl!" Wayne's voice mingled with Jenna's as he found himself overcome with excitement, along with Lorna.

He was awed by the strength and beauty of the animals as they moved closer to the finish line.

"For Ever Dashin' wins by a length with Noble Dash finishing second. Please hold all tickets until the race becomes official," the voice of the announcer went hardly noticed by Jenna, who screamed and jumped excitedly about hugging Lorna, Wayne, and Tom.

"Oh, she did it. She really did it. I knew she could!" Jenna exclaimed as tears of joy now spilled down her cheeks.

"Come on," Jenna coaxed anxiously as she led Lorna and Wayne toward the winner's circle.

Racing ahead Jenna ran onto the track to fly into her father's arms.

"Oh, Dad, she did it!"

Jace squeezed her tight, the moment reminding him of another race a long time ago. Shanna had flown into his arms embarrassing him a bit as the crowd watched on. But today was different; his focus was on Jenna and the filly, not the crowd, not the other trainers, not anything else around him.

Kissing her on the cheek, he set her gently on the ground.

"She really did, honey, she really did." Jace's voice warmed her heart as she drew her attention down the track.

"Here she comes, Jenna. Run get in the winner's circle with Lorna and Wayne. Tom and I will bring her in."

Tom moved out onto the track to help Jace with Dash, who had returned from the backside of the track to stand before the cheering crowd, her nostrils flaring, her sides heaving slightly.

The tote board lit up behind them, the roar from the crowd growing louder. Five, two, eight and four showed the order of finish. Dash was first as the five-horse with the number two-horse, Noble Dash, finishing second and the eight-horse, Kizzy Pie, finishing third. MaKayhan had come in fourth, right next to Kizzy Pie.

Dash moved into the winner's circle, her head held high, a look of pride shining in her eyes. Quickly the photographer snapped the shot as Jace stood at Dash's head, Jenna at his side holding the silver trophy.

Leading Dash to the test barn, Jace glanced about the crowd. His heart was pounding, a rush of thoughts filling his head. He had so much, he really did. His daughter, his family, and friends around him, a promising gelding and Dash had just won a ten thousand dollar futurity against seven of the leading trainer's horses in the final gate.

He had so much. His eyes continued to search the crowd as he stood by the fence, Dash now hooked on the walker, the faces blurring to mix with a memory.

Closing his eyes he whispered softly, "Did you see her, Shanna? She was awesome, wasn't she?"

CHAPTER 16

The rising sun shimmered through the early morning mist that hovered among the treetops intermixing with the warm breeze that danced throughout the branches. Jace loved the smell of the fresh morning air, the pine trees as they warmed in the sun, and the wildflowers as they swayed along with the sweet mountain grass.

He had awakened early, his mind jumbled with thoughts, his heart yearning for something— he wasn't sure what.

Heading for the barn, he had decided to saddle Buck and go for a ride, a long ride, up past the fence line into the mountains. He loved the beauty up there. To him, this was heaven, or at least the closest thing to it.

He felt so small looking out into the vastness about him as Buck stood quietly enjoying some of the mountain grass. The sun warmed Jace's face, his thoughts warming his heart. *I feel good, really good.*

He wondered at the loneliness that had seemed to fill his heart so long ago. He still missed Shanna, but her memory and love seemed to fill his every being. Closing his eyes, he could feel her warmth, even though she wasn't there with him, a part of her was; he knew it.

Looking about, he noticed the changes that had come to pass over the past four years, but Shanna's love was still there, still the same, he could feel it. *It has probably been here all the time. I had just forgotten how to feel it.*

Inhaling the crisp morning air, he urged Buck forward down the sloping trail, the gelding still chewing on the last bite of grass he had managed to grab.

The sun had risen off the mountain ridge to spread over the fields. Riding toward the barn, he could see Jenna and Tom waiting anxiously outside. Moving closer, he could see the tears Jenna held in check as Tom moved to take Buck as Jace dismounted.

"What's the matter?" Jace asked as he looked from Jenna to Tom, then back to Jenna again.

"Oh, Dad, it's Dash. She can hardly walk, " Jenna's voice cracked as her father moved to put his arm around her shoulder.

"Have you checked her over, Tom?" Jace questioned as they all moved into the barn, Buck following behind being led by one rein.

"Yeah, I checked her real good. There doesn't seem to be much swelling, but when I run my hand over her right front shin, she pulls away in obvious pain. She has a slight bump on about the same spot where her wrap was torn, but the skin isn't scraped or broken. Her knee seems to be a bit tender, but nothing unusual considering that is the same knee that she hurt this spring.

"Why don't you take a look at her? I'll put Buck away." Tom smiled at Jenna as he turned to unsaddle Buck.

Hovering close to her father, Jenna felt a sense of relief to have him there. He would make Dash better; she knew he could.

"Well, Jenna, I'm not real sure what to think. Why don't you run in the house and call Dr. Daines? Tell him to bring his portable x-ray machine."

It seemed to take forever before Dr. Daines' truck came pulling down the lane. Stepping from the cab of the truck, he reached for the x-ray machine, and then turned to follow Jenna.

"I heard she won that futurity yesterday," Dr. Daines commented as he and Jenna moved closer to Dash's stall.

"It's too bad she got hurt. Most horses wouldn't have run after getting kicked like that in the gates. She sure is a gutsy filly."

Stroking Dash on the nose, Dr. Daines questioned Jace and Tom while he gently ran his hands down her legs as she flinched occasionally.

"Jace, could you get her to move out into the alley? I think I can get better x-rays out there."

Dash moved slowly, cautiously alongside Jace until she stood in the open alleyway. Dr. Daines took numerous views of her leg and knee, not wanting to miss anything. After finishing the x-rays and further examination of her leg, he still could not find anything definite.

"Icepack her leg with the ice boots for about thirty minutes," Dr. Daines said and moved from the barn carrying the x-ray machine and plates, Jace walking by his side.

"I think she is just bone bruised, but you will need to lay her off for about a month. I'll call and let you know the results of the x-rays."

"Do you think she chipped her knee? " Jace questioned knowing well that a chip was a common injury to a racehorse.

Dr. Daines turned from the truck to face Jace after placing the plates on the seat.

"I really don't think so. Her knee doesn't seem to bother her much, but her shin sure seems to be tender. I will call you as soon as I can after reviewing the x-rays."

Jace stepped back as Dr. Daines started the engine of his truck.

"Thanks for coming so quickly. I'll get the ice on and wait to hear from you. "

Smiling Dr. Daines waved first at Jace then at Jenna, who now stood nervously at her father's side as the vet turned to drive away.

"Well, Jenna, let's get the ice boots on her, " Jace remarked as he moved toward the barn.

"Dad, is she going to be okay?" Jenna asked quietly, fear clutching at her heart.

Jace hesitated as he turned toward his daughter. He could sense her fear and concern, and didn't blame her one bit, for he too had a bad feeling. It wasn't anything real definite, just something deep inside that made him feel uneasy.

Smiling at Jenna, he said what he hoped was true, what he himself wanted to hear, "I think she will be just fine. Dr. Daines is probably right. She is just bruised up a bit. We will give her some time off and she will be good as new. "

Dash stood quietly, the ice numbing the pain in her leg. Jenna brushed her gently while they waited for the time to pass. Talking quietly, Jenna told Dash how good she had done, and how she was going to be just fine.

Jace moved about finishing the chores, Jenna's voice comforting both Dash and her father as he too listened.

Thirty minutes passed and Jace removed the ice boots from Dash's leg. The swelling seemed much better; the bump along the side of her shin much smaller.

Leading Dash to her stall Jenna thought she was walking much better. Jace watched intently, thinking the same thing, but knowing well the relief from the ice would be mostly temporary.

Latching the stall door, Jenna turned to look first at her watch and then her father. It had been over two hours.

Why hasn't Dr. Daines called yet? Jenna thought to herself.

Jace seemed to sense her thoughts as he himself noted the time.

"Come on in the house, Jenna. I'm sure he will be calling any moment, besides it's your birthday, remember?"

Tom too moved toward the house, glancing at the phone extension in the barn as he passed by.

"I'm sure he will be calling soon, " squeezing Jenna's hand, Tom tried to reassure her as his eyes met Jace's, concern shared between the two of them.

The sound of the phone ringing broke through the silencer stopping the three of them in their tracks. Glancing first at Jenna, Jace ran toward the house, Jenna and Tom close behind.

"Hello?" Jace answered anticipating the voice on the other line.

"Yes, Jace, this is Dr. Daines. I am sorry it has taken me so long to get back to you. Some of the x-rays are a bit fuzzy, and my equipment is a bit old, but I should still be able to pick something up, if it were there. After reviewing them, I can't see any fractures or chips of any kind."

Jace sighed with relief as Dr. Daines continued; "I think it would be best to lay her off about a month. That should be enough time for a bone bruise to heal. Just start her back slow and see how she acts. I'll check back in about a week to see how she is doing, but let me know if you need anything sooner."

Finishing the call, Dr. Daines remembered something he had thought of.

"Oh, by the way Jace, she is quite a filly, seems to give her all. Anyway, I will check back next week. Tell Jenna to take good care of her. Keep the leg iced once or twice a day, and slow, short walks.

"Thanks, Dr. Daines. Jenna will be relieved to hear the news."

Saying good-bye, Jace turned to report what Dr. Daines had said.

Lorna stood in the kitchen finishing Jenna's birthday cake. They had wanted to stay for Jenna's birthday and then head home in the morning.

Unfortunately things were not turning out the way they had planned. Jenna was too worried about Dash to care much about her birthday.

Moving into the kitchen, Jenna could see the beautiful birthday cake surrounded by numerous presents in the center of the table. Smiling meekly, she wrapped her arms about Lorna.

"It's a beautiful cake. Thank you."

In spite of everything, Jenna's birthday turned out to be quite pleasant. The good news about Dash helped to lighten everyone's hearts and the evening became quite enjoyable. Jenna was pleased with her gifts— all being something useful or special, and having everyone there together made it the best.

Dash seemed to improve quickly, moving with more ease, less pain. Jace watched her intently over the next few days. Often, if he looked real close, he could see she was sore. But if a person weren't looking for the slightest clue, they would think she was just fine.

Running his hands down her shins, he watched closely for Dash's reaction. Only when he pushed real hard would she pull her leg away. She seemed to have either a high pain tolerance or maybe she wasn't hurt very bad.

"You can put her in her stall, Jenna. She looks real good. You've done a great job." Turning toward Dancer's stall, his voice trailed off, "Come help me with Dancer when you get her settled."

Petting Dash's nose quickly, Jenna turned to latch her stall door, then hurried to meet her father at Dancer's stall.

"Well, Jenna, Dancer is in the ninth race, coming out of the two hole. It's a two-year-old allowance race, which can be pretty tough, but I guess we will just have to see how he does. We will need to leave tomorrow afternoon. Tom talked to Don, and he is going to stay and take care of Dash. "

Jace led the big gelding out toward the walker, Jenna at his side.

"Aren't you going to run Junior?" Jenna questioned as she glimpsed the flashy gelding spin about on the walker.

Shutting the walker off, Jace moved to snap Dancer on the open hook. Gazing at Junior, Jace shook his head not knowing what to really say.

"Yeah, Jenna, I entered him in an open maiden race of only three hundred yards. I really think this will be his last race, though, he just doesn't seem to have it as a race horse."

Jenna hesitated, her heart sinking slightly. She understood what her father was saying, but still it made her sad. She always had such faith in the horses, all of them, even Junior.

"What if he does good? What if he can run in the top three?" Jenna questioned looking toward her father.

"I don't know, Jenna. We'll see, okay?" Jace answered trying not to dash her hopes, but it was obvious that Junior just couldn't run, at least not fast enough, even though he really tried.

Some horses have the speed and don't try, but Junior, he truly tried. He would always put forth a tremendous effort, but he just couldn't outrun the bigger, longer legged horses.

Tom watched Jenna, sensing her thoughts and questions.

"You know, Jenna, Junior has a lot of potential. It just doesn't seem to be in racing. He would be a real good show horse or maybe even a good barrel racer."

Agreeing with Tom, Jace mentioned the sale at the end of the summer he was thinking of putting Junior in. It was an open sale for riding and performance horses.

"I really think it would be the best thing for us and Junior."

Jace watched Jenna closely, trying to judge her reaction, her thoughts.

Pausing slightly, he continued, "There is a young gelding at R and O Farms I would like you to see Jenna. He is a lot more money, but we would be dealing directly with the owner, not going through a sale. Would you like to go see him?"

Nodding slightly, Jenna tried to understand and she really did, but it was just hard. What her father and Tom said had made sense. "I do understand, Dad, really I do."

Turning, she moved into the barn, leaving the two men to gaze from her to each other.

The roar of the crowd drowned out Jenna's screams as Dancer moved toward the finish line. He was running against some of the finalists of the Silver Dollar futurity. These were tough horses and he was moving into the lead.

"Come on, Dancer. You can do it!"

Tears filled Jenna's eyes as the powerful gelding pulled ahead, his blue blinkers leading the row of horses along his side.

Jenna loved the feeling that spread through her— the rush and excitement of the race, the love and pride for the horse. People filled the winner's circle shaking her father's hand. Tom stood beside her for what seemed to be only an instant before Dancer was led away by her father to the test barn.

The same two men that Jenna had seen her father talking to in the past, followed alongside.

"Come on, Jenna, I need you to help me get Junior ready." Tom's voice turned Jenna's attention away from her father and the two men as she moved to follow Tom.

"Who are those two men with Dad?" Jenna questioned as she and Tom walked toward the barns. "I have seen them before, but I'm not sure who they are."

"Oh, they are just a couple of horse owners. They have been talking to your father about Dancer," Tom answered cautiously, knowing what Jenna's reaction would be.

"You mean they want to buy him?" Jenna questioned, continuing on without waiting for Tom's answer. "He can't sell Dancer. They wouldn't know how to handle him right. Like when he gets nervous, I'm the only one that can get him to settle down."

Jenna stopped in front of Junior's stall, waiting for Tom's answer.

"Jenna, they are just talking, and you know the horses are a business. You sell some and buy new ones. But don't get all worried, they are only talking."

Tom opened Junior's stall to get him ready, Jenna quietly by his side.

"He won't sell Dash, will he?" Jenna's voice cracked with fearful emotion, her eyes stinging with the thought.

"I don't think so, Jenna. She has done real well this year, and someone would have to offer an awful lot of money," Tom tried to reassure her. "Don't worry. I really don't think he would. Now help me with Junior or we won't have him ready in time."

Her head spinning with a mixture of thoughts, Jenna went about prepping Junior without really thinking about what she was doing. Instead, she was thinking about Dancer and Dash. She understood why Junior would need to be sold at the end of the summer, and even felt guilty that selling Junior would be okay, but not the others.

Pausing, she gazed into Junior's eager eyes. "I love you too, Junior, it's just different."

Hearing her father's voice, Jenna turned to see Dancer by his side.

"Have you got Junior about ready?" Jace questioned Tom as he hooked Dancer on the walker in front of the barn.

Jenna turned her attention back to Junior.

"Now come on, boy. You can do it. Try real hard, okay?" Jenna coaxed, wanting so to prove her father wrong.

How can he think of selling Dancer? Selling Junior is bad enough. Doesn't he care? Anger filled her as she imagined the possibility of Dancer and even Dash being sold.

"Are you about ready, Jenna?" Jace asked as he moved to check Junior.

"Yeah, just about." Jenna's voice was somewhat harsh and angry as she moved away from her father, leaving him and Tom to finish with Junior.

"What is wrong with her?" Jace questioned, wondering at her mood. "She seems mad at me for some reason."

Pausing from what he was doing, Tom looked at the younger man.

"She asked who the two men were with you and what they wanted, so I told her."

"Well, that explains it all right."

Jace led Junior from his stall, heading toward the saddling paddock, Tom at his side. "I guess I better talk to her about it later."

Leading Junior into the four-hole saddling stall, Jace glimpsed Jenna at the rail surrounded by numerous people. Searching the crowd, he hoped to see the woman, wanting to see her, yet fearing the emotions that would follow. Not seeing any sign of her, he returned his attention to the horse at his side.

Junior moved well out onto the track, Larry Knudsen upon his back. This would be the first time for Larry to ride Junior. Larry rode for Jace off and on over the past few years and had just brought Dancer down the track for a win.

Noticing Jenna by the rail, Larry smiled and waved as he moved Junior alongside the pony horse to warm up.

Jenna waited in the grandstand thinking to herself— a silent prayer. *Oh, please do good, Junior. Come on, you can do it. If you can just run register merit.*

To do that, his race time would need to be fast enough for the distance to give him an eighty-speed index.

The gates flew open, the bell ringing loudly, the horses digging in, the dirt flying from behind their powerful hooves. Junior moved out well, keeping pace with the horses next to him.

Jenna cheered Junior on, even though he couldn't hear her as he crossed the finish line third. That was the best he had ever done.

Running down to meet her father, Jenna proudly announced where Junior had finished in the race.

"Oh, Dad, he did so much better. He ran third and was only three-quarters of a length behind the winner."

"He did a lot better, Jenna, but how fast did the race run?" Jace questioned, feeling the race wasn't very fast.

Turning toward the tote board, Jenna searched for the time as the results lit up.

"18:09, and if Junior ran at least 18:14, that would give him an eighty-speed index for three hundred fifty yards at this track."

"Well, that is pretty good."

Jace turned to greet Junior and Larry as they moved to stand beside him.

Jumping to the ground, Larry began unsaddling Junior, the horse's sides heaving, his nostrils flaring.

"He gave me his all, Jace, I'll have to give him credit for that .If only all horses would try as hard, but he just doesn't have the stride."

Patting Junior on the neck, Larry praised him momentarily before turning toward the scales.

"Thanks, Larry," Jace said to the young rider as he stood on the scales to be weighed. "You did a real good job for me."

"Any time, Jace. I always enjoy riding for you." Hesitating momentarily, Larry continued somewhat jokingly, "But next time, how about letting me ride that filly you have?"

Smiling, Jace knew who Larry meant and thought that might actually be a good idea, for he knew Larry would always give a good honest ride, but never risk the horse getting hurt.

"When I bring her back after this lay-off, I'll have to take you up on it."

Larry knew Dash had gotten hurt and was pleased to hear Jace was planning on bringing her back.

"I'll watch for her. Thanks, Jace." Stepping off of the scales, Larry waved as he headed into the jock room.

CHAPTER 17

Standing at the paddock, Jenna felt like she was in a dream, the weekends seeming to blur one with the other. The past two weeks had been but a wisp of time as again Dancer moved from the paddock onto the track, the white silks of the two hole contrasting with his dark brown hair and his black mane and tail.

Jenna's heart pounded, her concerns over the race influenced by what her father had told her. Watching Dancer move to warm up on the backstretch, she remembered her father's words, although a bit jumbled, in her mind.

"... sell Dancer, it's a good price. He is just a horse, Jenna; there is always another good one. The horses are a business, we can't keep them all."

How could my father say those things?

The ring of the bell pulled Jenna from her thoughts as Dancer rose from behind the open gates. Dirt flew from beneath the powerful hooves as ten horses tore down the track. The roar of the crowd grew louder as the horses moved toward the finish line.

Dancer battled for the lead with the four-horse running by his side— the power of each stride matching one with the other. Crossing the finish line, it was hard to tell for sure who won.

It was definitely a close race as the "photo" sign on the tote board indicated, but from where Jenna had stood, it looked like the four-horse had beaten Dancer by a nose.

Running down to the finish line, Jenna met Tom and her father.

"I think he ended up second, but it was close."

Jenna was still happy about running second but couldn't help being a bit disappointed. Eagerly she watched the corner of the track as the horses came back to the grandstand area, the roar of the crowd praising the winner.

Dancer galloped closer, the sound of his breathing, loud and rhythmical almost like a motor as he came to stand before Jace. Handing his blinkers to Jenna, Jace turned to lead the beautiful horse toward the barns.

Jace barely acknowledged Larry as he commented on the race. Jenna listened closely wanting to hear what Larry had to say. Stopping in her tracks, Jenna struggled for a breath.

Did I hear my father right? Trying to still her pounding heart, Jenna quickly moved to catch up to her father as Larry turned toward the scales.

"What do you mean, that was 'a good race for his last one?' Aren't we going to run him anymore?" Jenna questioned, fear rising inside her.

She had heard him tell Larry that it was Dancer's last race. Her head spun with reasons as she waited for her father's reply.

"That was our last race with Dancer. I sold him this morning." His words were cold as ice, empty of feeling, but they cut her to the quick.

Jenna froze, unable to move, her emotions inside taking her breath away and tearing at her heart.

Dancer moved away led by Jace as other horses began passing her on their way to the barns. Frantically, Jenna struggled to get away, away from the horses surrounding her, away from the horsemen on the track, away from the crowd that watched on, as her tears broke free.

How could he sell Dancer? Running blindly, Jenna finally stopped beside an empty stall. Falling to the ground she sobbed, her tears seeming to come from every fiber of her being.

Jace paced in front of Dancer's stall. It had tore at him all morning. He had thought about how to tell Jenna, how not to hurt her. *So, what did I do? I blurted it out like it was nothing. But it had been a hard decision.*

He knew it would hurt Jenna, and to be honest it had hurt him too. He liked the big gelding and had struggled long and hard over the decision. Four thousand dollars was a lot of money, not that Dancer was not worth it, for he was.

Shaking his head to himself, he knew how Jenna would feel about the money. To her, it would not have been enough, not near enough.

Tom understood Jace's decision and felt it had been the right decision for business reasons. Sighing with emotional exhaustion, Tom was glad he wasn't the one who had had to make the decision.

Hearing footsteps behind him, Tom turned to see Jenna's sullen face. The tears had been wiped away; the only evidence of their existence was that of her red swollen eyes.

Her words seemed to come from somewhere else, their tone strange to her ears.

"Can I at least tell him good-bye?"

Jace turned, Jenna's words stinging him like the lash of a whip. He had not heard her coming and suddenly all the things he wanted to say were gone. Instead, cold empty words answered his young daughter, who now stood proudly before him.

She wasn't going to let him see her cry, wasn't going to let him see her pain, for she knew he wouldn't understand.

"Jenna, he is just a horse. Don't let yourself get all upset." His words were empty of all feelings or caring as he moved to open Dancer's stall.

"Hurry and tell him goodbye. I told them I would bring him over to their barn, and I am sure they are waiting."

Wrapping her arms around Dancer's neck, Jenna whispered softly in his ear, "Be a good boy, Dancer. I will miss you."

Her tears choked her words back as she clung to him, wanting to remember everything about him, his feel, his smell, the beat of his heart.

Confused, Dancer nudged Jenna gently. He didn't understand her tears, her sadness.

"Come on, Dancer," Jace urged the gelding, almost pulling him from Jenna's arms.

Leading Dancer away was hard. Jace didn't want to hurt Jenna. *But sometimes she is so unreasonable. Besides it isn't like I sold Dancer to just anyone. John Matthews is well known for the care he gives to his horses. In fact he said Jenna could come and see Dancer anytime.*

Rounding the corner of the barn, Jace could see John Matthews waiting by a freshly readied stall. Dancer moved quickly into the clean stall, the fresh hay and sweet grain enticing him.

Handing him Dancer's papers and signed transfer sheet, Jace accepted the check in John's outstretched hand.

"How did your daughter take the news?" John questioned, knowing well the attachment Jenna had for the horse and the horse for her.

"Not too good really, but she'll get over it," Jace answered coolly, not wanting to admit he hadn't really even said much to her about it.

"Well, Jace, I was wondering if you could have her stop by and maybe tell me some of the special things to do to make him feel more at home. I also want to tell her she can come and see him anytime."

John stroked Dancer gently on the nose. "Most of all, I want Jenna to know I will take real good care of him."

Nodding, Jace mumbled a reply, promising to have Jenna come over before they left for home.

Turning away Jace thought to himself, *That is, if she will even talk to me.*

He had seen the fire in her eyes, heard the hurt and anger in her voice.

Jenna quietly put Dancer's tack into the trailer, trying hard to hold back the tears. Buck whinnied softly as Jace approached the trailer.

"Jenna, John Matthews would like you to stop over and tell him some of the things Dancer likes before we go. Why don't you go over and we will swing by with the truck to pick you up?"

Turning away from the trailer, Jenna stood before him, but looked only at the ground.

"Where is he at?" she questioned, not even knowing who John Matthews was.

"He is in the end barn on the east side. John bought Dancer to run on the chariot and the flat track next summer, so it's not like you won't get to see him," Jace commented, trying to justify his decision to sell Dancer.

Walking toward the other barn, Jenna's heart seemed to sit in her throat.

How can I talk to this man? How can he understand how I feel? How can he take Dancer away?

Rounding the corner, Jenna recognized the man petting Dancer as one of the two men she had seen the day before. Stopping, she thought of running away before he saw her, but it was too late.

Dancer had seen her and whinnied softly, his attention going from the man to the young girl he knew so well. John Matthews turned to see Jace's daughter cautiously moving toward him. He could see the trace of tears upon her cheeks, the sadness in her eyes.

" Jenna, I'm John Matthews. I'm glad you came over. I want you to know I didn't mean to hurt you and I hope you understand the love and admiration I have for horses. I don't know if it will help you feel any better, but I want you to know you are always welcome to see him. I want only the best for Dancer, just as you do."

Holding back the tears, Jenna's heart eased at the sound of the man's voice. She noticed his gentle touch with Dancer and how the gelding seemed to like him.

"He sometimes gets nervous, but if you scratch him on the neck and talk to him, it helps."

Jenna moved closer to Dancer's stall door, still a bit wary of John Matthews. "He really just gets a little scared and then he acts up a bit, but he's not trying to be bad."

Bringing her hand out from behind her back, Jenna held out a white shadow roll with three blue diamonds across it.

"This is Dancer's shadow roll. I made it special for him because he always has his head up so high, so I made it extra thick to get him to keep his head down."

Handing it to him, Jenna's voice cracked just a bit, "When you run him, could you use this shadow roll on him for me?"

Pausing, she struggled to keep from crying, not able to say anymore.

Taking the shadow roll from Jenna, John lifted her chin to gaze into her eyes.

"Jenna, it is okay to be sad, and it's okay to cry, but I promise you, I will never hurt him. I will always take good care of him and I would be very honored to use your shadow roll."

A small smile spread across Jenna's face. He really seemed like a nice man. *Maybe it won't be so bad after all,* she thought but it still hurt.

"I will leave you alone to say good-bye, but remember to come and see him anytime."

With that John Matthews turned to leave Jenna standing alone in front of Dancer's new stall.

Again the tears broke free as her arms wrapped around his silken neck.

Jace stormed through the barn, the tension within driving him crazy.

Jenna quietly moved about doing her chores, avoiding him like he had the plague. He knew what the problem was and he would be damned if he was going to let her get to him.

The sound of occasional sniffling made him angry. *For hell's sake, it is just a horse, besides it isn't like I put him down. I sold him to one of the best owners in the area, and for a very good price. I haven't done anything wrong, so I don't have any reason to say I'm sorry about it.*

Watching Jenna made it even harder for him, for he really did feel bad that she was so hurt, even if he didn't understand why she was acting the way she was.

At least Shanna had talked to him when he had sold Duck. But Jenna completely ignored him and would only acknowledge him by doing what he asked without saying a word.

Jenna watched her father in glimpses, knowing well he was upset with her. *He has no right to be mad at me, though, for I haven't done anything.* She wasn't even so much mad at him about the fact that he had sold Dancer, but how he had told her. He seemed to have no feelings, his heart as cold as his words. She knew how he felt; he had told her many times.

"They are just horses and everything has a price."

But to Jenna they were more than just a horse, each being special in its own way. Most of all, there were some things that you couldn't or shouldn't put a price on, such as love, life and friendship.

Turning to stroke Dash, Jenna felt there was absolutely no price high enough for the filly. Dash was her friend. *How can anyone put a price on love and friendship?*

The days passed with a quiet tension lingering about. Jenna had begun to act more like herself, but still she had a reserve and distance about her. Dash was doing well, showing no signs of discomfort during or after her works.

"She is doing real good, Jace. I can't feel anything unusual. She is working strong and smooth, and doesn't seem to favor her leg at all," Don remarked after her work.

Jace stroked her leg watching closely for any sign of discomfort. She stood still not seeming the least bit bothered by the pressure on her leg.

"Well, let's spray her down. Jenna, is her stall ready?" Jace questioned turning to face his daughter who now stood quietly by the side of the barn.

She hadn't said a word or even made a sound but he knew she was there. Wherever Dash was, Jenna would be close by.

"Yes, it's all ready, so is Junior's," Jenna answered somberly, realizing it didn't take as long to do the chores now that Dancer was gone.

Tom moved to take Dash's lead rope as Jace sprayed her down with the cool water, then scraped the excess moisture from her body, leaving her damp hair shining in the afternoon sun.

Dash moved eagerly, an alert and eager gaze radiating from her eyes. Jace continued to watch her intently for any sign of discomfort as she moved about the walker.

Jenna moved closer to her father. She knew it would soon be the last weekend of races of the season at Greenland Downs, and Jenna wanted to know if they were going to run Dash that last weekend.

Hesitating momentarily she spoke quietly, her voice sounding strange, even to herself. "Are you going to run Dash the last weekend?"

Jace turned realizing she was talking to him. Still a bit put out with Jenna's silent treatment, he was tempted to comment on her change of heart concerning talking to him, but decided it wasn't worth making things worse. Besides he missed the close relationship they had been developing. He missed her smile and the little squeezes she would give him for no particular reason.

"She seems to be doing okay. Dr. Daines checked her yesterday and felt she was sound. There is an allowance race of three hundred fifty yards. I thought I might put her in on Labor Day. What do you think?" Jace questioned, wanting to know what she thought.

Surprised, Jenna hesitated thinking her father's question over in her mind, all the while surprised that he would really care what she thought.

"Well, she doesn't act sore and I would like to see her run one more time at Greenland," Jenna replied, gazing first at Dash and then at Junior. "What about Junior?"

"Both Junior and Dash are paid into the futurity at the end of September at the fair race meet. I think we will just wait and run him then. The sale I want to put him in is two weeks after the finals."

Jace noticed Jenna flinch slightly at the mention of the sale.

"And Dash?" Jenna questioned, not daring to even meet her father's gaze, fearing what he might say.

"Right now, I'm not planning on selling her. She has done real well this year, in spite of some of the problems. Dancer did real well also, but Dash seems to put her whole heart and soul into winning. To be honest, Jenna, I have had a few offers for her, but nothing has even been a tempting offer."

Jace thought to himself for a moment. *The offers I have received have been respectable, damn near tempting.*

"Besides, if she can continue to show as much promise, it would increase her value as a brood mare and she would make one heck of a brood mare."

Jenna turned to gaze from Dash to her father. She never knew how to take what her father said. *Will we keep her as a brood mare, or will the increase in her value make him sell her? Do I dare to hope that Dash will be with us forever, like Dot?*

Thinking to herself, Jenna realized she hadn't really even thought about the fact that her father wouldn't keep all the horses, but he really couldn't. She realized that now though— now that she really thought about it.

Jace's voice broke her train of thought, not realizing how long she had been silently thinking.

"Jenna, you know I didn't sell Dancer to make you sad and I am sorry that it upset you so. It was a good business thing to do." He paused momentarily, "Not everything is about you, Jenna. I didn't sell him because of you, but in spite of you. I knew how much you liked him, but you like Junior and you like Dash. Sometimes decisions are made because of someone and sometimes in spite of someone. This time it was in spite of you, but I want you to know it was a hard decision for a lot of reasons. I liked him a lot too. But, I feel I made the right decision."

Turning, Jace moved slowly away, feeling he had said more than enough, his heart still wanting her to understand.

"I hope someday you will understand."

Jenna watched her father disappear around the corner of the barn. At first his words had seemed harsh, but as she listened, his tone had become softer, quieter, even sounding a bit sad.

She did understand some of what he said, and tried to understand the rest. *Does he understand me though, or even try? So often he makes me feel stupid for even saying or feeling the way I do. Even if I think what he says is stupid, I try to think it through, to understand.*

Moving to pet Dash, Jenna wondered at some of the other things her father had said in the past.

She had heard them said more than once. *"Every thing has its price." That is one thing I will never, ever understand.*

CHAPTER 18

Jace threw the covers off, turning to sit along the side of the bed. The cool breeze played with the curtains as it spread a slight chill throughout the room. His head weighed heavy in his hands as he ran his fingers through his hair, an exasperated sigh breaking through the stillness.

His night had been filled with dreams and jumbled thoughts, making it impossible to sleep.

Rising from the bed, he left the room slipping quietly past Jenna's door to descend to the room below.

A few embers glowed orange in the fireplace, their slight warmth lingering close to the rock hearth.

Adding some fresh logs, Jace poked at the embers, new flames beginning to rise up along the pine logs. The golden glow from the flames spread through the darkness of the room, coming to rest on the beautiful image before him.

The memories of her seemed to reach out from the depths of his mind. *How I long to hold her, to just touch her.*

Tracing his finger along the picture, he gazed from Shanna's eyes to Jenna's. *Oh, they are so much alike, so much of Shanna in Jenna. So many of the things*

Jenna says are things I have heard before from Shanna— their hearts and feelings, one and the same.

"Always a price," he had said it so often, Shanna always disagreeing. Closing his eyes he could almost feel her touch, his memory of the dream, of her, of the past, burning strong in his heart.

She is right; as always, there are many things that could never, should never, have a price. So much of what I had and what I now have could never have a price.

It is hard, though, trying to change what I think and feel. Often though, he wondered what he really did think and feel. Searching his memory, he could remember a time so long ago, a time when he had maybe seen things more the way Jenna seemed to.

He had been young and different, so different from what he was now. Things he felt he could never have done then had become fairly easy now—no thoughts, no feelings, just easy to do.

He remembered a time when his father had put a gelding down.

Funny, I can't remember why now, but I remember how I felt, how I begged my father not to do it. Can't we do something else? How could my father or anyone else make the decision to end a life, any life?

It seemed so long ago, but since then Jace himself had put a couple of horses down. *It wasn't easy, but at the time it had been the right thing to do, had been for the right reason.*

Lowering himself into the recliner, Jace continued to gaze at the picture as his eyes closed, his mind drifting with the present and the past, entwining in a dream. The dream, her words, her love, soothed his troubled thoughts as he slipped into a deep and peaceful slumber.

The morning sun filtered into the room spreading a bright new warmth. Jace stirred slowly in the recliner, his body somewhat stiff from the night's sleep.

Stretching out toward the fireplace, he noticed the soft gray embers resting in the now cool hearth. The house was quiet, the morning sun just beginning to rise above the mountaintops.

Moving toward the front door, he stepped out onto the porch, enjoying the cool freshness of the breeze.

This would be the last weekend of races at Greenland Downs. He was somewhat relieved about the season nearing an end yet, a bit disappointed.

Reaching the barn, he started to check and load the horses' tack. They would be leaving around noon, after the horses had eaten, to head for the track. Staying overnight was a bit inconvenient as far as his other horses, but it gave the horses running a chance to rest after the two-hour drive.

Moving from stall to stall, Jace played affectionately with each of the horses, lingering at Dash's door. The filly seemed eager for his attention, reaching to tug gently on his shirt.

"Good morning, Jace," Tom's voice broke the silence in the barn, startling Jace a bit. "You must have gotten up pretty early," Tom commented noticing all the chores were done.

"Well, I never do sleep very good before the races."

Jace headed toward the truck as he continued to talk to Tom, "I'm going out to the back pasture to check the herd before we leave. Do you want to come? "

"Sure."

Tom moved to follow Jace, glancing up momentarily at Jenna's window.

Smiling to herself, Jenna waved at Tom as he glanced toward her. Tom's movement drew Jace's attention toward Jenna, a warm smile spreading across his face as he moved to step up into the truck, waving briefly before driving away.

The truck came to an awkward stop, the weight of the trailer causing it to rock slightly. Jumping from the truck, Jenna ran to ready the stalls, eager to get Dash out of the trailer.

Lowering the ramp on the trailer, Jace moved to lead the filly out into the afternoon sun.

Dash moved excitedly alongside him, her nostrils flaring, her eyes gazing out toward the track. She knew where she was. She knew the sounds, the smell, and all the activities about her. Spinning quickly in her stall, Dash turned to look out the open top section of the door. She watched excitedly, eagerly waiting while Jace, Tom, and Jenna got things settled.

It hardly seemed like they had even left the track for the night. The sun, now that of early morning, warmed Dash as she stuck her head into it's warm glow. She knew the routine and waited anxiously, eager to move onto the track.

Waiting in the gates, Dash prepared herself both physically and emotionally. Larry too set himself, ready for the gates to open.

Dash exploded from the gates. Jenna watched anxiously as she moved down the track. Staring in confusion and disbelief, Jenna watched as Dash drifted from her six-hole position in front of the seven-horse. Her hindquarters crashed into the front of the seven-horse as they collided momentarily on the track. Dash dug deep trying to regain her stride as the horses thundered down the track.

Holding her breath, Jenna stood almost in shock as Dash ran from the back of the pack, her heart driving her on as she neared the grandstands. Larry tapped her gently on the shoulder as she moved past the other horses, the announcer declaring a late run of the filly as she flew across the finish line.

It was too close to call. Jenna screamed with delight, knowing Dash was either first or second.

Running from the grandstand, Jenna turned as the announcer called for the horse ambulance to move onto the track.

Searching the track for the injured horse, Jenna's heart stopped, her throat closing as she recognized Dash standing on the corner, Larry at her side, stroking her gently on the neck.

Oh, God, no, please no! Jenna heard her mind screaming in her head as tears spilled down her cheeks.

Jace had come down the track and jumped into the truck pulling the horse ambulance just as it headed toward the trembling filly.

Looking around helplessly, Jenna was relieved to hear the ladies driving the regular ambulance offer her a ride to Dash. They knew Jenna and tried to comfort her as they neared the filly.

The truck had turned around, backing up close to Dash, who limped awkwardly as Jace and Larry coaxed her into the trailer.

"I'm sorry, Jace. I thought she was going to go down right after we crossed the finish line. All the way down the track she felt strong, then all of a sudden as we crossed the finish line, she changed," Larry explained, a sick feeling spreading through him. "It was like she was only running on three legs. I hope she will be okay. I tried to get her stopped... before it was too late."

Jace knew what Larry meant by "too late."

"You did the right thing, getting her stopped as fast as you did. Thanks, Larry."

Jace shook Larry's hand as he turned to see the tear streaked face of his daughter.

"Dad, is she okay?" Jenna looked from her father to the young jockey who had turned to walk slowly down the track, declining the ride offered by Dr. Summers.

After something like that he needed to walk, to think, if for just a moment, before again he mounted another powerful yet fragile beast.

"Jace, are you going to ride with us?" Dr. Summers, the track vet, asked, ready to move the trailer.

"Dad, can I ride with Dash? Please!" Jenna pleaded, looking from her father to Dr. Summers.

"It's okay with me. Besides, maybe she can get her to hold still as we take her off the track."

Dr. Summers moved to the ramp, waiting as first Jace nodded to Jenna, the young girl scampering into the trailer to stand beside the shaking filly.

The movement of the trailer caused Dash to stumble slightly, not wanting to put any weight on her right leg. Looking out the back of the trailer, Jenna could see the number four-horse in the winner's circle.

Dash had finished second, running the second fastest time she had ever run, only to be disqualified from the race for interfering with the seven-horse.

It didn't seem fair, but right now, all Jenna could think about was Dash. *What is wrong? Oh, please, God, don't let it be bad, please.* Jenna prayed silently as the truck came to a stop at the test barn.

The creak of the ramp caused Dash to move slightly, limping terribly as Jace coaxed her from the trailer to stand quietly in the test barn area. Dr. Summers drew up a syringe to ease her pain so he could check her over better.

Jenna stood quietly outside the fenced area, unable to go inside to watch as Jace and Dr. Summers worked on her.

Gary Petersen, his owner and trainer, led the number four-horse, Perfect Kirk, into the test barn.

"That was a hell of a race your filly ran, Jace. I hope she is okay."

"Thanks, Gary," Jace answered barely noticing the man who had hooked his horse on the walker and come to stand beside him.

"You know, Jace, I'll give you nine thousand dollars for that filly right now, as is."

Jace turned his attention from Dash to Gary Petersen, hardly believing what he had heard.

"What?" he questioned, wanting to make sure he had heard right.

"Okay, I'll give you nine thousand five hundred." Gary raised the price seeing the hesitation on Jace face.

Nine thousand five hundred dollars, Jace sighed to himself as he glanced toward Jenna who stood waiting by the fence. *Damn, that is a lot of money for any horse.*

Everything seemed to stop around him, his mind spinning with everything that had happened, a soft voice seeming to come from somewhere deep inside. *"Some things don't have a price, Jace, any price. "*

Looking back at Gary, Jace did what he knew was the right thing.

"Thanks for the offer, Gary. It is a very tempting and flattering offer, but she's not for sale. "

Jace looked again at Jenna, who stood watching, not knowing what the two men were talking about— only love and concern showed in her eyes.

Gary Petersen glanced from Jace to Jenna.

"I understand, but the offer stands, anytime, if you change your mind. "

Gary patted Jace on the shoulder as he moved toward his horse circling on the walker.

Taking a deep breath, Jace could hardly believe what was happening, what he had said, but turning Gary down had felt good, he felt good.

Pain broke through the hazy fog of her drugged mind as the trailer jolted to a stop. Gazing through the railings of the trailer, Dash looked about. *This isn't home; this isn't the racetrack. Where are we?*

Her nostrils flared as she breathed the air. *It smells different, the air cooler and stronger with the scent of pine and sagebrush.* Moving uneasily, she flinched as the sharp pain radiated up her leg.

"Easy, Dash," Jace's voice came from the back of the trailer as the sound of the door opening drew her attention behind her.

His gentle hand stroked her side as he moved in beside her; reaching to untie her rope.

"Come on, girl," Jace coaxed as he turned to lead her out.

Dash paused. It hurt to move. Her legs seemed heavy. She wanted to follow the man she knew as Jace, but it seemed so hard, too hard.

"Come on, Dash. Come on." His voice pulled at her as he tugged gently on her halter.

Stepping carefully, she moved to follow, each step ever so slow. She could see Jenna holding the back door to the trailer as she stepped cautiously from the ramp. The cool air seemed to clear the fog from her mind as she quickly searched her surroundings.

I don't know this place. I can smell other horses; hear them and other sounds. Her heart seemed to beat faster, pound harder. *I don't know these strange sounds, these other people that are moving closer.*

Stepping back she gazed first at Jenna, then at Jace.

"Easy, girl, it's okay." His voice tried to reassure her but fear filled her heart.

Why am I here? Are they going to leave me here? No! Take me home; take me home! Dash's mind screamed out as a low nicker rose from her throat.

"It's okay, sweetie. I won't hurt you." The new voice was gentle and warm as the man reached to stroke her nose, her nostrils flaring as she leaned her head yet closer still to Jace.

The man's hands smell different. The strange smell, strong and bitter as they moved down along her neck to her shoulder. Their touch was gentle, even a bit soothing as they traveled down her leg, until a sharp pain rose to meet their touch.

Pulling her leg back, Dash longed to get away, to be home.

"Jace, can you get her inside? I want to get some x-rays of that leg." Dr. Clark pointed toward the side door on the large building. "You can take her in through there."

Moving slowly, Dash walked as close to Jace as possible. Jenna followed along her side. It felt better to have them close by, but something was wrong, she could sense it.

Jenna was so quiet, an occasional sniffle concerning Dash. The girl was sad, Dash was sure of it, for Jenna's voice betrayed her feelings as she tried to comfort her.

"Just put her in that stall while I get things ready." Dr. Clark motioned to Jace as he moved into another room.

Dash followed Jace into the stall turning quickly but awkwardly, her leg hurting as she tried to follow him out.

Why did he close me in? Where is he going? Dash watched nervously as Jace disappeared into the other room, Jenna by his side.

Jenna, come back! I'm scared. Don't leave me here alone! Whinnying loudly, Dash called to Jenna as she leaned against the stall door.

She usually didn't whinny much, but she was scared.

Jenna turned her attention away from the large machines as the loud whinny echoed through the building.

"Dad, was that Dash?" Jenna asked, never hearing the filly do more than nicker.

"Yeah, I think so. Maybe you better stay with her. I have never seen her so nervous, in fact I didn't think she was scared of anything."

Jace moved to the doorway where the filly could see him. "It's okay, girl. We're here."

"I'll get her another shot to settle her down a bit before we start the x-rays. Then she'll be okay. It's just new and different here," Dr. Clark tried to reassure Jenna as she moved toward the anxious filly.

Nickering softly, Dash seemed to sigh with relief as Jenna came closer. *I don't understand what is going on. The past few days have been so confusing, filled with shots, leg soaks and wraps, trailer rides here and there, the pain ever constant in my leg.*

Jenna's soft touch eased her fear, but still she watched nervously about her.

Jace was quite impressed as he gazed about the exam room. There was just about every kind of equipment available for diagnosing and treating horses. A large operating table could be seen through another doorway in yet another room. He was amazed at how clean everything was, the conditions as clean and proper as any hospital he had ever seen.

A vision flashed through his mind. *How I hate hospitals.* A deep, uneasy feeling began sinking into his heart as he remembered those last days with Shanna.

It was different here, yet some things were the same, the smell, and the equipment. Taking a deep breath, Jace turned to answer Dr. Clark, his question drawing Jace's attention back to the filly.

All the questions seemed a blur as Dr. Clark and Jace moved Dash from the holding stall to stand next to the exam table. Moving her into position, they fastened the straps around her as Jace tried to sooth her fears while Dr. Clark inserted the needle into her vein.

"She'll be okay, Jenna. It will only put her to sleep long enough for us to find out what is wrong."

Dr. Clark tried to reassure her as the filly began to slump against the straps. Pushing a few buttons, the table that looked to be a wall, slowly tipped back, holding the filly against its cold hard surface. Dash lay as if she were dead, her body completely limp and relaxed.

People moved about the room each seeming to know exactly what to do without saying a word. A young lady moved closer to Dash's head as Dr. Clark pulled the overhead equipment into place.

"You'll have to step out of the room for the x-rays. You can come back in as soon as they are done," Dr. Clark motioned to both Jace and Jenna, stating it would just be a few minutes.

It sure seemed a lot longer than a few minutes to Jenna, but soon the door opened for them to come back in. More equipment yet had been moved closer to Dash, who still lay motionless.

"Jace, take a look here," Dr. Clark pointed to the large monitor screens.

Jace wasn't sure what they were or what he was supposed to be looking for, but he watched eagerly with Jenna at his side as Dr. Clark explained.

"This one shows the thermography in her leg, color imagery showing the variations of temperature. The x-rays show a definite green willow fracture about three and one-half inches lengthwise on her cannon bone running right to the core. I am amazed that she didn't blow that leg in her last race. You can see the intense heat around the fracture.... "

Dr. Clark's words seemed but a buzz in Jace ears as he looked at the devastated face of Jenna.

"What are our options?" Jace asked, fearing the answer.

Dr. Clark glimpsed Jenna's tear-streaked face almost reading her thoughts.

"Not all fractures require that a horse be put down. Her fracture is serious, but she is a strong filly. We could pin the fracture, but I think with proper care and time the leg will heal just fine, in fact be stronger than the other one."

Dash felt strange, her body there, yet seeming apart from her, seeing it but not really feeling apart of it. Everyone seemed to be moving so slowly about her.

Oh how sleepy I feel, my eyes so very heavy. Even the pressure on her leg wasn't enough to make her pull it back. It hurt but she didn't care. In fact, she wasn't so sure she could get it to move even if she tried.

The brace on her leg seemed warm, almost soothing, something she could actually feel as Dr. Clark finished wrapping the last part of the brace securing it in place.

She could hear all the voices, the new ones and the ones of Jace and Jenna, though they sounded different, slow and distant.

The room began to turn and spin, her body floating and tipping slowly, a strange hum filling her ears.

What is happening? Am I dying? Her mind struggled to make sense, to connect with her body as she felt it come to a stop with a slight bump.

Responding to the tug on her halter she followed Jace. *I am here. Jace and Jenna are here, and I will be safe as long as I am with them.*

Oh, the trailer! She could see the trailer with Jenna now standing by the back door. Dash knew she was walking but she couldn't feel the ground or the ramp as she stumbled slightly trying to move into the trailer.

Sighing deeply, Dash leaned against Jace as he tied her lead rope through the tie ring in the trailer.

"It's okay, girl, we're going home." Jace patted her gently, and then turned to step from the trailer.

"Home," he said. "Home!" Dash relaxed along the side panel, her thoughts still fogged, almost rolling with the movement of the trailer.

Jace drove quietly, not saying anything to Jenna, who sat motionless staring out the side window. He hadn't told her about the offer Gary Petersen had made him on Dash. At the time he had felt good about turning him down, but now he wasn't so sure.

For Jenna it had been the right thing to do, but what now? Can Dash run again? Will she even want to? Often when a horse is injured it can take all the desire out of it. Well, I could use her as a brood mare, one hell of an expensive brood mare.

Glancing at Jenna, Jace tried to put it out of his mind. He wouldn't have felt good about it even though Gary had said he would take her "as is."

Feeling his gaze upon her, Jenna turned to smile meekly at her father. She could just imagine what he was thinking. He hadn't said hardly anything about Dash since the race and when he did he seemed so cold and distant.

Fear though, kept her from asking anything about Dash.

What can I say? Jace thought to himself as he looked briefly into the depths of her eyes. He could see the worry, the questions. *But right now I have so many feelings about the whole thing, most of all, why Dash? Of all the horses, why her? She is the best I have ever had and now this. First it was her knee, now the fracture, of all the bad luck. Still she seems to always come out on top, like she is indestructible. Can she still run? Does it really matter? Sometimes it is hard to decide what really matters. Is it the wins, the races, the money? Nine thousand five hundred dollars is a lot of money. Or is it the horse?*

Looking to the furthest distance of the road, Jace's mind and heart tried to sort things out.

CHAPTER 19

Dash watched the trailer pull up alongside the barn as she walked gingerly along the rail fence. The grass corral felt good as she enjoyed the fresh morning air. It was cool enough that her breath showed mistily about her flaring nostrils.

Over a month had gone by and her leg was healing well. The brace kept her from being able to feel much like running. Its pressure made her content to trot lightly through the pasture, glad to be out of her stall.

"Jenna, you better put Dash back in her stall before we go," Jace hollered over his shoulder as he turned toward Tom. "I think you are really going to like this gelding. He is a big classy bay with real good bloodlines. I think Jenna will like him too."

Jace glanced toward Jenna as she led Dash into the barn.

"Do you think she has forgiven me yet for selling Dancer and then Junior?" Jace questioned Tom, his gaze fixed to the barn door waiting for Jenna to reappear.

Tom smiled at Jace, pleased that the younger man cared how Jenna felt about things. "I think so. "

At the auction, when they sold Junior, Jenna had been quiet and a bit tearful as she wrapped her arms around the gelding one last time. They had gotten a fair price for Junior from some people that planned on training him to run the barrels. They would take good care of him, but still it had been hard to say good-bye.

Jace had watched Jenna closely. This time he had discussed selling Junior with Jenna before taking him to the sale. Jenna had hated the idea of selling him but agreed with her father as he explained his reasoning.

Regardless of how well Dash and Dancer had done, the costs had been high, especially with Dash's vet bills, and the time very demanding. Since he was going to keep Dash, he only planned on buying one yearling, a gelding from a quarter horse farm about one hundred miles away.

Jace had seen the young gelding on one of his trips and just couldn't get him out of his mind, in spite of the price. He just had the feeling he should buy the young horse even for three thousand dollars.

"Well, Jenna, are you ready to go?" Jace questioned as he stepped up into the truck, anxious to see how she would like the gelding.

Jenna smiled gingerly. She wasn't sure if she wanted to like the new horse; it hurt too much whenever she had to say goodbye. Holding back a tear, she tried to pretend she was excited, at least enough to please her father. But inside, she tried to shut her feelings in and everything else out.

I won't let the gelding get inside my heart. I can't, for right now my heart hurts too much, even seeming to overwhelm all the love and goodness there is inside.

Jace wasn't sure what to think about Jenna's mood. He had thought she would be excited, but her eyes didn't shine with excitement, instead they seemed so sad and distant, the lack of her usual chatter making the drive seem twice as long. Even Tom was unusually quiet.

Pulling into the drive, though, Jenna couldn't hide the true excitement that filled her. She had never seen anything so beautiful. Two large barns stood before her surrounded by large green pastures filled with horses. She had never seen so many horses.

One pasture was filled with mares and the young foals. Some of the babies lay lounging in the grass; the sun warming their soft bodies while others ran about bumping and playing with each other. The mares seemed not to notice as they ate the sweet grass.

The other pasture held about a dozen yearlings. Their bodies were no longer soft with baby hair, but sleek and shining, their muscles rippling as they ran about, anxious with the arrival of the new trailer. Another smaller barn stood off to the side next to a horse walker.

Mr. Randall walked out of the smaller barn toward them. He was much different than Jenna had imagined he would be, being quite tall and almost frail looking, his movements slowed by his age. His gray hair was short and neat, his wrinkled face tanned and gentle, a gleam shining in his eyes.

He spoke not to Jace, but to Jenna as he smiled warmly. "Would you like to look around?"

"Oh, yes! Could I?" Jenna's excitement seemed to burst forth with her words.

"I can tell you must love horses," Mr. Randall smiled as he motioned toward the pastures. "You can go wherever you want, just be careful— you know horses."

Turning to face Jace, he extended his hand. "Mr. Brenton, I'm glad to see you had a safe trip. Shall we go see him?"

Jace knew who "him" was. He was the gelding he had that feeling about.

"Please call me Jace, and this is Tom." Jace motioned to the older man who stood beside him. "And that.... " Jace pointed toward Jenna as she ran happily toward the pastures, "is my daughter, Jenna."

"Pleased to meet you, and please call me Les."

The young gelding stood patiently in his stall, his head out the opened top portion of the stall door, watching intently the men moving toward him. His ears flicked back at the sound of a noise behind him but his gaze never left the men, his brown eyes fixed and unblinking, his nostrils flaring slightly trying to catch their scent.

Stopping before him Jace reached his hand slowly toward the colt's nose, then up to stoke his black forelock that ran down along his brown head falling upon the white strip that ran the full length of his face to the end of his nose.

"We call him Jet. His mother is Easy Goddess, so we named him Goddess a Jet, kind of a play of words, like 'Got us a Jet.' Hopefully, he will live up to his name."

Mr. Randall slipped the halter on the gelding to lead him from the stall. "Anyway, I think you'll be very pleased with him, he seems to be very levelheaded and eager to please."

Jet walked calmly from the barn into the fresh morning air, the bright sun causing him to blink. Slowing his pace just enough, Jet quickly took in everything around him, the large truck and trailer before him, the younger horses running about in the pastures beside him and the girl who came to stand next to the two men.

Feeling a bit uneasy, Jet whinnied nervously, hesitating but for a moment before he stepped into the new trailer, his eyes wide and wondering.

"Jenna, will you stay by him and keep him calm while we finish the paperwork?" Jace asked as he turned away, not waiting for a reply, before walking into the office with Tom and Mr. Randall.

Jenna stepped up cautiously onto the edge of the trailer next to where his head was turned trying to see her better. He seemed a bit scared and Jenna reached to stroke his nose, then held back. *I'm not going to start that, no, not this time. I am not going to get attached to another horse.*

Jet tried to move closer to the girl. Her presence comforted him, though her voice seemed a bit cool in tone as she spoke to him.

"Easy, boy, you're okay." Glancing toward the office, Jenna wished her father would hurry.

Jet moved uneasily, not sure what he sensed from the girl who moved away from him each time he tried to get closer. Whinnying nervously, he watched Jenna look from him to the office and back to him again. He could sense she was uneasy and it made him uneasy as he again whinnied, the sound echoed by the other horses watching curiously from the field.

Seeing Jace and Tom coming toward the trailer with papers in hand, Jenna jumped quickly from the trailer to get into the truck.

Tom and Jace followed shortly after thanking Mr. Randall. Jenna smiled and waved good-bye as the older man smiled in her direction.

Les felt good about where the colt was going. They would take good care of him, give him the attention he needed and the best chance at running he could get. Les Randall knew Jace Brenton was a young trainer, but he had a good track record with the horses he had run. Jace seemed to bring out the best in the horses he trained and Jet had a lot to offer, if he was handled in the right way.

"Well, Jenna, what do you think of Jet?" Jace questioned as he pulled the truck out onto the main road headed for home.

"He seems okay, a bit nervous though." Jenna glanced out the back window of the truck as if she could see the young gelding fidgeting within the trailer.

"He is just a baby, Jenna, but I'm sure with your mothering, he will adjust just fine."

Jace smiled from Jenna to Tom, missing the apprehensive glance that crossed Jenna's face, but Tom saw the look and understood it. She had been hurt by the loss of horses she had become attached to. She was trying to hold back, to protect her heart, but her love of horses wouldn't let that happen, though, of that Tom was sure.

Jace led Jet down the barn alley to the stall next to Dash. She watched eagerly nickering softly. Jet whinnied nervously like a baby looking for his mama, pausing to press his soft nose up against hers. Breathing deeply of each other's scent, a welcoming comfort spread through him as Jace moved him into his new stall.

Moving about, Jet found he could raise his head over the top rail to nuzzle with Dash momentarily before she moved away to face the girl moving closer to her stall.

"Well, Dash, what do you think? Do you like him?" Jenna asked as she reached through to scratch her affectionately along her neck.

Dash was such a little mother over everything, that Jenna felt sure she would enjoy his company. She seemed to miss Dancer and Junior. For the last month or so she had been the only horse in the barn with both Dot and Buck out in the pastures.

Moving from the barn Jenna went to stand by the rail, whistling to Dot, who stood grazing at the other end of the pasture.

Raising her head to the sound, she pricked her ears forward, moving first into an eager trot, then into an anxious gallop. Dot could see the small bucket in Jenna's hand and knew that sweet oats lay inside as she buried her head into the bucket. Jenna laughed quietly.

"Oh, Dot, you are such a pig when it comes to oats," Jenna teased as she looked toward the mare's belly.

She hadn't been riding Dot lately, but Jenna felt the mare still looked quite slim. As if he could hear her thoughts, Jace had moved to stand beside Jenna at the fence.

"She looks a bit slim for a mare that is supposed to be in foal, doesn't she?" Jace asked looking from the mare to Jenna.

It would be just his luck; the way things were going, for Dot not to have taken, making it another year before he could hope for a foal.

"Is it because I rode her?" Jenna questioned, concerned and disappointed at the thought of Dot not being in foal.

"I'm sure it hasn't got anything to do with her being ridden. In fact, that should have helped her stay in shape. It is just sometimes hard to get mares in foal after they have been on the track for a while. I'll have Dr. Daines come out and check her. If she's not in foal, you might as well ride her. Get some kind of use out of her at least, for all the hay and oats she eats."

Jace's tone was light as he patted the mare gently on the head, and then headed back into the barn, leaving Jenna to stand quietly at the pasture rail. *How I wanted Dot to have a colt, have dreamed of helping to raise it.* Jenna's mind wandered as she envisioned a young colt by Dot's side. *Well, if not this year, maybe next year.*

Jenna was amazed at how fast time seemed to slip away. Jet had been with them more than a month and was doing quite well working on the chariot with Buck. He had also grown quite fond of Dash and would often whinny like a baby if he were away from her for very long.

Dash was healing rapidly, Dr. Clark feeling that she could start back with light works on the chariot at the first of the year. Till then, Jace figured he would keep working Jet with Buck. It was more work than the poor gelding had had for a long time, but it was good for him.

Unfortunately Dr. Daines had confirmed their fears about Dot. There would not be a foal this year.

Gazing out the barn's open doors, Jenna could see Dot running along the pasture fence, the fallen leaves flipping up behind her hooves to again float softly to the ground, resting alongside the newly fallen ones that had fluttered from the now semi-barren branches.

The car that drove down the lane alongside Dot had long been expected. Leaving her father to finish with Jet, Jenna raced from the barn to greet Lorna and Wayne as their car pulled to a stop in front of the house.

It seemed like forever since she had seen them, but it had really only been a few months and Lorna and Wayne had called often to see how everyone was doing, including Dash.

Lorna smiled as she wrapped her arms about Jenna. She was glad to see how happy she seemed. Even Jace seemed to be a lot happier, though he was still quiet and a bit reserved as he moved toward them, his hand outstretched toward Wayne.

"Well, Jace, let's see this new gelding you have. I heard he is quite the horse." Wayne turned to head into the barn as Jace smiled to himself, glancing briefly at Jenna, who had paused quietly at Wayne's remark.

Following Wayne into the barn, Jace felt a sense of triumph. Jenna had acted so cool toward Jet, only doing the very basics of care. Never had he seen her fuss over him like she had all the other horses. But knowing she had talked about him to Lorna and Wayne made it evident that she liked him, in spite of her actions.

Jenna didn't notice her father's smile for she had turned to hug Lorna lovingly, whispering softly in her ear, "He is a real sweet horse. I think he has adopted Dash as his mama. And oh, Lorna, Dash is doing so good. Come and see her."

Jenna continued to chatter happily as she led Lorna into the barn. Dash stood at the front of her stall waiting as if she knew they would be coming to see her. Nickering softly at Jenna, Dash tried in her way to coax Jenna into letting her out. She was feeling so good and the stall was getting so boring.

Jace and Wayne stood right next to them, for they were still looking at Jet in the stall next to Dash's.

"Dad, can I let her out for a little while?" Jenna questioned, the filly gently pushing against her with her nose.

"Yeah, that would be fine," Jace, answered continuing to talk to Wayne about Jet. "Maybe I'll put him out with her for a minute."

Before Jace could finish talking, Jet started to whinny loudly, for Jenna had already begun to lead Dash from her stall and was halfway down the alley.

Jenna giggled softly; whispering to Lorna who was walking by her side, "See what I mean? You take Dash away from him and he starts whinnying like a baby. If you put her away before him, he does the same thing. He seems to think he belongs with her."

Arriving at the small pasture's gate, Jenna turned to see Jet leading her father up behind them, anxious to stay with Dash. Opening the gate, Jenna led Dash through, and then unhooked the lead rope from the halter. Jet's whinny rang through the air as Dash took off without him, her tail high in the air as she ran through the soft grass.

"Oh, take it easy, Jet. She's not going very far," Jace, scolded Jet as he led him through the gate to turn him loose.

Whinnying loudly, Jet turned to catch up to Dash, flipping dirt and grass behind him.

"I sure hope he grows out of this baby stage soon," Jace commented as he shook his head and moved to stand by Jenna, Lorna, Wayne and Tom who all stood watching at the rail.

Jet covered the distance between himself and Dash in no time, whinnying all the way. Dash knew he was coming and watched him out of the corner of her eye. Though she was excited to play with him, she exerted her self-control and only turned to nicker softly when he stopped by her side.

Then without a warning she nipped him affectionately and turned to dart the other way, turning briefly to see if he would follow. A game of tag was always fun, besides she felt good, felt like playing as she sprinted along the rail Jet close beside her still whinnying.

Stopping short, Dash surprised Jet by popping him in the nose with her own— her way of telling him to hush. He didn't need to be whinnying all the time.

Jet's feelings appeared to be hurt as he stopped, a bewildered look in his eyes, his head hanging slightly.

"That's it, Dash. You tell him!" Jace hollered to Dash, who had again moved closer, coaxing Jet to resume their play.

Jet wasn't sure what to think, but again turned to follow. Starting after Dash, a soft nicker could be heard if only for a moment, before he moved along her side, the two running in unison, their tails high, and their manes blowing in the breeze.

"She'll teach him."

CHAPTER 20

The days passed and with them so did the autumn season. Frost now greeted each new morning, staying well past the sun rising off the mountains, the brisk air protecting it from the sun's warmth.

The horses' sleek bodies were now fuzzy with the new growth of winter hair, their breath circling about their soft noses as they moved happily about the walker. They seemed to enjoy the crisp air, unlike Jenna, who despite her sweater and jacket, felt uncomfortably cool. Jace continued to wear only a denim shirt, enjoying the escape from sweating in the humid heat-filled days gone by.

Jenna watched quietly the things around her. She was in an unusual mood and wasn't really sure why. She figured her father would lovingly tease her about it being a "girl thing." *He has become so different over the last year and a half, or so it seems to me. But thinking about it, maybe it is I who has changed.*

She seemed to understand him more and he in turn her, so maybe therefore it was both of them. But what really mattered was the way their lives had changed. The peace and happiness each seemed to feel, the way they had become with each other. Still there were uncertainties and misperceptions as there always would be, for in spite of how well they knew each other, they were different people with different thoughts and feelings.

Glancing at her father, she wondered at some of the feelings she knew were there. He held them deep inside, only a sad glint within his eyes to betray them upon his otherwise smiling face.

Smiling to herself, Jenna thought it odd how you could be so happy, yet still be sad. She often felt that way. A lonely ache deep inside for reasons she knew not.

Her father was the same way. Not that he had told her, but she knew. For one of the many things she had learned was, often, if you just watch, really watch, and listen you can learn so very, very much, about people, about horses, about yourself.

Jace's voice broke through her thoughts drawing her back to reality and the obvious lapse in time that had occurred. Jet was already in his stall, the sound of his whinny echoing behind her father's words.

"Jenna, will you bring Dash in?" His voice was pleasant and casual.

It wasn't really a question or an order, just a comment. She had gotten so much better around her father and the horses. At first she had been so frustrated with his moods and expectations. He seemed to want her to read his mind. Now with all the work they did together and her wide range of experience with the horses, she almost could.

Well, at least I have a good idea of what he needs or wants.

Moving closer to Dash, Jenna had the irresistible urge to ride— not a "real ride" ride, just a ride into the barn. But since Dash only had a halter on and no saddle, it would be a bit harder, for the filly was quite tall and Jenna definitely was not.

Leading Dash close to the fence rail, Jenna had a slight uneasy feeling. It was one thing to jump from the rail onto Dot's back, but probably a totally different thing for Dash. For one thing Dash was still a racehorse, no one had done it before, and in case it spooked her, all Jenna had was the halter and lead rope.

As always the urge and Jenna's lack of common sense where Dash was concerned, won out. Climbing up the rail, she talked softly to Dash, who looked at her cautiously.

"Easy, girl, it's okay. I just want a ride."

Stroking her neck gently, Jenna leaned out from the rail and put her hands at Dash's withers, then leapt from the fence to her back. Dash moved only but a step, looking back at the young girl with an almost annoyed expression, for her weight had thrown her off balance just a bit.

"Sorry, girl. I didn't mean to land so hard."

Urging Dash forward with the gentle kick of her heels, they headed toward the barn.

Jace had moved toward the barn door wondering what was taking Jenna so long. Jet was still whinnying, and frankly, it was driving him nuts.

"Jet! Knock it off!"

He could see now what had taken so long as Dash entered the alleyway of the barn, Jenna happily upon her back.

"Well, it's about time. Poor Jet's in here having a fit," was all Jace said as he smiled to himself and finished with the work he had being trying to do.

Jenna had to admit to herself she was a bit relieved. A year ago, her father would have gotten upset and given her a lecture about racehorses, Dash being one, and using common sense.

Jet's whinnying had subsided into a soft quiet nicker, his eyes fixed on the filly's every move. Dash moved alongside without responding to him. Jet almost looked heartbroken as she moved past him into her stall.

Jenna giggled softly as she reached in to stroke his silken nose.

"What's the matter, boy? Is she ignoring you?"

His big brown eyes looked deep into hers, his head dropping slightly, almost pouting. Jenna quickly glanced about to see where her father was and found herself alone.

It was bad enough that she was finding it hard to stay away from Jet, but she didn't want her father to see her fussing over him.

Dash moved to the corner of the stall closest to Jet and Jenna where the rails allowed her to see what was going on. She could hear Jenna fussing over Jet and she wanted some attention too.

"What's the matter, girl? Are you feeling left out?" Jenna teased as she reached with her other hand to scratch Dash on the neck.

Jet eagerly raised his head and moved closer to the corner to where he could almost touch his nose to Dash's. Blowing softly, his nostrils flaring slightly, he coaxed to Dash, eagerly awaiting her response.

Jenna's heart felt a little tug as Dash blew her warm breath against Jet's soft nose, her deep throaty nicker responding affectionately. Maybe Dash was a bit like herself. It wasn't that she didn't like him, she was just being cautious.

Jace purposefully banged the back door to the barn to let Jenna knew he was back. He knew she occasionally fussed over Jet, but preferred not to be seen, which was okay with him. He was just glad to see her paying attention to him.

He also enjoyed the attachment that Jet had for Dash. He could learn a lot from her if she would just be willing to teach him.

"Well, Jenna, he sure seems to be settling in well, don't you think?" Jace questioned as he moved closer to the stalls where the three still stood.

"Yeah. I think Dash kind of likes him."

"And what about you, what do you think about him?" Jace coaxed.

"I like him. He's real nice. I just know that someday you'll sell him, so I don't want to get too attached, that's all."

Jenna scratched Jet lightly on the nose, unable to hide her affection for the young gelding and no longer feeling a need. Her father knew how she felt and she knew it, besides maybe he would understand.

Jace smiled and hugged Jenna lightly to him.

"I know, and I am sorry that it hurts. I guess I had forgotten what it feels like. I just got too good at blocking it out. But Jet can learn a lot from you. You have a special way with the horses and they respond so well to you."

Jenna smiled pleased with the compliment. "I just love them, that's all. The rest just comes with time."

Christmas neared and with it a series of heavy snowstorms, many of which seemed to last for days as Jenna longed for the warmth of the sun. Jace felt sure this would be a record year for snow and cursed as he again plowed the drive.

Lorna and Wayne were planning to come the next day, but Jenna feared they wouldn't be able to as the snow continued to fall mercilessly.

Dash and Jet on the other hand seemed to love the snow, as they would move along the track, the snow flying up from behind their hooves. Best of all, though, was when Jace would turn them out in the small pasture to run. Now that was what was fun to watch. The two seemed to regress into immature babies that ran and bumped each other, turning to flip the snow high into the air before burrowing deep into its softness, rolling and moaning in sheer delight.

Peering out the window one more time, Jenna searched for signs of a car. Lorna and Wayne had left that afternoon and planned to be there before dark. Glancing one more time at the clock, her heart fretted with concern for it was well past dark, the sun having set almost an hour ago.

"Don't worry, honey, I'm sure they will get here soon. Lorna's probably just driving slow because of the storm."

Jace had come to peer out the window beside her. The snow, now coming down in large flakes, twirled helplessly in the brisk wind. Just three hours before, the sun had been shining, the sky clear except for a few stray clouds.

Jace wouldn't admit it to Jenna, but he was also feeling a bit concerned.

Suddenly a pair of headlights could be seen in the distance, turning toward them to move slowly down the lane.

"See, I told you. I bet that's them right now."

The week passed quickly with all the fun and excitement of Christmas and having Lorna and Wayne there. The weather had eased leaving clear skies that allowed the warmth of the sun to make being outside enjoyable.

Even Lorna had gone with Jace and Jenna on the chariot around the track. Dash and Jet were working well together as they moved simultaneously, their strides matching one with the other.

Dash showed no signs of soreness and continued to improve in strength. Jet slowly grew in maturity and poise, always trying to mimic Dash. Whatever she did, he felt he should do as he bowed his neck and puffed a deep breath through his flaring nostrils to mingle with Dash's in the cool air.

"Oh, Jace, they are truly beautiful. I can see why you love this so. All their power and beauty held in the tips of your fingers with only a set of leather reins to ask your bidding." Lorna closed her eyes for a moment, enjoying the warmth of the sun upon her face, the chariot rocking beneath her as they galloped along the now soft track.

"Well, Lorna, would you like to feel something really awesome?" Jace questioned as he winked at Jenna on his other side.

With the three of them in the chariot, it would be a little crowded, but both Jet and Dash wanted more. A little blow down the backside of the track would be good for them. Besides, there was nothing quite like two horses in a full run with a chariot.

"Sure..." Lorna answered a bit apprehensively, for she wasn't sure what Jace had in mind.

"Get a good hold on the handle and get your feet planted well on the grill." Jace grinned as he moved to wrap the reins once around each hand, giving himself a firmer grip that betrayed his intent as Dash and Jet felt the reins grow taut.

Their movement changed, their muscles becoming flexed and ready as they waited, somewhat impatiently for the cue.

"Oh, Jace, wait a minute. I don't know about this." His intentions had become clear to more than just Jet and Dash and suddenly a twinge of fear seemed to spread through her.

"It will be fun, Lorna. Really, I promise you will love it," Jenna tried to convince her lovingly as she took a hold of Lorna's free hand. "We're ready, Dad."

Lorna smiled meekly as she gripped the handle. Jace glimpsed the slight hint of fear in her eyes before turning back to face the now impatient horses before him. Moving into the straightaway everything became a blur as Lorna heard him say once more to hold on, then yelled both of the horses' names and told them to "git."

Suddenly the chariot seemed to become airborne as the two horses moved in unison, the sound of their hooves and the chariot wheels thundering in her ears. Gasping for a breath, she tried to relax as their movement eased and they seemed to fly across the earth. Their speed made it hard for Lorna to catch her breath as the wind teased a few tears from her eyes. Her heart no longer pounded in fear but exhilaration as they began to move into the next corner and Jace pulled back on the reins.

"Whoa! Easy, you two. That's enough for today," he said turning to face Lorna.

She couldn't help but love him. His eyes shone bright, a huge smile spreading across his face, for with one glance he knew she had loved it too.

CHAPTER 21

Jace was glad to see the new leaves budding on the trees as he fingered them lightly. Dot grazed quietly on the small blades of grass that had finally begun to break through the cool earth. Even the sun shone in an almost clear sky instead of the cloudy overcast skies that had seemed to last for weeks on end.

The snow had been gone for quite some time but the cold weather had lingered well into April.

"Well, Dot, how about it? Want to go for a ride?" Jace asked the mare, who in response raised her head, her eyes intent on his.

She had watched him hook up the trailer but thought nothing of it and still was unsure of the meaning of his words, but she knew her name and knew he was speaking to her.

Just then Jenna's bus pulled to a stop at the end of the lane, opening its doors for her to bounce down the steps and race toward the trailer she knew would be waiting.

When her father had told her he was taking Dot back to the stud farm, she had begged him to let her come.

Considering it would just be a long drive down and back, he was thankful for the thought of having her company. He had become quite fond of her endless chatter and enjoyed listening as she talked about school, friends and, of course her favorite subject, the horses.

"What stud are we taking Dot to? Is it the same one as last time?" Jenna had a habit of always asking double questions and rambling on before you had a chance to answer, especially when she was excited about something.

"What color is he? Oh, Dad, I'm so excited! I hope she has a filly."

Jace laughed to himself as he waited for a pause from Jenna. "Okay, let's see if I can answer these in the right order. Noble Pride is the stud. No, it's not the same one as last time, but it's at the same place. He is a dark brown almost black and is about seventeen hands high. I'm glad you're excited, but I hope it's a colt," Jace finished, a mischievous glint in his eyes.

He often teased about the fillies and how moody they were, calling it a "girl thing," and proclaiming there were enough moody females around there.

"Oh, Dad, you love us moody girls and wouldn't know what to do without us."

Jace knew she was right. With everything they had gone through with Dash, he couldn't begin to imagine her not being there. And Dot, he could hardly remember her not being there. Besides she was a part of Shanna he would hold onto forever. Even though she could be the moodiest, orneriest one of them all, she could also be quite lovable. And as for Jenna, what could he say? He knew now he could never live without her.

After what seemed like an eternity, Jace pulled off the main road and headed down through rows and rows of houses. The traffic was quite heavy and he cursed under his breath as someone pulled out in front of him, causing him to brake hard, Dot's weight rocking the trailer as she lost her balance temporarily.

Glancing around, Jenna couldn't imagine a horse farm anywhere near them. All she could see were stores, schools and hundreds of homes, about as close together as they could get. Surely there wouldn't be room for any horses around there.

Turning into what looked like someone's driveway, Jace headed into the center of the block, where behind a row of large trees it seemed to open up into a new world. Small pastures lined both sides of the lane filled with what looked like half a dozen yearlings in each.

Further down, the lane turned into a large circle, with three large barns surrounding them. Two walkers turned slowly, filled with young, eager two-year-olds out for their evening walk.

Glancing all around, Jenna could hardly believe it. There had to be at least a hundred horses there as she noticed even more small pastures behind the barns, all filled with what looked like brood mares and new colts.

Stepping from the truck Jenna hardly noticed the man and woman coming toward them.

"Well, Jace, we're glad to see you made the drive safely. Shall we get her unloaded? You know Carolyn really likes this mare of yours and we would sure like to see you get a good colt out of her."

Jenna turned at the sound of the trailer door opening and Dot's loud whinny echoing through the air, many of the surrounding horses answering curiously.

Her father unloaded Dot and headed to the barn on his left.

"Well, Jenna, are you coming?" Jace questioned as he looked back to find her still taking everything in. "Maybe you shouldn't, though, because I'll never get you out of the barn."

Jace had been there many times and knew that barn held all the mares that were due or had delivered their colts just recently, along with some of the ones to be bred.

"Here, Jace, put her in this one." Carolyn opened the door to the fresh stall, and then turned toward Jenna. "If you would like, you may look around while we get her settled."

Checking with her father, Jenna headed down the alley. Peering into each stall, she found almost all of them had small colts sleeping next to their mothers, who paid very little attention to her.

Gazing back at her father, Jenna could see he was a bit preoccupied with completing all the arrangements for Dot. Turning again toward the young colt within the stall, she was surprised to see he had gotten up out of the soft straw and now stood at the rail, his soft nose almost touching her.

Reaching slowly, she stroked his nose as he licked at her finger, a soft giggle esçaping Jenna as the young colt tried to suck her thumb.

"Well, Jenna, would you like to see him?" Jace asked as he came to stand beside her, his business completed.

He hadn't said who "he" was, but Jenna knew and turned eagerly, wanting to see the stud horse she had heard so much about. Moving down the alley in the other direction, Jenna stopped occasionally tugging at her father's arm to look at a colt or filly.

There had to be about twenty stalls on each side as they moved slowly to the far end of the barn.

There the last two stalls changed in appearance, their panels being much higher, their rails narrower, and the main size almost twice as big.

Hearing the approaching visitors, both of the horses moved to the front of their stalls as Jenna peered in. The stall on her left held a large sorrel horse; a narrow blaze ran the full length of his face. His muscled body seemed much larger than any horse Jenna had ever seen before, but she noticed he was not fat, just very filled out and muscular.

He turned away and moved to the back of his stall appearing bored and disinterested with the visitors.

Turning around to face the other stall Jenna could see a large dark brown horse standing at the front of his stall near her father, who waited for her reaction.

The large stud horse stood close to Jace, watching Jenna casually in an almost aloof manner. His intense eyes held hers as she moved slowly closer. His deep color was what Jenna would surely call black, yet her father had told her often, there were no true black horses— almost all of them had brown around the muzzle of their noses and the soft hollow of their flanks.

A small white star peeked out from under his forelock accentuating even more the intensity of his color. He had an aloofness about his manner, yet appeared interested in her as she moved closer yet to his stall.

"Oh, Dad, he is beautiful!"

As if the horse understood, he raised his large head and arched his powerful neck turning to strut slowly along the front of his stall.

Jenna hadn't been around many stud horses and hadn't realized how large and muscular they generally were. *Oh, isn't he an awesome sight!*

Jace smiled to himself. There was no reason to ask; he could tell by Jenna's smile, she definitely liked him too.

CHAPTER 22

For the month of June, the weather seemed more like February as small flakes of snow fluttered to the ground.

Jenna stepped carefully along the edge of the track, the surface puddling with mud, water, and snow. *What a rotten day for races.* Even her coat didn't keep out the cold chill from the breeze that twirled the flakes helplessly and teased a tear from her eye.

Dash moved closer to the starting gates, along with the other nine horses, for the last trial race of the derby.

It would be her first official out since she had been pulled up on the corner and was taken off the track in the horse ambulance. Dr. Clark had declared her leg sound and felt she was ready to run.

Trying to ease the pounding of her heart, Jenna grasped her golden charm and waited quietly, hardly daring to breathe. The last horse loaded and almost instantly the bell rang, the gates freeing the ten horses.

Jenna was surprised by how quickly the gates had opened as it appeared were some of the horses.

Dash broke quick but lost her balance in her hindquarters as the wet ground beneath her broke away, only the power of her front legs pulling her on. Pressing harder she neared the halfway mark as she came upon a large puddle, mud and water flying behind her, the weight of it slowing her stride if but for a moment.

Jenna held her breath as they neared the finish line. Two horses on the inside of the track appeared to be out in front, but Dash was coming on strong in the nine-hole as they crossed the finish line.

"After reviewing the photo, the nine-horse, For Ever Dashin', is the winner, Mr. Taylor's Short second, and Flyer Jet finishing third, " the announcer's voice echoed over the loudspeaker to mingle with the roar of the crowd as the numbers lit the board— nine, four, three, showing the order of finish.

It had been close between the four-horse and Dash. Both horses and riders had circled on the track waiting for the decision. Jenna had stood quietly by her father's side, fearing she had been beaten, yet relieved she had run so well.

Dash showed no signs of soreness and moved smoothly toward the winner's circle at the announcement of the winner, Jace and Jenna at her side.

It would take awhile before the ten fastest qualifiers for the final gate would be announced; yet Jace dared not even hope. Theirs had been the last trial heat and the track had gotten deeper and muddier with each race. Even though she had won and beaten some of the faster horses in the whole group, the race had been slower because of the track conditions.

Dash walked quietly on the walker while Jenna watched on. The snow had stopped but still she sat huddled in the chair against the cold breeze that continued to blow.

"Dad, what if she doesn't qualify?"

Jenna too knew the chances were not too good.

"Well, we'll just wait and see, but if she doesn't, we'll just run her in some open races for awhile. Besides we need to focus on Jet for the Silver Dollar Futurity trials. He hasn't run anything but a schooling race since he wasn't able to draw in this weekend and the trials run in two weeks."

Jenna shivered as a breeze gusted past. "I sure hope it's a lot warmer than this."

"It should be. It was just the cold front that moved in. Who knows, in two weeks you'll probably be complaining you're too hot," Jace teased, for Jenna was never one to like it very cold or very hot.

"Get her stall door open and we'll put her away. They should know the qualifiers by now."

Jace moved to pick up Dash's lead rope as Tom came around the corner, a white sheet of paper in his hand.

"I was beginning to wonder if you got lost," Jace commented at the sight of the older man. "So, where did we finish?"

"She was the eleventh fastest. I tried to argue, as did many of the other trainers, that the track conditions were not equal for each race. Therefore, time trails couldn't be considered fair, and get them to take the first and second place horse of each trial. With the five trial heats that would make an even ten. But they wouldn't go for it, "Tom finished, an expression of disgust upon his face. "She was only eleventh by one one-hundredth of a second too."

Jace just shook his head. *What else can I do? That is just the way racing goes. Sometimes you have the luck and sometimes you don't.* But he had to admit, some people seemed to get more than their share of good luck and others more than their share of bad luck.

"Well, let's get her loaded and head for home."

Jenna finished grabbing the few things that had not already been loaded, and then waited at the back of the trailer as her father led Dash in.

Dash stepped in eagerly. Though she loved to go to the races, she was always ready to go home.

Jenna hadn't felt tired, but realized she must have fallen asleep soon after they left the track, for that was the last thing she remembered and now they were almost home. Gazing out the window, she marveled at the colors of the evening sky as the sun began to dip into the mountain ridges, its rays leaving bright beams, breaking through the few scattered clouds, that came to rest upon the earth.

"Look, Dad, a glory hole!"

That was what Shanna had always called them and Jace smiled inwardly as he thought of her. She was the one who could always find the silver lining in everything, just like Jenna.

Jace was in a pessimistic mood. Nothing had seemed to go right lately. The weather had been wet and drizzly, making it hard to get Jet galloped on a regular basis.

Today had begun with clear skies and warm temperatures, a perfect day for races. Yet still he felt a gray cloud hanging over him, for Jet had drawn the two-hole and the inside of the track was generally deeper and slower. *But what does it matter? Jet hasn't gotten the works he needs, and his chances of qualifying out of almost two hundred horses, well, it's just a long shot, probably a waste of time and money.*

Dash nickered to Jace trying to coax him into letting her out of her stall.

"Sorry, girl, you're just along to keep Jet happy. He doesn't seem to be able to do anything without you. Now be a good girl and be quiet," Jace scolded affectionately as he stepped into Jet's stall to finish the final adjustments on his tack.

"Bring your horses to the paddock for the seventh race," the announcer's voice echoed over the loudspeakers causing Jenna's heart to give a start.

When will I get used to the routine? Am I always going to be so nervous? Trying not to think about it, she opened the stall door for her father as he led Jet out.

"Go get 'em, Jet. You can do it," Jenna coaxed as he walked by.

Jace smiled and wished he could be so optimistic as he patted Jet on the neck. "Yeah, you give 'em hell, boy."

Jet loaded quietly into the gates aware of everything around him, his eyes focusing through the grill of the gates, beyond and down the track. His heart pounded as he got himself set. He knew Jace stood behind him and felt the gentle touch of the man's hand upon his hip. He hadn't done this very much but he had the main idea. Get out fast and run hard.

Suddenly the gates opened and Jet sprung forward. He had been watching the gap in front of him and had seen it widen that split second before the bell rang and the whole gate popped open. Digging hard, he ran with all his might, not even realizing he had been holding his breath until about his third stride out.

Breathing deeply, he dug harder; the tap of Larry's whip on his hip asking him for more, which he gladly gave. He knew he was right alongside the other horses as he raced on.

Larry's strong arms pushed against his neck, Larry's voice thundering in his ears to blend with the roar of the crowd as they neared the finish line.

Suddenly Larry stood up and began to pull back on the reins.

Is it over already? Am I done?

Moving into the corner, Jet slowed his pace, his nostrils flaring, his heart pounding, his whole body exhilarated.

Coming back, he could hear the roar of the crowd getting louder and louder. Larry patted him vigorously on the neck as he stopped in front of Jace, who stood waiting in the middle of the track. Jet could see Jenna and Tom running out to meet him, but was confused by the tears in Jenna's eyes as she wrapped her arms about his neck.

Is something wrong?

"Oh, Jet, you did it! I knew you could!" Again Jenna wrapped her arms about his neck, and then kissed him briefly on the nose.

The announcer's voice rose above the crowd to announce Goddess A Jet the winner.

Walking into the winner's circle, Jet finally figured it out. He had done well.

CHAPTER 23

Jace glared slightly at Jenna, annoyed by her persistence. She continued to insist that something was wrong with Dash. Her last two races had been tough competition and the mare had barely finished in the top five.

She showed no signs of soreness in either of her legs and continued to put forth a strong effort, but something just wasn't right.

"Jenna, she is running against all the boys. Almost every horse in the last two races were geldings, in fact she was the only mare in her last race. At three, the geldings are just bigger and stronger, and allowance races are just real tough. If you would let me run her in some claiming races, I'm sure she could get some wins." Jace tried to rationalize with Jenna, but, at the mere mention of claiming races, he could see the fear fill her eyes.

"Someone would claim her though, wouldn't they? And all the claimers listed have only been for three thousand or five thousand dollars."

Jenna's gaze dropped as she felt the sting of tears coming to her eyes. "You told me you had turned down that offer of ten thousand dollars, don't you think someone would try to claim her for that much less? Please, Dad, I know that she could be winning; I just think something is wrong."

Jace knew she was right. Someone would claim her in a heartbeat. He still had people asking about the mare even though he had made sure the word was out that she wasn't for sale.

"Well, if it will make you feel better, I will call Dr. Clark and see what he thinks."

Jenna was relieved, for even though Dr. Daines had checked her over, he didn't have some of the equipment that Dr. Clark had. Besides, Jenna just knew that something wasn't right; otherwise Dash would be winning.

Jace turned his attention back to Jet. The eager colt had managed, with his win in the trials, to qualify for the consolation gate of the Silver Dollar, which that in itself was quite an achievement.

The day of the finals, Jet had appeared eager and ready, but had not broke well from the gates. He didn't seem to have his heart into it, seeming distracted as he neared the finish line at the back of the pack.

Jace had been truly disappointed as obviously was Jenna as she patted Jet on the neck. Larry jumped lightly from the ground stating Jet just didn't seem to kick it in, apologized for not getting more out of the colt, and thanked Jace for the opportunity to ride for him.

Walking from the track, Jet had wondered what was wrong. *We aren't going into the circle, some other horse is. Jenna seems kind of sad and Jace seems to barely know I am beside him,* he thought as they moved toward the barns.

Dropping his head slightly, Jet wondered at the mood. *Something is wrong. It isn't the same as last time.*

Then had come the trials for the Dash for Destiny Futurity. Jet had won his trial heat with an impressive two lengths lead, finishing the trials as the fastest qualifier.

Jace had to admit he had been more wrapped up in Jet than what was happening with Dash and right now he was a little worried. *It is not always the best to be the fastest qualifier, for some reason it almost seems to be a jinx, and Jet is being far from consistent. Running real well, then running at the back, then turning around and blowing them away. What will he do this time? Does he have it figured out?*

"Well, Jet, just do it again, one more time for me next week." Jace patted him firmly on the neck, and then turned to find Jenna waiting patiently at his side. "Come on in the house and I'll call Dr. Clark. Maybe he can squeeze Dash in tomorrow if he's not too busy."

Jenna smiled quietly as she listened to her father's side of the conversation.

"Thanks a lot. I sure appreciate you working her in tomorrow. We'll see you about noon."

Jace hung up the phone, Jenna's arms wrapping tenderly about him. "Happy?"

The soft kiss on his cheek and the smile on her face were all the answer he needed.

The drive seemed to take forever as Jenna shifted in the seat her bottom getting tired from sitting so long. Three hours of rolling hills and open ranges had gotten pretty boring, but slowly they climbed along the foothills up into the base of the mountains where the sage and pine trees blended to create a carpet of green, their aroma filling the breeze.

Dash shifted nervously in the trailer. The air smelled familiar, it wasn't home, but she had been there before as an uneasy feeling spread through her. Nickering softly she moved closer to Jace as he turned to lead her from the trailer.

"Well, Jace, what seems to be the problem?" Dr. Clark asked as he moved to run his hand expertly down Dash's front legs.

No heat or swelling could be detected in either leg. Moving nervously, Dash's stepped cautiously away.

"Easy, girl. I won't hurt you," Dr. Clark spoke softly his gentle voice calming her as he continued to examine her. "Jace, walk her straight away from me, then turn her around and trot her back."

Watching intently her every move, Dr. Clark never changed his expression. Dash showed no signs of a missed step, a limp or anything as far as Jenna could tell, so she was surprised when he calmly said something about her right hindquarter and asked Jace to bring her inside. He had only looked at her for about five minutes.

Moving into his ultrasound room, Jenna was again amazed by all the equipment. It seemed that with each trip there was always some new piece of equipment.

"Crosstie her over here and we'll see if I'm right. I think she probably has a torn muscle in her right hindquarter. Has she slipped or fallen lately?"

Jace tried to think back, he couldn't recall that she had, and quickly reviewed her last few races.

"She won her first race out.... "

Pausing for a moment, it came to him.

"It was real muddy that day, though, and now that you mention it, I remember she had her hindquarters slip out from under her as she broke from the gates, but was able to recover and win. She hasn't acted sore though."

"It probably doesn't hurt her as much as it restricts her from full extension, for at that point it does hurt."

Dr. Clark ran a strange looking piece of machinery along her hip and down along the back portion of her buttocks, explaining as he continued to check her about injured muscles putting off more heat and the color variations in thermography, while pointing at the screen in front of them.

Jenna noticed a large red area on the screen while Dr. Clark confirmed her fears. Dash had a large tear in her muscle just under her buttocks. With that kind of an injury, she could not extend her stride, could not run with all her power. Dash was done for the year.

"It could take a good six months for a tear like that to heal. But I'm glad it's not something worse." Dr. Clark continued to tell Jace what to expect and what kind of treatment she would need as Jenna's mind drifted from the conversation to her own thoughts.

She had known something was wrong but the confirmation of the fact only made her angry. *Why Dash? Why is it always her and not someone else's horse?*

The trip home seemed twice as long. Jenna gazed out the window, the rolling hills and mountains seeming but a blur, as her thoughts played over and over in her mind. *Am I selfish? Shouldn't I be happy that Dash will be okay?*

Instead she was sad and a little mad, mad that Dash wouldn't be running anymore. Sad because she loved to watch her run; to see her win. Mad because it didn't seem fair, seemed they always had the bad luck.

Looking back toward the trailer, she was grateful that Dash would be okay, and it wasn't as bad as the last time. *But what about Dash? Isn't running what Dash loves most? Does she run because she loves to, or does she run for us?*

"You know, Jenna, we're really lucky it's just a torn muscle and not something permanent..." Jace's words startled her, for it was like he read her mind, "and I guess we could even run her one more year, if that's what you would like to do."

Again he seemed to know her very thoughts.

Gazing into the depths of her father's eyes, she realized he knew her better than she knew herself, for his soft words continued, answering for her the very questions that seemed to haunt her mind and trouble her heart.

"Jenna, sometimes it's hard to tell if your luck is good or bad, if something is right or wrong, fair or not fair. And often it's how a person chooses to look at it. We could look at her final gate. We could say why did we have such bad luck for her leg to get kicked, for the kick to cause a green-willow fracture? Or we could say how lucky we are that her leg didn't blow in that race, or the following one, that we didn't lose her.

"I know you love to watch her run, to see her win. And there is nothing wrong with that. If she is sound and healthy, there is no reason we couldn't run her one more year, but we will have to wait and see. I can't make any decisions at this time. I'll need to wait, to make the best decision for her. But remember, Jenna, one of the things I have learned in my life is that it's not always fair. You just have to do the best you can, to be the best you can."

Jace's words trailed off, his mind thinking back on how his life had changed, how he had changed.

How truly lucky I am for all the wonderful things in my life. His hand slowly drifted from the steering wheel to grasp the small hand of his daughter. *Oh, to be so very, very lucky.*

CHAPTER 24

Jet loaded eagerly into the two-hole of the gates with Larry upon his back. The final gate for the Dash for Destiny Futurity was almost complete as they loaded the last two horses. Larry wore the bright blue racing silks Jenna had made as a gift for her father.

Jace stood behind Jet, one hand on his large hip that flexed eagerly awaiting the gates, the other hand holding his tail taunt.

Jet's ears were pricked forward, his head turned slightly to one side as he watched the three-horse out of the corner of his eye. The anxious horse kept lunging forward, banging the sides of the gate nervously. Headers continued to work with all ten horses trying to get the perfect start. Jace kept Jet in position from behind while the header was supposed to make sure he was straight in the front.

Finally the gates grew quiet, if but for a moment, it seemed like forever as the starter seemed to be waiting for something.

Why doesn't he pull the gates? We can't stand here forever. Suddenly the gates lurched as Jace felt Jet move away from him. The three-horse had lunged and Jet was not going to be beaten out as he exploded with all his might.

The sight that followed moved everyone into action as headers rushed in front of and behind the gates. Jace could hardly believe his eyes as he looked quickly behind him at Larry, who lay sprawled out in the dirt, the ambulance crew rushing to his side.

Turning his attention back to Jet, he could see Vaughan, one of the starters, moving through the front of the gates with amazing speed and grace for the large man that he was.

Jace felt sick as his eyes came to rest on Jet. He had seen the three-horse make a false start and given his all.

Only thing was the starter hadn't opened the gates. Jet had exploded with such power that the header was unable to hold him and he had slammed headfirst into the front grill.

He now sat at the back of the gates on his haunches, obviously knocked cold as he sat without moving. The starter and the headers quickly opened the front of his gate as Vaughan moved alongside to grasp the side of his bridle. Trying to rouse him, Vaughan coaxed and tugged him forward.

They couldn't open the tailgate or he would fallout onto his back. Pushing up from behind him along his sides, Jace and another header managed to get him off the ground as he suddenly came to, lunging drunkenly forward, his world spinning, blood dripping from his mouth and nose.

Moving to take Jet from Vaughan, Jace marveled at how he now moved forward with an eager balanced stride, while Jace led him around to the back side of the gates.

Jace could hear the announcer declaring a delay and a problem with the favored horse in the race, the number two-horse. He knew Jet was favored to win this race. He had been the fastest qualifier with an impressive two lengths win in his trial heat.

"Well, Jace, let's take a look at him."

The track vet moved to Jet's head, looked into his eyes, cleaned out his nostrils and removed a front tooth that had been knocked free, except for one small piece of flesh that managed to hold it in place.

"I think he looks okay. Can't really see any reason to scratch him."

Jace couldn't believe what he was hearing. *How can Jet run after something like this, be expected to?* Yet, Jet seemed pretty good, but Jace knew he stood practically no chance of winning after what had happened.

By saddling and putting Jet on the track, Jace had committed him to run, without a vet scratch he was obligated. If he refused to run him, Jace could be fined and lose racing privileges.

Looking again at Jet, he realized how much money the track could make off of this. *Jet is the favored horse. Most of the bettors' money is on him. His chances of even finishing in the top three are not all that good, the track will make a bundle off the lost bets.*

Jet nudged him gently on the arm, confused by everything that had happened.

Didn't I do what I was supposed to do? Didn't I do it right?

Gazing toward the barns his loud whinny coaxed for Dash.

"It's okay, Jet. Easy, boy."

Jace hesitated as the starter called out to mount up. Larry had only had the wind knocked out of him and now stood waiting at Jace's side.

"Is he okay?" Larry questioned.

Jace's shrug was his only reply for the moment as his mind struggled with everything. *Can I really load Jet back into the gates and expect him to run? How can the vet and the stewards expect him to run after this? Well, that's easy. They don't have anything to lose.*

At that moment Jace had the strongest urge to lead Jet off the track, take the chance of being fined or even suspended.

"Mount up!" again the steward announced as Jace turned to see Jet was the only horse without a rider up, the others already beginning to circle around him.

Jet nudged him questioningly, only knowing the other horses were going to leave without him.

"Jace, is there a problem? " the starter asked in a tone that almost defied there to be a problem as he moved closer, then turned to direct the trainers and headers to start loading.

"You can load him last, Jace."

His words seemed to finalize everything. As far as they were concerned, Jet was running.

"What do you want to do? " Larry questioned as he waited for Jace to say something.

He could see the hesitation and didn't blame him. *Jet hit hard. How can any horse run, really run, after that?*

"Jace, load him up! "

Turning quickly, Jace felt he had no choice. He couldn't risk a fine or a suspension.

"Okay, Larry, watch him close. If anything seems wrong, anything at all, pull him up."

Legging Larry up, Jace turned to lead Jet toward the gates. Jet didn't hesitate, yet he seemed cautious and unsure as the tailgate closed behind him.

Jet had barely gotten set when the bell rang and the gates popped open. He hesitated if but for a moment before lunging forward.

Larry felt good with Jet's powerful strides as he moved about three to four lengths away from the gate right alongside the other horses. Suddenly Jet seemed to slow as he gasped for a breath, his nostrils flaring, blood flying back to cover Larry's hands and arms.

Oh God, no! Larry's mind screamed as he immediately pulled back on the reins trying to slow Jet's stride, praying the young horse didn't drop from beneath him.

Jet fought the pull of the reins as the other horses began to pull further ahead. Able to draw a breath, he continued to drive forward, his gaze intent and focused though the blood continued to drip from his mouth and nose.

Larry was amazed at Jet's determination as he continued to pull back, rising up off his back to stop him, though he only showed signs of slowing. Crossing the finish line, they were only a length and a half off the full gate of horses as cheers and moans rose from the crowd.

Jenna ran from the stands, her heart pounding, tears filling her eyes. Even from where she had stood she could see the blood coming from Jet.

Finally Jet stopped just before the corner as Larry quickly leaped to the ground to inspect the now slowing flow of blood.

Jet's head dropped, his mind beginning to spin as a dull pounding spread between his eyes. Rain seemed to be falling upon his head as he felt liquid run into his eyes and blur his vision. Shaking his head, he tried to focus on the young man beside him.

Larry's breath caught in his throat as he moved to unhook the now blood-soaked blinkers from Jet's head, the young colt appearing dazed and confused.

Jace jumped from the back of the truck then ran to Larry's side. A four-inch gash split right through Jet's white stripe between his eyes, the blood running to mix with the slow drip that continued from his nose. He stood quietly, moving only enough to get closer to Jace.

Jace could feel the heat in his face as anger filled him. He knew if he even said anything, it wouldn't be good as he noticed the track vet moving toward them.

He was a new vet at the track and at that moment Jace wanted to kill the son of a bitch.

Gazing back at Jet, he knew he should have told them all to go to hell, taken Jet off the track, refused to run him. But he hadn't, he had loaded him into the gates.

Jet's trusting eyes met his. Now the colt's eyes showed only pain and confusion.

"I'm sorry, Jace. I tried to stop him sooner but he wouldn't. I thought he was going to drop dead on me."

Their gazes met, yet Jace couldn't say anything, he could only pat Larry on the back as the young jockey turned to slowly walk from the track.

"I guess I should have scratched him for you after all. I didn't even think to look under his blinkers." The track vet moved closer to Jet inspecting the large gash upon his head. "You can bring him over to the test barn and I'll be happy to fix him up for you."

Jace met the man's gaze if only for a moment, shaking his head disgustedly before turning to lead Jet away.

"No, thanks."

No one said a word as they watched the dazed horse follow at Jace's side, his head seeming to rest against the man's shoulder.

Jenna had moved onto the track and was now running fearfully toward them.

"Oh, Dad! Is he okay? Don't you want the vet to check his head?"

"I wouldn't let that man touch him with a ten-foot pole!"

Jenna sensed her father's anger, though she didn't understand it, for she was unaware of everything that had happened. She knew Jet had false fired and hit the gates, but felt it best not to ask further, for she had never seen her father as angry as he was now.

Taking the blood-soaked blinkers from her father's hand, Jenna reluctantly left their side to cut through the grandstands.

"I'll meet you at the barns."

Moving through the crowd, Jenna quickly thought of what her father would need for Jet's head. They always carried a first aid kit for the horses, just in case, and she mentally checked off what she thought would be needed.

A loud voice to her side broke though her concentration.

"What the hell was wrong with that damn two-horse? The son of a bitch cost me fifty bucks!" The man spoke not to Jenna, but a group of people beside him and didn't even notice the horrified expression that crossed her face or the tears that filled her eyes.

Running faster for the barn, Jenna's mind screamed angrily at the man. *Stupid fool! What does he know anyway? He deserves to lose fifty bucks, for he obviously doesn't come to the races out of love for horses or admiration for their strength and speed. He is here for his love of money.*

CHAPTER 25

Jenna closed her eyes, listening closely to the sounds around her. The wind whistled musically through her hoop earrings as the sound of Dash's breath came harder and faster, keeping pace with the rhythm of her hooves as they floated along the soft earth.

Jenna loved moments like this, with the sun upon her skin, the wind caressing her cheeks and playing with her hair. She could hear and feel everything, almost swear she could hear the rhythm of Dash's heart beating with hers, together as one.

Dash's strong muscles rippled beneath her to carry them effortlessly into a moment of sheer delight. This was what Jenna loved, and if she were to imagine heaven, this would have to be a part of it.

Exercising Dash had become one of Jenna's jobs. Don still rode her once a week but Jenna got to work her the other times. It was something they both seemed to look forward to and even the rides in from the walker had become a routine.

Jet would begin to whinny about the time Jenna had Dash lined up at the fence rail to jump lightly on to her back. Dash always waited patiently for Jenna to climb up the fence, seeming to understand the need for more height. And Jet, well, he had become quite predictable as Jenna listened for but a moment before leaping effortlessly onto Dash's back, Jet's whinny right on time.

"Oh, Jet, she's coming. You know Jenna's routine. Now just be patient." Jace turned to see Dash and Jenna entering the barn. "See, I told you they were coming."

Jet moved closer to the corner of his stall, his eyes intent on the two moving toward him.

"We could hear you bawling clear outside, Jet. When are you going to grow up?" Jenna teased affectionately as she slid gracefully to the ground.

Jace moved to take Dash from her and turn her into her stall. Jenna turned to stroke Jet's soft nose. A pair of blinkers still surrounded his head.

Once home from the track, Dr. Daines had arrived to find Jet standing quietly in his stall. His head hung low, a small trickle of light fluid oozing from behind a pair of blinkers that held clean gauze over the gash between his eyes.

"I know it's not the greatest, but it was the best I could come up with to keep it closed and covered." Jace had gone on to explain briefly why he had preferred not to have the vet at the track treat him.

Removing the blinkers, Dr. Daines was impressed with how well it had closed. It had been too long really to stitch it and with the blinkers in place he couldn't really see a need.

"Even though it's a large split, I think the best thing to do would be to change the dressing and put the blinkers back on. They seem to be holding it together nicely. Once it scabs over you can put on some of your mesh blinkers without a dressing and let the air get to it. I think it will heal up to where you won't even be able to see it. But with all the trauma and internal bleeding, we best put him on some antibiotics and give him some bute to keep him comfortable."

Looking closer into Jet's slightly glazed eyes, he continued, "You have already given him some bute, haven't you?"

Jace smiled. "Hell, yes. I gave it to him as soon as I got him off the track and back to his stall. Walked right past one of the stewards with the syringe in my hand too. I was just waiting for him to say something to me. Pretty stupid of me I know, but I almost wanted them to try and fine me!"

Dr. Daines couldn't blame him much, but even having a syringe on the track was illegal unless you were a vet. But everyone had them and gave their own legal injections, you just didn't flaunt it, didn't let it be seen. Trainers had been fined and even suspended from the track when found in possession of just a syringe.

Oh, how stubborn pride and male ego can cause a man to be so foolish.

"I guess I was just lucky they didn't do anything. " Jace felt very foolish at the moment as he thought about it.

"I probably would have done the same thing, " Dr. Daines smiled as he lit a cigarette, then awkwardly dropped it to the ground. "I'm really trying to quit, I just keep forgetting. "

Jenna sat quietly beside the old well, the large tree shading her as its fall leaves fluttered down to rest beside her. She didn't really know what had brought it on, but lately her thoughts had turned to her mother.

It had been almost four years, but in many ways it seemed like a hundred years ago. So long ago that she could hardly remember her face, only the visions that reflected pictures would appear in her mind.

Closing her eyes she tried to see her mother, to see her smile and laugh, but only the image of the portrait would appear. Squinting her eyes tighter, she tried harder to remember, so hard that small tears began to squeeze out the corners of her eyes.

Dropping her head into her arms, Jenna cried like she hadn't cried for a long, long time, her small shoulders quivering.

Jace stopped at the edge of the lawn. He could see Jenna's small figure beside the well and hear her muffled sobs. Pausing, he thought to turn away.

It would be easier to walk away than to face what ever was troubling her. Looking again at Jenna's small, trembling form, he knew she needed him, and that he needed to be there for her.

Saying nothing, Jace knelt beside Jenna drawing her into his strong arms. It felt good as she in turn wrapped her arms about him, her head resting upon his chest, her tears slowly beginning to subside.

"Dad, I really miss Mom. Do you miss Mom?" Jenna's words caught him by surprise for she had not really said anything about her mom for quite some time.

Occasionally he would notice Jenna's small hand clinging to the golden necklace she continued to wear around her neck, a quiet and thoughtful look upon her face. But he had avoided asking her what was troubling her, for that was easier, at least for him.

Looking now into her eyes, he knew easiest wasn't always best and sometimes the things that are the hardest are the most important.

"Every day, Jenna, every day."

"I'm afraid I'm forgetting her. I close my eyes and I can see her facer but it's always a picture, not really her. "

Jenna's tears renewed, her words muffled in her sobs. "I don't want to lose what I have left of her, even if it is just memories."

"I know what you mean. But I've learned something over the past year or so, sometimes it's not so much what you see but what you feel." Jace held Jenna tight within his arms. "Now close your eyes and just think about things you remember. Don't try to see her. Just try to feel her in your heart, for that is where she is and always will be, and that is something you will never lose. It took me a long time to learn that. I think I owe it to you, for when I see you, I see her and when I hold you in my arms, I hold a part of her."

Jace grew quiet, his emotions getting to him as he held her tighter.

Closing her eyes, Jenna's heart seemed to swell as she thought of her mother; warmth spreading through her to meet the warmth of her father's arms about her. She held her breath not wanting the feeling to end for it filled her with a love and peace she hadn't felt for a long time.

"Do you feel it, Jenna? Do you feel her love? Because it is there. It is the one thing we will always have within our hearts, and maybe the one thing she took with her. Sometimes I feel a part of me is gone and maybe that's the part she took with her, for the love we give to others and the love they give to us, that is what's forever. "

The quietness of the house seemed to haunt him as Jace paced about the rooms. Jenna had long since been asleep and Tom had gone home after a few hands of cards. The sound of the front door closing had been the last sound he had heard, as the stillness seemed to overcome every corner of the house.

Only the beating of his heart could be heard *(or was it felt?)* as he gazed about. Oh, how time could fly by, the tiniest moment changing everything.

Climbing the stairs, his body seemed to be without feeling, all except for his heart *(or is it my soul?)* that seemed to be feeling everything.

Jenna's words still echoed softly in his mind, *"Forget her... miss her... love her... "*

Oh, how I loved her. I just didn't realize how much. Or maybe, I just didn't understand love the way I feel I do now. Stopping at the dresser mirror, he gazed at his reflection. He still looked the same, but he had to admit he felt like a different man.

In spite of losing her and missing her, he felt more complete than he ever had— complete in his heart, mind and soul. Things he never particularly believed in or even thought about, now seemed a very important part of his life.

Slipping into the softness of the bed, he didn't feel alone as he smiled to himself. Suddenly he was a man who believed in heaven and angels, of true love that lasts for eternity from life and beyond, and most of all the power of that love.

CHAPTER 26

Winter came with its full vengeance as the temperature dropped and snow fell to blanket the earth from constantly overcast skies.

Peering around her father's back, Jenna was surprised at how hard it was to tell Dash and Jet apart from behind. Jet was now as big as Dash and even moved like her as they eased down from their gallop into a slow trot. Moist vapors circled about their heads, their nostrils flaring with each breath, their sides heaving rhythmically.

Clouds of steam rose mystically off their warm bodies, disappearing into the frosty breeze as they moved along the track.

Jenna usually rode in the chariot with her father, enjoying the ride as the horses kicked up the snow, the roll of the chariot rocking them gently. But lately the temperatures had made the usual trip unbearable. The cold wind would chill you to the bone as it teased tears from your eyes, only to freeze them on your cheeks.

The chariot no longer rolled smoothly, but bumped and jarred as the Wheels fought against the frozen earth.

Even the horses stumbled on the hard earth, their hooves filling with packed snow, their strides becoming awkward and uneven. Still they moved eagerly along the track, the two working in unison.

Jace stepped stiffly from the chariot, the cold imbedded deep into his joints from the trip. Only his mouth and eyes could be seen behind the masked face turned red from the wind, his mustache frosted from his breath.

Jenna giggled to herself, subconsciously comparing her father's frosted whiskers to those of the horses. A sudden shiver quickly doused any humor she had seen, as she thought about how cold he must feel.

Standing behind him in the chariot, he had blocked her from the wind as her arms wrapped firmly about his waist, her head snuggled close to his back. Still she trembled with the cold that crept up from her fingers and toes as Tom and her father unhooked the horses.

As though he sensed how chilled she was, Jace turned to smile lovingly, his moustache no longer frozen, his face less red. Jenna had on layers and layers of clothes. Jace had laughed and teased about how many layers, but at that moment, he actually wished he had more and could see by her trembling she still did not have enough.

"Jenna, why don't you go in the house and fix some soup and warm yourself up a bit? Tom and I can finish out here."

Smiling gratefully, Jenna hesitated just long enough to pat Jet and Dash affectionately before running for the house. They were much too sweaty for a hug, besides her teeth were beginning to chatter.

Rushing through the front door she turned to quickly shut the large oak door against the frosty breeze that tried to follow her inside. Peeling off a few layers of clothes, she moved to kneel before the glowing embers as she reached for a new log, then gently blew into the red glow, teasing it up along the untouched bark.

Sitting there upon the hearth, her teeth no longer chattered, her toes were no longer numb with cold, but still she couldn't bear to leave the fire's warmth.

Reaching yet for one more log she was somewhat saddened by the empty corner beside her. Christmas had come and gone much too fast, her memory of it already blurring with mixed images of Lorna and Wayne visiting, cutting the tree with Tom and her dad, the many presents for all, the wonderful dinner Lorna had fixed, their loving hugs as Lorna and Wayne had said their good-byes.

One memory stood out though and she could almost see the tree again standing in the corner as she carefully decorated it with Tom.

Then it had happened. His hand had reached to pick an ornament from the box, and then moved to place it awkwardly on the tree. It was the first time Jenna had ever seen her father help decorate a Christmas tree as she tenderly wrapped her arms about him. Reaching for the delicate angel, she had handed it to him.

"Dad, could you put it on the top please?"

It was Shanna's angel, a bit worn but still beautiful as he placed it securely on the top of the now shimmering tree.

The slight rumble of her stomach reminded her of the soup she was going to heat. It wasn't as good as Lorna's, but opening a can was a lot easier as she reached into the cupboard for a couple of cans. Now some fresh biscuits would be easy enough, though, and she hurried to mix the ingredients.

Stepping in through the front door, Jace was met by the sweet smell of baking biscuits as the warmth from the fire caressed the cold from his face. Tom closed the door behind them just as a few stray snowflakes twirled inside to rest at their feet, quickly becoming but traces of moisture on the floor.

"Oh, Jenna, that smells so good." Jace moved closer, his hand caressing her hair tenderly as he kissed the top of her head. "Thank you."

She could still feel the cold chill upon his hand as she led him into the kitchen. Smiling to both him and Tom, she motioned toward the table where their bowls of soup sat waiting.

"Come sit down while I get the biscuits."

She loved dinnertime, loved sitting together as a family, talking, listening, just being there together.

Turning the page in her book, Jenna glanced over the edge to see her father and Tom deep in concentration, the small chess figures seeming not to have moved since the last time she had looked their way.

The sound of the television seemed but a distant hum as everyone was focused on other things, though Jenna knew both Tom and her father were listening to the news of the day. Some of the things sounded too awful to be true as she paused to listen to a story, a sad story, and she shuddered at the thought of it.

Burrowing deeper into her blanket, she returned to her book— a fanciful tale of princesses, knights and mighty dragons. Chuckling to herself she thought it funny that what she had thought was her dragon, was truly her knight. Though he could still resemble the dragon, she knew it was just a disguise; that inside was her knight in shining armor.

Looking at the room about her, she knew this was her castle and here she would always be safe and protected. Her thoughts began to blur as her eyes drifted closed and they became dreams of wondrous things.

Stirring slightly the princess moved to wrap her arms around the strong knight as he lifted her from the depths of the dark pit. Carrying her upon a winged horse to the uppermost tower of the castle, he gently laid her in soft blankets, their warmth enveloping her. The sound of the dragon's fiery cry echoed in the wind as the knight tenderly kissed her.

"Good night, honey. I love you."

"You are my knight in shining armor and I will always love you." Jenna's words were but part of a wonderful dream as she wrapped her arms about her father one more time before again burrowing back into the warmth of her covers.

Smiling to himself, Jace glanced once more at the book he had taken from her small hands, the image of a beautiful princess catching his eye.

"And you, Jenna, you will always be my princess."

CHAPTER 27

Jenna glanced once again at the test in front of her trying to concentrate on the question, but as before, her mind continued to think of other things, no matter how hard she tried.

Dot was not due for another two weeks, but Jenna had a feeling today was the day. Besides it was doing all the things her father always talked about; when calving time came.

"All you need is a storm and a full moon and they think they need to have those babies."

He always says it about the cows, why not the horses?

For the past two weeks the weather had been wonderful. Spring was definitely coming a bit early with everything looking more like the first of May instead of the middle of March— until that morning.

Last night the full moon had risen high off the mountains, the breeze caressing the earth with a cool briskness announcing the coming of a spring snow.

Waking that morning, Jenna had rushed to her window to find the pastures covered with fresh fallen snow. Dot stood in the corner of her pasture beneath a large tree; her head tucked low, her butt blocking the rest of her from the cold wind.

Reading the question one more time, Jenna marked an answer as she noticed some of the other students were done. Looking down the page, she could see she only had a few more questions left. Still she struggled with her concentration as her eyes glimpsed the fluffy flakes falling past the window.

Before leaving for school she had begged her father to let her stay home so she could see Dot have her baby. He had laughed, somewhat humored by the idea, reminding Jenna that Dot wasn't due yet and showed very few signs of being near ready. He said just because there was a storm and a full moon, it didn't mean that she would have the baby that day.

Reluctantly she had left for school, reminding him to bring Dot in out of the storm. Glancing about Jace had said something about the snow stopping and he would bring her in, in a little while. He told Jenna not to worry, and to hurry before she was late.

Now all she could think about was getting home. *He is probably right, though, and I will get home to find Dot snug in her stall just as fat as ever.*

"Okay, class, pencils down and pass your tests forward." The teacher's voice startled Jenna as she hurried to mark the answer to the last question.

Ten more minutes of school seemed to last forever as Jenna's mind drifted off again.

Finally the bus stopped in front of the lane leading to home. Jumping eagerly from the last step, Jenna waved and rushed toward the house. The pasture was now empty, the only sign left of Dot being there were the hoof prints in the snow leading to the barn.

As she got closer, Jenna could see there was more than just Dot's and her father's footprints as she noticed a few small prints alongside of Dot's that disappeared leaving just Dot's and her father's. Rushing for the barn, she almost collided with her father, the surprise momentarily stopping the words that were ready to spill forth.

"Okay, okay. I don't need to hear it. You were right," Jace spoke quickly to avoid hearing it from Jenna.

When he had headed out to do chores, Dot had been standing in the corner of the pasture enjoying the break in the clouds that allowed the warm sun to beat down upon her. Deciding to leave her out for a while longer, Jace had moved into the barn to be greeted by whinnies and nickers from within.

Noticing the skies were becoming darker and that small flakes of snow were again fluttering to the ground he had headed out to get Dot.

The mare lay just about where she had been standing, moaning and straining in obvious discomfort, the tips of her foal's hooves protruding beneath her tail.

"Tom, it looks like Jenna was right, and boy, will I hear about it!" Jace yelled back toward the barn just as Tom emerged from the doorway.

"So, we're going to have a colt, huh? Isn't she about two or three weeks early?" Tom questioned as both he and Jace moved closer to Dot, who watched them intently.

Again another moan of discomfort escaped her writhing body, the foal's hooves extending further out followed by the soft tip of its nose, only to disappear as the contraction ended.

Jace knelt next to Dot, talking quietly as he stroked her neck. "It's okay, girl. We're here and soon that baby will be too."

Another pain gripped her abdomen, the contraction forcing the foal's nose and most of its face out along with the front legs, the soft hooves pushing into the fresh snow. Again the contraction ended and the soft nose retreated back inside as Dot turned to see what was happening.

The contractions began to come harder and faster and soon the soft nose was followed by the eyes and then the ears. The amniotic sack remained intact as the foal's front shoulders passed through, followed by a small gush of fluid, then the hips and hind legs of a small bay filly.

Removing the sack from the filly's nose, Jace cleared the remaining fluid from her nostrils as her eyes struggled to focus.

"Damn, she sure is little."

Dot nickered anxiously as Mother Nature's instincts kicked in and she turned, eager to clean and care for the shivering little filly now trying to move her wobbly legs.

"I guess we better get her inside," Jace commented to Tom as he noticed the filly shiver as a brisk breeze caressed her wet hair.

Tom agreed, moving to the barn to get Dot's halter.

"She's so small you could probably just carry her in while I lead Dot," Tom commented on his return as the filly struggled to stand, her legs buckling as she toppled nose first into the soft snow.

Jace laughed as he took her into his arms, her weight not being more than a bale of hay, if that.

"Well, so much for luck."

Tom looked curiously at Jace, unsure of his meaning.

"Today is St. Patrick's Day and already the little thing has had anything but good luck, born two weeks early and in one heck of a snowstorm," Jace mentioned as the once fluttering flakes began to fall faster and heavier, creating a thin blanket upon the filly's back before they arrived at the barn doors.

Dash nickered loudly as she paced at the front of her stall, sensing their approach as they all moved into the barn. Dot continued to keep a close eye on her baby that Jace held tenderly in his arms. Though she had never been a mother before, she was fast becoming an expert, and pinned her ears protectively at Dash as they neared.

"Oh, Dot, she's not going to hurt your baby," Jace scolded as he moved into the stall next to Dash that was filled with fresh straw to gently lower the filly into its warmth.

Dot moved quickly in beside her nickering and carrying on while everyone watched, especially Dash as she nickered softly her eyes fixed on the new babe.

Now looking into Jenna's eyes all Jace could see was excitement as he continued, "I'm really sorry you missed it. I just didn't think she was near ready, but I guess she showed me."

"Oh, that's okay, I just want to see it. What is it anyway? Is it a filly? I hope it's a filly."

Jenna ran past into the barn, too excited to really be upset about missing everything.

Dash nickered excitedly as Jenna entered the barn moving in her stall to the corner where Dot now stood eating her hay. Jet too tried to peek over the top rail of his stall, past Dash's stall and into the one on the other side.

He knew the mare; he had seen her in the pasture and watched Jenna sit upon her back while he walked on the walker. Something was different though. He could sense the excitement shared by both Jenna and Dash as they stood peering within. Whinnying loudly, Jet reared high above the panels still trying to see and breathing deeply of the new scent that drifted toward him with the breeze.

"She's pretty small but that's because she is so early. You can go in and see her if you want." Jace opened the latch allowing the door to open slowly.

Jenna giggled softly as the small filly tried to suck on Dot's belly, then her front leg, and so on, sucking everywhere but the right spot.

"Oh, you silly girl! You are looking in the wrong place." Jenna moved slowly, putting her arms around the little filly, who stood wobbling next to her mamma.

Guiding her gently, Jenna led her to the right spot and pressed her soft nose up against Dot's teat. "This is the spot you're looking for. "

No sooner had Jenna pressed her nose up against Dot's soft flesh did the small filly decide this was definitely the place she had been looking for, and began to suck hungrily.

Dash watched intently, a low nicker vibrating deep within her throat as the filly finished nursing and moved closer to her corner of the stall. Dot continued to eat her hay unconcerned for the moment as her baby moved closer to Dash, their soft noses touching in the gap of the corner.

"Oh, Dad, isn't she beautiful?"

Jace smiled at Jenna as he looked at the little filly. She was small, but she was beautiful. Her hair was now dry, her bay coat soft and fuzzy. The small white spot on her forehead looked like a heart, her soft nose having a small white snip to match. Both front feet were black with both of her hind feet being white.

She held her head high and showed no fear as she eagerly explored everything and everyone around her. She truly was a beautiful filly.

CHAPTER 28

Jace's heart pounded, the feeling of his pulse racing through his veins, filling every part of his being. The room about him was dark, only the slight hint of the sunrise to come touching the night sky. The curtains blew gently in the breeze announcing the coming rain that was just beginning to caress the mountain ridges.

Trying to slow his racing heart, Jace lay quietly as he focused on everything around him, an eerie feeling spreading through him like a cold fire.

There was nothing that should have woken him. Everything was quiet, yet he felt like someone had yelled his name, not from beside him, but from deep inside his mind and soul. *Something is wrong, really wrong, I can feel it.*

With each second that ticked by, the feeling grew worse as he began to feel sick, each breath burning in his lungs.

It sounded so close, that again he felt sure someone was in the room, though he could see he was alone— the voice *(or is it just a thought?)* thundered in his mind.

Suddenly it seemed so clear, like someone was truly yelling at him, screaming over and over in his mind.

Throwing on his pants and boots, Jace headed for the barn, his body numb, except for the racing of his heart.

"Oh, God, please!"

His gut feeling seemed to know; though his mind tried to tell him he was crazy. Flipping on the light, he waited, almost frozen in place.

Jet whinnied ... Buck whinnied ... and still Jace held his breath; waiting for the nicker.

"Dash?"

But only silence filled the barn as he gasped for a breath, his body moving forward on its own. His mind raced with explanations as to why Dash hadn't nickered. *She is sleeping or just doesn't feel like it.* But his heart knew better and told him so with each step as he neared her stall.

Dash stood in the back of her stall, partially hidden in the shadows, her head drooped and listless. Her body looked spent and wasted, a hint of moisture remained in her once silken hair now matted with dried sweat and sawdust. The sound of the latch to her door raised her head only slightly as she turned toward him.

Jace now stood beside her, stroking her gently as he took everything in. The stall was in total disarray, one of her buckets lay half buried in a pile of sawdust. The hook broken on the side panel caught his eye, drawing his attention to the hole below, its jagged edges holding small pieces of hair and dried blood.

Returning his attention to Dash, he could see the blood oozing down her left hind leg. Crouching beside her, he could see it was bad, but nothing really serious as again his mind tried to tell him things were not that bad. But looking again at Dash and then her stall, he knew it probably couldn't get worse.

She had colic, and she had it bad, he only hoped it wasn't too late.

"Jenna? Jenna! Wake up, honey."

Jace shook her a bit harder than he meant to, but he needed her help. Then, just as her eyes fluttered open, the thought came to him, *what am I going to tell her?*

"What's the matter, Dad?" Jenna questioned, her mind still fogged with sleep as she tried to focus on her father.

Jace took a deep breath as he struggled for the words. "I need you to call Tom and tell him to get up to the barn, and then call Dr. Daines and tell him I need him as soon as he can get here, then come out to the barn."

Jace turned to leave, hoping to avoid any specific questions, but suddenly Jenna was wide-awake, fear creeping through her as she grasped what her father had said.

"Dad, is one of the horses sick? Dad?"

Jace turned to face her worried eyes, not knowing what to say.

"Is it Dash?" Jenna persisted, tears already filling her eyes.

He couldn't answer, but his eyes said it all before he could turn away.

"Is she going to be okay?" Jenna continued to question.

Again he turned to face her, the words strangling him.

"I don't know, Jenna. I don't know. Just hurry."

This time he left, turning to race out of the house and into the early morning glow that now rose off the mountain ridges into the dark, scattered clouds that seemed to close in around him.

Tears stung Jenna's eyes, her mind whirling as she dressed and headed downstairs to the phone. Her mind too tried to convince her heart that it wasn't that bad. *Besides, Dash is invincible. She will be okay, she always is.*

Through both of the phone calls, Jenna was able to convince herself even more, that everything would be all right. It always was and only a small bit of doubt and fear remained to tug quietly at her heart.

Entering the barn, Jenna could see Dash standing in the alleyway next to Jet's stall. The gelding nuzzled her through the rails as Dash's head hung against her halter rope.

Jace was kneeling next to Dash's left leg cleaning the oozing blood, which had almost stopped.

"Is it very bad?" Jenna asked as she came to kneel beside her father.

Dash had raised her head in response to Jenna's voice, and now looked longingly toward her. Jace noticed the very mild response, but was pleased to see any positive reaction from the filly as he stood to brush some of the remaining sawdust from her hip.

"Well, Jenna, the cut isn't what I'm worried about. I'm afraid she might have colic."

Jenna looked from her father to Dash, a bit confused. The last time Dash had had colic, she kept trying to lie down and roll, and would bite at her belly because of the discomfort. But right now she seemed very quiet and tired. She wasn't trying to lie down and roll or any of the other things horses did when they had a bellyache.

"Jenna? I said, did you get a hold of Dr. Daines?" Jace again questioned Jenna, bringing her back from her thoughts.

"Yes, he said he could be here in about twenty minutes at the most," Jenna answered, but her eyes never left Dash.

Seeing her matted hair and the remains of sawdust in her mane, nostrils and eyes, she tried to brush the filly off with her hands with little success. Jenna ran to the tack room for the brush and a soft towel.

Dash stood quietly, barely responding to Jenna as the young girl cleaned the sawdust from her nostrils, which was something the filly hated, then took a damp cloth to clean the sawdust from the corners of her eyes.

Brushing her gently, Jenna watched her father meet Tom as he came into the barn. The two men stood together talking quietly for quite some time, but Jenna didn't think much of it, she just continued to coax lovingly at Dash, who nuzzled her meekly.

Jet paced back and forth along the front of his stall nervously, stopping by Dash to nuzzle her nose and blow into her soft nostrils. He was puzzled by her response, or lack of it, since they had become very close. Concern seemed to echo in his throat with each breath, for he too, knew something was very wrong.

Jace heard the sound of Dr. Daines' truck before anyone else and quickly moved with Tom to meet him at the front of the barn. Again the men talked quietly but this time Jenna hardly noticed. She knew Dr. Daines had arrived but was intently working with Dash.

Jenna hated to see the filly hanging her head so low that the lead rope seemed to be the only thing holding her head up. Gently Jenna would coax her to step forward, closer to Jet, only to have her step back and again hang her head with all its weight onto the lead rope.

"Hi, Jenna." Dr. Daines' voice drew her attention away from what she was doing, though it bothered her greatly to see Dash standing that way.

"Hi," Jenna answered. "I was just trying to get her to hold her head up. It looks so uncomfortable, the way she hangs it down against the rope, but she just steps right back and does it again."

Dr. Daines smiled sadly to Jenna as he took everything in. It didn't look good at all and he hadn't even examined Dash yet.

"It's okay, Jenna, she's probably just very tired. It's really not hurting her or she wouldn't do it. But why don't you cradle her head in your arms while I check her over real quick," Dr. Daines suggested, feeling it would be good for both Dash and Jenna.

Taking his stethoscope, he first listened to her abdomen hoping to hear the rumbling and gurgling of normal active bowels. Nothing. Moving the stethoscope he listen again and again, and still he could hear none of the normal sounds he so wanted to hear.

Moving up to her chest, he listened to her heart, that, though it was slower than a human's heart rate, was much too fast for a horse. Checking her temperature, which too was abnormal, being almost three degrees higher than it should be.

Through it all, Dash stood quietly, hardly noticing the man as she rested her head in Jenna's arms. Jet's warm breath caressed her ears as he hovered close by her head.

"Here, Jenna, let me see her."

Dr. Daines gently took her head into his arms as Jenna stepped aside. Turning on his little penlight, he looked into her eyes, and then pulled her lips up to look at her gums. Jenna noticed how pale they were but didn't realize that too was bad.

"Okay, Jenna, you can have her back. Uh, Jace, I will need to do a rectal on her and then probably tube and grease her both ways. I'll give her a muscle relaxant, then I can tell you more when I'm done."

Dr. Daines headed for his truck to get his supplies.

"What about her leg? Aren't you going to stitch it or anything?" Jenna questioned, puzzled why he had hardly even looked at the cut, for she thought it looked quite bad.

Dr. Daines glanced first at Tom and then Jace.

"Well, Jenna, it's not too bad, and really doesn't need stitches, but I'll wrap it up before I'm done."

All of the men knew that the cut was the very least of their worries.

Dash flinched only slightly as the needle entered her vein, the liquid spreading a fuzzy warmth though her. She knew the man was sticking a tube up her nose that gagged her for a moment, before it slid into place in her stomach. She had had this done once before and didn't like it much, but the medicine made it so she didn't really care at the moment.

A small amount of greenish liquid came up the tube and into a bottle on the other end. When Dr. Daines felt sure her stomach was empty, he then poured a large amount of mineral oil through the tube and into her stomach. The mineral oil would move down through Dash's system and lubricate her digestive tract.

He would then do the same thing rectally.

Pulling on the long exam glove, Dr. Daines began to slide his arm gently into her rectum. A horse's bowels are quite fragile and he had to be very careful as he extended his hand slowly in. Jace watched quietly as Jenna only peered over Dash's hip while she held the filly's head lovingly in her arms.

Dash felt cold to the touch and Jenna cursed the rain that had begun to fall, the sound echoing through the barn as she tried to hold her closer to keep her warm.

Looking about for a blanket, Jenna didn't notice that Dr. Daines had not gone in very far before stopping, and she completely missed the unspoken words the men all shared, their eyes all fixed on one another.

Turning to grasp the blanket she had spied behind her, Jenna heard the soft-spoken words that made her heart stop.

"Her bowel is twisted off. The kink is about fifteen inches in and it's tight. I can grease her from this end but I don't have the facility here for what she needs. She will need surgery as soon as possible, so you will have to get her to Dr. Reese. He is the closest and the best."

Dr. Daines turned to finish, his heart sick with what he knew and was sure Jace and Tom knew— it would be a miracle if they could save her.

"Will she be able to run again?" Jenna's naïve question surprised them as they all realized she didn't really know how serious it was.

Glancing all one at the other, none of them wanted to tell her, could bring themselves to tell her, what they all knew in their hearts. Silence hung heavy around them as Jenna waited quietly, wanting someone, anyone, to answer her.

Finally Jace spoke, his words empty of emotion, they had to be for him to say anything, "Well, if we are lucky, we can maybe breed her and use her as a brood mare."

It was the best he could do right now. If he said anymore, it would tear Jenna apart; it would tear him apart.

Jenna looked so disappointed as she cradled Dash's head tenderly in her arms. She hated to think of her not running, for Dash loved to run, but the thought of Dash with a colt brightened her thoughts.

Jenna remembered how Dash had nickered to Dot's new filly, her eyes intent on every move the filly made when her father had brought them into the barn to get out of the spring snowstorm that had moved in. Dot had even allowed Dash to nuzzle her new baby at the corner of the stall.

The memory faded as Jenna realized Dr. Daines was done with Dash.

"Well, Jace, I've done all I can do. I'll contact Dr. Reese and let him know you are on your way. If you can leave within the hour, that should put you there about..." Dr. Daines and Jace both looked at their watches simultaneously, "ten-thirty."

It was almost eight o'clock, he had been there well over an hour and the drive would take at least an hour and a half. If they left by nine o'clock, they would get there about ten-thirty.

Dr. Daines voice quieted for Jace's ears alone. "You better hurry, Jace. I'm afraid she's in bad shape. I'm sorry I can't do more. I really am. Good luck."

Turning to face Jenna, he took a deep breath, he knew how much she loved the filly, but there was nothing more he could do. Trying to smile, the words almost choked him, his eyes unable to meet hers.

He couldn't lie to Jenna, but he couldn't tell her the truth either. "Dr. Reese is real good, Jenna. She'll be in good hands."

Gathering up the last of his equipment, he headed for the barn doors.

"Please, let me know how she does." His words were meant for no one in particular, but they were sincere as he stepped out into the drizzling rain, the sun beginning to peek through a small break in the dark clouds.

Backing the truck up to the trailer, Jace tried not to think of what he was afraid was going to happen. Even if they got her there in time, he knew her chances were not good. Dr. Daines had even said she was in bad shape.

The surgery is a risk for a healthy horse, and it will cost three thousand dollars just to put her on the table, regardless of the outcome. But the money isn't really the issue, not this time; this time I will do whatever it takes, whatever it costs, if not for the horse, for Jenna. Besides she is a tough mare, who knows, maybe she can pull through this. She has seemed to improve.

Turning her back into her stall after Dr. Daines had left, Dash had actually taken a drink and turned to nibble some of the grain he had put in her bucket. It was a good sign.

"It's okay, girl, go lie down; we'll be here. "

Dash had nudged him tenderly, lingering close by his side. A sad emptiness seemed to hover about them as he held her head tenderly in his arms.

"It's okay, girl, ... you can rest now. "

Leaving her in the stall, Jace felt he had said those words before, in a different place and a different time.

Though they had been hurrying, Jenna felt like it was taking forever as she finished the few things in the house.

Her father had called Don, explaining they wouldn't be galloping the horses after all but asked if he would mind stopping by and feeding for him, since he wasn't sure how long they would be. He had then left the house with Tom at his side to hook up the trailer, reminding Jenna to hurry.

Locking the front door, Jenna rushed from the porch. It had only been forty-five minutes but it seemed like hours. She could see her father and Tom were still hooking up the trailer as she rushed through the open door of the barn.

Stopping suddenly, Jenna turned back to grab Dash's brush. She would keep the filly company until her father was ready.

Jet stood in the corner of his stall, his head high above the upper rail as he watched Jenna coming toward him. Moving quickly he paced to the back corner of the stall, his soft nose blowing warm air to the filly he knew was on the other side, before he moved back to the front, his eyes intent on Jenna's every move.

"Hi, Jet," Jenna casually remarked.

As she neared Dash's stall, a sudden chill spread through her, seeming to strangle her breath and still her heart, though she could feel it pounding harder than ever before. Gazing through the rails, Jenna couldn't see Dash and knew she was lying down. But something held her back, she couldn't seem to feel or hear anything as she slowly let her graze drop to where she knew Dash was lying.

Oh, God, no! Please, please no! Please let her sides rise with a breath.

"No!" The words burst through, the very air burning her lungs. She found herself moving without any feeling to Dash's side.

"Oh, Dad! She's dead! She's dead! Please, no.... "

Her words trailed off as she collapsed beside the filly, her arms wrapping around Dash's neck and chest, her tears falling freely.

"Oh, Dad.... "

Jace froze in place as Jenna's words cut through his heart. *Oh, God, why?* His heart seemed to be ripping his chest apart as he ran for the barn, Tom close by his side.

Jet paced anxiously back and forth along the side panel, stopping each time to blow a warm breath to Dash. He knew she was there.

He could smell her and almost touch the soft tip of her ear. Her head lay resting in the corner of her stall, close enough for the tip of her ear to meet the gap in the corner.

Blowing harder to get her attention, he startled at Jenna's scream, and then froze. He didn't understand the words, but he understood the agony and sensed the cold chill that filled the barn.

Now he knew that something was terribly wrong and he too called out, his whinny piercing the air.

Stopping at the stall door, Jace gasped for air, the scene before him knocking the very breath from his body. Jenna sat huddled in the sawdust, Dash's head now resting in her lap as she tried frantically to close the now empty eyes that gazed out into nothingness.

Hot tears burned his eyes as his mind whirled. *What to do? What to say?*

"Sometimes, Jace, you don't need to say anything. Just hold me and tell me it will be all right."

The words came to him as clear as the day Shanna had said them and he moved to take Jenna tenderly in his arms.

No words were spoken as the two sat huddled by Dash, Jenna's sobs wracking her small body as she tenderly stroked Dash's soft neck.

After what seemed like forever, Jace spoke quietly in Jenna's ear, his words loving and tender. "I'm sorry, honey, I'm so very sorry."

Turning to her father, Jenna wrapped her arms around him, holding onto him with all her might.

"Oh, Dad, why? Why her? Why?"

Her tears took over, her grief being more than she could bear as her words faded into uncontrollable sobs.

CHAPTER 29

The hammering echoed through the barn mingling with Jet's whinny as Jace connected the hammer to the steel peg of the stall.

Jet continued to pace back and forth nervously blowing air through his flaring nostrils, his sorrowful cry driving Jace crazy.

"Jet! Knock it off!"

He didn't mean to be harsh but this was almost more than he could bear. Dash's still form and lifeless eyes haunted him even though he had covered her. Glancing up from the stall panel, he blinked to clear his eyes.

Again he drove the hammer against another steel peg. He would have to practically dismantle the stall to get Dash out.

Jenna had left the barn unable to watch, but pleaded lovingly as she hugged Dash one last time, "Please, Dad, don't put the chain around her neck to drag her out, anywhere but her neck… please. "

He had promised without thinking. Now looking at her still form he wasn't quite sure how he would get her to the small pasture. Tom had already begun to dig a grave using the tractor at the site Jenna had chosen. Glancing out the barn doors, he could see Tom beneath the large oak working in the moist earth as the rain again began to fall.

As Jace pulled Dash's front panel down, Jet reared high above the side panel his eyes wide with fear, the thud vibrating against the earth. Tom had hung large blankets between Jet and Dash's stalls trying to shield Dash from his view.

Buck paced quietly across from Jet unnerved by everything as he peered through a small gap in the blankets. He too sensed something was wrong, his eyes wide, and his nostrils flaring with each breath.

Tom slowed the tractor at the front of the barn, and then cut the engine as it jerked to a complete stop. Jumping to the ground, he met Jace halfway down the alley, dragging the front portion of the stall. Leaning it against the outside of the barn, the two men returned to Dash's stall.

Few words were spoken as they strained against her weight, trying to edge her closer to the open section of her stall.

"If we can just get her to the opening, I can bring the tractor down," Jace's voice cracked slightly, the physical and emotional strain tearing at him. "If you can reach that blanket behind you, we'll try and edge her onto it. "

Jace pointed to Jenna's favorite fleece blanket lying at the side of the stall. He hated to use such a nice blanket but had found it hard to refuse as he gazed into Jenna's tear-filled eyes.

"Jenna doesn't want her scraped up. I told her I would do my best."

Jace glanced away from Tom finding it hard to meet his gaze. He was struggling harder with this than he would have ever imagined, and though his mind tried to remind him she was just a horse, his heart told him she was so much more.

Though the day was cool, Jace felt a stream of perspiration run along the side of his face. The two men continued to struggle, trying to get her through the opening. They had managed to get most of her on the blanket, but they just couldn't get her out into the alley.

Looking at the tractor, Jace tried to figure out another way, but looking at Dash he knew there was no way the two of them could do it.

"Tom, take a break. I'll be right back."

Moving to the tack room Jace lifted the lid on the large trunk. Reaching deep into the bottom he withdrew a pure sheepskin blanket. It was one of the last gifts Shanna had given him, in fact he had pretty well forgotten about it until that moment.

Moving toward the house he tried to practice what he would say to Jenna. He understood her feelings and the thought of putting a chain around Dash's neck didn't appeal to him either. But they needed to get her out of the barn, needed to bury her.

Knocking lightly at Jenna's bedroom, Jace opened the door to find her gazing out the window. She had seen him coming and suddenly he knew he need not say anything, for she knew what he had come to ask, he could see it in her eyes as she moved to wrap her arms around him.

"It's okay, Dad. I know you tried. If you put the blanket between her and the chain, it will be okay." Stroking the blanket gently, her voice quivered slightly, "Didn't Mom give this to you?"

"Yeah, don't you think Dash would like it?"

Nodding, Jenna struggled with the tears. "Dad, do horses go to heaven?" The last word was but a whisper as she tried to be strong, tried not to cry.

The question caught him by surprise for he wasn't really one to think much about heaven. He had always felt there was such a place and that was where Shanna was now, but hadn't really thought about it where animals were concerned.

Without thinking too much about it, though, he said what he felt in his heart. "I'm sure they do, honey. I'm sure they do."

Jace walked slowly back to the barn, the rain had slowed, the sun trying to peek through a small break in the clouds, but still the gloom surrounded him. He dreaded what he had to do, but felt it was something he would have to do alone. He knew Tom would gladly help, but nearing the older man, Jace just felt a strong need to be alone.

"Thanks, Tom, I think I'll get it from here if that's okay. "

Tom understood as he rose from the bale of hay he was sitting on. He was actually quite thankful, for he was feeling a bit emotional for the old man he was.

"I'll go in and check on, Jenna. Let us know when you get her to the pasture. Jenna wants to say good-bye."

Tom figured he would remember but felt it was okay to remind him to get Jenna before covering Dash for the last time. Moving toward the house, Tom was glad to get away.

"But, Jace, come and get me if you need some help." With that Tom gazed at the sky, amazed that the sun could actually shine after what had happened.

Jace started the tractor, then slipped it into gear moving slowly down the alley, trying not to scare Buck and especially Jet. He was thankful for the hum of the tractor drowning out Jet's whinnies as he continued to pace and call to Dash.

Shutting the engine down, Jace was surprised to find the barn quiet except for the sound of air blowing through flaring nostrils. Moving past Dash's still form, he stepped to the other side of the blankets to find Jet wide-eyed with fear.

"Easy, boy. It's okay," Jace coaxed, extending his hand to stroke Jet's nose.

Jet breathed deep of his scent, his eyes still wide as Jace tried to calm him.

"I'm sorry, Jet, but she's gone. I know you don't understand, but she can't hear you, can't answer you."

Jet calmed with Jace's gentle touch and soft tone. His eyes no longer shone with fear but became shadowed with sadness. His nostrils still flared with each breath as he buried his nose into Jace's arms. He could smell her scent on the strong arms that held him and, though it was different, he was comforted.

Jace moved reluctantly away from Jet, who immediately began to pace slowly, whispered nickers echoing deep within his throat.

Glancing one last time at Jet, Jace stepped again to the other side of the blanket. Dash lay halfway out of her stall, her still form cradled in the blanket Jace had managed to wrap around her.

Picking up the sheepskin blanket he moved to kneel beside her. He would need to pull the blanket back from around her head to wrap the soft sheepskin in place followed by the heavy metal chain that rested in the dirt beside him.

Touching the soft blanket he paused, his hand lingering to press tenderly on her form. He could feel her soft nose, her firm jaw, and muscled neck as he ran his hand reverently over her.

"I'm sorry, girl. I didn't know. I would have come sooner, if I had only known."

He struggled with the vision of her writhing in pain, rolling and pacing as the pain in her abdomen became unbearable. He had seen horses lose their minds as they thrashed frantically in pain. She must have been relieved when her bowel ruptured, for then the pain had finally eased.

Bowing his head, he took a deep breath and slowly drew the blanket off her head. Focusing on her neck, he slowly wrapped the sheepskin followed by the large chain snugly in place. He felt it was he himself with the chain around his neck, as his throat grew tight, each breath burning in his lungs.

She was still warm to the touch as he stroked her lightly before whispering softly in her ear, "I'm sorry, girl."

Drawing the blanket back over her head, Jace noticed the barn was filled with a cold, empty silence. Jet no longer paced or whinnied and suddenly he felt so very alone.

Still kneeling, Jace struggled to rise; his body felt weighted with lead. Gazing up into the rafters of the barn, he again thought of what Jenna had said about heaven.

"Take care of her for me, Shanna.... "

Forcing himself to finish, he moved to start the tractor. Its engine drowning Jet's whinnies that had renewed. Slipping it into gear, he began to drag her ever so carefully out of the barn.

Suddenly Jet reared higher than Jace had ever imagined he could, his head rising high above the stall panel.

Instantly their eyes met and locked, the absolute fear and anguish of Jet's gaze knocking the very breath from Jace's body as Jet's gaze reflected the betrayal he felt. All Jet knew was Jace was the one taking her away and suddenly his entire world seemed to crumble as his head disappeared from view, his body banging the side panel as his front hooves found the soft surface momentarily before again trying to rise.

Whinnying louder, he tried to beg Jace not to take her away as he watched the tractor clear the barn doors, then turn out of sight.

Getting Dash into the grave was easy in comparison to everything else as Jace closed his eyes, his mind hearing and seeing everything that had happened. He felt numb inside; it didn't seem real. It all seemed like a bad dream he wished he would awaken from.

The skies had again filled with dark clouds that seemed to close in upon them. Jenna knelt beside Dash's head still covered by the soft blanket, stroking it tenderly as she said her good-byes, her words muffled with sobs.

Tom stood beside Jace, his eyes red and puffy, and an occasional sniffle made Tom feel a bit uncomfortable with how emotional he was being.

Jet continued to whinny desperately, the sorrowful sound echoing out from the barn.

"Oh God, why?" Jace questioned as he raised his gaze to the heavens fighting back the tears that stung his eyes, his heart tearing apart inside, for everything was more than he could bear.

He couldn't bear to see Jenna so torn apart; couldn't bear to hear Jet's whinnies echoing in his mind, couldn't bear to feel his own heart breaking. His words were but a whisper that shook the heavens as the thunder exploded around them.

CHAPTER 30

Jet paced the stall anxiously, his whinny echoing throughout the barn. Nipping at the small leaves in his hay, he turned away disinterestedly only to raise his head high over the top rail, his gaze searching the alleyway. Whinnying again, the sorrowful sound sent a chill through Jace as the empty stillness followed.

Moving to the back of his stall, Jet faced the corner, his head drooped, a long deep sigh escaping at the end of an almost whispered nicker.

Jace moved close to the stall, his voice coaxing to Jet, "Come on, boy. I have a carrot for you. Come on."

Jet turned his head to gaze momentarily at the man, and then turned again to face the corner, his head seeming to droop even lower still.

A sick feeling spread through Jace, as his gaze fixed on Jet. He had never seen a horse grieve so. Babies often went off their feed and whinnied a lot when they were weaned from their mothers, but Jet had hardly eaten anything for three and a half days and was continuing to call to Dash waiting for some reply. Jace even found himself waiting for the deep throaty nicker of the mare.

Jenna wasn't doing much better than Jet. Often late at night he could hear her crying. Never knowing what to really say, he would hold her in his arms until her tears would subside or she would drift into an exhausted and fitful slumber.

During the day she kept her distance from the barn, hardly being inside since they had buried Dash. Jace couldn't blame her though, for it was hard for him to gaze into the now empty stall.

Looking again at Jet, he knew things were not good. If Jet didn't snap out of it soon they could lose him too.

Tom moved quietly down the alley to stand next to Jace. "He still isn't eating?"

"No, not even a carrot."

Jet loved carrots; they were his favorite treat from Jenna. Looking out the barn doors, he could see Jenna sitting just inside the pasture rail. Dot's filly nuzzled at her hands, coaxing to be scratched. Jenna showed little interest and only briefly scratched the little filly who showed complete ecstasy, if but for a moment, before Jenna's hand would again drop listlessly to her side or reach to brush a stray tear from her cheek.

She couldn't imagine there could be any tears left, only emptiness seemed to fill her.

Tom's gaze followed Jace's to rest upon Jenna. Her head was bent low, resting upon her knees as she sat motionless, the filly still milling around her.

Dot paid little attention as she grazed on the soft grass, only raising her head occasionally to find the whereabouts of her baby.

"They both look lost without her." Tom glanced from Jenna to Jet, their images reflections of one another.

Jace knew right then what needed to be done. *I can't let Jenna make the same mistake I made. I can't let her shut everything and everyone out, shut herself away from the things she loves. I did and I almost lost the most important thing in my life. In fact, if it hadn't been for Dash…*

He dismissed the thought; not wanting to even imagine what things would be like, what he would be like.

Tom watched from a distance, waiting and wondering as Jace headed toward Jenna, the sound of his voice drifting back to the barn.

"Jenna? Jenna, I need your help."

Jenna turned to see her father striding purposefully toward her. Her body moved slowly feeling weighted as she stood from the softness of the grass, her movement startling DeeDee who turned and bolted to her mother's side.

"What?" Jenna's voice was as empty as she appeared to be, her face pale, her eyes sunken and red from crying.

"I'm sorry, honey, but I really need your help. I know it will be hard for you, but I'm worried about Jet. He won't eat anything, not even a carrot."

Extending his hand, he offered Jenna the carrot. "Will you try? He might take it from you."

He knew why Jet would turn away from him, knew why Jet wouldn't take the carrot from his hand. Jet had watched, had seen Jace pull Dash's lifeless body from the barn. He hadn't understood it all, but he knew in his mind that Jace had taken her away.

The memory of his whinny, of the look within his eyes haunted Jace and he knew it would be a long time before Jet would again trust him.

"Jenna, I'm afraid if he doesn't start eating soon, we could lose him too."

A sick feeling filled her stomach. *Oh no, not that! I can't handle losing another one.* Looking toward the barn, her heart began to pound harder, faster. *Can I bear to go inside? To stand next to Dash's stall? To feel its emptiness?*

Just then Jet's whinny rang sadly through the air, almost as though he were calling to her.

"He needs you, Jenna... and you need him. Just like I needed you and you needed me. Only I was too dumb to know it. Don't make the same mistake I did. Love him as I love you now, and he will love you as she did."

Jenna paused at the barn door. She couldn't still the pounding of her heart or the trembling of her body. *Why is it so hard? It is just the barn, just an empty stall.*

Jet's whinny seemed to coax to her as her father's arm wrapped lovingly about her shoulders. She smiled meekly at him, his eyes soft and loving, his touch seeming to give her strength.

Holding her hand out for him to stay, Jenna moved slowly inside. "I'm okay, Dad. I can do this. "

Tom had moved outside to stand next to Jace as Jenna moved deeper into the barn. It was just the barn; she knew that. It was still the same. It smelled the same, looked the same, nothing else had changed.

Buck raised his head from his hay to whinny softly as she neared Dash's stall. The door was closed, the hay bin empty. She knew it would be easier to hurry past, yet she couldn't.

Tears filled her eyes as everything began to blur. Reaching to lift the latch, she slowly opened the door. The sawdust still showed the imprint of Dash's body and Jenna knelt to touch the spot where her head had rested.

Closing her eyes she could almost feel the soft silken hair, the smooth muscles, the warmth and life that had always been there.

"Close your eyes and just think about the things you remember. Don't try to see her. Just try to feel her in your heart, for that is where she is and always will be, and that is something you will never lose." The words seemed to come to her as clear as the day her father had said them concerning her mother. *"When I see you, I see her, and when I hold you in my arms, I hold a part of her."*

Jet nickered a soft, throaty nicker at the corner of the stall. Jenna's heart nearly stopped. For with her eyes closed, it had sounded just like Dash. Maybe it sounded like her because she wanted it to.

Again he nickered softly, coaxing to the girl he knew was crying softly on the other side of the panel. Jet had never nickered like that before. He had always been such a baby, whinnied like a baby, always been so worried about himself. But now as Jenna knelt crying he was worried about her, longed to comfort her as Dash so often had.

He could see her through the gap, her small body continuing to tremble slightly. She seemed not to even hear him and his head drooped slightly lower as one last nicker came from deep inside.

"... *A part of her,"* Jenna could almost swear it was her mother's voice, but her father's words that seemed to come from within her heart.

He was a part of her. Jet had learned everything from her. *"When I hold you in my arms, I hold a part of her. "*

Brushing a tear from her cheek, Jenna rose warily from the softness of the sawdust. Fear seemed to grip her as she slowly moved to open Jet's stall door.

He had never been overly affectionate. He liked attention but just wasn't very affectionate himself. *What if he turns away from me; rejects the love I have to give? Can he love me as Dash did?*

Shaking the thoughts from her mind she realized it wasn't fair to expect him to be like Dash. He wasn't Dash; he was Jet and special in his own way.

At the sound of the latch, Jet's head rose slightly. He had listened to her soft footsteps as they moved from Dash's stall to his. He waited quietly, patiently, which was unusual for him. His eyes were fixed at the door as it opened to let Jenna in. He remained still, not sure of her or himself.

He nickered, coaxing softly as his eyes met hers. Stepping forward, his nose raised to meet her outstretched hand.

"Oh, Jet!" Jenna cried as she quickly moved to wrap her arms about his head and neck, something that he normally wouldn't have liked or tolerated.

But Jet nuzzled his nose against her side, her touch, her scent, and her arms about him comforting him as her soft words filled his ears.

"Oh, Jet, I miss her too, but you have to eat. Please eat something," her voice pleaded as she released his head.

Realizing she had left the carrot in Dash's stall, she moved toward his grain bucket. Scooping up a small handful of oats, she placed her hand by his soft mouth.

"Please, Jet, for me."

Slowly he lipped at the small kernels till her hand was empty. Pricking his ears forward, he gazed past Jenna down the alley as again the sound of a small whinny drifted into the barn.

"Oh, did you hear DeeDee?" Jenna questioned as she turned to follow his gaze.

The small filly could be seen running awkwardly at her mother's side in the front pasture. Looking into Jet's eyes she could see a sad yearning as he continued to try and see her.

"Do you want to see the baby?"

Jet's gaze shifted to meet Jenna's, a new light radiating forth as though he had understood.

"Dad!" Jenna hollered out toward her father and Tom. "Dad, can we bring Dot and DeeDee into the barn for a while? I think it would really help Jet. I think it would give him something to care about."

Soon DeeDee was walking cautiously into the large barn, her eyes wide and curious as she looked nervously about, making sure to stay close by her mother's side. Jet watched eagerly, a soft nicker rising from deep within his heart, his eyes intent on her every move.

Jace led Dot to the front of Jet's stall, talking quietly to her. "He just wants to see her. He won't hurt her, so just be good."

Dot pinned her ears momentarily at the eager gelding, then turned her attention toward Jace, as he again spoke her name. "Dot."

He only said her name but she knew what he was meaning and conceded reluctantly as DeeDee raised her nose to meet Jet's at the lower rail of his stall. Jet blew gently from his nostrils, a soft nicker following as the little filly responded affectionately nipping at his nose through the rail.

"Can we put them in Dash's stall for a while? I think it would help him," Jenna questioned apprehensively.

There was a part of her that never wanted another horse in that stall and a part that felt DeeDee belonged there.

Jace's answer seemed a buzz in her ears as he explained they could be in at night and a few hours during the day, but still needed to be in the pasture most of the time. She missed the part about the need for more room, exercise, and fresh grass, for her mind had wandered.

"Dad, can I name DeeDee? I mean her real name, her registered name?"

The question caught him by surprise. He hadn't even thought about a real name for the filly. They had just called her DeeDee for the time being.

"What did you have in mind? "

"Well, I don't know if you noticed but Dash died exactly one month from the day that DeeDee was born and so I would like to name her after Dash."

Jenna paused; the thought bringing a sting to her eyes as she found there were still more tears inside and fought to control them.

Jace waited patiently sensing her struggle.

"Noble from her dad's name, Dashin' from Dash's name, and Delight from Dot's name, and call her Noble Dashin' Delight."

"Noble Dashin' Delight, that's a good name, Jenna, a real good name."

Jace moved to pet her affectionately as she continued to nuzzle Jet, the gelding noticing him move closer.

Turning his gaze from the filly, his eyes searched Jace's. They were soft and gentle the words that followed the same. "You take good care of her for me, Jet."

Their eyes met and held as Jet nuzzled Jace's hand, if but for a moment, before turning back to Jenna and DeeDee a deep throaty nicker rising from deep within.

CHAPTER 31

Jenna fingered the keys on the piano lightly. Her mother had insisted she take lessons when she was younger, but after a year of little success or enjoyment on Jenna's part, had given up on her daughter being able to play better than herself.

Shanna had taken lessons and loved to play. Often as a young child, Jenna had curled up in the chair beside the piano to listen while her mother played. There was one song Jenna could remember, just a little tune her mother had made up, but it had become her favorite.

There were no words to it; it was just the feeling it gave her inside that Jenna loved. Closing her eyes, Jenna could almost hear the soft notes come from beneath her fingers as they gently touched the polished keys.

Gazing out the window she could hardly believe it had been almost two months since Dash had died. In some ways it seemed like forever, and in others, it seemed like only yesterday. Her heart ached, the pain becoming fresh with the very thought of it all. *How things have changed, one little thing and your world is never the same. And if you had the power to changes things, could you? Would you?*

A friend had commented that it was too bad it wasn't the other one.

Thinking of Jet, she had known her friend had meant him. But she could never have made that kind of a choice and was actually grateful to not have the power to change things, but only the power to get through them.

Fingering the keys again, the tune seemed to come from some where inside their very tips.

She had often tried to play the song but had never seemed to be able to get it quite right. But suddenly it seemed to fill her, comforting her as the sweet sound floated through the room.

Stopping at the top of the stairs, Jace felt a little tug at his heart. Jenna was playing Shanna's song. He had loved to hear Shanna play and had almost forgotten that she ever had. But that tune, that simple little song, that was Shanna. Sweet and gentle, the tones caressed his heart as his eyes rested upon Jenna.

Sensing his presence, Jenna turned to face her father, who now stood close by her side. His arms tenderly embraced her as he kissed her lightly on the top of her head.

"I love you, Jenna." The words were soft yet strong, for they meant the world to her.

As quietly as her father had appeared at her side, he had disappeared, only the sound of the closing door announcing his departure.

Gazing back out the window, she could see him move into the barn, only to return with Jet at his side. The gelding immediately whinnied to DeeDee as she ran about in the small pasture.

Stopping short at the sound, she turned, her high-pitched whinny answering his. Dot paid little attention and only raised her head slightly before resuming her grazing of the sweet blades. Moving closer to the large tree, DeeDee eased herself down to lie in the soft grass.

Watching intently, Jenna hadn't realized she had risen from the piano and now stood at the window. It was not a big deal really, but at first she had the urge to make DeeDee move, for the filly lay right were they had put Dash to rest.

Moving to the pasture, Jenna watched DeeDee as she raised her head, their eyes meeting for but a moment, before the filly burrowed her head back into the softness of the new grass. Stopping at the fence, Jenna's throat grew tight. DeeDee lay just as Dash did, the filly a small image of the one beneath her.

Sitting on the top rail of the fence, Jenna watched the golden horse swing gently on the delicate chain. She had taken it off to gaze wonderingly at it. The delicate wings could be those of an angel, the strong muscled body that of Dash.

Closing her eyes, Jenna thought of her mother, thought of Dash, and imagined them together. *Maybe they are racing across green meadows. Maybe Mom is holding the filly tenderly in her arms. Maybe they are thinking of me or maybe they are with me, if only in my heart.*

Again the tears stung her eyes as she returned her gaze to the golden charm still swinging gently in the breeze.

"Jenna, are you alright?"

Though Jace's voice was quiet, Jenna started at the sound of his words. She had not heard him come up behind her and was unaware of the fact that he had stood there for quite some time.

Brushing the tears from her cheeks, she apologized for crying again, "I'm sorry, Dad. I don't mean to keep crying, but I was just thinking about Dash."

Jace smiled as he moved to brush a stray tear from her cheek. "And what were you thinking?"

Jenna looked at the golden charm now resting in the palm of her hand. Struggling with the words, she fought for control, as her throat grew tight.

"Oh, you'll think it's silly," she managed to squeak out softly.

"I would never think anything important to you was silly. "

Holding the charm closer to her father, the words came soft and sweet, the slight hint of a tear filling her eyes.

"I was just imagining now that Dash is in heaven, that God has made her an angel, and she has wings and can fly like Pegasus."

"Angels may come in all shapes and sizes. They may be right here with us, and we just don't know it." Jace thought of Shanna's description of Pegasus— *an angel sent by the gods to protect Perseius.*

"If Dash wasn't an angel before, I'm sure she is now," Jace said softly.

Jace woke slowly from the dream. He couldn't really remember the dream, he could only remember dreaming and feeling a comforting peace within himself. Gazing about the room he languished in its warmth. The morning sun's rays cast small beams of golden light that danced about the room as the curtains blew gently at the partially open window.

Stretching slowly he realized he had overslept, yet felt no need to rush. Instead he slipped on his Levi's, and then moved toward the window, the soft curtains almost beckoning him closer.

Parting them slowly Jace looked toward the track, his heart telling him before his eyes, what he would see. The image floated magically upon the soft earth of the track, the two moving as one.

Another day, another time, it would have been Dash and Jenna sneaking out for an early morning ride. Or even further days gone by, it would have been Shanna on Duck, and from the distance, if he didn't know better, it would be hard to tell.

The beautiful bay horse moved with mystical grace, the small delicate form complimenting his power, her beauty enhancing his, it could be any memory, any dream, and any moment in his life.

But it was Jenna on Jet. It was here and now, and as ever changing as life could be; some things were different, yet they remained the same.

THE END

LORI PRINCE PETERSON

was an R.N. of Northern Utah. She earned her Associate of Science in Nursing at Weber State University. She was laid to rest in Logan, UT on November 30th 2013.

www.ingramcontent.com/pod-product-compliance
Lightning Source LLC
Chambersburg PA
CBHW030428310726
48979CB00009B/1673/J

* 9 7 8 0 9 9 6 5 2 0 6 5 2 *